DISCOVERING PERHAPS

DISCOVERING PERHAPS

Book 1

W. L. SIMON

DEDICATION

To Matthew
Always, forever, & then some.

THE HOUSE BY THE WOODS-
BEGINNINGS

"Move!" Rory whispers. He looks around to see if anyone saw them enter the hole. The beady eyes darting in the dim light under the steps catch his attention. He picks up a pebble from the dirt and aims right between those red orbs. "Hey, I told ya to be quiet and stay outta sight. Are ya stupid?"

Dirty clawed hands reach up to stroke the injured spot.

"I know. It's not your fault." Rory speaks more to himself than to his companion. A shake of the head as he moves past the twitchy guy. "You're useless. Why do I bother?" At the wall of brick, he searches the ground. The dry powdery dirt dips in one particular place. On his belly, he reaches his own dirty claws as far as possible. He pulls back several fists full of the gritty earth.

"Follow behind me." The words are unnecessary. He speaks out of habit. Head first, Rory crawls under the brick, pushing the silt away. On the inside of the crawl space, he waits. Just when he thinks no one is coming, a twitchy nose pops out, sniffing the air.

"What took so long?" He turns to the side, avoiding dirt flying from the shaking mass beside him. "Don't bother. We will get dirty again."

"I don't suppose you've ever been here?" Only briefly waiting for a reply he knew wasn't coming, Rory continues to walk along the brick wall. "I've scouted around to see how many humans dwell here." They reach an unidentifiable spot when he leads the way deep into the crawlspace.

"My nose senses something is here. If I can find this one thing, growing my reputation will be easy. Everyone will know I deliver the goods." The pair stop. Noses raise and whiskers twitch in unison.

Above their heads, boards squeak in a procession. Muffled voices and the hum of music filter to their ears.

"That's them alright." They relax, and Rory looks around in the dark with his beady eyes. "I'm positive they've got something I can use. It will put me on the map. I will use it to make a name for myself. It will get my empire established faster than any other job." After a quick glance at the mound of fur beside him, Rory walks forward to a small strip of illuminated dirt. "I've heard whispers of a special object needing found." Near the spot of light, Rory extends up on the tips of his clawed feet, to ductwork poorly attached.

"If you suck in that belly of yours, we can just fit up next to this pipe." A muffled, rustling noise fills the crawlspace under the house. Rory pauses, listening to sounds on the other side of the wall. "Come along, but be quiet." He thought louder than the whisper he spoke.

They stand beside each other on the elbow of the duct. Claws gripping the lath boards holding the plaster wall intact. "These older houses are simple to scavenge. It's as if they made them just for us to climb around inside the bones." Using his expert vision in the total darkness above them, Rory spots his next move.

"I want to get a look at this room. That old grate up there will let me see everything I need." Rory knew his mental connection, along with the micro expressions they share, will communicate his intentions. "We must be silent and hope the music keeps them oblivious to our attendance at their party."

"What does that say?" Rory peers through the metal grating near the ceiling of the sitting room. "Look at that?" He bumps his shoulder on the twitchy guy next to him. "It's a party for the last Monday of the month? What in all the realms is this party?" Rory listens to the people.

"Momma, can I put toppings on the ice cream?" The dark-haired little girl wraps a yellow steamer around the back of an over-stuffed chair of dark blue.

"Of course you can, my little Violet. It won't be a party without ice cream and all the fixings." The lady hangs steamers in a wide doorway to the kitchen.

"What is this?" The man wraps an arm around the woman's waist.

"A party Daddy!" The girl jumps up and down. This causes her blue glittery fairy skirt to flutter around her little legs.

He scoops her up in one arm. "Is that so? Can I have a hug from my girls before I go up to wash? Then am I allowed to join the party?" The three stand in the streamers of yellow and green embracing.

Rory makes a yak noise in his throat. "This sweetness makes my teeth hurt." He sees nothing in the room to cause his nose to tingle. "It isn't here." The cramped space doesn't allow for a good view of the surroundings. He needs to try somewhere else. "Go back, Stooge." He smacks his hand on the shoulder of the silent crony.

The party distracts the humans from the scurrying noise they make moving back to the space beneath the house. Still, Rory shushes his companion repeatedly. No point in letting your guard get lazy. He knew one day he wanted his reputation to include his stealthy abilities. If only this caper produces the goods to launch his retrieval business, he will realize the dream soon.

The dry powdery earth in the crawlspace covers the once pink pads of the bare paws. Flexing clawed toes in the silt, Rory scratches his furry belly while his eyes search for the next entry into the old farm style house. He stands peering through the darkness as his whiskers vibrate with each twitch of his nose. Rory flings his hand at the rat next to him. When his hand didn't land on the expected shoulder, he turns to look.

"Stop that!" Rory hisses.

The feral rat stops brushing his paws on his snout. Stray cobwebs dance on the tips of his whiskers in obvious irritation to the rat. Still in his crouched posture, he is ready to scurry on his four feet. Red, beady eyes flick to Rory and away.

"This is the very reason I call you Stooge." Giving a sigh, Rory turns sauntering to another point. They step around a pillar of bricks. He stops after walking in a dip of the earth and up the other side. Then he reaches up to find a hollow for them to explore.

"Leaving the cobwebs alone is too much to ask, right? We're going to get those whiskers of yours dirty again. Now, come over here." Rory stands waiting for the other rat to move. "What are you looking at?" His quick survey of the crawl space observes nothing lurking in the shadows. "You feral guys are so nervous." With a shake of his head, He reaches up into the shaft.

The walls are newer construction, causing the surface to be harder to navigate. Rory soon finds a small ledge where they can stand.

"What is this?" Rory digs his clawed fingers under the wood panel. With little effort, it lifts. Stooge wedges his nose under to sniff the air. When no one screams, as humans do, they stick their heads out to assess the room.

Rory smacks the ear next to him, then pulls back into the dark interior of the wall. "Get in here!" When the door is closed again, his excitement bursts. "I haven't seen one of these in some time. That room is off the kitchen. I could make out those machines used to clean clothes." He turns to jump on gears on a side wall.

"Somewhere in this tunnel, we will find a platform the humans can use to deliver junk." Checking to see if the cable is sturdy, Rory scurries up fast.

"What are you waiting for?"

Soon, the pair maneuver onto the shelf and open the panel to find a bathroom on the second level. Stealthily, they drop to the cool tiled floor. Rory reaches the door leading to the hallway. No sign of humans.

"Stooge," Rory looks for his companion. The dim glow of a nightlight on the counter illuminates movement in the sink. "Stooge!" The harsh whisper gets his attention. Rory breathes easier after seeing the rat drop to the floor. Rory scurries to the end of the corridor. An open door shows a bed with a quilt and warm light glowing.

On his four feet at the doorway, Rory hesitates. He glances at the stairs, then at the room. Empty. The wood boards of the old house squeak as the pair of rats cross the threshold.

"The parents' nest, I bet." Rory stands up to survey the room. "You must stay with me and touch nothing." He looks into Stooge's eyes, trying to communicate with every fiber of his being. "I mean it."

They climb onto the footboard at the end of the bed. From there, Rory sees the top of the dresser near the bed.

"Typical. Predictable. Humans are all the same." Sniff, sniff, "flowery perfume for the lady, and musky spray for the man." He jumps to the floor, continuing to maneuver into a chair next to the chest in the corner.

"I'm sure something is here. I just have to find it." Rory looks over a built-in bookshelf filled with books and objects to the ceiling. "Humans make no kind of sense. I can smell human stink easy! Sprays can't mask it. We animals, feral and otherwise, know more about them than they will ever learn." He pushes off the back of the chair to stand on the white shelf. Books stand from one end to the other. Laying in front of the worn spines are several items of no real value.

"Junk, ordinary seashells. If mermaid tears saturated the shells, I could work with that." Rory says. The second he reaches for the ledge above, his whiskers tingle.

"What do we have here?" On the shelf in an empty spot between the books, it sits. Rory climbs up and walks to the space. His long fur-less tail curls around for his hands to grab. Whiskers vibrate.

A leather pouch rests on the painted wood looking ordinary. One of Rory's paws reaches out and a low hum begins from inside the stiff material. "Yes, that's it." The whisper of a lover's call. He drops the appendage and slides clawed fingers into the bag. The vibration increases in intensity when he works the top open wide enough to see.

"Oh, yes, you are special." Rory says. His dirty rat paw reaches inside for the gold chain. "Almost got you, you're mine." He talks to himself. Each word a drawn out mumble. The rat's claws scoop up the strand to maneuver it into his palm.

"Don't get attached to the treasure, darling."

Feral instincts take over in his fright. His hand out

of the pouch, Rory crouches, arches his back, keeping four feet on the shelf. His nose points in the voice's direction. The moment his eyes land on her, he eases back up to stand. His beady gaze never wavers from her while he puts himself between her and the bag now laying with the chain spilling out.

"I won't say it's good to see you Contessa Fusco." Rory twitches his whiskers, realizing he missed seeing something so vital. He hadn't considered the open window a threat, his focus so intense on the hunt.

"I appreciate that. No pretending, such a relief." The great horned owl stands leaning in the opening, her ankles crossed.

Not used to seeing this breed of predator up close, it takes a moment for Rory to notice his stooge. He picks at his dirty claws, understanding his colossal error.

"Let's not do anything hasty." Rory answers, knowing in his gut it's too late. The other rat shaking with the knowledge, too.

The feral rat stops quivering in shock and squeaks. Faster than Rory could say wait, the enormous owl removes the talon, pining the rodent to the windowsill, just long enough for her pointed beak to gobble him whole. Without ruffling a feather, she continues to pose. This time, the tip of her wing plays with the tail dangling from the corner of her beak.

"Was that necessary? He didn't deserve that." Rory says.

"Oh, but he asked for it." Contessa said.

"What did you expect him to do?" Rory asks.

"You should thank me. His noise would have brought the humans here any minute. Then your caper is at an end." Contessa swivels her head to see the door, then Rory.

"There is no caper. This is just a scouting mission. For fun, if you will," Rory grins a dirty toothed smile.

"Come now, Rory rat. Who is your client?" Contessa emphasizes rat in her enunciation.

A smirk that doesn't reach his eyes fills his face. "I could ask the same of you, Contessa." Rory says. She doesn't see the chain that slipped from the bag.

"You're going to make me eat you, too, aren't you? Please, don't. A girl must watch her figure, you know." With a slurp, the tail disappears inside her beak.

An instinctive step back and Rory feels the chain under a foot. It makes the slightest crunch when his weight settles on it. That sound, no human can hear it, but the creature of the night hears every loop of metal dig into the painted wood shelf.

"That must be it, then? The object you alluded to in the pub? You know, I alone believe you have a gift for hunting." She drops to the arm of the chair in the corner, creating no sound.

Rory feels his heart rate increase, making it difficult to form a plan of escape with the treasure. With each second that passes, he understands the object will not be his today.

"You be a good boy and lower it to me?" She waits.

The rat doesn't move, buying time.

"Don't make me come over there, Rory." Her talons squeeze into the fabric hard enough to puncture.

He turns away from her.

"Yes, that's right, go slow." Contessa says.

Before Rory puts the half-formed plan into action, the sound of humans in the hallway fills the silence between them.

"May I have many bubbles, Momma? "

"Yes, my sweet Violet." The lady answers.

A door closes, muffling the voices. More footsteps continue getting closer.

"I'll tuck you in when you get out." The man says near the doorway to the bedroom.

Rory jumps at the same time Contessa lunges at him. The chain catches his claw; the object moves with him, but he doesn't have control of it. With arms outstretched, the rat hits the back of the bird of prey and glides on her glossy feathers. The rodent makes a frantic grasp to avoid collision with the floor.

Contessa jerks when he pulls her quills, at the same time the floorboards creak. The human stands in the doorway.

"What! How did..." The father of the family watches the owl flapping, trying to get back outside as a rat yanks out tail feathers while avoiding the beak, lunging for him.

The man grabs the blanket from the bed. He aims at the chaos in the room's corner and tosses it. The wings of the large bird tangle in the fabric. Then, he lifts the pair to the window, hurling the squirming mass into the night air. The rat jumps at Contessa's feet as she flaps, trying to free herself. With freedom comes a snap filling the moonless sky.

The owl tucks her useless appendage to her side as Rory maneuvers to brace for impact. He realizes he has injured an eye. But it doesn't matter because the fall might kill him.

One wing tries to manage a glide to cushion the landing, but no use. A hard thud and then rolling to a stop in cool grass. Stillness fills the early night. Deep shadows cover the pile of disheveled feathers. Rory lifts his head from the plumage. He sees the man at the window, looking out into the darkness. The chain hanging from his hand with a pendant swaying in the open window.

His attention back on Contessa, he knows his plight is not over yet. As he finds his way to stand in the grass, one clawed paw inspects his eye. A bleeding gash from his eyebrow to cheek across his eyelid.

"Are you going to help me?" Contessa's voice weak in the quiet.

Without a word, Rory runs for the forest.

2

THE HOUSE BY THE WOODS-WITNESS

The book lay open on her lap, forgotten. Only with her out of habit, with no genuine wish to read. She sits gazing across the lawn. She can hear a cricket chirp breaking the stillness, a sound organic to the comfort of summer nights. Now changed in her memories forever. Violet is unaware when it happened. Each shrill call of the insect signals change in her life.

Hands gripping the painted edge of the porch floor, Violet gives little thought to this spot. It is best not to notice. Absently, her thoughts turn to running across the grass and the woods closing around her. Letting go of everything she wanted to hide from today, tomorrow, and her unknown future.

Violet desperately wants life to be normal. The ordinary routine of her sitting here listening to the laughter of her parents cleaning the kitchen up after supper. Quietly here reading a book, she can ignore the sound of crickets. Carefully, she tries to remember the last time it happened? When had it been? She had to take a deep breath. Her grip tightens on the edge of the porch.

She sits rigid, avoiding looking back at the house. The downstairs has been dark for days. A shake of her head for clarity doesn't help. At eight years old, she cannot recall difficult times. Her family was fine until now. How could this happen? Why? One day, she might understand. She raises a fist to rub where her heart is to calm the ache.

"Violet…" came the soft voice of her father.

Eyes closed tight, her breath catches as the screen door creaks.

"We need—" clearing his throat, he tries again, "come in, please."

Her sight draws to the tiny ant walking along the step near her scuffed gym shoes. If only she were the bug instead.

Time both crawls and flies by, filled with dread and uncertainty. She will remember the stillness in the house as being a specter they hadn't invited. The squeak of the screen closing behind her. The sound of her dad's old work boots on the stairs. Followed by the tingle in her fingers rubbing across the texture of the wallpaper as she trudges along the hallway. Eyes fixed on her parents' bedroom door, Violet holds her middle tight.

Frozen on the threshold, she watches. Her dad walks around the bed, sitting to embrace her mother's hand. His tenderness, both common and too intimate to watch. She can't look away from the tragedy playing out in front of her.

Her father whispers, "Marietta," Touching her

gently, he uses the endearment most familiar. "Etta, babe, Violet is here." His eyes never leave her pale face.

Cautiously, she grips the doorway, watching her mother's bony torso rise higher with each breath. Her chest, once a pillow for her head. The beating of her mom's heart in her ear while being read a bedtime story, but never again. The pink nightgown emphasizes how frail this special woman has become. She can't take her eyes off her mother's frail hand as it slides across the worn quilt. Thoughts of her braiding Violet's tresses come to mind. Violet didn't want the fuss of having her hair done. She always wished her black tendrils were the same as her mother's blonde strands. Now, a soft cap covers fuzz.

The familiar voice calls her out of her memories.

It is her turn to act. But convincing her feet to trudge across the floor feels impossible. She tries to ignore the medicine bottles, thermometer, bedsore cream, and protein drink with a straw's bent end at the ready. She sees them. Visible evidence of the illness stealing her mom. So much is different now. Violet rubs her palms on the denim of her shorts.

"Mom," the choked sound foreign to her ears.

"Come sit with me," her mother pushes to rise, but doesn't change her position. The effort making her face paler.

She eases her hip on the side of the bed. Violet gravitates to her mother's eyes. The spark of light, once magnetic, is now dim. Pain and tiredness cloud what was once vibrant and filled with love.

"I need you to listen to everything I say. It is

important that you understand. I didn't plan for this. I wanted you to be older, but I'm out of time." A dry cough replaces her exhale. "That brown bag on my bedside table. Open it."

Violet pushes her fear away, trying to gain control of her little frame, and swallows hard. She struggles to reach past the unfamiliar medical supplies. While holding the stiff pouch, pulling the drawstrings takes effort. A slight scent of leather mingles with the newer hospital smell in her nose. She upends the bag, letting the contents fall into her palm.

A peek at her mom and Violet can see the pain she is hiding.

"My sweet girl, it's yours." She lays her hand over Violet's fingers. "A treasure you must keep safe and never lose. It belongs to you." Her mother rests on the bed.

Etta turns, "David…"

He speaks after glancing from one to the other. "Your mother's family has handed this down from generation to generation. We know little of its history. Only that it's never to leave the bloodline."

With a tug on his hand, Etta encourages him to continue.

A shake of his head and David rolls his eyes. He continues. "Your mother remembers someone said it… does something. We are uncertain what that is. Mom could never get it to work." As he looks at Etta, he becomes serious. "It's important, dear."

She tries to care for the pocket watch object in her hand. She flips it from front to back, not seeing it.

Misery creeps into the parts of her where this woman lived. Violet feels the pain her parents can't hide as her mother grows weaker with each breath. Today is more significant than any other. It must be the end. Why now and not later? Any time but this one, the dumb family heirloom might be exciting. Not in this minute. Looking at her mom makes everything insignificant by comparison. Having her normal again is worth every stupid thing they have.

"Wear it, always. Can you do that for me, my Violet?" Her mother's whisper fills the room.

Tears fill her eyes, seeing how small her mother has become. Violet doesn't want this jewelry, especially because it means mom won't be with her anymore. What words should she say? Despite her efforts, nothing surfaces in her churning mind.

"In the attic maybe, my treatments make me forget so much." She takes shallow breaths, her gaze locks on Violet. "In that old family trunk is a wooden box that goes with that necklace. I couldn't open it either. It's for you now. Or pass it on to your kids one day." With that last whisper, a tear falls to the thin skin of her cheek. Her body rests deeper into the pillows.

It is time for goodbye. A voice in her head yells, "Run! Escape!" A huge sob fills her chest. Violet escapes the room without looking back. Not tracking the wall paper, ignoring warnings of no running on the stairs. She wants more air than the suffocating blanket of death covering the house allows. As tears blur her vision, she jumps, missing the last step, and burst through the screen.

Then she descends the porch, unaware of the loud thwack of the door. Now Violet understands why their home faces the woods, not the driveway. She can seek refuge in the trees, but what is she hiding from? The new world that doesn't include her mother.

Her entire life, her parents walked with her in this grove. They trust her to visit her favorite spot alone, but only if they know. They'll figure it out, at least dad will. She must get away. It is overwhelming. The necklace thumps on her chest, reminding her to run faster. Despite shadows she hurries, she barely sees the path, but knows where to go.

Tears flow. Upon seeing the cement land marker ahead, emotions bubble up, making it hard to breathe. She remembers the curve in the trail. Her feet avoiding the bolder under the brush, she flings herself to the ground at the post. The vegetation and dry leaves soften her landing.

Sobs rack her body. She can't stop. The echo in her heart tells her nothing can be the same for her and her father. That's the last thought Violet thinks as she falls into the sleep of a broken-hearted girl of eight whose mother's death is imminent.

"You were right to gather us." Lady Zia didn't pass the stone pillar. She strains to see the littling's face, avoiding crossing the gateway. "Do you know the cause of our border alert? The girl?"

The stag stands next to the littling. "It's not obvious without moving her, and I don't want to try that."

"I trust you will find out." Zia looks at the girl. "She isn't much older than my Bijou." Stepping apart from her companions, she extends her hands. "I don't sense her having ever crossed into our realm before this." Brows knit and eyes narrow. Yet, odd familiarity emerges yet unidentifiable. "I am sensing this world, but it's not from the child." Lady Zia relaxes, dropping her gaze to the cobblestones under her feet.

"If I may, Lady Zia, may I please? It's foreseeable, even perhaps-able, that she's not intended to be here." As he continues, the white rabbit stammers thumping one enormous foot and bouncing. "Best, better, bestest if you will, that we go away and forget we have seen…her." Horatius Hare turns his back on the matter, adjusting his monocle.

Lady Zia runs a hand up the long ear of Horatius to soothe.

"No, I'm afraid we cannot. She might require our help, or we may need hers." Her attention focuses on the guard, Lady Zia orders, "Be sure she awakens and returns to her people. But don't let her know you're guarding her." Then, making eye contact with each member of the council, she nods her head. "In time, we'll discover what this means. We watch her until we understand more." Everyone but the stag follow her, turning back to their world.

After the shimmer between the lands disappears, the deer assumes the pose expected in the ordinary realm. He nudges her foot. As told, he leaps over brush to watch from behind trees. The stag watches the littling rub her eyes, then touches the necklace. She walks out of the woods, chin on her chest.

Lady Zia and the Advisory Council still gathered after the portal closed. She surveys the variety of Maplehaven citizens in the group. The two governors of the ancient village, husband and wife, seek their guidance on major issues. Lady Zia allows the gathering to fall into random talk, as happens when not guided. She intends to break up the conversation among those assembled before the evening ends.

Something in the air changes before she can speak. The scent? The energy flowing through it? She turns her head to see the tree blooming in Circle Center. This is unprecedented. No one understood the lack of flowering.

"Randolph, what is on your mind?" The tingle on her neck alerts Zia to his presence. He moves soundlessly.

"First, who is not in the village, my lady?" spoken for her alone. As his wolf sharp eyes survey the end of day activities of shopkeepers and residents. He turns, taking in everything by sniffing the air.

"There above the trees near Raven Glen." Focused on the bright light, Sir Randolph pivots one ear around to catch the murmurs.

"Have you seen the likes of this?" Hands clasped behind her hips, Lady Zia contemplates the view.

"It's doubtful anyone has," the voice of smoky honey growls. "If you'll excuse me, I'll investigate." The gray wolf gives a tip of his brown and black top hat and separates from the others. As always, he vanishes as if he possess magic.

Lady Zia, known for her serenity, hides her uneasy feelings well. The residents of Maplehaven rely on this. Sir Randolph's words come back to her. Someone isn't here? She observes the quaint village. Instinct tells her something is coming. Until she knows more, she will continue to be the picture of normalcy.

A white mare sits in a mossy clearing. Her mate, a black stallion, stands near her. Their offspring curled on a bed of moss. Just born and being tended to by her mother. She raises her head to nuzzle into her mother's nape. A rumbling snort by the steed causes the newborn to twitch her spiky main of hair, sending a ripple of twitches along the ridge of her neck. The velvety snowy coat of the foal glows in the glade.

The radiant light illuminates those that traveled through the forest to bear witness. They are the ones who answered the call of a vague knowing. Those present are unaware of what called them here. As eyes adjust to the silvery glow, gasps erupt from the crowd. The air fills with sounds of wings flapping, caws, chirps, growls, and hoofs scraping the ground. Fireflies float around until they surround the celebration with twinkling through the trees. Soon, a stillness settles over the tiniest creature to the largest.

A product of this moment, a unique happening untold in historic scrolls of prophesies. This rare soul of an unknown purpose for this reason, a proper welcoming, begins.

First, the fairies bring fragrant blossoms. Each Fairy hovers, passing flowers from one to another. They arrange them in the fine hair of the newborn's mane. The mother cleans a spot high on its forehead, pushing the new locks aside. Meanwhile, flapping wings overhead draw attention from onlookers. Birds of every color and song pay tribute by sprinkling seeds in the clearing. Now, a sacred space forever marked by what will become an intricate growth of plants. A humming fills the air. The gathered crowd separate. And the whir becomes a buzz when the purple metallic crown of an ancient ruler moves forward through the witnesses. The blur of her wings surrounds her black and yellow form. Queen Eldora lands, surrounded by her swarm. The length of a full-grown rabbit, the Queen Bee bows. Kneeling, she unwraps the gift from the hive. Small worker bees continue buzzing while dropping delicate blooms in a ring around the assemblage.

The mare stops licking the brow of the newborn. Hoof scraping the ground, the dark horse encourages the Queen's approach. A vibration of her antenna has several of the swarm land on the honeycomb, removing the wax cap. Queen Eldora dips an ebony hand into the rare treasure of the hive. She places a golden dollop of concentrated honey on the favored spot. With a nod, the queen and her colony leave through the onlookers.

Last but not least, the dapper white rabbits. Each wearing a variety of fancy hats, bow ties, collars and monocles. One following another, too many to count, walking upright and bouncing. The fluffle offer the softest fur. With the grunted snort of the mare, the hares go forward. Each rabbit uses their fluff to rub and buff the palest, pearly coat as the creature continues to grow.

Next, a sudden hoot from above draws attention to the center of the clearing. On the head, the favored spot sprouts a nub. As they watch, it grows, swirling turns, forming a shimmering twist of bone longer than the legs underneath the growing body. The shaky limbs gather to lift the creature from the nest. The rabbits hop back into the crowd. Muscles quiver as it raises off the ground. A cheer erupts from those gathered, including dwarfs, deer, even gnomes.

Bell-like musical tones descend from the sky. A lone phoenix sings its enchanting song as its glides fluidly through the tree tops. Stunned silence settles upon the witnesses. While the unicorn continues to grow, the blaze colored bird lands on its back. Everyone falls to a knee in hushed reverence. Unaware of onlookers, the phoenix nods its head and Unicorn flips her mane as something unspoken passes. As a result, the plumage of the fowl swishes to cover its hindquarters. Red and gold feathers mingle with vivid white strands of the tail. The chest of the feathered beast rises, followed by its wings extending wide. With a whoosh, the phoenix flaps its feathers on to the unicorn's sides. It pulls up, taking flight, circling above the canopy.

In awe, the witnesses watch the rare being fly through the trees. A breeze sweeps from the clearing, drawing eyes to the full-grown Alicorn, wings fanning the air. With front legs pawing at the sky, she calls into the dusky night.

Making note of the phenomenon are two professors watching and recording the birth from their conveyance. The young apprentice moves levers, pushes buttons, and peddles the chain to move long spider-like stilts over the brush. The effort provides the trio a better view of the Alicorn. They are so engrossed by the amazing events unfolding before them; it strikes them dumb. In contrast to their usual chatty behavior, the scholars leave robust discussion for later.

Despite not being present, villagers sense something unidentifiable in the evening air. Maybe just the rustling of tree leaves. It could be energy zinging through the sky. Meanwhile, deeper in the forest, shadows are watching. Many draw back into the darkness. But others gather information to report to those that sent them to this place. Which version of these events that will become popular knowledge remains to be seen? Soon, every enchanted land will hear of it.

3

THE HOUSE BY THE WOODS-SEEK

"Mr. Landry, I appreciate you coming in today." She gestures to the empty chair beside his daughter, closing the door behind him. "Please, have a seat. We'll have you back at work as soon as possible."

"Vi, what's this about?" He looks in her direction while stiffly fitting into the too small armchair.

One quick glance at her dad and she knows he truly has come from his job. He hasn't begun drinking yet. Violet relaxes a fraction, thankful that vice always waits until after work.

Shrugging a shoulder was her only reply. Father and daughter wait as the lady sits behind the desk.

"I'm Ms. Anders, your daughter's high school counselor." Busily unbuttoning the single button of her dark orange jacket, Ms. Anders opens the file in front of her with a flick of a wrist.

"You may remember, Mr. Landry, I've left you several phone messages." One brow lifts as she levels her gaze at Violet's father.

"Sure." Despite his comment, his neck flushes red.

Violet took care of important things or pushed them under his nose for him to sign.

"Violet,"

"V," corrects Violet.

"Vi," states her dad.

"Miss Landry," Ms. Anders raises an eyebrow, "sits at a crossroads for her future. I've sent letters and left phone messages for you."

His hands clinch and release as he drops his gaze to the front of the desk.

"Dad?" It was out before she knew it was coming. Arms crossing her chest.

"I can explain. Vi—Miss Landry has a good chance at getting into a great collage if she applies herself this year. If she follows the plan, she and I have discussed." Ms. Anders waits for Violet's father to respond.

"She will graduate then?" Her dad asks.

A slight grin shows on Ms. Anders' face. "Yes. That was never an issue."

"Why am I here?" He looks from the counselor to Violet and back again.

Ms. Anders pauses, missing a beat. "I'm sorry for the misunderstanding, Mr. Landry. I hoped that you and I could convince your daughter to apply herself more fully so she will have the best future possible." Eyes softening, she breaks from the stiff demeanor. "It's a small town, and I know of your family's tragedy."

Absently, biting the inside of her lip, Violet feels what is coming and assumes her dad does, too. While it doesn't happen much anymore, it can sneak up on her.

As if sitting on a spring, he jumps out of his chair.

Violet's school counselor stands and says, "Not having her mother to guide…" then Mr. Landry interrupts.

"Vi will decide for herself." Turning to his daughter, "I'll be late. I have to get to work." He leaves the office without hesitation.

Violet's shoulders droop, then instinctually she pulls them back into place. At one time, this episode led to tears being shed. Before… it, he had been so present. They had been a close, happy little family. That being so long ago, she could forget how it felt. At least she tried to make it easier to face the bare minimum he gave her.

Every day, they each follow the same routine. Sadly, no need for communication or interaction unless absolutely necessary. Most times, school is the only thing marking time for her.

"If I promise to consider what you said, can I go?" Violet asks.

Defeated, Ms. Anders nods consent.

Violet drives her old car home from school. She wants to escape everything to consider what she should do. The morning's meeting with the counselor bugged her repeatedly throughout the day. "It's time to decide my future." Speaking to herself may be crazy, but she didn't have anyone to seek for advice. It never felt safe to let anybody close after she was gone. No family to speak of, their friends drifted away because no one could stand the constant grief. She has been alone. Not liking where her thinking was going, Violet tries to reason with herself. With no plans, the past is more appealing than she likes.

What could life have been? If her mother had lived, would she be different? If only this, that, and the other? Violet rubs the place where her heart sits in her chest. The pain does not dissipate. Nothing can change those lost years.

Her dad drowns himself in alcohol and work to avoid the grief of living without his love. And it works for him in a dysfunctional way. But not for Violet. Laughter and celebration, two elements missing because her mother had died. This realization forces her to see the list of reasons to stay wasn't truly a list. But will he miss her when she goes away to college? Did he care?

Because her dad doesn't notice her having a job or friends, it's time. Time to figure out her own path. Mom expected it of her, right? Still, Violet ignores the hurt, remembering the life she should've had.

Pain, grief to be exact, comes to the surface when she thinks of changing the future. They both suffer every day. Violet can see no other choice. She waited long enough, regardless of her father's plan to change or not. Pushing away thoughts that he may never get better, Violet's teeth bite into her bottom lip.

Tears fill her eyes as she pulls into the driveway. The little girl of nine, deep inside, always reminds her to have hope. That voice is getting difficult to hear.

She pauses, looking in the rear-view mirror, swiping dampness from her face. Short dark hair, she keeps chopped under her chin, has purple streaks. Her only rebellion aside from a lack luster outlook. Violet's coloring of black tresses and summer tanned skin, the same as her dad, distracts from her similarity to her mother. Whenever Violet sees her own reflection, she notices it.

It is time to get moving. A deep breath, she opens the door. Noticing the woods tempts her as she rounds the side of the house. Violet drops her backpack at the stairs. Indecisive, she looks from her home to the forest.

Violet startles to attention. Loud flapping wings and squeaking erupt in the quiet afternoon. She locates a raven above the lawn struggling to fly. Open-mouthed, she sees a brown squirrel dangling from its talons by one leg. The bird swoops near the stoop and drops the creature into a bush, squawking. With noisy chatter, the bushy rodent tumbles through the foliage right beside her. Violet shakes her head in disbelief.

With the raven's caw, she jumps into action. The blackbird on the porch roof causes worry he will try for the squirrel again. Despite her hair tangling in the branches, she sees the creature shaking on the ground.

"It's okay, little fella." Arm outstretched, she ignores the scrapes caused by the shrub on her bare arms. "I won't hurt you." She touches his fur and sends up a brief prayer he does not bite her.

After getting to her feet, she eyes the raven. Violet cradles his victim tighter, feeling an odd sense of being scrutinized by the silky feathered creature on the roof.

"You can't have him. Go away." Shaking her head as she walks up the stairs. "Now I'm talking to ravens." Opening the door, she plans what to do next. "A box for the squirrel listening to me speak. Oh, nuts." Violet heads to the mudroom.

"I don't know who I am anymore." Looking at the little face. A tiny paw reaches up to the neck of her t-shirt. Afraid he's going to scratch her bare skin, she grasps his leg, careful not to startle him. He withdraws and curls into a ball against her.

"Once I get a box, we can examine you and see what's hurt. Which, I assume you are, since you're letting me carry you." With a shrug, she knows her mental state needs attention. Still, the animal in her arms feels more urgent than herself.

After looking carefully, he wasn't injured as severely as she feared. Except for his outstretched limb, he curls into a ball. Violet checks the leg for broken bones through the fur. One eye peeks from under the fluffy tail, watching her. She makes him a bed after finding no obvious issue. Old towels for padding the box and a pleasant spot on the screened-in porch for fresh air.

"This is the best I've got." She worries her lip with her teeth while looking over the arrangement. "You can sleep here and I'll let you out in the morning. I still hear that raven making noise. At least you'll be safe tonight." She sets the box on the floor.

Familiarity of the scene evokes a memory. Slowly, she remembers a chipmunk in a container, same as this one. Her mother telling the critter she will help him.

Violet grabs her necklace, tucking it back inside her t-shirt. She continues trying to gather elusive threads of the impression. The squirrel squeaks and fidgets, Vi murmurs comforting sounds to the rodent. She drops the pendant and the recollection. Calm, it lets her rub a furry cheek.

Violet gazes into dark eyes as warmth fills her. She spins the dangling necklace. Tempted to sit here enjoying the critter's company, she rises to her feet. Violet moves to the screen door, flips the latch loose.

"I'll check on you when I get up, if you're still here." One last look at the fur-ball curling up and burrowing into the towel. Violet can't help but hope to see him in the morning.

An hour after darkness falls, a raven calls into the night. As soon as the squirrel hears this, he pokes his head out of the box, whiskers twitching. With eyes darting to each doorway, he listens for the slightest sign of danger. He positions himself for an escape.

The bird perches on the stair railing, watching and waiting for the brown rodent to open the screen.

"Get out here." The low caw from the onyx beak calls.

Although the squirrel knows the humans are in bed, he is cautious, pausing halfway to the exit. His eyes dart around, whiskers twitch, and he sprints to the door, sliding to a halt.

"We're late. Come out here." The raven insists.

Once outside, the squirrel speaks. "That's enough.

They might hear you." At the bottom of the stairs, he looks back up at the raven. "Like I'm looking forward to flying with you after this afternoon. You were not very careful." The squirrel rubs at his ankle.

"Sketes, you made it difficult with your thrashing about. You are fortunate I didn't let you fall." The dark gaze of the raven pins the squirrel.

"Berenger, we had to make it look real," Sketes stammers, trying not to cower at his menacing companion.

Berenger swoops, grabbing Sketes up under his front arms.

"You found what we came for, correct? And did not blunder the mission." The raven heads for the woods.

"The claws, hey, watch it! Yes, yes, I got it." Wiping a paw down his snout, "Please hurry. Flying with you isn't very enjoyable."

Berenger flies near the treetops. The night creatures are stirring as they glide through the forest. Over, under, around and swoop, the unlikely pair fly in the moonlight.

"It's just up ahead." Berenger calls out.

"Oh, good." Sketes tucks up his tail between his legs, grips it with both paws and buries his face in the fluffy fur.

The gateway was visible only by a glint of moonlight. With a shimmer, the two pass into the enchanted land. During the shift, the pair received their belongings as they had not wanted them in the ordinary world.

Berenger swoops low and releases his passenger.

Sketes hits the ground running, while adjusting his blue shirt collar with one paw and settles his cap more snuggly on his head.

"I'll never get used to shifting between worlds." Sketes runs on his hind legs.

"Enough complaining. I'll meet you there." Berenger flies up just above the rooftops. Moonlight dancing across the darkened windows throughout the village. Yellow lamp light glows along the lane. White and caramel colored stone cottages tucked together. From the sky, Berenger glides to the center circle. On a chimney, he watches for his entertaining friend. Not that he admits to friendship with a squirrel.

The cobble stones are warm from the heat of the day. Contrasting with the cool night air, Sketes shivers. Eyes darting to the dark crevices in the tiny space between houses, behind flower pots, and around unlatched gates, he continues to run. Running on his four feet. But pausing randomly and raising up on his hind legs, he listens for unusual sounds in the night. Mumbling to himself as he goes.

"You're not a rodent, you're a squirrel." Over his shoulder, Sketes sees iridescent wings flutter from a window box of flowers. A fairy, maybe. Any other time he would stop to investigate, but the others were waiting, so he keeps moving.

"Squirrels are brave. We go anywhere. Nobody notices us." His whiskers twitch at the smell of a cat. "You're on enchanted land. Maplehaven is a safe place." Not all enchanted lands are. He wipes a paw under his cap.

At the center circle, Sketes spots a streak of white glinting in the moonlight. Berenger drops to the ground in front of their destination.

"It's about time." Berenger straightens the silky scarf around his neck. He hops to the door, taps the wood with his beak.

"If you'd carried me all the way here, you wouldn't have had to wait." Fidgeting with his own neck wear, Sketes grumbles.

Turning with the point of his black beak close to the twitchy nose, Berenger speaks low. "My flying technique distressed you. Did it not?"

Sketes's wide eyes lock on the ebony point. "True, ac — accurate enough."

The dark chuckle of the raven ends as the door opens.

"Get in!" A young girl closes the door behind them. "The governors are waiting in the study for you. You're late, you know. Unnecessary worry you've caused them." Her brown curly hair bounced around her pale freckled face.

With a flap of wings, Berenger lands on the edge of the hall table. Eye level with the housekeeper. "My sincerest apologies, Fern." Giving a bow of his head, he removes his elegant top hat. "Dear, please forgive us. I hope we didn't keep you from your duties."

Stopping to wag a finger at the beak, the dwarf places her other hand on her hip. "Now behave yourself, Berenger. I've known the likes of you long enough."

"Long enough for what?" Sketes smirks.

"Nothing out of you, either. Just get going, both of you." Hands wringing her apron as she hurries away.

"Such late hours. Nothing good comes of late hours. Ma always said…" they could hear Fern grumbling as she waddles off through the doorway to the living quarters.

The two visitors enter the office, seeing the family waiting for them. Hurriedly, the raven flaps his wings. Landing on the elegant perch stationed at the far end of the impressive desk.

"Lord and Lady Stone, young Miss Stone, good evening." Berenger says.

Scurrying to the miniature staircase, Sketes scrambles to the top of the desk. The family rise from their seats by the fireplace.

"Berenger, Sketes report." Lord Stone ignores the greeting.

Stepping forward, Lady Stone lays a hand on her husband's arm. "Callahan Stone, please." Turning to the pair, she asks, "You're so late. Was there trouble?"

"It was my fault. Please forgive me, Lady Zia, Lord Callahan. I had to be sure they were asleep before I could leave." Sketes confesses.

"More that he slept in the crude quarters the young one made available for him." Berenger remarks.

As the daughter laughs, her mother quiets her with a glance. Berenger preens.

"Did you get what we need?" Lady Zia sits at the desk to be eye level with Sketes.

Hands removing his cap, he kneads it as he speaks. "Yes, I sure did. It took finesse, but it's in here." Sketes taps his temple.

"Can you describe it to Bijou?" Rising from the chair, Lady Zia gestures for her daughter to take the seat.

"Absolutely. We squirrels have a nose for details. That's why the Maplehaven Reporter employs mostly squirrels. It's the best newspaper in the enchanted lands because of us." Puffing up his chest, he walks near the sketch pad Bijou opens.

"Just don't expect him to remember where he buried his winter rations." Berenger remarks with a roll of his eyes.

Bijou grins at Berenger before turning her attention to Sketes. "Close your eyes and see it in your mind."

His small round ears relax back, eyes close, and whiskers twitch. He gives a detailed description of the necklace, as he recalls it dangling above his head.

Lord Callahan motions for Berenger and Lady Zia to join him across the room. After sitting near the unlit fireplace, they speak in hushed tones.

"Did you learn anything useful?" Lord Callahan asks.

"What could they possibly learn, Cal? This was only to see the talisman." From her seat, Zia looks at her daughter and Sketes with their heads together, talking animatedly.

"For what it's worth, I believe the reports of sadness are correct. The home feels sad. I can say she was very gentle and kind." Berenger walks from the back of the leather sofa to the arm. "I don't believe the girl, Violet, is aware of the enchanted. She spoke to

Sketes. But it wasn't with the idea of him understanding. It was the typical way the ordinary behave to us lower creatures." Stroking the tip of his wing along the white scarf at his neck.

"We are sure this—this trinket is Violet's only link to our world?" Cal looks from Berenger to his wife.

"Yes, dear, the little we have gathered over time suggests this. It's clear, too, that she knows less than we do." Lady Zia said. Again, glancing at the pair at the desk. "The gate patrols report that she never tries to use it to enter our world. We are sure it will allow her to do so. They have been successful at preventing her from passing through to the enchanted lands." Lacing her elegant fingers together on her lap, she grins. "They have become good at distracting her. Now that Violet is older, she isn't in the woods very often."

Lord Callahan asks Berenger, "Did you see any others watching her?"

"No, not anyone focused on the girl. I believe a scavenger was scouting around until the resident stray cat chased the rat away." He says, then smirks.

"A coincidence, or could he be looking for something?" Lady Zia asks.

"There's no way to know. With Rory Rat, he is working for someone or scavenging for profit." He says. With a raise of his black beak, he sniffs.

"That's it!" Sketes shouts.

The trio joins the others at the desk. The sketch shows an object resembling a pocket watch. One side displaying compass markings mingled with numbers of a clock surrounded by intricate filigree.

"On the back, what are the emblems?" Lord Callahan asks, looking at Sketes.

"Well," shifting from one foot to the other, "I couldn't tell. It was twirling on a chain around her neck."

"Hum," hopping from his spot on the desk to the perch next to it, Berenger comments, "more likely you fell asleep."

Chattering away with clicks, squeaks, and angry sounding squeals, Sketes scurries across the desk and up the perch in a blink.

"Now calm down." Lady Zia soothes with a hand along Sketes' fluffy tail. "It's late, and we have had more excitement this evening than normal." With graceful ease, she moves to fill the seat vacated by her daughter. Zia writes out two notes. "Sketes, take this to Professor Bibli before you go home. And Berenger, you do the same with Professor York." She looks at her husband. "We'll visit them tomorrow. They may know something about this artifact."

With a turn, Lady Zia finds her daughter waiting in the entry hall after closing the door behind Berenger and Sketes.

"You did an excellent job with Sketes tonight. And your skills with the pencils are improving." A hand out, she touches her girl's springy curls. Bijou's hair, so like her father's minus his gray strands.

"Thanks, it was fun. I love watching the two banter as they do."

Lady Zia waits for her to find the courage to speak her mind.

"My friends are day tripping to the, um, ordinary world for shopping." Bijou fidgets with the drawing pencils she carries.

"That's nice." Zia's expression softens with a smile.

"I want to go with them."

"Bijou, you know how I feel about you going there without me or your father." Lovingly, her mother wraps her arm around her shoulders.

"I had to ask. If I don't, I may never see the ordinary world. Perhaps one day…" Bijou faces her, shrugging.

The disappointment her daughter tries to conceal causes an ache in her mother's heart. She gives her a hug, knowing the topic will come up again. "For now, let's be patient for what comes tomorrow. I suspect we have an adventure ready to unfold before us."

4

LAND FOUND THROUGH THE
WOODS-KNOWLEDGE

The door opens as Lord Callahan raises his hand to knock a third time. "Ah, Gryphin, how's the best apprentice in all of Maplehaven?"

"Well, uh…" Raising darkened goggles to rest on his head. "That time already? It must be, you're here. I'm well. And the only apprentice in this land." With a step back, he gestures them to enter. Gryphin produces a grungy rag from one of his many pockets and rubs his smudged face. "How, well, um, how are you, Lord and Lady Stone?" Stepping back, the willowy young man looks out the door as they enter.

Lady Zia takes the rag from his hands. Bracing a hand on his chin as she wipes the dirt from his face, despite him being a head taller than her. With a soft smile, she murmurs. "She's not with us this morning." She returns the cloth to him. "It would please me if you drop by our home for a visit soon."

Looking everywhere but at the lady in front of him, he pretends she hasn't spoken. His ears turn scarlet, matching the curly red hair rioting on his head.

"The professors are waiting for you in the Community Library. I, uh, must get back to my work for Professor York." With a stumble, Gryphin tromps to the long hallway leading to the professors' laboratory.

"Why do you encourage the boy?" Callahan Stone shakes his head as they move to the large, expansive room attached to the entry.

"It's not my gifts telling me there could be an excellent match there." His wife says. The twinkle in the sidelong glance is unmistakable.

As the pair enter the library, their gazes raise to the center of the domed ceiling. Round windows pour in light from all directions. Painted in brilliant colors around windows and beams, a magical sky filled with many winged beasts and magical creatures alike. Bookshelves fill every wall on the first floor. At each corner sits a winding serpent inspired iron staircase. Rising to the dark wooden catwalk circling the room with more shelves. The third story is the place for rare books and artifacts from history. Locked cases hang on the walls between shelves and cabinets. Only one winding staircase on the second story at the center of the far wall allows access.

"Takes my breath away every time we enter the room." Lady Zia sighs.

"I agree. As a boy, I spent many hours here buried in books." With a sentimental gaze to his partner, Lord Cal turns, reaching for her hand.

"I remember too." Following a wink, Zia looks

around the room for the professors.

"Professor Bibli, Professor York." Cal calls out as he crosses to the study tables piled high with books.

"No, no, you can't think that. Drawing that conclusion won't work." Pacing away from the table and back again shaking his head, Professor Hewitt York steps on the footstool, his position before disagreeing with his colleague.

The large round glasses worn by Professor Bibli enhance the size of his eyes. As always, his patience is bottomless. The resident enchanted world historian and current presiding book worm waits.

The well-proportioned man of very short stature concludes his ruminations, stroking the white tuft of hair covering his chin.

"You're brilliant, Bib." Spoken low, raising his wise old eyes to the gold ones of his long-time friend.

"Gentlemen, are we interrupting?" Lady Zia asks.

With a wiggle and squirm, Professor Bibli moves from behind the books. "No, not at all." The bookworm speaks in his quiet voice. "I'm curious about what you have discovered." The trinkets dangling from the many nubs used as hands jingle as his blue grin spreads wide.

"We are hoping you can find answers for us." Raising the flap of the cross body satchel, Lady Zia pulls the drawings of the necklace free.

"There isn't time for this, Bib. We have important things already needing our attention." With a shake of his head, the white halo of hair flutters. Like cottony clouds sprouting from his head, Professor York long ago stopped trying to tame the stubborn locks.

Lord Callahan greets the man with an outstretched hand. "You're quite right, Professor. How's that apprentice working out for you?" With genuine curiosity, Lord Callahan's brow creases.

"He's too busy for the likes of this. Another apprentice would be outstanding." The wise man squints up at them. With another stroke of chin hair, he contemplates.

"Gryphin Tizly was a significant find. We thank you for that, Lord Stone." Professor Bibli says. The slight bow of the head shows the worm's blue and purple back.

"An interesting young man, indeed. Few like him, I'm afraid." Lord Callahan addresses the pair after pushing a stack of books down the table.

"We need a moment of your time," Lady Zia says. She places the drawing on the table.

Heads bent, the professors mumble in somewhat of a shorthand speech created from a lifetime of working together. At first, words between the colleagues come so brisk it seems unintelligible. Almost as suddenly as it began, it ends with them studying the papers in silence.

"Anything at all?" Lady Zia breaks the silence.

"We are familiar with" Professor Bibli raises his gaze to Lady Zia.

"But not exactly." Professor York's bushy brows lift from his eyes.

"We know when it's from." With a nod, the worm's tail wiggles around for better positioning.

"Yes, and who it's from." Professor York says.

"We can't say for sure, you understand," Bibli jingles his way through the objects hanging around his body. When he finds the feathered fountain pen, it passes up to his upper most right nub. He writes in tight small letters a list of information. The pen moves to the next appendage as the entry grows. He inscribes what he knows of the object in question.

As does Professor York, pulling a silver filigree writing utensil from a pocket, he makes notes of his own. When finished, they both step back to gage each other's conclusions.

"Okay, how about one of you explain what you think you know?" Lord Callahan, stepping closer, tries to read the tiny writing.

"Yes, follow me." Professor Bibli jingles his way off the table onto a chair and to the floor. Rippling constrictions of the lower half of his body propel him across the room to a pedestal holding a very large, ancient book. Both professors climb up on the bench and flip pages, searching the text.

"Yes, that's it. Excellent memory, old fella!" Running a bony old finger along the page, Professor York taps a note at the bottom. The scholars look from the passage in silent communication.

Used to the eccentric manners, the Lord and Lady wait. On each side of the pedestal, they try to understand detailed and colorful text.

"The Widowed King, are you sure?" Lady Zia raises her eyes, looking at her husband.

"Yes, it is." Lord Cal leans closer.

"We mustn't mention that, must we, Hewitt?" Professor Bibli's soft voice whispers.

"Like you, I don't believe all of it but, yes, do." On a sigh, Professor York steps down and walks to the wall near the library entrance. A wooden box fronted with a metal door embossed with colorful pigeons hangs above three risers. The professor uses the stairs and opens the door. He pulls the flared end of a black funnel towards his mouth, he then turns the small crank, making a whirring sound. Below the mechanism, he presses the second button and speaks into the contraption.

"Young Tizly?" He waits for a reply.

"Yes, Professor?" The speaker on the top of the box emits a crackle and goes silent.

"We need help with a scroll on the artifact's level, please." He pushes the mouthpiece back into the fixture. Then a slight shake of his head and he leans in, "right away Tizly."

"Ahem," clearing his throat, Professor Bibli confesses to Lord Cal and Lady Zia. "I'm not sure where to begin. You are both aware of the popular understanding of the enchanted history, I suppose."

"What does that mean?" Lord Cal crosses his arms over his chest.

Coming to stand beside the Bookworm again, Professor York prods. "Just tell them." Professor York leaves the group to retrieve the scroll on the third floor when the apprentice enters the library.

Yet by adjusting his glasses and clearing his throat, Bibli stalls for a few more seconds. "You see this and other likenesses of the widowed king, Vergilius Starosta, he wears an amulet of gold and silver much like this drawing." With a glance, the professor gages the progress of Hewitt and Gryphin.

"But does that mean the girl's necklace belonged to him?" Lord Callahan was growing restless with the unclear answers.

Bibli pulls his attention back to his audience. And for a quiet moment, he considers the Lord. Decision made, he warms to the telling of history.

"It's not as clear as that. What Professor York and I know is more complicated. We were just beginning our field studies at the time of the final reigning king of the enchanted realms. I was in one region, and Hewitt was in another. It was the topic our acquaintances enjoyed most."

"So that means…, forgive me, Professor Bibli," brows drawn together, Lady Zia interrupts. "The last monarchy existed one hundred years ago…" looking from Bibli to Hewitt. "… You can't be."

"Ah, you have always been an attentive student, perhaps because of your empathic abilities." His warm smile makes his eyes sparkle brighter. "We seem to live long lives. King Starosta did not. He had twin daughters, as everyone knows. What history books leave out is the family rift just before he died. Few alive today remember those times."

Professor York interrupts the sentimental pause by calling out from the upper level.

"There's more, keep going, Bib." The shout bellows in the dome above the room.

Morning light fills the room through the glass canopy of windows. The sound of clomping boots on metal treads grows nearer. The apprentice and teacher make their way down two stories of the spiraling stairs.

"There is not much known about the family problems, but we recall a rift. One daughter stayed in the enchanted lands, the other one to the ordinary, never seen again. At least that is the tale. We believe, as things are, it was more complicated than it seems. By the time Hewitt and I returned from our research in the far lands, the King was dying. He had vowed to end the rule of kings in our land."

Professor York instructed his apprentice to arrange the scroll on top of the book. He opens the yellowed parchment to the section that pertains to the current topic.

"Now, you're leaving out very necessary details," Professor York admonished his old friend.

"It's most depressing. Important, but so sad." Professor Bibli's eyes softened, looking away.

"True enough. I remember the King's daughters were opposite to each other in looks and manner. One dark if you will and the other light. Not good versus evil, keep in mind. Very different things. Yes, we shouldn't confuse the two." York punctuated his words with a wag of a finger in the air.

"Now, don't mislead them. Share the facts, not story-book tales." Bibli shakes his head.

"If the rift was between the girls, choosing opposite paths, enchanted and ordinary, in this case. What happens to the monarchy?"

"I'm not understanding how any of this relates to the necklace." Lord Callahan says.

"I'm getting there. If it had been agreeable, it wouldn't be a problem. If it was not, who knows?" Lady Zia said. Growing more animated as she grasps the threads.

"Precisely!" Professor York points to the scroll. "Here we see a foretelling of future events. Now, mind you, we don't believe this, but some do. The sisters looked alike, but for light hair and the other dark. The prophecy tells of a switch. It's difficult to say what because of the wording."

"You must understand, the daughter going to the ordinary world received the necklace." The bookworm interjects.

"True, the dark girl's actions caused that." Professor York agreed.

"Dark haired sister." Bibli corrects.

"You've skipped something, I think." Lord Cal looked from one professor to the other.

Bibli moves to the floor from the pedestal with a soft thud. His body rippling as he propels himself to a section of books and disappears on the shelves.

"We must study this scroll for a full understanding of what may be. Omens, prophecies, and such are never simple. Interpretations are muddy water. I will research the necklace and Bibli the foretelling. That is the way." Professor York mumbles under his breath.

"I can help you, Professor Bibli." Lord Callahan follows the sound of books shifting at a spot head high, in the middle of an aisle of shelves.

"Yes, please, Cal, take this volume to the table."

After removing the book from the shelf, Lord Stone receives a nod of appreciation from the bookworm. He carries the leather-bound edition to the place where the drawings remained. Followed by the others, they wait for Professor Bibli.

Using the feather end of his fountain pen, Professor Bibli points to the entry on a page marked Chronometers and Navigational Devices Enchanted.

"AHHH, yes… hum." Professor York pulls a monocle from the clip on his shirt and moves closer. "This reference book is one of many. But not likely to catalog all enchanted objects known. They find more every year. We must test each to understand them before we make records. We never have an updated list."

Professor York adjusts his aim to direct attention to the particular devise. "It's possible we are dealing with this object. We don't have a likeness to compare to your drawing. A notation of the amulet is in the craftsmen's journals. That caused the entry to be made. A snail with three dots is the maker's mark. The historian calls it the Proclivitas Amulet. However, it only says it will allow passage between the worlds via gateways." He becomes quiet and leans back.

"It's believed to have powers unknown."

The expression on Lady Zia's face matched the contemplative pacing of the wide circle in a patch of bright light from the windows overhead.

"Let me see if I understand what we've gathered. Violet's necklace came from the enchanted world. The twin daughters of the Widowed King had a fight that tore the monarchy apart. The device is likely the Proclivitas Amulet, but we don't know what its exact purpose is." Zia stops, turns, waits for the professors to confirm the summary.

"As best we can say, yes. We will give it more attention now that we are sure of the period in time the amulet originated." Professor York closes up the books. "I have things to get back to in my lab. I'll inform you when I've finished my part of the study."

The gentlemen once again pick up the private speech. Lord and Lady Stone make their way towards the entrance.

"There are gateways scattered everywhere, what if…" wringing her hands, "… what if she passes through unprepared?" Looking up to her husband, concern is obvious.

Reassuringly placing a hand on her back, stopping her in the entranceway. Before opening the door, he turns her to him. "You're thinking with your mother's heart." His warm smile calms her. "We will do what we can to keep her safe. As the governors of this village, we need a plan. I have the beginnings of one. Let's gather the council."

Zia grins in response to the twinkle in his eyes. "It must be clever. You never want that." With a wink, she turns to open the door.

"Lord Callahan, a moment?" The miniature man waited for permission to approach.

"Did you find something, Professor York?" The couple turn from the exit of the building housing the

Community Library and Research Facilities.

"No, not on that matter. It's concerning a missive my apprentice delivered to me upstairs. I don't wish to alarm my colleague. However, I feel you, as governors, should know." He pulls a fold of parchment from his vest pocket.

"Please tell us what's so important." Lady Zia clasps her hands behind her back, waiting for him to continue.

"An acquaintance in the West Lands has written that the realms have experienced several burglaries." Running a finger across the words, he is silent.

"Professor?" Looking from his wife to the ancient man.

"Yes, well, he included a list of items, four when he wrote this correspondence, unaccounted for." He strokes his chin hair. "It doesn't seem they have any relation to each other. I recall one was on display at a ceremony, and another being transported for further study." He looks to the library, then back to the governors. "I believe they could be thefts of opportunity, yet we should still be vigilant."

"Notify the aerial security reserves. They can watch for suspicious activity. Does that satisfy you?" Lord Cal rests a hand on his hip.

The grin gave Professor York's aged appearance a goofy mad scientist look that always produces smiles around him. "Of course. Should have thought of that myself. We will run an inventory here. Just to be sure." Thumbs hooked in his vest pockets, the slim man turns to go.

"Uh, Professor, any idea if the variety of artifacts mean anything?" Smile disappearing, Lady Zia asks.

A sudden change in posture, then he runs a hand across his shiny brow. "Interesting question, nothing that I can think of. But, I am positive it involved multiple people to, say, gather the objects. Two of them were too far apart for a single person to collect them."

"Even with the portals and gateways scattered about everywhere?" Lord Callahan's eyes grew dark.

"Yet still, one object in the ordinary world is remote to the likes of our travels." A brow raised. The professor sighs. "You have given me more to consider than I had thought worrisome."

"Let's stay ever aware. And be sure to send us word if you hear of more misplaced objects." Lady Zia said.

5

THE PLACE BETWEEN WORLDS-
INTRODUCTIONS

Violet sits in her car waiting. Her fingers tapping on the steering wheel. She adjusts the rear-view mirror that doesn't need adjusting. A glance shows a discarded straw wrapper in the door pocket. She reaches for it and grabs a receipt for gas out of the empty seat. The trash, deposited in a bag found on the floor of the empty passenger side, she taps her fingers on the steering wheel.

Wait, avoid or stall? What does it even matter? In the rear-view mirror, Violet confronts herself. This childish behavior wasn't fooling anyone. After all, moving home was her own idea, no pressure from her dad. In fact, the surprise was mutual and not part of her original plan.

Yet, here she sits, still delaying the drive home. At least she made it to the town. Besides, her dad was still at work. No one waiting at the house for her.

Occasionally, the life that could be if her mother still lived poked at her. A childhood habit, she supposed. But today her mind couldn't help but go there. Today definitely held inspiration for the parties her mom loved creating. Homemade decorations in the living room and dining room. The ordinary became celebrated and as special as her mom could make it. Today is one of those days. She insisted dad skip overtime at work to be with them for celebrations. Unaware she was smiling, Violet recalls one of the last parties her mother insisted they have. The party for the first night of the lightning bugs, her mom insisted they have it on the porch one of the last summers she was alive.

Violet watches the rain splatter on the windshield of her car, trying to put the past out of her mind. Her entire plan feeling doomed. The rain making her hurt worse. Moving home with the purpose of fixing things with her dad now feels ridiculous. She had gotten the idea from a mental health class she now regrets taking.

A rumble of thunder draws Violet's attention back to the rain. Still falling just as hard as when she parked. Might as well do something she likes before doing something she won't. Shopping is good for her spirits. This bookstore caught her eye as she was driving around town. Books have always been her escape route. A new place to shop for books is perfect for her veracious reading appetite.

A wish for an umbrella is useless as she rushes from the car. Violet opens the shop door greeted by bells announcing her entry. She wipes her feet on the worn rug, giving her eyes a moment to adjust to the light inside the bookstore. With a shake of her head, rain drops dislodge from her shoulder length hair.

Violet surveys her surroundings. A sudden urge to explore piles, shelves, nooks, and books. Odd friendly sculptures cover the space on the walls not filled by shelves. Dark wood moldings border the ceiling of the long room. Amber colored light fixtures drop from medallions on the ceiling, giving the room a warm glow. So many stacks of books on tables and overflowing bookcases fill the space to bursting.

"Good morning. How can I help you?" A lovely, white-haired lady pops out from behind a stack of books at the counter.

"Hi. I'm just looking." As intrigued by the woman as the shop, Violet moves near the counter.

"No problem, look around. Have you been here before?" Without waiting for an answer, she continues rounding the end of the counter. "It's awfully wet out there this morning. It promises to clear up this afternoon. Don't worry." Her grin never leaving her soft cheeks, she says, "My manners! I'm Candy Shepherd and pleased to meet you." Facing Violet, she waits.

"Vi, I'm Vi." Unsure why she didn't say V as she has since high school. The pet name her father preferred was not her favorite.

"Good. Now we're friends. I'm sure you haven't walked through that door before today, so I'll tell you what I tell everyone new. I don't have everything, but I can get it. Much of my inventory is old. Be mindful of that, please. Other than that, I'm here to help. You take your time and enjoy. We're not new, flashy, or online, so don't ask for Wi-Fi whatawhosits because I don't have it." A breathy chuckle, then Candy looks Vi over with eyes, taking in more than appearance. "Are you from around here?"

"Yes, I'm moving back home after being away at college. And I don't remember this shop being here." Violet says. Distracted, her eyes move to the sculpture of a white rabbit's head wearing a top hat protruding from a picture frame. "I'm sure I would remember this place."

"We have passed this store down in my family many generations. I suppose you never looked close enough to see us," Candy says. She pulls a feather duster from the waistband of her apron. With a flutter of feathers, she dusts the sculpture on the wall. Soon, she is moving around, whisking puffs of particles into the air.

"Oh, do you have any books on pet rabbits?" She felt relief as she remembered the predicament a rash decision created for her.

"You have a pet rabbit!" Dropping the duster to the counter, Candy holds her right index finger in the air, thinking. "The fifth shelf, second segment of row D. Follow me, please." She disappears in the main aisle.

Vi follows her. Pausing, the vibrant blue eyes of a fox mesmerize her. At the end of a row of shelves over stuffed with books, a sculpture of a fox with a fancy hat is on the wall. With a shake of her head, Vi rushes on, ignoring the draw each character has on her.

The animal sculptures sprinkled amongst the books are unique and require a closer look. Reaching the aisle Candy is in, Vi tries to focus.

"Yah, an old tenant in my building left the rabbit. I didn't know what might happen to her over the summer if I didn't bring her home with me."

"What a nice thing to do." Candy said. She pulls a low stool to the exact spot she stated. As she sits, she pulls one book and then another, holding them up for Vi to take.

"I think that will do." Candy says. Her warm smile erasing years from her face.

"Thanks for finding these." Vi says. The door bells jingle from the front of the shop. Vi jumps, stepping back, letting Candy pass to make her way to the counter.

Alone, Vi turns in a circle, wondering what to explore first. This stop had been impulsive and a delay tactic. Avoidance is not a luxury she can afford. She realized moving had to be done alone, so she had moved most of her belongings last weekend. With loose ends tied up at school, she is home. Living with her father will prove difficult. But this shop could serve as an escape when she needs it.

Vi wonders through one aisle after another. Gradually making her way deeper into the store. She can't believe she never noticed such a unique place. Somewhere a clock keeps its rhythmic count. Free hand out, tips of her fingers glide along the warm wood of a shelf. Her attention migrates to the sculpture at the end of the aisle. Eyes that appear illuminated keep contact with hers as she moves forward. Still, her fingers slide on the shelf. One book catches her knuckle and falls. Vi startles, breaking her gaze with the wolf on the wall, turning to pick up the book. Her head collides with the leg of a stranger browsing shelves behind her.

She fumbles and drops the books, her hair falls into her eyes, the locket swings out from under the neck of her t-shirt. Vi plops to her bottom, frowning at the dark shoes of the stranger. Ready to apologize, it dies on her lips as she runs her eyes up the black jeans to the baggy untucked shirt and open gray hoody.

"Careful." The quiet word said without inflection of any kind. The young man ignores her.

Violet sits awkwardly, taking up the entire walkway between her mess of books and splayed limbs. She comes to her senses and piles her books back onto her arm. She stands in a rush to scoot away. Violet tucks her hair behind her ear, and tries to ease back against the shelf of books behind the aloof guy. She looks at her feet, hoping to keep from tangling them again. Just another step and she could avoid more embarrassment.

He spins to face her. "Wait." He says. Wearing old-fashioned glasses that do little to hide his dark eyes as they dip lower than her eyes, in an assessing manner.

"Don't you want to apologize for assaulting me?" A hint of amusement creases one corner of his mouth. His eyes raise to hers.

"Sorry, excuse me, please." Unsure why, she feels breathless, looking up at his unreadable expression. A slight warmth fills her cheeks.

His hand raises to remove his glasses. He tucks them into the pocket of his hoody. Eyes flick away, then back to hers again.

"I haven't seen you in here before, have I?"

Growing more self-conscious of her chest, where his eyes keep dipping, her ears grow warm too. With tremendous hope that her V-necked t-shirt is covering her bits appropriately, she refuses to reach up to check. Her increased awareness of being mostly alone, deep in an unfamiliar bookstore with a total stranger, had her assessing him. A stranger at least a head taller than herself. A low hum of alarm fills her gut. Violet takes a step sideways toward the main aisle before answering.

"No, I haven't been here until today." Another step, moving closer to a safe distance between her and this total stranger.

Low on the shelf from behind, she hears a noise coming from the books. Thinking someone must be looking at books on the other side of the shelf, she glances at the bottom of the shelf. Then a second, more intense look.

"Did you see that?" With a leap, Violet is standing next to the stranger. Concern of his intentions disappear in an instant, replaced by a more urgent primal fear.

He moves to face her, resting his shoulders on the offending shelf. He scowls at her. "You falling at my feet, sure."

"Not that, there, listen. Can't you hear that?" Violet's voice raised an octave or two as she points at a lower shelf near his feet. "I'm sure I saw a tail, a rat's tail." Her chest heaving, she moves to see around his legs. Not seeing movement, she wonders if something is moving on the books. Or maybe damaging the books altogether?

"I would appreciate you moving out of the way." Violet insists.

"You're sure you're OK?" He asks. But she can tell he has no actual concern. Not moving as she requested, his feet planted in place.

Violet tries harder to see what is happening, resorting to bending over, intent on understanding the possibility that a rat was trying to eat or nest in the books.

"Look," He taps a foot on the shelf behind him, "see, nothing is there. You sure you didn't hit your head when you bumped my leg?" Annoyance fills his voice.

Nothing jumps out of the shelf. The noise stops. She could have imagined it, maybe. It wouldn't be the first time she glimpsed something completely impossible. Something that her very active imagination created. Violet had always reasoned it was because she spent too much time alone after her mom had died. Reading too many fantasy novels with her active imagination was as good an explanation as any.

Embarrassment crashed over her anew when she looked up at the stranger in front of her. Violet, toying with her necklace, noticed his eyes drop again. She tucked the only jewelry she wore back into the shirt. Violet wants to slip out of the tight aisle.

"No, I'm fine, honest. Again, I'm sorry, um, for

this." Just wanting to get away and escape this odd encounter, Violet looks to the open end longingly.

"At least let me introduce myself. I'm William, or Will, if you prefer." He waits, holding out a hand.

"I'm Violet, but I go by V." Slowly, raising her hand, she decides it can't hurt. With the handshake, he wraps his fingers around her hand. The warmth and soft vibrating purr running through her palm surprises her. Her first impression of William was threatening to melt away. Her impression originally pegged him as an intellectual, spending more time in the library than out of doors. William's hand, while gentle, was firm and labor rough. Shoulders not slim and bony, but well-used muscles. The snap judgment was far from reality.

"Mouse then." He gave a brief nod of his head. "Maybe we'll bump into each other again." The slight raise was back at the corner of his mouth.

"What? No." Violet tugged her hand, but he held firm.

"Which one do you object to?" The question keeps her in Will's company longer.

"Mouse? Both actually, but you are not calling me that or anything because we won't be seeing each other again." Violet said. Her hand resting on his forgotten.

"You're afraid of little mice, obviously. Besides, you're the size of one." Will said. At the last statement, his gaze lowers to her shoes, then back up to her face. Ever so slowly, he leans closer.

"I'm not afraid." Violet says, breathlessly.

"Then see me again." Will, grin gone, his dark eyes serious.

The feeling of his firm hand holding hers is perfect. When she notices his other hand cover the top of the one he grips, Violet is aware of the slippery slope under her feet.

Violet pulls her hand free, then backs out of the aisle. Sliding her palm on her thigh did not make the buzz go away.

"Until next time, Little Mouse." The words spoken just for her.

No, nope, not doing that! She told herself in no uncertain terms. No men, guys or jerks are on the priority list at this moment. With her daddy issues ready to poison her decisions, Violet shudders. She reminds herself to stay focused. Getting into veterinary school had been difficult, and she wants it to be her primary goal.

Dad had to be her focus now. Before classes begin, progress with her dad needed to happen. What that could be is still unknown. Only time will tell, but perhaps there could be a new way forward. Nothing could make her happier than having him back to who he had been before her mom had died.

"Hey! What's the big idea? You bent my whiskers." The rat rubs his snout, sitting on a shelf looking William in the eye.

"Don't blame me. You were not to be noticed. That was the agreement, remember?" William points a finger at the rodent. Because of the aggravation, he pulls back, exhaling a breath, gathering himself.

"You are being paid to scavenge inconspicuously, Rory. And do not forget next time." The whisper held the heat of a threat.

"Those fancy glasses, did they find anything? I'm not sensing squat today. We may have wiped this gem of a treasure trove out already." Nose in the air twitching, Rory's eyes dart around with an excited gleam.

"I found one thing in particular." William looks at the end of the row where Violet had left.

"Now, boss, now isn't the time to go flirty. "Your mom wouldn't approve." Rory said, giving distracted attention to an old volume with faint lettering on the spine.

"Step-mother. This is a mistake you don't want to make again." William says, steel lacing his words. He moves to the end of the row, looking both ways. "In case you forgot, you work for me. This is not the time for other contracts. Now let's get going. She'll be waiting for a report."

Hastily Rory disappears in the books, only to pop back out on the floor. He stands upright, adjusts his duster and pulls his vest in place. Tail swishing behind him as he rushes to catch up to William.

"We have nothing to tell her. She will not be happy with that."

"You didn't see what I did with the darshana glasses. I won't disappoint her." Each step taking the unlikely pair deeper into the store. The owner being engaged with customers according to the bell jingling and murmur of voices, they hurry. At the back of the bookshop is a sitting area. Oddly enough, a coat tree stands in the center of the wall. A variety of hats appear forgotten on the wooden limbs.

With purpose, William and Rory reach for theirs. Rory's dark top hat looks old and well worn. While William's is a nondescript blue baseball style cap. They slap them on their heads, then step into the shimmering opening next to the hat rack. The portal closes behind them.

"Please consider what I said, Ms. Grail." The willowy man dressed in a dove gray vest with a white shirt steps out of the front door. He looks down his tailored pants to his slate gray leather shoes and taps a silver tipped walking stick on the outside of one foot. And then lifts his gray hat trimmed with a black silk band, he places it on this bald head. Anyone looking at him would figure the hat was to protect his pink skin from the sun. His pale blue eyes meet hers.

"You have no cause to come around here. My business is none of your concern. You don't know as much as you think you do." Ms. Grail said. She moves back from the threshold, preparing to shut the man out of her house.

"If you cooperate with me—," He tries to speak when the dark-haired lady whispers in his ear. Words for him alone.

"Mother Brune, is everything OK?" The young man with disheveled brown hair steps through the stone archway at the courtyard's front. A family estate that has seen better days now it has a shabby feel with the ground's overgrown foliage draping over the stone wall at the front entrance.

The sharp glare disappears the instant Brune looks away from the pale man. Only when the young man nears does she speak.

"Darrock, we were just having a slight differing of opinions. Besides, the Marquis is leaving." Brune Grail wraps her hand through the crook of Darrock's arm.

"Ms. Brune, as I've told you before, my title is unnecessary. It's an old family relic best left in the past." The Marquis admonishes her.

"How are you, Pravat?" Darrock asks, his gaze meeting the odd man while placing a hand atop the one at his elbow.

"Well, thank you. It's been awhile, hasn't it Young Mister Grail?" Marquis Pravat asks.

"Yes, I've only been back a short time. Just helping with a few family matters." Darrock surveys the grounds before his gaze meets with Pravat again.

With the visitor on his way, the pair shut the door. Darrock holds Brune in place. "What was that about?" He asks.

"That terrible man hates me." Brune looks up into his dark eyes. She placed a hand on his cheek, a warm smile fills her face. "You're here and he won't bother me now." She turns to look around the entrance filled with paintings, antique side tables and family heirlooms. "You know what his kind are like. They only care for the past and the value of objects from another lifetime." Her voice trails off as her thoughts disappear to a different time and place.

"Mother Brune, be sure you tell me if he bothers you again." He says encouraging her to move with him through the hall. "Now, come sit with me. I have news."

In an instant, Brune's attention focuses on Darrock and what plans they will make.

6

LAND FOUND THROUGH THE WOODS-TRIP

"How can you live this way? I've been cleaning this place since I moved home. You haven't even noticed." Violet, arms crossed, waiting in front of the door. She holds back tears, waiting for her dad to respond.

"You just got here." He sits on the stairs putting on shoes. "It's not as bad as you make it out to be." After tying his last lace on the dusty boots, he stands towering over her.

"I've been here two weeks." It took effort, but she swallows the lump in her throat.

"Can't be." His scowl softened with confusion.

"Dad."

It was there, that hint of care, maybe something more. She could see it on his face, in his eyes. She just wants a reason to believe. A tiny glimmer that her father still cares about having a relationship with her. That is why she came home. One last attempt with her dad. It will only work if he is present and sober.

"I'll cook supper…"

"You know where everything is. I've got to go." Just like that, he withdraws from any connection with her.

"I mean, let's eat together."

"I'm going to be late." He looks from Violet to the exit.

So she moves aside, while her hope drops like lead to the floor.

He steps past her but stops outside the screen door.

Violet turns to look at his back covered in a faded plaid shirt, one of many he wears to work.

"Vi, why did you bother coming here?"

"For you, Dad." A whisper was all she could force past the emotions choking her.

The pause feels endless as he hangs his head, motionless.

"You shouldn't have. I'm not worth it." His long stride took him from the porch.

"But I am." She said. The words hang in the air, with no one to hear her declaration. A deep breath, then another, and her eyes focus in on the woods. Past the screen she could see the lush green shadows and raises her hand to push the door, but stops. Turning to look at the cobwebs dancing in the foyer's corner as a breeze blows into the house. First, she must clean the rabbit cage. Then, she needs time to pull herself together, so that is what she will do today. If he can bail on her, she can bail on housework.

Moving up the stairs to her bedroom. She grabs supplies from the bottom of her closet. Violet hurries to toss the lid of the plastic tub, pulling out cleaner and fresh hay. She lifts the dusty caramel colored rabbit from the cage. After a quick cuddling rub, she lets her loose on the floor and scrubs the habitat.

"That's better, girl. I'm not saying you're a messy bunny, but you have your moments." Violet turns to find her in the room.

"Cacey, don't go under there." She rushes to scoop her up just before the last fluffy white bottom of a paw disappears under the bed. Once in the enclosure, Violet latches the top back into place.

"I don't have a clue what I'm doing with you." A statement that applies to the human living here as well. At least Cacey is a comfort when snuggled. A smile pulled at her mouth.

With everything put away, Violet leaves the room and the house. The dew covered lawn makes her canvas shoes damp as she walks to the woods. With determination to leave her cares behind, she longs for the shaded, earthy air surrounding the trees. Early morning sunlight warms her back as she nears her haven. She gave no thought to finding the overgrown path of her childhood. But she follows it. A deep breath of mossy dampness and her spirit lifts.

A few years absent from this place hasn't dimmed the tranquil effect it has on her. Like a soundtrack of her early life with her parents, birdsong fills the air. So familiar, yet new at the same time. A fallen tree that had been standing when she had been here last. Foliage that is more lush than ever. The path she had once run on, now covered with ferns and limbs. Violet moves slower than expected. She didn't mind.

Violet nears the tapered land marker. She rubs the necklace. She never noticed a round dimple in the center of the back. Her toe snags on a tree root. Startled by a prick to her skin, her attention goes to the pendent. And she falls to her knees. In a move to sit upright, her breathing hitches. Blood. Just the tiniest droplet on the pad of her thumb. Somehow, she must have damaged the locket, causing this to happen. When she feels the dampness of the ground, she stands, brushing debris off of herself. Not looking where she is going, the boulder hidden under the brush catches her heel and, as she notices the mechanical hum and warmth of the pendant on her chest, Violet tumbles. She lands on her backside, past her favorite spot next to the cement pillar.

With a shimmer and ripples in the air, Violet is sitting on a cool cobble stone road. Not the damp, leafy ground of the woods, as expected. Unable to move, she forces a breath in and out of her lungs. Blinks. Blinks again. She jumps up, turns around to see a village lane lined with stone buildings. Stepping back in reflex, the rippling and sparkles stand between her and the enchanted world. Under her feet lays trampled brush. Chest heaving, she leans with a hand braced on a knee and one on the post.

"This can't be happening." Violet says, her eyes closed.

With slow realization, she straightens to see the stone marker more clearly. Her fingers find three slash marks carved into the pillar. Above those are two circles sunken just enough to be felt but not seen. With further inspection, the carvings must be ancient.

"Why haven't I noticed this before today?" With a hand on the post, Violet reaches the other one out. A shimmer ripples through the air. Her hand falls to her side. She turns away from the gateway and is mindful of the boulder under the brush, and steps back.

"No, this can't be happening." Deep breath, hand in her hair.

"I'm asleep, like I used to do near the post." Steps trampling the green leaves around her. She looks at her thumb, not able to find any trace of the blood. The necklace is quiet and no longer warm.

She faces the place she had fallen through to... somewhere. She takes a step forward. Then she takes another with her hand reaching out. She squeezes her eyes closed and takes another step.

The pendant warms and makes a low noise as shimmers fill the air and Violet steps on the stone street again. Slowly, she opens her eyes one at a time. A glance over her shoulder reveals a slight ripple in the air as the forest fades to show a stone wall.

A decision had to be made. She can go back to the safety of her home or explore this place, even though it is likely a dream. A dream during a nap she couldn't remember taking. Violet looks down the street to lovely window boxes filled with cheerful flowers. She moves forward.

Sweet floral scents bring an earthy comfort as she takes quiet steps past each residence. Most buildings are a light color stone with varying colors of shutters and window boxes. At the corner, Violet realizes she has seen no one yet. She peeks her head around the corner, trying to decide which direction to turn.

One direction has a gathering or something happening. Lots of people run around with animals. Maybe a zoo had a catastrophe because the animals are wearing hats and vests. No, it must be a circus. Maybe a circus derailed allowing the animals to escape.

Violet chose the chaos in the circular park area. A tree stands to one side with pink blossoms, unlike any she has seen in her life. The green grass is such a vibrant color as to be unnatural. Yet something feels very familiar.

This place she has never visited before feels oddly like home. With this realization, Violet raises a hand to run through her hair. The hand pauses as she reaches the edge of the spectacular scene.

It appears one woman is directing others to catch a rat. Just then, the slim woman calls to a dear with a large rack of antlers to corner Rory with two other deer. Just as the creatures move away as directed, the lady spins around as if surveying the chaos. Suddenly, she is locking eyes with Violet.

Hand moving from her hair to her pounding heart, Violet feels her knees unlock in the most disastrous way. This is too real to be a dream. The rat is wearing a brown coat and talking. The animals are talking, ALL the animals are speaking.

As Violet feels the world tilt, and a buzz fills her head, the lady wraps her arms around her. The lady's arms are strong as she keeps Violet from dropping to the ground.

"I've got you, young one. Such a fright you've had. Deep breaths now, that's it." She says. A smooth, melodious voice continuing to soothe as Violet tries to find strength in her legs again.

In the next instance, the chaos fades away. The rat is finally captured. Everyone but the deer with the biggest antlers leave. Everything from finely dressed rabbits to swarming bees wonder away from the park. They send curious looks at the olive-skinned lady with the beautiful voice and Violet.

In her obvious state of shock, Violet is led to a home. It is larger than the few Violet passed on her way to the clearing. Most buildings had been what she was sure were businesses. But none of that was making sense yet. Later, she could sort that out. Right now, the talking animals and the familiarity of some of them had her head plunged into confusion.

Still feeling the warmth of the lady's arm around her waist, Violet enters the house to be greeted by a girl much shorter than herself. A girl, seemingly human and yet not exactly. Maybe she is a little person. That was the only thing her mind could make fit with what she was seeing.

The kind murmurs around her were little more than a hum that she couldn't pull into focus. Once seated on a sofa near a fireplace filled with lit candles on this warm summer morning, Violet tried to find calm. She closes her eyes and takes a deep breath. She opens her eyes to see a face filled with worry sitting on the sofa across from her. Unsure how to process anything, she lets herself take in each moment. To accept the adventure as simple as a vacation to a foreign land.

So this land has talking animals. She tries to push that thought aside and takes deep breaths. Looking around the cozy room with walls the color of buttercream and wood aged with a warm glowing patina. Books on shelves from floor to ceiling flank a window opposite the fireplace. Paintings and tapestries of dancing rabbits, fairies and creatures unknown to her fill the room with an age old mood. The perfect place to explore was it not for the fact she is now in a world separate from her own.

Violet catches herself and reins in her thoughts. Now is not the time to freak out over the impossibility. Yet she hasn't fallen into another land before this. She places a hand on her fluttering heart.

"Violet, dear, please have a drink of water for me. It will help with the shock." The woman hands a glass to Violet. "I know it's difficult to concentrate. The first time passing through is a shock to the system." She continues speaking, stroking Violet's hand. Cautiously, the lady moves to sit next to her.

"That's it, look into my eyes. I'm Lady Zia Stone. You have wondered through a gateway in the woods near your home." She says, as if speaking to a much younger child.

Violet could not help but feel as if she was a simpleton for the muddled thoughts racing through her head. Then she grasped one thread.

"You called me by name. How do you know who I am?" Violet asks.

"We have been aware of you from the time you were just a littling. You have nearly come to our land many times over the years." Zia said. She takes the glass from Violet's other hand, she turns to put it on a table at the end of the sofa. This gave Violet time to consider the information.

"We concluded you couldn't use the gateway. The Proclivitas Amulet, until now, behaved as a beacon, but had not turned on completely yet. We didn't know if you could ever activate it." Zia said.

"Wait, what's the Procli—vita thing?" Violet asks.

"You're wearing it." Lady Zia points to the pendant hanging on the necklace Violet has worn for the many years her mother has been gone.

"No, you're mistaken." Violet lifts the metal piece that now feels heavier than it ever had. She looks down to study the piece closer. It surprises her to see it is different. Not in any dramatic way, just something more than it was.

"My mom gave this to me. It's a family heirloom." Violet can feel the confusion creasing her forehead. She looks into the eyes of the lady in front of her for answers. She is not at all sure she is ready for those answers.

"Then that adds a piece to our puzzle. We know the origins of the piece, but not how you came to have it." Zia said. The warm smile disappears at the commotion coming from the hallway.

"Fern, what is the matter?" Lady Zia stands waiting for an answer.

With the two windowed doors open, the entry hall

is visible. Spilling from the hall into the room with Violet and Lady Zia are two rabbits in fancy hats. Wide eyed, Violet stares as the rabbits shove what looks to be a birdcage on a pedestal between them.

"No, I refuse to be responsible for the thing!" The white rabbit wearing a hat of various cream colors says. He shoves the cage to his companion.

"Impossible! Imponderable! You will not make me responsible!" The white rabbit with a hat of various grays and a white feather crosses his arms.

The cage swings from one shoving paw to the next, and crashes to the floor. A moan follows the loud crash. With no hesitation, Lady Zia steps between the two hares and looks at the cage with one elegant eyebrow raised.

The housekeeper stands in the doorway, wringing her apron in her hands.

"I'm so sorry, my Lady. They just burst through the door and I couldn't do a thing with 'em. You know what their lot is like." Fern eyes the two rabbits as they adjust their hats and ties, mumbling of the others' blame.

"I don't blame you, Fern. Thank you." Zia speaks to Fern but her attention was on the cage on its side on the rug.

"Are you in one piece?" Zia asks as dirty brown fabric moves to reveal the rat trying to sit up. His movements making him appear drunk. Likely from the jostling, the rabbits had done with the cage.

A hiccup burst forth and then a small voice says "If I say no, will you promise not to let them touch this jail again?" From the seated position, the rat takes stock of his whiskers. He runs his hands along the hairless length of his tail. Then he reaches into each of the pockets of his long coat. This took several moments, as there are pockets on the outside and inside of the dirty brown garment. Satisfied, he pats the jacket in place and sighs.

"Wait, my hat, where's my hat?" He runs his rat fingered paw through the rumple of fur between his ears. He looks under himself the best he can as the cage still lies on its side.

Lady Zia grabs the ring on the top of the domed bars and picks the prison from the floor. "Hold on Rory." She warns.

Violet can't believe her eyes. Watching the two rabbits standing on hind legs with fluffy tails touching the floor as they stop snarling at each other waiting for dismissal from the Governor. She looks at each one and nods for them to leave.

The pair hop their way out of the room. Violet notices something on the floor. After picking it up, she realizes it's a shabby little top hat. The frayed, dark fabric is still warm from being worn.

"Now be still and I will get to you in a minute." Lady Zia says as she places the cage on the large desk.

Violet notices an intricately adorned wooden staircase along one side of the desk. Small enough for a creature of the same size as the rat. Violet lets her eyes wonder around the room. It is clear many things are on a variety of scale. Presumably, to accommodate the various species that may be present.

"Hey, girl?" The rat calls to Violet.

While the rat is speaking, Violet responds as normal as possible despite his beady red eyes.

"Yah, that's it. Over here." Rory rat braces each bony hand on the bars of his pedestaled prison. His nose, with disheveled whiskers, sticks out through the bars. "You're holding my hat."

"Oh, sorry." Violet takes it to him, pushing the tattered top hat through the bars.

"Are you settled now?" Zia clasps her hands together in front of her hips and pins the rat with her glare.

Rory scratches his belly after unbuttoning his grungy vest. Oblivious to Lady Zia's impatient mood, he says, "Got any food around here?"

Violet was past the point of shock over a talking rat. Now on to his arrogance and lack of concern for the shiny padlock keeping him in the cage. A cage big enough for him to stand and sit but not stretch out to sleep. She supposed they intended this cage to transport and not to house.

Without warning, a door slams out in the hallway, followed by thumping on the floor.

"Lady! Lady Zia, sorry, so sorry. I must report." Breathless, the girlish voice continues with no acknowledgment from the Lady.

Eyes moving from the rat to Zia, Violet was slow to see who ran into the room. Rushing so fast, the housekeeper, Fern, didn't bother to follow the guest.

"It's most dire. Dire, indeed. I've lost my charge. She was there and then gone. I did have trouble getting out to follow her. That is no excuse. My duty is to report on her comings and goings and I lost her." The excited rambling report pauses as she takes a deep breath. In her hasty run into the room, she had scrambled up the stairs to the top of the desk.

"Cacey—," Zia says

With a twitchy tail, Cacey looks from the Lady looming over her to the side where her charge stands with mouth gaping.

Rushing around the desk, Lady Zia shoves a guest chair over in time for Violet's legs to give out on her. In a daze, she plops down staring at the caramel colored rabbit no bigger than a squirrel, standing upright looking at her. Not just any rabbit, her rabbit. The one she had just filled a cage with fresh bedding for. The one that had just tried to scurry under her bed. The one she let snuggle in her lap while watching movies. The one that was abandoned at college.

Right now, Cacey, standing wide eyed with a twitchy nose, looks at her frozen in place. Wearing a hat with lace and feathers still bouncing from the quick dash up the stairs. A fancy brooch sits under her chin holding together a shirt collar. An elegant outfit, sure, but this was her rabbit! It could talk. It could give a report.

Lady Zia crouches in front of her. "Please, Violet, take a deep breath. Let me explain. Just relax." A hint of panic in the eyes assessing Violet lost something. From the first moment of meeting this lady, there had been nothing but warm reassurance coming from her. Gone now, like everyone in Violet's life. First the promise of care and warmth, then taken back. Not one person has enough loyalty to care for her long term. Not even her parents.

Where was her head? This revelation, a clarity unlike any she has come to before this moment. The shock must have caused it. This must be a dream. Maybe she fell, hit her head and now she is going on her own Wonderland trip. Or maybe even a tornado dream like Dorothy. Whichever, she could just wake up now and get back to reality.

7

LAND FOUND THROUGH THE WOODS-LEARNING

Lady Zia's hands folded, rest on the smooth wood surface of the desk. The rat sits leaning his back on the bars of the cage while she watches him in all of his scroungy splendor. Rory Rat is the best purveyor of anything one is seeking to acquire. Loyal only to himself, or rather to whatever benefits him the most.

"I'm waiting for you to answer my question, Rory." Lady Zia says.

"What can I say? I'm a private businessman. I can't divulge my client. Not without damage to my reputation." Rory says, casually using one dirty claw to clean under the ones on his other hand.

She knows he is trying to push her to exasperation, so she doubles down on her resolve to stay calm and draw out the information she wants.

"I do understand your need to earn a living." Lady Zia reaches into a desk drawer to pull out a flyer in varying sizes. She studies the smallest on the stack and hands it to him between the bars of the cage. Rory wipes his dirty paws on his vest, stretching for the paper.

"You can't be serious?" Rory looks directly at the Governor for the first time.

"Oh, I am. Your confinement in this jail is merely to make sure you will stay still long enough for our conversation. Once I let you free, and I will do so no matter what you do or do not tell me, I will post this wanted poster if you refuse to cooperate." Despite his concern, she casually reaches back into the drawer and pulls a thick file out. She places it neatly on the corner of the desk.

"No, that's not right, *Lady*." Rory sneers her title. He drops the paper to the bottom of his cell. Both boney paws grip the bars as his snout pokes between them.

"I have enough complaints and suspicious activity reports to call for the guards to investigate you." Zia says, hand resting on the file. "It doesn't matter if we find reason to prosecute you. We can detain you for a prolonged period to be sure we impact your business. I know how much you love to trade and scavenge. The council could see fit to impose travel restrictions that might cause long-term difficulties for you."

For the first time since arriving in the Governor's study, Rory's whiskers went still and drooped. Even his nose loses color. With a hard swallow, he makes a decision.

"I can't tell you much. My safety would be at risk." Rory muttered.

"That is a problem. I'm not unreasonable. Let's do

this so that you don't put yourself at risk." Zia says. She rests her hands on the arms of the chair and leans back. Her attention turns to the fireplace across the room. The glow of the burning candles filling that space is all that she sees. Lady Zia let her energy gather. Turning to the rat, she focuses.

"Can you tell me how many objects you have been gathering that might have magical essence?" Zia asks.

Rory pulls back from the bars, counting his fingers in a manner that makes no sense to anyone but himself. Because of his pondering, his color returns to normal and his eyes sparkle as he thinks of his treasure hunting.

"I can say I have procured seven such items for a single client." Rory says, giving his whiskers a twitch. "However, you might like to know that I am not the only source this person has." Something calculating crosses through the bushy brow, squinting over his beady red eyes.

"What can you tell me?" Zia releases reassurance as strongly as possible in the rat's direction. Also, trying to keep her lines of discernment open.

Rory looks toward the hallway doors. He leans closer, dropping his voice. "I'm uncertain about who exactly is instigating this gathering of objects forward. I thought it was one person and then got wind they could be in a predicament with another. That person could push them to do these things."

"So you don't know for sure what this is about?" Zia asks.

"I do." Rory pushes his shoulders back and pokes

out his vest covered belly. He hooks a claw from each paw on his vest and smirks. "Lady, it's what everything is about, *power.*"

Her focus relaxes. Lady Zia tries to think of questions that might yield more information. She knows her small amount of empathic abilities are exhausted at the moment. But she wishes her husband and co-governor were back from his investigation to see whatever she might be missing.

"I'm sorry my mom couldn't walk you home herself. Her job can be a pain sometimes." Bijou says.

Violet could only force a small smile as they descend the front steps of the governor's house.

"Violet, are you okay?" Bijou laid a hand on her arm to keep her from moving past her.

The kindness in the governor's daughter's eyes pierce something Violet hadn't known was numbing her to the surrounding scene. The view of the village's circle center is something out of a fairytale. Old world buildings lining the roads around the green space still creating a city block. One building catches her interest. The Apiary Confectionery Café had bees swarming the building.

"What is happening with the bees?" Violet asks.

"Oh, we should go there!" Looping her arm through Violet's, Bijou continues, "my treat!"

Her enthusiasm was contagious, and Violet squints to see more. A dream or not, her curiosity won out over the disbelief she has for this new world.

Her intrigue grows stronger the closer they get to the café. After walking past a couple of buildings, they turn to cross the narrow road. That's when she heard a soft hum in the air. A gentle scent of something sweet and floral floats to her. At home, instinctually, the buzz tells her to be careful around the bees. But this somehow feels less alarming.

At first glance, the bees appeared to be a chaotic swarm. The closer Violet and Bijou get, they seem to dance to an unheard rhythm. From the top of the building, bees, larger than in Violet's world, fly out of the building. Presumably the bees are flying off to find pollen, Violet considers. Some bees glide down the front of the building to tend to the flower boxes overflowing with lush blooms of many colors. More flower boxes sit under windows on the second and third floors. Both floors have six narrow windows facing the round green space in the center of town.

Below the sign featuring the word café, gold letters spell out The Apiary Confectionery. They sit boldly over two large windows showcasing the biggest window boxes on the entire block, if not the whole town. Slowly, they walk past windows at the entrance. Bijou calls out a greeting to the buzzing worker bees tending to the green vine with lavender flowers trailing up the brick building.

When Bijou opens the door, ushering Violet inside, a bee turns to the girls. The bee lifts a top hat made of strips of green satin fabric in greeting. Violet stumbles.

"Careful, mind your step." Bijou stifles a laugh but can't hide her smile.

"But, that…" Violet turns to the window to watch the bees harvesting the sweet bounty hidden in the vines. Each bee has a hat or neckwear, a few have both. Then her gaze lands on one with a green hat.

"She winked at me!" Violet said too loud.

"You might want to close your mouth." Bijou pulls a chair out and guides Violet to sit at the nearest bistro table. "She is playing with you. The bees know you're not from here."

"How? I've been here a couple of hours." Violet tries to pull her gaze to her companion.

"The bees know everything." With a shrug, Bijou looks around the café. "Besides, your gaping fly trap is enough to tell that." The chuckle dies, half finished.

"Miss Stone." A slight nod as the man stops near the table.

"Hello Mr. Pravat." Bijou says.

"It's nice to see you. Your father will be returning soon, I hope?" Towering over the young woman seated enhances the man's impressive height.

The question sounds like a statement of fact and didn't go unnoticed. Bijou responds equally evasively. "Mm, you know how things go. I'm being rude. Let me introduce my friend Violet. She's visiting my family."

"How rude of me." Turning his attention away from Bijou, something that might be called a smile stretched his thin lips even thinner. "So nice to meet you, Violet. Are you staying long?"

"Nice to meet you." A kink forms in Violet's neck as she leans back to meet the pale man's gaze. Bijou answered before she can respond to his question.

"Violet has an open invitation to visit with us." Bijou's warm gaze meets Violet's.

Still not processing normally, Violet hadn't gotten as far as her next visit. Was that even possible and did she want to come back again? Before that thought finished, the server came to the table.

A glow the size of a tennis ball with iridescent wings floats near the table and grows into a shimmering human-like person the size of a child at the table. Anxiously, Violet tries to put what her eyes were seeing into a context her brain can understand. The only comparison she can think of is a Syfy movie hologram. She can somewhat see through the person, yet every detail, including the pointy ears, is visible.

"Hi Bijou, what can I get you and your friend?" The voice tinkles musically.

"You must excuse me, Ladies. Please enjoy your refreshments. Violet, I do hope we meet again." A slight bow and Mr. Pravat was on his way out of the café.

After ordering honey tea and cakes, Bijou turns to Violet.

"You must consider coming back for another visit. There is so much I can show you here," Bijou said and smiles.

"How old are you?" With a small shake of her head, Violet clears her throat. "I'm sorry. I don't know what's wrong with me." Violet looks around the café. She takes in the warm glow of the room, smelling honey and a lovely earthiness mixed with fresh baked treats. The peaceful ambiance created by the hum of bees mingling with so many species of magical beings, Violet could see herself enjoying this place once she got used to the creatures. And then she thought of the animals talking, drinking from teacups, and wearing the most fascinating hats.

"I take that back. I know what is wrong with me." Violet grins back at her new friend.

"Don't worry, I can't imagine what this must be like for you. I've always known of other worlds. It's part of our teachings that every young one receives. But to answer your question, I'm a couple of years younger than you." Bijou looks at her lap. She fidgets with the leather skirt, smoothing and straightening it on her lap. It reached her knees but slits up both sides shows leggings.

Violet waits for the young woman across from her to share what's on her mind.

"Yes, I know. My height and poise make everyone think I'm older than I am. That can be a bother, you know." Shyly, Bijou looks from her lap to Violet as she rests her hands in her lap.

The admission gave Violet a clearer idea of what life might be like for the daughter of the governors. She could imagine becoming friends with her easily. Self-consciously raising a hand to the necklace, as is her habit. Violet recognizes an odd feeling.

"Um," leaning over the table, Violet lowers her voice. "I think something is happening with my locket." A slight vibration coming from the pocket watch style pendent is obvious to the touch.

"What do you mean?" Bijou glances around the

room and leans into Violet.

"It's alive? I don't know how to explain it. It's like a cell phone on vibrate except it's very faint." Calmly tucking the necklace back into her shirt, she hopes no one could tell it was moving.

"We don't have those devices here. I'm familiar with the concept you describe. When did it start doing this?" Bijou smiles and forces herself to relax. Her mother had warned them to keep the locket out of sight until her father returned from his investigation. Stolen magical objects have gotten to be a serious problem. This was obviously a special piece.

Violet had to think hard on the question. *When had it begun?* She had been so distracted by the café, bees, and the pale man that greeted them as soon as they sat... Wait!

"I think it was when that man, Mr. Pravat, was here." Violet said.

When Bijou looks out the window to see Mr. Pravat speaking to someone just past the view, the window afforded her. She looks back at Violet. "Let's get you home right away." Bijou reaches to a small pouch on the belt at her waist and pulls out coin for the bill.

Just then a parade of Bees and the floating ball of light, Violet knew to be the server, glide through the air with the tea and cakes Bijou ordered.

"Perfect timing. Thank you." Bijou ignored the dishes floating to the surface of the table as the coins glide away and speaks to Violet. "Now please, be quick. We should get going."

There wasn't time for Violet to think on the

amazingly magical sight she had just seen. Nor to revel in the most delicious tea and cakes that were honey, lemon, sweet yet light as air and spiced with unidentifiable flavors.

Swiftly, they finished what they could and made their way out of the café and back to the alleyway where Violet had arrived. Bijou embraces the shorter Violet and spoke words Violet had heard said in the café several times as friends went their separate ways.

"Safe crossings." Bijou said as she brought her right hand to rest on her own heart briefly.

With a nervous smile, Violet reaches for the necklace and turns to the brick wall. She takes a deep breath, closes her eyes, moving forward until the surface of the ground feels and sounds different from the cobblestones. Eyes open, the forest of her childhood is before her. Violet spins around to see Bijou shimmer and fade away. Trees and underbrush taking shape before her eyes.

With pounding in her chest, her knees go weak, and she drops to the dried leaves beneath her feet. This was unreal and couldn't possibly have just happened. Deep breaths, she tells herself. Violet grips the pendent and holds a hand out in front of herself.

The shimmer was there. A cobblestone alley way lined by stone buildings comes into view. She pulls her hand back, and the shimmer disappears. Violet feels childish for wanting to try the test once more, so she drops the necklace.

She made a rash decision, completely unlike herself. The plans she had for the day could go suck pig's feet because she needs answers. And the only way she knew to find them was through books and the internet. First, she needed to go see Candy at the bookstore. Despite it being in the ordinary world, the Book Shepherd store would be the place to have books about this enchanted world.

Violet rushes through the door of the bookstore. Side stepping two women talking about grandkids as they made their way out of the shop. While mentally forcing herself to slow down, she looks for Candy. As she glimpses her white hair disappear down an aisle, Violet feels a slight vibration in the necklace under her shirt. The pause was just enough for her eyes to rest on the sculpture hanging behind the checkout counter.

That rabbit, white, and wearing a fancy hat in the same style as… How could this be? Coincidence maybe? But, could it be happenstance that she returns from another world to see a sculpture of a, a what? Person or being straight out of that world, impossible. However, coincidence is crap.

Violet let herself move down the center aisle, looking at the sculpture at the end of each one. A wolf, fox, bear, even a dragon all dressed as the animals she had seen just that morning. Near the back of the store, Violet rubs her damp palms on her jeans. She notices the pendant on her necklace still vibrating on her chest. A final step brings her to the sitting area. Candy sits with a book open in her lap. The chair she sits in seems to be made especially for her. The warm wood legs support traditional lines in garish colors that didn't feel as harsh as Violet imagined it would in a living room.

"Hello, how nice to see you," Candy said. Leaning to pat the cushion of the loveseat next to her chair.

"Have a seat, my dear. I was just about to read a passage from one of my very favorite books. When things get out of whack, seeing the world differently is exactly what we need." The old leather book had faded gold filigree and words Violet couldn't make out as Candy flips to the page she was looking for.

Violet sinks to the seat offered, struck speechless. Before she can find coherent words, she is perched on the edge of a cushion, waiting. It occurred to her, as she looks at Candy's white hair, something differed from the last time she was here. And this woman seems older than her first guess. Even so, she is timeless. The small glasses perched on the end of her nose glinting gold in the amber light of the store. Her flowing top with a gray-blue pattern hid her figure but gives an elegant impression. The gold and silver chains mingle in folds of fabric, allowing their tiny jewels of rich colors to glint as she flips through the pages of the book.

"Here we are. Listen to this…" lifting the book to a comfortable reading angle, Candy pauses.

"It's there, just beyond the corner of your sight. Just over your shoulder or on the edge of your awareness.

What is IT you ask? IT is a world that you may only glimpse, if you're lucky. If you catch your breath just in time. Or if you turn your head fast enough.

Possibly, you could look behind a bush, or under a low branch. Maybe you will find it if you look in the hollow of a tree.

How will you know what to look for? Ah, yes, knowing that would help you find IT. Cast about around forgotten places for discarded and unnoticed things. Things like buttons, scraps of cloth, or bits of ribbon. They do like used and forgotten bits and baubles.

Now to explain who THEY are. Let's cover who they are not first. THEY are not you or me or the boring or the ordinary. It can be said that THEY are quite remarkable and odd. Yes, odd is best to describe.

Some have fur, some have feathers, and for sure a few have scales. You may know them by common names and walk right past a sir, a madam, an empress, or even a prince. Not just anyone is allowed to see the truth behind the ordinary."

On a sigh, Candy closes the book and rests back in her chair. The soft dreamy expression rests on the hat filled coat rack across from her.

Violet gives a side glance at the coatrack, unsure if she was supposed to wait for Candy to say something. After a moment, she couldn't help but speak.

"That was—was exactly what I needed to hear." Leaning back in her seat, Violet shakes her head. "No, I didn't mean to say that." Elbow propped on the armrest of the worn loveseat, her hand rests on her forehead. "What is wrong with me?"

"I suspect you've had an interesting morning."

Candy lifts the book from her lap and places it on the low table in the middle of the seating area.

"How could you know that?" Violet asks.

"Of this world, I know very little of what is possible to know. I'm at peace with that." Candy smiles as she leans to rest a soft hand on Violet's arm. "You, however, seem to struggle with something you've discovered."

Violet closes her eyes. When she opens them, she leans towards Candy. On the way here, she was sure of what to say. She had planned to say everything and went over every detail of descriptions of what she had seen. Violet pauses, the soft eyes across from her feeling warm and reassuring.

"Thanks" Violet drops her gaze to a book on the low table in front of her. She reaches for a thin paperback, the calm spreads to a grin.

"I read this with my mom when I was…maybe seven." She leans back, her mind wondered to the memory.

The tinkling of the bells on the door brought Candy up from her chair. "You sit and enjoy that story. Because of the morning you've had, take your time." She winked and was gone.

Without thinking to do so, Violet curls up in the cushion's corner and opens the book.

8

THE HOUSE BY THE WOODS-TRYING

Violet becomes aware she had fallen asleep. Her head resting on her arm on the cozy loveseat in the bookstore. She blinks repeatedly and opening her eyes to see the book she had been reading, now rested on her lap. The events of the morning play in her mind.

She pushes aside memories of the trip when something catches her eye. She sees denim covered knees of someone sitting on the low table facing her. A startled gasp escapes her as she jumps.

"What are you doing?" Violet asks.

"Nothing, sorry. It's okay, sorry." Will held up his hands and leans back away from her. His wide shoulders still block any view she could have of the rest of the store.

"Are you watching me?" Violet glares hard at him while pulling her legs out from being curled up underneath her on the cushion. She plants her feet firmly in between them.

"No, I saw you sitting here and wanted to be sure you are ok." Clasping his hands together, he rests his elbows on his knees. "This isn't how I expected this to go."

The slight crease of a smile at one corner of his mouth draws Violet in for a second. The sleep fog fades completely. She hears other shoppers are in the bookstore. A breath she hadn't known she was holding rushes from her lungs.

"At least you knew to expect something." One hand smoothing her hair down, she was sure it was a mess. Violet turns to pick up the book she dropped moments ago.

"Hey, let me take you for a coffee as an apology for scaring you." Will stood, his hand out in invitation.

And knowing that if she looked at him, it would be hard to refuse. She stands, keeping her eyes on the book. Violet realized there was irritation growing in her gut. Why did he just assume she would go with him? What is his track record with women?

"No, thank you." Squaring her shoulders, Violet turns to face him.

"Really?" Will's smile was not reaching his eyes.

"I've had an endless day and I need to go home." Forcing aside the trip from the morning, Violet had to think of her relationship with her dad. Determining how far to push him is the priority. She couldn't live in the same house with him as things stand. She steps forward to make her way to the front of the shop.

At the last moment, he moves over. A crease forms between his eyes.

"Okay, Little Mouse, take my phone number. We can do it another time, then."

"Don't call me that. I don't even know you. I'm not even sure I like you." The intimacy of waking up to see Will watching her sleep had her speaking more openly than she might otherwise. Violet recognized it to be a ridiculous idea that bumping into him at the same bookstore twice meant she could trust him. As a single girl on a college campus, she learned how to stay safe. She had even taken a self-defense course with her roommate.

"How can you get to know me if we don't talk?" Will reaches out, putting a scrap of paper with his phone number inside the book that she clutches to her chest.

"How do you know I'll take this home?" Violet asks.

"I don't." With a shrug, Will took a step back. "Text anytime, Mouse." With a half-hearted tip of a nonexistent hat, he spun and walked away. Seconds later, Violet heard the bells jingle as he exited the shop.

The emotional upheaval of moving home to live with her dad felt insurmountable, given the other things piling on top of it. The list keeps getting longer. We have alternate dimensions, a bookstore that was always there, but she had never noticed, bees that wink at you, mysterious guy that didn't quite seem as genuine as he appeared, pet rabbits on a mission...

She needed to get home and clean her rabbit's cage. WAIT, knowing what she does now, will Cacey come back? What did that even mean? The day had become too much to figure out. Questions spun through her mind in circles. She should find books on other worlds.

Then she can try to make progress with her dad.

Violet walks into the house, setting groceries on the kitchen counter. After taking books to the dining room table, she prepares a light meal. Her mom springs to mind while washing the grapes and blueberries. A path well-trod, so she pushed the memories away. She finds a wooden cutting board, and arranges fresh French bread, a block of mild cheese with a slicer, and the fruit.

Violet looks at the warm rotisserie chicken still in the store container. She didn't want it after all. So she left it on the counter to cool. She gazes out of the window while washing her hands at the sink. Twilight casts a beautiful purply, pink hue around the trees and structures. Deep shadows are already covering more than the sunlight. Scanning the area she can see from the kitchen, movement catches her eye.

Near the back steps, a tiny creature emerges from the shadow of the garage. A fluffy rabbit sits gazing up at the door to the porch. Violet recognizes Cacey but doesn't move. She is not sure how she should feel about it, raising a hand to her warm cheek. Violet remembered a few times of crying her heart out over the decision to come home and the wound it would expose. All the time, Cacey sat in her lap trying to nuzzle her to get petted. She said private things, not knowing Cacey could understand, let alone repeat them.

Still watching the shadow in the growing darkness, Violet warred with forgiveness. The rabbit turned into the shadows. Impulse pushed Violet from the window and through the porch. She didn't open the screen door but spoke to the darkness.

"Why did you come back?"

From the edge of a shadow, Violet could hear sniffles. "Tell me why you came here." Violet encourages her.

"I want to apologize to you." What began in wavers, grows to a steady voice. The compact figure moves from the shadows into the soft yellow light of the fixture above the door. Cacey sits on her hind legs. The back of one paw swiping across her cheek.

"Then get on with it." Violet speaks from the dark porch, hidden by shadows the light cannot reach.

"I'm sorry I deceived you." Cacey tilts her head to the side. "Rather, I'm sorry that finding out was such a shock." Again, Cacey rephrased, "you deserve a better attendant than myself to look after you. My aunt got assigned to you originally. She wouldn't have messed this up. What with her sixth pregnancy and all, she couldn't do it." A small hop nearer to the steps and Cacey slumps down until her tail rests on the ground.

"Stop, Cacey." Violet speaks from the darkness. She reaches for the latch, only to pause. Her bottom lip suffers the brunt of her unease. The screen door squeaks as she pushes through and lets it close behind her. Violet sits on the steps and wraps her arms around her knees.

"Cacey." She stops, only to try again. "What do you want from me?" She asks, feeling embarrassed by the memories.

Another hop closer.

"Violet, will you forgive me so we can start over?" Cacey stands at attention rather than the cuddly rabbit that Violet had known her to be.

"I forgive you." Violet let out a sigh of release. The crazy situation just couldn't be helped. If Cacey had spoken to her in her bedroom, she probably would have fainted dead away.

"I'm sorry for blubbering all over you before we moved here." Violet said.

"Oh, no, not at all. It was part of my training at the academy. The ordinary often treat pets as emotional support in difficult times. It's an honor, really." Cacey reassured as she hopped up on the steps to sit next to Violet.

"I'm not sure I want the details, but I'm curious about how this works. You being abandoned and moving home with me? What gives?" Her grasp on reality wasn't super strong at the moment, but filling in gaps of understanding might help. At least she hoped it would. It could push her right over the edge, needing serious psychiatric treatment.

"Well," Cacey took a deep breath, "they left my cage in a recently empty room. Staff assumed the student abandoned me. It's easy to slip things past the ordinary. They are so distracted by technology these days."

Her speech growing faster. As she warms to her story. Gesturing wildly and bouncing on her spring filled rabbit legs, she couldn't believe Cacey had been so upset just moments ago.

"Okay, calm down." Violet tries to keep distance

emotionally from Cacey, but her endearing charm was making it difficult.

"Sorry," Cacey rubs a paw down the back of her floppy ear. "I'm still a little green."

"What will you do now?"

"I face a review council because you discovered me." The rabbit slumped, growing quiet.

"That wasn't your fault, exactly." Violet turns to look closer at Cacey's distress.

"I lost track of you. It may be what gets me hopped out of the program." Eyes moving to peer into the shadows, Cacey continues. "It's always been my dream to be an agent of the realm." Voice dropping to a whisper, she says, "I might never be more than a cadet now."

Violet realizes this little being is exactly that, a being with feelings. So whatever secrets this world holds, there are emotions, dreams, and desires that matter. Not just her own are important. Despite having been shocked by this talking rabbit, Violet still cares for her. A feeling of responsibility for her is becoming more apparent. Even though it's obvious Cacey is very much a capable being. At some point, Violet knew she would have to realign her view of who Cacey really is. That wasn't happening in this moment.

"Cacey, do you want to stay here tonight?" Violet asks.

"What exactly does that mean? In what capacity?" Cacey looks concerned.

"Like a slumber party for us girls." Violet says.

"Whew!" Ears perking up, Cacey bounces on her

hind legs. "It would be too humiliating pretending to be a domesticated pet now that you know the real me." Cacey fluffs her fur and it vibrates all over before smoothing back down. "Personal hygiene has never been more demeaning than the time I spent in that cage. Ugh, you cleaning up after me, as if I'm a newborn kit."

"I know you're a rabbit, Cacey." Violet says.

"Grin if you like, but baby rabbits are called kits. I'm not a baby. In our clan, I am an old maid. I could have had two litters by now." Cacey says.

"My apologies. And I promise to work on the image I have of you as soon as I can." The urge to stroke the fur down Cacey's back tempted Violet. She knew for certain it would be too awkward at this point.

"You can sleep wherever you want tonight. I will miss your company, truly." Violet looks at the soft eyes of her friend. Despite spending so much time together, the thought of friendship with this talking rabbit is a surprise. It shouldn't, given the shared confidences. Cacey not speaking back to her didn't diminish the relationship one bit.

"Cacey, you are always welcome to come visit me. But, I have no idea what the rules of your world are or what your life is like outside of, um, your job. Just know, you will forever have a place with me."

Then Cacey stretches up as tall as she can, her eyes grow wide and fill with tears. When she lands against Violet she squeezes her the best she can with short rabbit arms, and Violet leans closer. As the last of the daylight disappears, clouds drift away to show moonlight. The sound of crickets grows louder. The pair on the steps release a breath as they enjoy the serenade in the silver light.

"Nothing." Violet leans back in her seat at the dining room table. "This is pointless." She closes the laptop and pushes it away. She reaches for the cutting board with food she had prepared a while ago.

"I told you earlier" Cacey yawned, "You must go back to Maplehaven" Half-closed eyes look up from her snuggled position on the table.

"What if I can't get there?" Violet pops a grape in her mouth. "Why am I able to go? I have too many questions." She shakes her head and looks at Cacey.

"The professors can answer anything." One paw reaches up to rub one ear, causing it to lie over one eye.

"Cacey, I want to hear about these professors tomorrow. You head up to my room and sleep wherever you want. You don't need to worry about the cage." Violet scoops up the sleepy bunny, carrying her to the stairs. "Go on up. I'll clean up my mess and be up when I finish."

Without a word, Cacey hops up each step, half asleep. Violet stifles her own yawn on the way back to the dining room. She places the books in a canvas bag. Then grabs the cutting board she used to serve the light meal. In the kitchen, it was difficult to keep reminders of her mother locked away. She floated around the room prepping meals for their little family with efficiency and grace. Her mom was always humming as she opened drawers or pulled a pitcher of lemonade from the fridge. Slices of lemon floating in the pitcher. Memories that Violet wishes she could lock away.

The time spent away at school had been an unexpected relief from the past for her. Now, it was like ripping open the wound all over again. It was no wonder her dad was stuck in the pain. He has never gotten to escape the constant reminders.

As if she had called him home, his truck rumbles up the driveway. Violet continues to pull out containers for the cheese, carrots, and grapes she had not eaten. When hearing the pickup door slam shut, her eyes go to the window over the sink. She can see his progress up the back steps. Before she finishes cleaning up, he is in the kitchen's doorway. He was a silhouette in the darkness of the room behind him. The dim light over the stove did not reach him.

"Dad?"

Frozen for a moment longer, then he swayed slightly as he steps into the kitchen.

"Are you okay?" Violet smells the beer or whatever alcohol had been his choice tonight. She keeps her hands busy, waiting for him to answer. As an adult, this was the first time she wanted to confront him. Her mind races to find the best direction to go with him.

"Fine. Just forgot for a minute." He turns on the water and grabs a cup from the dish rack.

"What?" Violet stacks the containers and goes to the refrigerator.

The glass clinks on the bottom of the sink when he finishes. Hands braced on the edge of the counter, he hangs his head. Violet closes the fridge and leans against the door, waiting.

"You were humming."

"So?" Violet crosses her arms over her chest.

So much time passes, she doesn't think he will answer.

"It…it was as it used to be. You're like her."

"Dad" The instinct to go to him compelled her to push off the appliance at her back, but she didn't allow herself to take a step.

In a blink, it passed. He wrestles the connection to the ground and stomps on it.

"No! Go to your room. Leave me alone." His dusty boots tromp to the living room and he drops into the old faded chair.

"Dad, if we could just."

"No, I said go to your room." He untied the boot laces.

"I'm not a child. That won't work on me anymore." Violet speaks softly, moving in front of him to sit on the coffee table. She waits for him to lean back in his seat.

"What can I do?" Violet's hushed tones were the only sound. The stillness of the house in the middle of the night fills the silence between them.

Head resting with eyes closed, he responds. "Just go away." Arms draped on the armrests of the chair, his hand dangles off the end.

Violet looks at the work-worn hands. As a little girl, his hands had been different from now. She remembered him picking her up for a ride on his shoulders. Just as calloused and tattered today, but not the same. Back then, they didn't have dirt under the nails, his cuts got bandaged until healed and they were always ready to help and hold. Once he even stroked her hair after a fall in the rocks while riding her bike. So long ago.

"I need things to be better." Violet clears her throat.

"I promised your mother I'd take care of you. That's what I've done, isn't it? You finished school, you went to college. Now you are going to vet school or whatever. I have paid for what I can. That's all she left inside of me." Only opening his eyes a crack, they were closed before he finishes speaking.

Drowsy with alcohol, the conversation ends. Violet looks intensely at his face. So sad overall, gray fills in the shaggy hair at his temples. Lines just taking shape on his forehead and next to his eyes. His job of construction work kept him outside much of the day. Years of the weathering showed. It seems to Violet that he had become the supervisor at the company he had worked at during most of her life. That was the only thing he cared to maintain.

When was the last time she had seen him smile? He has frown lines beginning to show on his face. Not much in the way of laugh lines. A life with no joy. There must be a path to connect with him. Why should this be the only way for them? Feeling her eyes moisten, Violet stands. One last look at the only person to know the same grief of losing the one person to love them each in the most amazing way. Violet shakes the tears away. The ache of sadness clings to her the same as an invasive vine winding up a tree in the forest.

Maybe she should go back into the woods.

9

LAND FOUND THROUGH THE WOODS-EXPLORE

"This is the best thing to do, right?" Violet slows her steps on the path to the land marker.

"You woke me up with this grand plan. Why are you asking me now?" Cacey pushes herself up higher in the backpack to lean on Violet's shoulder.

"I know." Teeth gnawing her bottom lip, Violet reaches up to still the fluffy ear bouncing on her cheek with each step. "It's just that, in daylight, it sounds childish." With the portal in front of her, she stands, feet planted. Violet rubs the pendant on the chain around her neck. A humming wherrr vibrates the metal. "Is this actually possible?"

"No need to whisper. There is so much more than you can imagine." Cacey grew more excited with each breath.

"But wait, let me—" Violet struggles to pull off the backpack before Cacey falls, trying to free herself. Before it reaches the ground, the rabbit hops out of the bag.

"I want to see my family while you visit the professors. So do you mind if I go?" The excitement fills her smiling face as she bounces on her hind legs.

"As much as I love having your company, yes, run visit them." Violet once more faces the space next to the portal. With a stomach full of nerves, she steps closer. "How does this happen?"

"You did it once already, just do the same thing as before." Cacey's bouncing being punctuated by wiggles of her fluffy tail.

"I didn't do it on purpose. I fell." Violet said. One hand reaching up for the chain to pull the pendant out of her shirt.

"Whatever it did that time, is it doing it now?" Cacey asks.

"I think I hear a hum. It's hard to tell with the birds chirping this morning." Violet glances around the lush woods. The narrow dirt path under her feet, hardly visible from the ferns and other ground cover.

"Maybe I should wait. In case something goes wrong, I should consider this more." Violet said, taking one step back.

"Nope, you did that half the night." Cacey said, hopping forward, causing the portal to shimmer open.

The dreamy ripple in the air shows a cobbled road with buildings lining each side. Cacey looks up at Violet and leaps into her home world and waves a paw, beckoning her.

Violet pulls in a deep breath, smelling the damp, woodsy scent so familiar to her. Without thought steps forward with one hand still holding the pendent and the other seeking to feel the glimmering. She felt nothing on the tips of her fingers. Under her feet, the soft dirt disappears, her foot lands on hard stone. There had been a jolt, or maybe it was a shift deep in her soul. She grips her solar plexus, seeking to steady something she can't name. The next breath she finally pulls in is so different from the last Violet can't identify much more than a floral sweetness.

"It's about time. I'm running late, we're late." Bijou pushes off the wall beside the portal.

Violet jumps. She hadn't seen her or adjusted to the other world she finds herself in now. And telling herself to take deep breaths and counting them until she trusts herself to speak is all she could manage.

"Bijou?" Violet asks.

"Yes?" Bijou stops to consider Violet. "You look odd, you okay?"

"Fine. What are you doing here?" Violet asks.

"Cacey told me you were coming." Bijou opens a pouch on the belt at her waist. "We all thought you should have this. That way we can communicate if you want help when you visit." Bijou steps to Violet and grabs her wrist. Before Violet can say a word, Bijou fastens a silver bracelet on her.

"What do you mean, to communicate with you?" Violet asks. Bringing the bracelet closer to see the intricate details. Silver and gold vines lace together under such delicate enameled leaves. It is hard to fathom the piece is metal.

"This is beautiful." Violet said.

"It is, isn't it?" Bijou asks. "It is one of my

mother's." Reaching her long thin fingers out, she touches a tiny button on the side of the center medallion of larger leaves. The top flips open to show a glowing stone resting on top of gears. "This is our world's cell phone."

"You don't have cell phone tech here?" Violet looks up in disbelief. "You can't be serious."

"Oh, I am. That technology doesn't work here. We don't have the same infrastructure as in your world. Our slang for where you live is the ordinary world. Our tech works in all worlds."

"But wait, what?" Violet asks. One hand reaches for Bijou's arm.

"First, let's get this figured out and then we will go to the professors and they will answer your questions. Okay?" Bijou speaks calmly.

"I'm not a child. I'm older than you are, remember?" Violet asks, but relents. "What do I do with this thing?" She gestures to the bracelet.

"When you want to contact one of us, you need to find a tree. Any vegetation works when you are skilled, but you are not. So find a tree and the bigger, the better." Bijou said.

"How do you know I'm not skilled? Maybe I'm more capable than you think." Violet looks up from the bracelet to the girl in front of her. Why is she treating her like a child? Violet tries to step back from her, but Bijou has a firm grip on her wrist.

"This isn't personal. You've just stepped into a world where you don't even know the most basic of principals of our physics and scientific understandings.

And we look very similar to the world you have lived in your whole life. Just know that not everything is as it seems. We don't have magic as in the old days, but things still happen that you won't understand, can't understand. Yet." Bijou said. The last word spoken with a grin.

"Fine. I'm sorry for being so touchy." Violet apologizes and rubs her free hand under her breasts. "I think stepping through that thing has messed with me."

"Regardless of how you feel right now, it gets easier. Or so I'm told." Bijou said. She looks at the portal for a long moment. "Anyway, once you find a tree, touch it. Hands are best, but a bare foot can work. Exposed skin is most important for a beginner. We all learn that way first." Bijou said.

"Close your eyes and envision who you want to reach. Like making a phone call in your world, but this is through the organic root structure of all vegetation of the worlds. They connect us through their root system. So you open the bracelet, touch the tree and visualize, that is all there is to it." Bijou steps away, releasing her grip.

"That can't be it. What happens next?" Violet asks.

"We need to walk." Bijou side steps, for them to follow her.

"Violet, I need to get hopping. Just listen to what Bijou tells you. She is a friend. I trust her." Cacey scurries ahead of the girls and, with one paw touching the spot where her heart was, she nods her head. Bijou returns the gesture.

"Rabbits never stand still. It surprised me she hadn't moved on already." Bijou said, setting a quick pace. Violet tries to lengthen her stride to keep pace with the taller girl.

"I can't keep the professors waiting. We're meeting my parents there." Bijou said.

"This is not how I thought this was going to go." Violet takes a double step to keep up.

"What did you think would happen?" Bijou asks while nodding a greeting to a lady and Raccoon wearing hats. The pair stand outside of a shop with a sign that reads 'Odds to go with Ends'. Violet stumbles, turning to where Bijou leads.

"Cacey didn't tell me she had told anyone I was coming. Honestly, I wasn't even sure how to come back here. It was an accident the first time." Violet said. Bijou walks past the governor's house where they had met before. Across from that is the park with the beautiful tree. Last time, she hadn't looked carefully at the flowers blooming all over the canopy. The pink blossoms seem alive, but surely it's a breeze making them sway. When each movement of the flower brings a change in color, yellow, purple and back to pink. Violet blinks, unsure if she believes what she sees.

"Magnificent, isn't it?" Bijou asks, stopping next to Violet. She continues when Violet doesn't answer. "I hardly remember a time before that tree bloomed. I was a little girl. While there are theories on what caused it, a record of the last blooming can't be found." Bijou said. Her hand coaxing Violet to continue walking.

"Nothing I say will do it justice." Violet said with a

smile.

"Let's keep moving." Bijou says gently. "I can't understand how you must feel finding out the world differs from what you thought." The younger woman smooths the front panel of her split skirt. "It is possible for us to be friends. Can we work on that?"

"Yes, I'd like that. The rest of this, I can't figure out how to feel," Violet said. With a sigh, she looks around at the walking and, amazingly, talking animals mingling with humans. "I will try." Said more to herself than her friend.

"Good." Bijou said, smiling.

The two continue, reaching the far side of the center circle. A large domed building sits with a wide opening in the corner. Citizens of all kinds came and went from the opening.

"What is this place?" Violet asks, slowing her pace as they pass by the white stone building.

"That is the International Gateway Station of Maplehaven." Bijou said. Slowing, she hooks her arm through Violet's. "The place you enter this land is actually a portal. Researchers have documented many portals, and people occasionally discover new ones."

"A portal, okay I understand," Violet said, waiting for Bijou to continue.

"Maplehaven isn't the only land your world is unaware of. My dad travels regularly to the High Council in the High Lands." Bijou said, her pace picking up as the circle center fades behind them. The Learning and Research center becomes visible ahead.

"We have a place called the Highlands in our world,

too. Are they connected?" Violet asks.

"No, High Lands is a mountainous land that…well, I guess it floats in the clouds. I haven't ever thought to describe it before." Bijou said. She looks up to the cloudless sky above the trees and buildings lining the street.

"I have so many questions!" Violet said, searching the sky to find the land.

"No, I didn't mean that it's here. You can't see it here. The only way for us to get it, is through the Portal Arch. The lands here don't connect the way yours do. You can't walk, sail, or fly from one to another. Well, very few have airships that can go from one land to another, but that is another thing all together." Bijou said.

"Look, this is all hard to explain in one conversation. Our world has very different physics than yours, the ordinary. Don't expect to figure it all out. Some here never travel from one land to another because they don't understand fully how enchantment works. It scares them." She pauses at the front of the enormous building. Bijou turns to Violet.

"I don't want you to worry. My family will help you. Just take it slow." Bijou said, turning she knocks on the door.

"Hello, come in, perfect. They are in the library." Gryphin Tizly pulls the door open before Bijou's hand lowers.

The young woman jumps at the rush of air, causing her skirt to shift.

"Hello Gryphin." Bijou recovers quickly. "This is

Violet. We're here to—"

"Yes, I know," Gryphin said, lifting his eyes from Bijou's face to rest on her hair as he continues to speak. "You are late. Um, if, well, it would be best for you to, I think you should hurry." He stumbles, moving aside.

"Is something wrong?" Bijou asks. Passing the gangly young man.

"No, why would you think that?" Gryphin asks. He closes the door and motions for the two to move on.

"You just said, oh never mind." Bijou said and looks over the oddly handsome face and flaming mass of red curly hair.

"If you must know, another artifact has turned up missing, probably stolen." Gryphin said. He tries to step around the girls to lead the way and stumbles on his untied boots. All while mumbling to himself.

"Gryphin!" Bijou said, standing her ground.

Halfway through the entry hall, he stops.

"Yes, Bijou." He said in a calm voice unlike the one she had used to gain his attention.

"If you tie your shoes, you won't trip." Bijou motions for Violet to follow and rushes past the silent young man.

"Bijou" Gryphin says.

"What?" Bijou looks back at the rumpled young man.

"It's nice to see you today." Gryphin said as his cheeks turn so red his freckles nearly disappear.

"Um, well, it's good to see you too, Gryphin." Bijou said, then continues on to the library, mumbling. Violet hurrying to her side.

"What was that?" Violet giggles with a knowing smile.

"Nothing, what?" Bijou asks looking over at her new friend. "No, no, don't go there. I'm not, well, he is the most exasperating person I've ever met." The last was nearly a whisper to herself.

"We will talk about this later, for sure." Violet said, glancing up at Bijou.

"Mom, Dad, Professors, I'm sorry we are late." Bijou said.

Violet turns to see Lady Zia standing next to a man with coco colored skin and hair the color of chocolate with gray at the temples. He looks very much like Bijou.

"I'm so glad you made it." Lady Zia reaches out a hand to touch her daughter's shoulder, then grasps both of Violet's hands.

"Violet, are you feeling well after your crossing?" Lady Zia asks.

"Thank you, I'm fine." Violet said, noting an unexpected warmth comfort her entire body.

"Mom, you shouldn't do that without telling her first." Bijou said.

"I'm sorry, you're right." Lady Zia said, releasing Violet's hands.

Before Violet could ask what they were talking about, she saw the most amazing thing yet. A giant worm wearing a hat and glasses, its body rippling in a slinking motion directly at them.

"What is that?" Violet asks in bewilderment.

"Step-mother!" Darrock calls from the hallway.

"I'm in here dear." Brune says. She sits at a writing desk in the parlor of the family home. After a glance at the doorway, she slides the papers into a folder, away from prying eyes.

"It's good to see you with color in your cheeks today, Mother Brune." Darrock crosses to sit in a chair next to the desk with his back to the window.

"Ever the flatterer, thank you," Brune says, patting the hand he rests on the desk. She looks through the sheer curtains to the sunny sky. "I hope you have news for me. It would make this lovely day so much brighter."

"But must we always speak of this project of yours? Surely we can plan something fun, a dinner party, remember the old days?" Darrock asks. Excitedly, he leans forward, intent on persuasion.

"Darrock, we've discussed this several times. We won't celebrate until it is done." Brune casts her eyes away.

"Dad expected us to continue—" Darrock said.

"No, we will not speak of your father." Brune said, interrupting as she stands. She walks to the empty fireplace. On the wooden mantel stand framed photos of members of the Grail family, many long passed and several remaining.

"Your lineage has a storied history. We should restore it back to its higher rank in society." Brune said. She snarls at the faces of the past. "Your father's line should not end like this."

"Don't do this. You know as well as I, members of the family are alive and well. So they're not my father's direct line, but we still have a few to continue the name. Myself included." Darrock said as he approaches the photos.

"I miss him." Darrock said quietly.

"Don't be so sentimental." Brune snaps and turns away. Just as her majordomo enters the room.

"Mrs. Grail." Dom said with a slight nod of his enormous head.

"Dom, it's good to see you. I didn't have the pleasure the last time I visited." Darrock steps towards Dom with his hand outstretched.

"Darrock, don't be silly. He is a servant." Brune walks to the nearest armchair to sit. "What is it Dom?"

Darrock ignores the admonishment from his step-mother. The gentle gorilla's much larger hand clasps his. Only then did Darrock take the seat facing her.

"I've finished the search." Dom stands his full six feet, awaiting her response.

"What did you find?" Brune asks, leaning forward in anticipation.

"Nothing Mrs." Dom said.

"How can that be?" Brune asks, collapsing back into the chair.

"Father had a will. I know he did." Darrock rose to pace the end of the room. "I've spoken to his legal reps, accountant, and business partners, anyone that he may have communicated with. Everyone assumed it to be here in his safe." Darrock said.

"At least the estate had provisions for you to

inherit." Brune taps her fingers on the armrest. "Just because we expected him to have made a personal provision for each of us doesn't mean he did. His death was so unexpected."

"No, I do not believe he left you without resources. You don't think he would do that, do you Mother Brune?" Darrock stops to look at her disbelieving.

"I don't know why he was in that wicked place when he died. I don't know what drove him to do the things he did in the last days of his life. It might be best if we just let it drop and focus on finding the artifacts." Brune said, dismissing Dom with a wave of her hand.

"Darrock, have a seat and tell me what you have found for me now." Brune said. Her eyes grow shiny and expectant.

With a sigh, Darrock sank back into his chair. His tailored black slacks and gray t-shirt allow him no hidden pockets.

"You can see I have nothing for you this time." Darrock leans forward to rest on his knees. "All security across the lands has increased. None of my sources can get the things we need."

"No! No! This can't happen now. You must try harder. Or will you fail me too? You can't fail me, Darrock." Brune moves to the edge of her seat, pleading with her stepson.

"I'm not giving up. Don't think that," Darrock goes to her. Hands on both shoulders, he raises her head to lean on him. Gently, his hand pats her back.

"I know you're such a good boy," Brune said, sniffling into his shoulder.

"You go up to your room now and rest." Darrock said, leaning her back to look at her. "Really, all that lovely color has drained from your face. You go and I'll talk to Dom about household things before I leave. Don't give up hope." Darrock said and guides her out of the parlor. After she ascends the stairs, he turns to find Dom waiting at the end of the hallway near the kitchen entrance.

"If you're not busy, Dom, I could use a sparring partner?" Darrock said.

"I thought you would never ask Mister Darrock." Dom said, moving to the back room containing sporting equipment and weapons for just such occasions.

"It's been far too long, my friend. The back lawn, as always?" Darrock asks.

"She won't like it, but yes, it has been too long." Dom led the way.

She bursts into her bedroom, at the last second remembers to close the door quietly. They had come so far. Brune flexes her hands, her rage at the delay courses through her. She won't stop until she has what is rightfully hers. That man took away everything she ever wanted. Every time she was close enough to put her hands on her dreams, he kept her from it. Now, even in death, he was continuing to deny her.

Whirling through her room to find the hidden key in the nightstand on the far side of the bed. Brune goes to the closet, which in this old estate was a small room with a window. When not in a rage, she likes to take her time strolling through the wealth of her possessions. The rooms, her rooms, her clothes, the jewels her dead husband had showered her with in the beginning. She deserves it and more. He could have given her so much more.

Instead, he took from her the one thing she wanted more than the riches. Her bloodline was what she needed now. It was in the journal. But that had to wait. More had to be gathered. She slides the clothes aside, causing the frankincense scenting the room to waft through the air. Knowing the door she needs to open will bring a musty smell she didn't want her clothes to absorb, Brune opens the window.

She unlocks the secret door. No one dares to enter her bedroom, so it didn't matter that she left doors open to air out the room. A small light on the wall was hardly bright enough to see her treasures. The objects are shiny gold, a few are silver with jewels, and one is silky velvet spun by ancient worms in a land lost in time. The one thing the objects have in common is a measure of magic.

At one time, the enchanted lands were full of a variety of magic. She needs as much as she can get. It is destiny, her destiny. It is so close.

"Yoohoo, lady please!" The voice came from behind a black cloak hanging on the wall.

"Not now! Shut up!" Brune hissed. She moves a bag from a small desk at the end of the little room, barely wide enough to turn around. The journal was inside of an ornate wooden box sitting on the desk.

"But please take this thing off of me, if only for a moment?" The voice pleaded.

"Oh, fine." Brune turns around to step back a couple of steps, pulling the fabric off of the mirror. "Now be quiet."

"Yes, you are so kind." The mirror said. A face with silver and black eyes and a hollow mouth floats in front of a celestial backdrop. A dim green light illuminates the face.

Brune moves back to the book, fumbling to get the box open. Then hunts through the pages.

"I can't tell you how lonely I am behind that thing. You have no idea." The voice enunciates each syllable in the most proper manner.

Brune ignores the floating face.

"It's here, I know it. I've read it many times. Where is it?" Brune mumbles to herself.

"Oh, dear, please. Why look through that book when you have me right here?" A brow raises and mouth smirks, waiting for Brune to turn.

"You are going to get covered back up if you keep talking." Brune didn't look at the annoyance.

The room went quiet. Until a low hoot came from the other room. Brune drops everything to greet her visitor.

"Owe! Be careful, don't crack me, Madam." Mirror glows red as she shuts the door behind her.

"What have you got for me?" Brune rushes to the window, her skirt rustling in her haste.

"What the others are telling you is true. It is more difficult to procure what you desire."

"Not you too! I thought you, with your reputation, would not fail me." Brune said. Hands on hips, she stares nearly eye to eye with the great horned owl sitting on the window's edge.

Saying nothing, the owl lightly flutters her wings. One made a gentle feathery rustling sound, but the other made an ominous sliding of metal on metal and a snapping of scissors closing as it stills.

"There is one small morsel of information."

"Well, tell me, Contessa." Hands balling into fist, Brune's breathing quickens.

"It is being said that signs are appearing. The old ones remember a long ago legend and the events that proceed it. They are keeping the details to themselves, at least for now." Contessa said.

"That happens all the time. I will not worry on that. I need the objects. How about instead of wasting my time, bring me the things I asked you for? That is why I'm paying you." Brune paces away from the window and turns to gaze out of the tall window at the sky beyond the bird.

"If I'm going to get my life back, we must stay focused on finding as many of these special artifacts as possible. Don't disappoint me, Contessa. You won't enjoy how I handle disappointments." Brune said. The backdrop of her clothing of dark colors hanging in her wardrobe room gave her confidence to threaten without fear of the others.

In her mind, she went to another time. Her family was a lineage of royalty, but today no one cared that she is the rightful ruler. If she had her place in the kingdom, none of this could have happened to her. She would have married a prince and not a minor noble widower. She would have money and power and not be hiding her plans. Most importantly, she would not be missing her beloved.

"My dear, you are not the only one with the ability to resolve one's disappointment. I'm helping you only because your endgame has benefit for me and my kind. You do not own my loyalty. You are listening to me, aren't you?" Contessa Fusco asks.

"Yes." Brune blinks hard and focuses on the owl. "And we have an understanding of expectations. Now, go find what I need and I will reward you well."

10
LAND FOUND THROUGH THE WOODS-ACCEPTANCE

"Ah, that is our friend Professor Bibli." Lord Callahan said. He looks from Violet to Bibli, then back at Violet. "I see," Lord Callahan moves to Violet's side. "My dear girl, this must be a shock. We didn't think how odd this may seem to you." He reaches for her hand to tuck in the crook of his elbow.

"Please forgive us for our carelessness. The matters at hand have preoccupied us. Your discovery of our world comes at a most stressful time. We promise to do our best to help you understand. Just don't be frightened. No harm will come to you in our land. I can assure you of that." Lord Callahan pats her hand, turning his gaze to his wife.

"Violet, I want you to meet two of the most knowledgeable beings in all the enchanted lands. Our resident bookworm and historian, Professor Bibli, and our inventor and historian, Professor Hewitt York." Lady Zia gestures to each of the respected beings. The small man approaches Violet to bow as he closes his right fist and lays it on the left side of his chest. With a warm smile to each of his friends, he moves to a wooden step stool next to a table with papers and books piled high.

Professor Bibli wiggles his way to Violet's feet. His head nearly reaches her waist. One small nub gestures for her to lower down to his view. When Violet did so, Bibli spends several moments gazing into her eyes.

Violet, on her knees, is just about even with the bookworm's gaze. His warm eyes draw her deeper than any she has ever seen. She worries about what he can see in her own. Surely, he couldn't actually see into her soul. But nothing in this land would surprise her at this point.

"It's my pleasure to meet you, Violet. I'm sorry I haven't made it a point to do so sooner. We have known about you for some time now." Professor Bibli said.

"It's nice to meet you, too. It's probably best we didn't meet sooner. I might have passed out if I saw you before today." Violet said with a grin, feeling her cheeks warm.

"I am rather unique to this world. I understand your land has caterpillars, but they are lowly creatures, and only noticed by their avian and insect predators." Professor Bibli gave a good belly laugh, causing the items he carries around his body to jingle together.

"That is about right." Violet can't help but smile at the blue figure before her.

"Oh, what a meal I would make!" Professor Bibli glances around his audience as he moves along the floor to climb up next to Professor York on the table.

Violet stands, moving with the others to gather around the table with the two respected professors.

"I think we should address the artifacts going missing first gentlemen. It's likely to take you much longer answering all the questions young Violet here has for you." Lord Callahan said.

"Very good Lord Stone. You are always right to the point and, as time is valuable for us all, I agree," Professor York said. He turns to his colleague to speak quietly in shorthand no one could understand.

"We feel it is important for you to know that the thefts have reached every land in the realm now. Every item taken is of magical significance. Our efforts to increase security have slowed down the culprits but not stop them completely. We agree," York turns to gesture to his blue friend, "the amount of magic being amassed in all the objects missing is substantial enough to cause great trouble."

"Oh, yes, that is indeed the case." Professor Bibli said quietly.

"Do you have any idea how they can use magic from multiple objects?" Lady Zia asks.

"Well, my dear that is a tricky question. There is an ancient text that was one of the first pieces stolen." Professor York said.

"That is to say, we now believe it is associated with this caper." Professor Bibli moves forward slightly. "The investigating officials in various locations have all agreed with us on this theory."

"I was skeptical at first, I admit." Professor York

strokes the white fluff of hair on his chin.

Suddenly, a light metallic squeak resonates through the room. Everyone looks up at the domed glass ceiling. Violet gasps. She watches a butterfly fasten a latch on a glass window after having just climbed through. The window is one of many with ornate metal work around it, creating the glass dome. Around the sunny space, the butterfly flutters her way down to the lower level of the room.

Landing as light as a leaf on a breeze on the table near the professors, she looks to the governors first.

"Please excuse my interruption." She nods to each of the governors. Landing on the table with the professors.

"Of course. I'm sure it must be important. It's good to see you, Commander Sera." Lady Zia said.

"I just need to share some information with Professor Bibli as he requested me to investigate a theory he has concerning the thefts." Sera said, acknowledging Lord Stone as well.

"Certainly, do as you must," Lord Stone gestures to Bibli.

Professor Bibli and the two foot tall butterfly move to the other end of the table. Violet watches in fascination for never having seen a lovelier creature. The near midnight purple color of Sera's body and outline of her wings frame the shades of plum in her wings, set apart from the pink flesh color of her face.

"She's beautiful." Violet whispers to Bijou.

"Isn't she?" Bijou agrees.

Lord Callahan and Lady Zia speak quietly with

Professor York while Sera and Bibli lean their heads together, speaking so that no one can hear.

"Uh, Bijou, would you? Maybe if you want to, we could go to the confectionery together sometime." Gryphin asks. His face turning red while his lips go pale and dry.

Bijou gives a little jump and turns to face him.

"I didn't know you were even behind me, Gryph." Bijou said with one hand on her belly. "Are you asking me out on a date?" She asks, glancing over her shoulder and back. "In front of my parents, no less?"

"My friends, Commander Sera, brings troubling news, I'm afraid." Bibli addresses the group.

"Don't keep us waiting. What now?" Professor York asks.

Everyone gathers closer to the table. Professor Bibli's body ripples and pushes his upright half closer to the group. Then, bowing his head, he gives an audible breathy grunt before he begins.

"I asked Commander Sera to take on an assignment." Bibli said. Turning slightly, he faces Violet.

"My dear, I want you to know that everyone here and more will come to your aid and protect you as much as possible." Bibli said.

"From what, exactly, do I need protecting?" Violet notes her heart skips a beat at the implication in his words.

"I'm sorry, that isn't where I should begin." Bibli turns to York.

"No, I can't fix this now. Continue and end where

you should have begun." Professor York said.

"Long ago, the magic in this land was strong. The separation between the ordinary world and the enchanted was great. We didn't have so many connections and methods of crossing from there to here, nor here to there. The very last king of our lands we call the Widowed King. He dispersed the magic." Bibli said, relaxing back to his quiet tone. His audience leaning closer.

"Your mother, and you, are descendants of one of his twin daughters. It is how you came to possess the proclivitas amulet." Bibli said.

"The device you wear around your neck," Professor York said, pointing.

Violet knew her mother had very little family. This fantasy is over the top. For her to wake up one day and learn she has royal blood, HA.

"But this isn't real, is it?" Violet looks at the surrounding faces. "You understand how ridiculous this is for me, don't you?"

Someone would have told her if all this was true. Wouldn't they? But who exactly would the 'they' be? Quickly running through her mind for any old family information she might have picked up over her lifetime. She moves to the side of the table to sit in a wooden chair. Now she had to look up to see the eyes of the beings that apparently know more than she does about, well, everything.

"My dear, there is more, but I will skip to what the Commander came to tell us." Bibli looks from Violet to the Governors. "I had requested that Aerial Security patrol the sky above you at all times to see if any of our citizens are interested in you."

"And what did you see, Commander Sera?" Lord Cal asks.

As light as air, the butterfly walks closer to the group. In a very efficient manner, she gives a report.

"The squad I dispatched to follow the subject," Sera gave a nod to Violet, "witnessed at least two specific subjects either trying to enter the home or following her movements through town. One, you have already spoken to regarding the thefts of magical artifacts. The other is notorious for working with the underbelly of both sides of the border." Commander Sera said.

"Let me guess, the Contessa?" Lady Zia asks. She receives a nod from the butterfly.

"I liaised with a unit of the ground patrol, and it seems the goal is to gain the amulet." Sera said, stepping back from the group.

"My necklace, take my necklace?" Violet asks. She clasps it protectively.

"It is possible," Professor Bibli said to Violet while looking at York.

"We are practically certain, yes Bibli, more so than I, that you cannot come back to our land should they get possession of the amulet." Professor York looks to the Governors.

"The most intriguing notion is that she, you, are here at all. This device awakened for a reason we cannot prove, without an understanding of how to do it. The girl, you, activated it and are here." York said, his hands stroking the white clouds of hair on either side of his head.

"Calm down, my good man." Lord Callahan places his hand on the smaller man's shoulder. "Some things we must see through to the end to gain understanding."

"I didn't come here just to be stalked by thieves. Nor do I want to get involved in this magic stuff, if that is even a real thing. Maybe I should reconsider coming here at all. I have plenty to deal with at home. I don't need this. Besides, my schooling starts up in a couple of months and I won't have time for any of this," Violet says. Her hand gripping the amulet tightly, then places it back inside the neck of her shirt.

"Here or there is no matter. There are ways to tell an object contains a special energy of any kind. Someone has seen the energy it carries. You can't know for certain who that might be. Visit here, stay at home, you won't know when you are in danger of losing the object." Professor York said. He ends the thought looking at his long-time friend.

"You see, my dear," Bibli lowers himself eye to eye with Violet, "they will come for this beloved keepsake of your mother no matter where you are. It's the magic they want. They seek power to harm our worlds." Professor Bibli gestures to Professor York as he slides back.

York opens a scroll, laying it on the table for all to see. He places crystal paper weights at the top and bottom. With great effort, he slides a contraption from the far end of the table to sit over the delicate parchment. On one side he cranks a gear, causing several more to move. His tiny hand toggles several switches and the screen lights up.

Everyone angles for the best view. Before their eyes, the ornate paintings on the ancient scroll became animated.

"Long ago, an oracle said there would come a time when a desire to separate the two worlds would drive one of the split line." Professor York narrates as the story unfolds on the screen.

The gold accented jewel colors move on the yellowed page depicting twin babies merging into fully grown young women that became broken-hearted by each other. The one with hair dark as night allowed the hurt to grow and twist inside until she hated her fair-haired sister.

"Every daughter, regardless of the father, had the same coloring as the mother. Until one day the light-haired line saw the dark-haired daughter." Professor York turned to look at Violet's black hair.

"Violet, are we correct that your mother had very blond hair?" Professor Bibli asks.

She looks from one professor to the other while fidgeting with the hem of her t-shirt. Her eyes actually saw the white hair of the drawing fill in with black ink as if someone held a brush above, letting it drip on the page.

Violet silently nodded.

"We must conclude the unknowns are preventing us from understanding. Brune is the only living relative we are aware of. She herself has the same black hair and there is no report of any others in that line. I have checked with other record keepers, to be sure."

Professor Bibli relaxes back in thought. "For this to be true, we need to find the white-haired offspring from her."

"Her husband died some time ago. They traveled plenty, but surely if they had a child we would know about it." Lady Zia said.

"There would be a notation of the birth somewhere, right?" Lord Cal turned to Bibli.

"It is possible that it went unnoticed. The travel makes it more difficult to track down information." Bibli said.

"Can't you just ask Brune about all of this?" Violet looks at the surrounding faces. "She is my distant relative, so maybe I can talk to her." Violet said.

"Um, that isn't as easy as you might think. She—well…" Bijou said.

"That isn't a good idea." Lord Cal said.

"I'll say it if no one else will. Violet, you shouldn't get too hopeful about making family connections with Brune. She is unpredictable and very difficult." Lady Zia said. Looking into Violet's eyes, she continues, "I'm sorry."

It was obvious Lady Zia wants to say more. This left Violet to roll her shoulders and take a deep breath. So she pressed down on the desire for family and found she respected the restraint on Lady Zia's part. Extended family had always been absent from Violet's life. Now wouldn't be any different.

"No, don't be. I don't know her," Violet said.

"I've heard Brune's son has come for a visit. Is there any idea what brought him home?" Lord Cal asks.

"I hear she has let the estate deteriorate, and he is trying to save it." Lady Zia said.

"Pardon my correction. He is only a son by marriage. The young man, Darrock, inherited nearly all of his father's holdings. It would be time for his training to have ended and he should become head of the family now." Bibli said, shaking his head as he continues. "Sad happenings in that family. His father was a good man, by all accounts. Tragedy in the ordinary land should not have taken him away. The timing was critical for the young man, too. Most impressionable age for the son."

"Sentimental Bib." Professor York pats his friend's back.

"Violet, sit and speak with the professors. Bijou will take you wherever you wish to go after you get your answers. If you don't mind, we would like Cacey to continue staying with you." Lady Zia said.

"I'm not sure how I feel about that. It seems odd now that I know who she really is," Violet said.

"You've always known who she is. Maybe not all the details, but her character is still the same. Cacey is a friend beyond all else. That is just her way. That said, it is up to you to work it out with her. I would feel better having someone that can alert us to any trouble from our world towards you. Not that I expect anything to happen." Lady Zia smiles reassuringly.

"That's settled. Young Gryphin, fetch us some tea while we get acquainted with young Violet here." Professor York moves a stack of books closer to a chair for Violet and sits on the books.

"Right away Professor." Gryphin said. Turning to Bijou, he stammers a goodbye only discernible by the closed hand over his heart and rushes from the room.

The governors make their way from the room as did the Commander. Leaving Violet to find some order to the world she now understood to be the origin of her mother's family.

Violet locks her car. The crossing into the enchanted land still filling her mind as she walks to the bookstore. The sounds of the vehicles seeming louder than ever. Was it possible that all the electricity used to power this ordinary world makes a humming sound? She began looking with a new perspective around her childhood hometown. So much of the ordinary feels foreign to her. The modern conveniences were even a little heavy, if she was honest.

Power lines drape from one pole to the next all around the square. Lines run from poles to buildings. Streetlights hang at the ready to turn on when the daylight dims. What she had once thought of as a charming town square now seems overly modern with clutter of conveniences that invade the senses.

When turning the corner, Violet makes her way to the front of the bookstore. For the first time, it occurred to her that this storefront would fit right in at Maplehaven. How odd it seemed tucked in between the updated stores around it. The hand painted, gilded lettering on the sign above the window and door had her wondering if the craftsman worked in both lands.

From what the professors shared with her, many straddle both worlds. Violet can't help but wonder why nothing showed up in her research about the enchanted lands. The explanation of misdirection didn't explain why knowledge of the enchanted hasn't leaked into her world. That would be a question for another time. Right now, Violet was more focused on asking Candy about the possibility of her bookshop being tied to the enchanted lands. It had to be. The artwork was like dimensional portraiture of those in Maplehaven. But then one moment it seems there are too many people to count in the store and the next they are gone without the bells on the door making any noise. Where did they go?

For the first time, Violet notices the window box overflowing with pink petunias and what she thought was a lime green potato vine. She reaches out a hand to touch the head of a deep red geranium standing among many running the length of the box. Attention focused on the earthy scent of the plants, she jumps at the sight of a chipmunk standing on the edge of the box, looking up at her.

The little critter bowed slightly with a fisted hand on its heart before it jumped down to run along the sidewalk behind her. So swift she may have imagined it. Eyes following the black stripes on the back of the furry creature, Violet felt a wall hit her solidly on the back.

"Sorry!" The deep voice came from above her head.

Finding herself being steadied by firm hands on her elbows causes a warmth to slither up her flesh. The voice pulls forth several emotions, one of which is unwanted.

"Will." Violet said. She rubs her hands on her arms to chase away the lingering feelings he causes.

"Guess we are even now, Mouse." He said.

"Good, no need to keep chatting." Violet said.

"Sorry?" Will takes a step back.

"No, I'm sorry. That was rude." Violet sighs. Her inner thoughts about avoiding entanglement were too close to the surface. But she realizes this topic only comes up when Will is near. How interesting that she hadn't given the possibility of a relationship any thought any other time. She needs to pin that until she has time to look at it closer.

"I'm a mess. Just ignore me." Violet glances at the door of the bookstore and bites her bottom lip.

"How about coffee, my treat?" Will tilted his head to the cafe across the street. "If you want to talk about it, I will listen." He said, all the while showing the slight upturn of one end of his mouth.

"I can't, really. I just want to see if Candy has a moment. You know Candy, right?" Violet asks.

"Sure, as well as anyone knows Candy, I guess." Will steps to the door, holding it open for Violet to enter before him. "I was heading here too."

Passing by his chest allows her to inhale his masculine scent. Nothing overly strong, warm, musky, wood and earth with a hint of something she can't name, maybe leather. She can't place it. Before she has time to figure it out, she is inside and looking for Candy at the counter. The scent is gone.

"Perfect! Exactly the pair I need," Candy said. She turns from ushering a group to the back of the store and grabs a basket off the counter.

"Hi Candy. Do you—" Violet didn't finish her sentence before she was holding a large basket to her chest. "What is that smell?" Violet asks.

"Isn't it scrumptious? These goodies are to die for. My honey lemon crumble muffins and mini apple crumb cakes. And these are coffee table books I need you to pick up." When Looking at Will, Candy gestures to a cardboard box on the floor at the end of the counter.

"What am I doing with them?" Will asks with a full smile, obviously game for whatever is happening.

"My Love Bugs book group arrived before I delivered these things. Now that you two are here, I won't worry about them. Thank you!" She turns so fast her skirt flares out in a colorful swirl.

Before she disappeared to the back, Violet calls out. "What are we doing with them?"

"Oh, silly me. Take them to Irving across the street. He owns the Cafe. I promised to get these to him today. Now I must go, thanks," Candy said, waving a hand behind her, causing a jingle of bracelets.

Alone with arms full, the two turn to each other with a shrug. Violet loops the basket over one arm and opens the door with her free hand.

"I didn't see that coming." Will said. "But now that we will be there anyway…"

"Yes, fine, as long as I can have tea." Violet rolls her eyes and shuts the door behind them.

So little traffic made crossing the street swift. Violet didn't look too deeply at the events unfolding before her. Given recent events, it is best to stay in the moment. If she didn't do that, she might find herself locked in a padded room.

"Do you drink coffee?" She asks.

"Yes, hot and black is my preferred way to drink it, but today I will go for iced." Will said. The bright sun making his choice understandable.

"Do you come here often?" Violet opens the door of the coffee shop to the rich aromas of the roasted beans.

"I've been here, but rarely." Will said.

The extent of her small talk used up it was good they had arrived at the destination.

"Irving?" Will addresses the middle-aged man behind the counter.

"Yes? Is this from Miss Candy?" Irving moves to the end of the counter and raises a section of the antique wood high enough to step into the small dining area.

Violet extends the basket forward, causing the scent of the baked goods to waft around them.

"Oh yes. I can smell heaven from here." Irving reaches for the basket, taking a moment to close his eyes, savoring the aroma. "That lady has so much talent for baking. These won't last long at all. Would you kids like one, maybe some coffee? On the house for the delivery service." He sets the basket on the counter for an employee to load a glass domed display while he reaches for the box of books.

She looks up at Will, considers declining, but follows through on her earlier decision. "Sure, I'll have whatever hot black tea you have." While Will gives his order, Violet looks for a seat.

The Cafe was an interesting mix of antique style with modern polish and simplicity. The dark wood tables were best for two seats and spread out with privacy in mind. Violet was surprised to see the floor had a night sky look of black with fading to dark blue covered in a high gloss. Glass pendent lights hanging from the ceiling cause flecks of silver to sparkle in a few places on the floor.

"No, this is on me. Next time you bring this one in here, you can pay." Irving winks at Will. "Here, you must try Candy's treats." He plates one of each of the treasures from the basket, setting them on the counter.

Violet moves to a spot on the counter to find sweeteners. The selection was surprising, honey and sugar as expected, but the rest were beyond her experience. Feeling adventurous, she decided to try agave in her tea.

The pair move to a table near the window. Violet glances across the street with a thought of how her plans had gotten sidetracked.

"Want to talk about it?" Will asked quietly, then sips his coffee, causing the ice to jingle.

"Sorry, I just can't seem to get out of my head lately." Violet said.

"Ah, anything important?" Will asked.

"No and yes, but I don't want to get into it." Violet waves a hand dismissively, then wraps it back around the warm mug of tea. "What about you? Do you live around here?"

"Not exactly. I come here because of work pretty regularly. This place has grown on me. I enjoy being here sometimes more than when I'm back home." Will gazed out the window. "I've not defined that so clearly before." Looking back at her, the corner of his mouth lifted as it typically does.

"Don't you have family to go home to?" Violet asks.

"Not much, but I have responsibilities to take care of. My father left me a lot to deal with now that I'm… out of school. How about you, family?" Will asked.

"Just my dad." Violet is not sure about that. She unctuously reaches for the necklace.

"My mom died when I was a kid. What about yours, divorce or something?" Will asked.

"Mine died too." Violet sips her tea and rubs her thumb on the pendant of the necklace.

"I'm sorry I brought it up. Are you a student?" Will relaxed back into his seat.

"Yes, you finished already?" Violet asks, trying to get an idea of his age.

"I studied abroad as my father wished me to do. What do you think? I'm probably a couple of years older than you." Will narrowed his eyes, looking her face over.

"I'd say so." Violet leans back in her own seat, returning his assessing gaze. "You keep reading my mind. What's up with that?"

"It's a gift." Will gives her his full smile and leans forward on his elbows.

Oh no, this was going to be much harder than Violet thought. That smile, the glint in his eyes as he locks them on hers causing a slow tingle somewhere deep inside. Her own smile forces its way out. She glanced away to break the spell.

"What are you studying?" Will asked.

"I begin veterinary school soon. I wasn't sure what I wanted to do so I wasted an extra year deciding." Violet said.

"Why wasted? Did you learn anything in that year?" Will asked.

"Of course, but not towards the degree I actually want and need." Violet hadn't expected the challenge.

"Not wasted. You did what it took to get ready for what you want. Don't beat yourself up." Will said, taking a drink of his coffee.

"I didn't say I was beating myself up. Anyway, you don't know me well enough to assume what I think." Violet leans forward on her elbows too.

"Hey, I just mean you should cut yourself some slack." Will said, leaning into her.

"I don't need your permission." Violet's brow creases as she, too, leans into the disagreement.

"Perfect." Will spoke softly as his eyes drop to her lips. His hand slowly moves to still her fingers on the necklace.

Violet felt the slow boil of the fight shift under the heat of his eyes. She drops her gaze to his lips. At the touch of his fingers on hers, she pulls back suddenly, slamming her back into her seat.

All traces of amusement disappear from Will's face,

replaced by something Violet can't identify. Even if she was up for more with him, this was too fast. What did she even know about him? So little it was startling that she was sitting here with him. Chemistry was obvious between them, so maybe she should get to know him a little and see what might be here. The bigger problem was, did she have the capacity to include this in her life right now?

"Sorry." Will spoke as he drops his gaze to the coffee in front of him.

"I'm sorry too. This is just a little fast for me. I've got so much going on right now," Violet said. She felt overwhelmed with current events to play games with him. Here forward, she just had to be transparent. For her own good, this would be her permanent tactic with everything.

"I understand that." Will said, more self-reflective than supportive.

"Let's try friends first." Violet said slowly. The last sip of tea finished and ready to put a little distance between herself and this attractive, slightly irritating man.

Her cell vibrates in her pocket. Surprised to get an actual call instead of the more common text. Violet pulls out the phone. Seeing her dad is the caller instantly sends dread to the pit of her stomach.

"Dad?" Violet answers her phone, her surroundings forgotten.

"Vi, I need you to pick me up." David said, snarling at her.

"Why?" Violet, no longer startled, leans an elbow

on the table. It was likely he got drunk again and couldn't drive. This had happened twice since she had been home. Thankfully, people around him know he has a problem and don't let him drive. It was awful early in the day for this to be the case this time.

"They won't let me leave unless you come get me. Just get here," David said.

"Who are they? Get where, Dad?" Violet hangs her head and closes her eyes.

"The nurse won't let me go because they gave me pain meds, so now I can't drive. I drove here fine, didn't I? I can walk fine, can't I?" David growls at someone other than Violet.

"Why are you at the hospital? What happened?" Violet perks up at that bit of information.

"A stupid new guy at the job site today screwed up cutting a board, causing it to kick back, and I was in the way when the wood went flying. No one would listen to me, so I had to come here. Just come get me." David calmed down by the end of his explanation. The medication must be taking the edge off his aggravation.

"I'm in town already, so I will be there soon." Violet hears the phone click off without acknowledgment from her dad. Typical.

"Everything okay?" Will asks trying to see her eyes.

"Sure, I'm sure he's as good as I can expect." Violet puts the phone away.

"Do you want company? I can help if you need it." Will offers.

"No, it's fine. I'm fine."

"Text me later. Let me know everything is good."

Will said as he follows her to the door.

"Okay." Violet agreed. Without another thought, she heads to her car and the mess awaiting her.

11
THE HOUSE BY THE WOODS-ESCAPE

"No, I'm not dropping you off," Violet said. Her dad dwarfed the passenger seat. His right arm sleeve rolled to the elbow with a white bandage taped to the forearm. Once she got him to sign the paperwork for the workman's comp procedures, he then wanted to fight about riding in her car. He just wanted to hop in his truck and ignore the advice to not drive until the pain medication wore off.

"Just pull over and I'll walk." David leans his head on the window.

A side glance was enough to show Violet why he wanted out of the car. His hand had a slight tremor. This late in the day, he would be drunk already.

"Dad, just relax and we can go home and have something to eat. You can lie down and rest." Violet softened her tone.

"You don't get to tell me what to do. I'm the parent here, not you." David adjusts his legs as best he can in the cramped car. "Who do you think you are?" His left hand makes a fist on top of his knee.

"Dad, I'm just saying we should get you home to rest after getting hurt at work." Violet keeps her eyes on the road and her voice calm. Every nerve in her body was on alert at the anger rolling off him. To get home from the hospital, Violet knew she had to drive near his favorite drinking spot. She focuses on getting home. A little farther and they would be on the edge of town.

"I'm getting out at the next stop sign. Go home, little girl." David used his left hand to swipe sweat from his forehead, despite the cool air the car vent blew at him.

"Fine. No reason to be a jerk." Violet said quietly, concentrating on the road.

True to his word, the door opened at the stop sign. He got out and didn't look back. Violet continues on her way home as the tears fall silently.

At the house, trying to avoid thinking too deeply about her dad, Violet let the tears fall randomly and forces herself to pick at a sandwich she put together. Giving up, she goes to her room. Moonlight lays a path on the floor, ending in the empty cage.

No Cacey tonight. The tears dampen the white pillow under her head. When turning onto her side, she looks out of the window to see leaves of a tree lightly dancing in a gentle breeze.

At last she reaches for her phone on the nightstand. Violet checks to see if she had saved the number for Will. Nope, what had she done with the number?

"The book!" Violet said under her breath. Jumping from the bed to hunt around the room. The bookshelf didn't have it, but the desk did. It was under several others, but it was there. With a flip of the cover, his number was waiting for her. Back on the bed, Violet enters the new contact and begins a new message. Now what to say?

Like ripping off a bandage, she types a random 'this is Violet, I'm home' and put the phone face down. Regret avalanches over her and the phone is in her hand. Why had she put her full name? She never uses that. Oh, if only she wasn't so stressed.

Nothing happens, no dots showing his typing, no message in response. She puts the phone back on the nightstand. Violet snuggles back into the bed. This time, she avoids looking at the empty cage. Tomorrow she would get rid of it.

Unsure how much time had passed or if she had fallen asleep or not, Violet picks up the phone to see she missed a call and a text. So she sits up and calls her dad back, no answer. The text was Will asking how she was doing. A fast message back saying things could be better, but she will chat tomorrow. Now she has to get dressed and find her dad.

Every time she got in her car to pick him up, it was a battle. All the years she was away at school, how had he managed? She certainly hadn't been here to save him. What would her mom want her to do? Or what would mom want HIM to do? Not this time. There just wasn't enough left in her to do anything but look for him.

As soon as the business district at the edge of town is in sight, so are the blue and red lights flashing.

Around a corner, she saw police cars and a few people on the sidewalk. The dark night was lit up with headlights but no sirens were screaming at them thankfully.

Violet felt her stomach tighten at the sight of her dad leaning on the hood of a police car. Everything in her soul screams this was too much. She couldn't do this. She kept moving forward to park in the parking lot. Shallow breaths were all she could manage. One foot in front of the other, toward the owner of the bar that had helped her get her dad in her car one other time.

"I'm sorry Vi. I had no choice but to call them." The big man shook his head. "He was spoilen' for a fight and no one wanted to take him up but, he just kept tryin'. It's not like him to be this way."

"I understand. It's not your fault." Violet said. One arm wraps around her middle and the other hand squeezes the necklace. "What now?"

"I don't want to press charges or nothin'" He assured her. "Hey, Officer John?"

"What's up Wade?" The officer standing with her dad looks over at them.

"This here is his daughter. Can't we let her take him home?" Wade asks.

The officer spoke to David. With a nod of compliance from David, the officer removes the handcuffs. Officer John steps over to Violet.

"You sure you want to do this?" He asks.

"Yes," Violet said.

"Your mom babysat me some before you came

along. I remember him before." Officer John gestures to her dad. He continued quietly, hands on his well-equipped belt. "Sad thing to watch. I'm sorry you have to handle this without her. Chances are you wouldn't have this at all if she were here."

She can only nod.

"Here's my card if you need any help with him. I'll do what I can." Officer John watches as her dad staggers to her car and clumsily gets into the passenger seat.

"Thanks" Violet said. She gets into the car trying not to breathe the foul odor from her dad.

"Vi, I—" David began.

"No, don't" Violet said. She drove home in silence.

The smell he brought into the car demanded the windows be down. And forever the smell of beer and God knew what will connect to this trauma, she knew. Something broke deep inside her. The fight evaporated. The need to hold on to him slipped away, and she didn't know if she cared.

In the driveway, with the car off, they sit.

"Vi, I'm sorry." David said.

"No, that isn't true." Violet just couldn't pretend anymore. She couldn't make it okay anymore.

"I never lied to you about who I am or what you should expect from me." David looks straight ahead.

"Yes, you did." Violet looks to the woods as tears fall to her lap. "Which you is a lie? The one sitting here right now or the one that was here when Mom was?" Violet swipes a hand under her nose. "Don't you think I remember what it was like before?"

"You were too young, of course you don't." David fidgets in his seat.

"You're wrong. I remember you. That is why this is such crap. That is why you hurt me so much with this…" Violet waves a hand in his direction.

"You don't know anything. Just go away, leave me alone." David said and reaches for the door handle.

"That lets you off the hook then, doesn't it?" Violet asks.

"I can't be who you want me to be anymore, not without her." David said and got out of the car.

"That is the most truth you've ever given to me." Violet got out of the car and walks to the woods. Soon she is running.

Inside the edge of the woods, Violet pulls out her cell phone to use the light. No longer running, she stumbles into the darkness the phone light can't reach. Finally, the stone pillar is visible in a shaft of moonlight. Violet rushes through to Maplehaven. She feels a slight twinge of disorientation, but keeps moving. Cobble stone under her canvas shoes makes running possible. Turning the corner to see the circle center, Violet realizes it's the middle of the night or at least very early and everyone is asleep here too. Even the hum of bees is quiet in the stillness of night.

Under the blooming tree sits an empty park bench. Violet walks through the grass to sit under the canopy of the tree. She curls up, using her arm as a pillow. The Govenor's home sits in her line of sight and it's obvious the occupants are sleeping. In the morning, she will visit them for a while and then decide what to do next. With that plan in place, she let herself relax into sleep.

"I was walking to the cafe and saw her sleeping here. The professors always want breakfast early and the bees know that. I pick it up early before they open. She was just here when I came through. You should wake her." Gryphin said in a whispered rush of words.

"If you will be quiet, I will," Bijou said. She gathers her dressing gown to cover her legs as she squats down in front of the sleeping Violet. A hand on her shoulder, she gently pushes her. "Violet."

Eyes flying open, Violet closes them just as fast in the bright morning light.

"It's okay." Bijou said.

"Oh, wow." Violet slowly stretches and sits up.

"Take your time," Bijou said, sitting on the bench next to her.

"I'm sorry to just show up like this. It was so late, I didn't want to bother anyone." Violet sits gripping the bench on each side of her legs. Head hanging as she works kinks out of her neck.

"Gryphin, go get Violet a gilded spring from the bees. Put it on my tab." Bijou turns back to Violet. "Want to talk about last night?"

Violet kicks her shoes off. She puts her feet on the grass and wiggles her toes. With a deep breath, she leans back on the bench. Without turning to Bijou, Violet told her about the events of the night before. When she finished the facts of the matter, she drops her head back to gaze up into the canopy of the tree.

Gryphin passes Bijou a mug of something steaming. Violet sees something in a glass that glistens like transparent liquid gold. Over one arm hangs a quilted bag, looking ready to burst.

"What is this?" Violet asks.

"The most anyone can get from the Queen is spring water and honey. But it has to be so much more." Bijou grins.

The heavy emotions lace with the story of her night slip away on the breeze. One sip and another, Violet forgot to examine the flavors. Crisp, cool water but a warm drizzle of honey and herbs she couldn't imagine. As soon as she swallows, the flavors disappear. Then she realizes the ache in her head is gone. With shoulders relaxed, Violet watches as a flower floats from the tree above down to her lap.

"Oh, now watch. Pick it up and it will give you a color." Bijou leans over close in excitement.

"Really?" Violet grasps the tiny stem under the petals as the colors shifted randomly until it slows and turns blood red, to rose, to settle on deep, royal purple.

"That is a new combination!" Gryphin pulls out a notebook, writing as he speaks. "Have you heard of this one, Bijou?"

"No, nor have I seen this shade of Tyrian purple until now." Bijou reaches out to touch the flower nearly the size of a tennis ball.

As Violet studies the velvety color, her free hand reaches for her necklace. Her fingers run under the neck of her t-shirt, searching for the chain. All of her attention hones in on her search, dropping the flower to the ground.

"Where is it? Do you see it?" Violet says, standing abruptly.

"What?" Gryphin asks, tucking the notebook back into a pocket.

"You wore it when you came here, right?" Bijou looks on the bench and under it.

"No, no, no!" Violet said, pacing as she feels her pockets and searches around the bench.

"We need to calm down." Bijou grabs Violet by the shoulders. Holding her still.

"Right!" Violet takes a deep breath. "Am I stuck here?"

"Let's go see." Bijou grabs her hand and the three race out of the park to the portal at the brick wall.

"Bijou, don't let go, please" Violet looks at Bijou as she steps closer to the spot of her crossing. When reaching out a hand, they wait to see the ripple in the air. A little closer, more hand waving.

"Nothing." Violet froze.

Bijou reaches out, and the shimmer appears. Gryphin reaches out, and it opens for him. Violet cannot see it or feel it.

"Just the wall, I'm stuck." Violet releases Bijou and can only see the part of her on the Maplehaven side of the portal, but not the shimmer of the transition. Gryphin goes all the way through and back again. Still, Violet can only see him vanish and reappear.

"What has happened?" Lady Zia leads her husband and several of the council into the small alleyway.

Violet's head whirls around at the suddenness of the group's arrival.

"Violet's necklace is gone. She can no longer cross between worlds." Bijou said, pulling her arm back through the portal quickly, tucking her hand behind her back.

"The guard alerted us to odd activity here. That must be you, young Tizly." Lord Callahan pinned him with his glare. Causing Gryphin to stop moving between the two worlds.

Lady Zia moves to wrap an arm around Violet, she squeezes gently, rubbing a hand on Violet's arm.

"Let's go home and sort out what's to be done. No worries until we are sure we have a need for it. Now, come so we can hear all that has happened." Lord Callahan ushers everyone away from the portal.

Violet looks back at the unchanging wall. Obviously, her dad wouldn't notice her missing today. But what would happen if she never got to go back? Or should she even care? Violet turns back to see the people surrounding her. The people that had been more concerned for her than her own dad had for too many years.

With each step into the woods, the birds hush. Every angry mumble has woodland creatures disappearing under brush and out of trees. At the sudden stop of motion, everything becomes still. Hands on hips turning in a slow circle, Brune looks for the signs found when on the correct path. She steps near a pile of rocks and crouches down, pulling vines and brushing leaves away.

Brune waves back her mass of wavy black hair. With long slim fingers, she caresses the surface of the rocks. Suddenly, her hand stops. Three shallow lines cut into a large rock. Next to them is a triangle on its side, pointing toward the path. It leads deeper into a thicker part of the woods.

A look at the sky shows thickening tree cover, causing less foliage on the ground for lack of light. Dead leaves crunch under boots. Her fingers find another set of markings in the bark of an oak along the trail.

"Where are you, woman?" Brune whispers to herself. She swats dry brush from her skirt. Her gaze becomes a squint to see the near nonexistent path. Few come this way, giving the forest floor an untouched ancient feel.

Light grows so dim and verdant under the thick canopy that one nearly misses the rock fence row around a piled stone cottage. For being built with the purpose of blending into the landscape of trees and rough stone outcroppings. Two tree trunks make the sides of the doorway, then arc to meet above it and form a united trunk with a rich green canopy sheltering the entrance.

Brune moves as swift as she dares, avoiding noise as much as possible. She had been told not to startle the hedge witch. No one knows of anyone that has dared to visit this place. One old journal had suggested placing some kind of offering next to the door and stepping back a safe distance. However, the gate on the stone fence is latched closed firmly by the looks of it. Getting to the door would not be possible.

The flat stone on top near the latch would have to do. Brune places a bundle of herbs, a spool of thread, and an old silver coin in clear view for anyone trying to see. All worthless items to herself but of value to the likes of this woman.

A step back and she waits.

Hands clench at her sides, then release.

Eyes fastened to the door, Brune continues to wait.

Then, shifting her weight from one foot to the other, she turns to the side, looking through the trees. Scrunching her nose at the damp odor of earth and composting leaves. A small sound brings her head snapping back to the cottage. There stands a woman bent over, examining the gifts at the gate mere feet from Brune. She can't see her face because of the wide brim of a hat shielding the woman.

"You are the hedge witch Wilga?" Brune asks softly.

"Not the answer you truly seek." She said. A small shuffle back from the gate, she stands with a stooped hunch of a woman used to working with her hands in the ground. Mud dried on the layers of her dark skirts, evidence of the physical toil.

"You speak truth, lady of the woods." Brune nods her head in acknowledgment.

"Not here, only I." Wilga said.

"I only mean you are the only lady in these woods. But please forgive if I offend." Brune's brow draws together.

"Some say that you are one that can create a spell to ensnare a magical beast. Is this true?" Brune wishes she could look at Wilga's face.

"Your eyes were on such a beast?" Wilga asks.

"You miss understand. I was told you know of such a beast and can charm it. I would like to know if this is true." Brune said, finding herself leaning as if to see under the pointed hat.

"What price are you giving Wilga?" She asks, waiting stone still.

Her fists tighten and open again. One went into a pocket in the skirt. When her hand came out, she held a small trinket box. Tarnished silver filigree adorned with a pearl snail on top. With no delicacy at all, she places the box on the stone.

Wilga waits until Brune takes a step back before reaching out with a green tinted hand and pointed nails dirty and chipped. For an instant, the nails seem red. Ever so slowly, the front brim of the hat raises until intense eyes level on Brune.

"Yours to give?" Wilga asks.

"My house contains many such worthless objects." Brune feels the weight of the gaze as she waits. Silver eyes streaked with blood assess her own dark ones.

"Objects you say. House, hum." The brim lowers, and the box disappears into her sleeves. "Now speak of the magical beast."

"Rumors are full of an Alicorn being spotted in the lands. Have you seen it?" Brune asks.

"I see more than some and less than others." Wilga said.

"Please, woman, just tell me!" Brune steps forward. Wilga steps back.

"My apologies. This is so important to me. I'm trying to find someone. She needs me to find her. Please help me."

"Mine to give, the creature is not. Your true intent with which it is yet to be seen. If it is here, as you say, for one and only one, it will come. Dare not interfere with events having not to do with you." Wilga said.

"You must tell me now, how can I find it!" Brune demands, hand on the gate. In the time she takes to blink, Wilga is in front of her. The cold, firm hands atop Brune's own. Eye to eye, Brune sees every wrinkle, wart, and grungy gray hair the old woman has. The smell of herbs and spice was at odds with the person before her.

"Something is out of place." Wilga said, looking deep into Brune's eyes. "Broken pieces you cling to. Old ways you desire." Wilga releases Brune's hands and steps back several paces. "Beware, the path you take, lost you may become." Wilga stands outside of her cottage door. "Still time to choose." The witch said, and the door closes behind her.

"Come back! Tell me what I asked. I paid your price," Brune yells to the cottage while rattling the gate. The bound branches of the gate withstand the abuse. Pulling and pushing couldn't force it open. Brune looks up at the sound of wings flapping. A large raven lands on the roof. Another perches in the tree at the front door. Yet another bird was on the ground in front of the entrance. Was it a warning?

One last kick at the gate and Brune turns to make her way out of the deep woods. Before long, the dead leaves gave way to green brush and dappled light. The journey from the cottage much faster without hunting for ancient markings in unknown places. Before leaving the edge of the woodlands, Brune stops.

What now? Examining her next moves in the shadows of the trees gave her a view of the town. Everyone going about their business in their tiny lives. They should be her subjects. Her family should have been ruling these stupid beings, it is her birthright. If she could get her hands on the horn of the Alicorn, there would at least be a chance to set everything right. She could bring Aubrey home. No one would have more power than she. No one could take anything away from her ever again.

From the direction of her home, Brune saw the Contessa searching the woods as she flew to them. She steps forward, making her presence known. But she moves back once detected by the owl.

"I have something for you, my Lady." Contessa Fusco perches on a branch just above Brune's line of sight.

"What could have you risking us being seen together, Contessa?" Brune asks.

"Believe me, it is worth the risk. First, we need to consider payment." Contessa said. One wing stretches giving a metallic slither as metal maneuvers on metal. The faint sound of scissor snip, snip sounds before it closes back to the side of the enormous owl.

"That monstrosity of a replacement for your wing

doesn't frighten me. Save it for lessor creatures." Brune crosses her arms casually, waiting for a more interesting topic to discuss.

"I would not dare try to intimidate you, Lady Grail." Contessa lowers her eyes and head slightly.

"Where is the object you believe I will pay dearly for? I don't notice it with you. Our usual arrangement isn't good enough?" Brune asks.

"Not even close to enough. You shall receive the piece as soon as we agree, not a moment sooner. Shall we meet at the same place as last time?" Contessa Fusco prepares for flight.

"Don't keep me waiting. I will be there shortly. And, Contessa—" Brune said.

The owl made a large circle in the air above the lady.

"This had better be as good as you say." Brune walks away without looking back.

12
LAND FOUND THROUGH THE WOODS-MEETINGS

"Governor Stone? Please, Governor." A voice calls to Lady Zia as she and Violet cross the cobblestone street. People of all races, including many Violet had never seen before, walk past them. A variety of hats and neckwear worn by beings interacting and shopping. Aside from the unusual creatures, it could be any business and shopping center in the ordinary world.

On the sidewalk, the Governor stops to find the source of the voice.

"What can I do for you?" Lady Zia pauses for the citizen.

"Thank you. Yes, I'm working on a story for the paper and would love to get a statement from you. It will only take a moment." The squirrel rushes through the explanation and adjusts her glasses. Pin and paper in hand, she takes a deep breath, ready to rapid fire the topic at the Governor.

"What a delightful idea. It will have to wait, I'm afraid. I must keep moving right now, Bridget." Lady

Zia said.

Face falling, Bridget lowers the notebook she had at the ready.

"Contact me this afternoon in the office and we will get you what you need." Lady Zia steps past the journalist.

"I think the disappearance of valuable relics would be a priority for the governors of Maplehaven. Shopping with friends does not seem reasonable." Bridget said.

"I appreciate your concern for my schedule. That is why I don't have time to give an interview. There are more important things I must attend. You have a good day, and I will speak with you later or when we have something worthy of the public's time." Lady Zia said, glancing at Violet as encouragement to follow.

A large building sitting on the corner, near the tree and bench Violet had slept on just that morning, must be the destination. Violet's amazement over the structure she had walked past with Bijou once before, clear by her open mouth. The building takes up at least two more spaces than the other buildings do. Across the entire front is a wide set of stairs, with people coming and going everywhere. The stone building doesn't appear to have doors, but wide open arches across the front.

"Violet, this is our International Gateway Station. From here, we can reach other lands in the realm and a few that aren't. We can even reach your ordinary world. The enchantments used to power these stations are the most concentrated in existence. If you are going to get back to your world, this should be the place to make that happen." Lady Zia rushes up the stairs with a hand pulling on Violet's arm.

Upon entering the archway, Lady Zia drops her hand. "Please dear, watch your step."

Violet tries to focus despite the chaos of so many people and species rushing around them. It was like watching a busy airport in a major metropolitan city. That was the only comparison Violet had for the abundance of beings in one place. This, however, is beyond amazing with animals, and varieties of race and enchanted beings she couldn't name or fathom. In wonder, Violet turns in a circle to see hats of every color with feathers, jewels, silks and satins. The simple cottons and caps of lower-class citizens are present too.

As a few birds in the air caught her eye, Violet looks up to see a great glass ceiling tiered in several layers above the entire building. Through the upper most glass, air ships appearing through a shimmering veil in the sky are visible.

While trying to make out the emblem on a flag of the closest ship, Violet feels herself falling into Lady Zia.

"Please, pay attention." Lady Zia wraps her arms around Violet to prevent a fall.

"Sorry!" Violet said.

"Watch out, coming through." A deep voice well above Violet's head calls out.

Violet watches as a giraffe brushes past her and out of the archway she had just entered.

"Here, I see Baldric." Lady Zia leads the way to an office halfway into the main room of the building.

"Baldric!" Lady Zia calls out.

Violet rushes to keep up with the graceful strides of the taller woman but comes up short when a large male rhinoceros turns to face them. Mouth gaping, Violet notices the way Lady Zia stands squarely in front of Baldric. No fear or intimidation is visible in her body language. This only slightly relieves Violet.

"Ah, the great Lady of Maplehaven. How marvelous for you to visit us on this glorious day!"

"You don't fool me, Baldric. Drop the pleasantries and let's get on to business." Lady Zia turns to glance over her shoulder at Violet. "I'm here for your help with a difficult crossing."

Violet moves forward, willing to brave the massive creature if it means getting back to her own world.

The gray horn shakes side to side slightly and a great base cough and grumble rumbles out of the massive chest of the finely dressed creature. "Yes, let's get to it. What is the location of the destination?" Baldric asks, while walking from his office area to a large console of controls in the center of the cavernous room.

"Are you familiar with the un-designated gateway in the alleyway behind the cafe on city center?" Lady Zia asks, motioning for Violet to follow her near the long row of portals. Citizens were entering the station from three of them and leaving through five of them.

Violet watches what looks to be a shower of shimmering air flowing both down and up at each portal. Large signs to the side of each one lists the destination but seem to rotate between two or three listed in changing times of ten-minute intervals.

"Of course I know that one! It's my job to know all the gateways, designated or otherwise." Baldric turns from the Lady to mumble about humans being difficult. His grunts and the occasional intelligible word interrupted hushed, garbled speech. Violet was sure she heard him say the name Brune.

"Now, Baldric, you know I'm not trying to insult you. It's just the way we speak. You, yourself, were being effusive just moments ago." Lady Zia said.

"Yes," grunted Baldric. "I had been dealing with a difficult citizen only moments before you arrived. That is the only way to speak with her for civility to be maintained." He pushes buttons and rotates something Violet thought was a polished stone ball sitting in a tight hole in the console. The black onyx color seemed deeper than the midnight sky.

"I have located the gateway. Is this the passenger to cross?" Baldric gestures with his sharply pointed horn on his snout.

"Yes, Violet is from the home near that spot in the woods." Lady Zia reaches a hand out to squeeze Violets. "She can't get back through that way, but needs to return home."

At the end of the row of portals, a ring of ropes cordoned off what looks to be an empty spot on the polished marble floor. In a half second, faster than Violet can blink, the air shimmers to life.

"Safe crossing." Baldric said, and his right hoofed hand touches the left side of his chest as Violet had seen many in the station do.

Lady Zia walks Violet to the area while a spider monkey in a vest and cap, holds open a section of the rope. She fastens it behind them after they enter.

Violet stands in front of the portal. She turns to Lady Zia, uncertain what to do.

"Just walk through and you will be back in your woods. We will do everything we can to find your amulet. I will bring it back to you." Lady Zia squeezes both of Violet's hands.

"I hope so. Can I call you?" Violet holds up her wrist with the bracelet they had given her.

"Yes, please do. You may not be able to cross back over without the amulet. But I will stay in touch too. Besides, Bijou will want to visit when I'm ready to allow it." Lady Zia said with a light laugh.

Violet took one last look around the room. Still amazed at the creatures carrying on with their normal daily lives. With a deep breath, she walks to the shimmering curtain. A gentle caress crosses over her skin as she moves through the portal.

Nothing. The hard marble floor is still under her feet.

Violet turns back around to reach a hand out to the portal. The shimmering light sparks around her hand, but the woods never appear. Suddenly, Violet is aware of several loud jarring bangs. The rhino had been walking back to his office but now was stomping his way through the roped-off section. He drags the barrier with him.

"What is this?" Baldric's voice booms throughout

the cavernous room.

"Please, stay calm, Baldric. We will sort this out." Lady Zia moves to his side.

One arm outstretched, Baldric tries the portal for himself. Between the hulking beast and Violet, her woods became a ghostly image.

"Now, pass through, miss." Baldric orders.

Violet looks to Lady Zia for approval. With her nod, she steps into the portal, only to be directly in front of Baldric. Inches from his great snout, Violet's hair flutters when his hot breath huffs out of his nostrils.

"Who are you?" Baldric asks turning his head to the side so one eye can squint at her closely.

Before Violet could speak, Lady Zia pulls her aside. "Baldric, you and I will speak privately. Give me a moment." Arm around Violet's waist, she moves her back near the entrance of the building but pivots to one side. An alcove containing what appear to be old-fashioned wooden telephone booths.

The marble floor ends in an arc around the seven booths clustered together. With stepping stones leading to the door of each one. A thick carpet of moss covers the surrounding ground. Mushrooms sprout sporadically throughout. Woody vines grow up the sides of the wood to gather above with a flush of green canopy. Very few citizens enter the designated place, and only one booth has the door closed.

"Now, while I sort this out, you might try to contact your father. Do you have your cell phone?" Lady Zia asks.

"Yes, but it doesn't work here. It won't turn on or

anything." Violet reaches into her back pocket, pulling out the device.

"I know, but we can work with it here." Lady Zia steps to one booth, gesturing for Violet to enter. A small bench on one side faces a small desk with several instruments on it.

"Set your phone on this moss pad. Then wait for a moment." Lady Zia instructs.

Violet did as instructed. It isn't long before fine vine-like tentacles sprout up to enter ports on the phone. To one side, a chunk of amber spins in a glass dome surrounded by moss and mushrooms. When the phone lights up receiving notifications, Violet looks at Lady Zia with enormous eyes.

"Go ahead, you can send messages from here." Lady Zia said, stepping back she, closes the door.

Violet taps the screen of her phone to see new texts from Will, but nothing from her dad. Tapping on her dad's message list, her finger hovers over the keyboard. Instead, she scrolls back over the previous texts. The realization it has only ever been a one-sided conversation causes her breath to hitch. Rarely did he ever respond. Even then, it was one word.

She had been gone all night. After a terrible event, and he wasn't even worried. She looks at the time on her phone. Half the day has passed. Sleeping in couldn't be the excuse for her dad not noticing her absence.

Her eyes wonder from her phone to the amazing contraption, making it possible for her to use her phone in this world. A spur of resolve has her backing out of her message history with her dad. In a blink, Violet pulls up the new message from Will. At least one butterfly fluttered in her belly. No, that couldn't be excitement? Yes, it had to be.

There! If Will noticed her absence, then her dad should have, too. Three texts listed on the screen. The final one expressed concern for her lack of response. Sending a reply was a must. She just needed to think what to say, because the truth was not possible. He would definitely think she was crazy if she mentioned this world. Violet looks out the window of the door to see Lady Zia talking with someone just out of view from the narrow pane of glass.

She began her response by typing her name in all caps. He needed to stop calling her Mouse.

"Darrock Grail, how nice to see you." Lady Zia addresses the finely dressed young man that had just entered the station through a portal.

"Ah, Governor Stone. It has been a while. You and your family are well, I trust?" Darrock asks.

"Yes, thank you. How is your step-mother, Brune? I haven't seen her in sometime." Lady Zia asks.

"She is good," Darrock said. A slight pause between them.

"If we can do anything to help, please let us know." Lady Zia offered.

"Now that I have run into you, I have a question for you." Darrock said, gently resting a hand on the lady's arm. He urges her to move to the side of the corridor. "I have been looking into family matters. So is it possible the original document of my father's will got filed in Maplehaven? Who would have information on that?" Darrock searches her face.

"Interesting question, I don't recall. I can look into it for you, if you like? As a governor, I have access to all the village records. I'll send word to you if we find anything." Lady Zia said, looking back over her shoulder at the booth Violet was using.

"Let's keep this quiet. I don't want to disturb Brune with digging up past troubles." Darrock said.

"Is there something wrong?" Lady Zia asks feeling a hum of the unsettled coming from him.

"No, just tying up loose ends with the family estate. Now that I'm home for good, I want to move forward. It would be easier to do, if I can put this history to rest. I'm afraid my father's books and papers came to me in a mess. Unfinished and disorganized, and I was too young at the time to understand much of it." Darrock said. He smiles, but it doesn't reach his eyes.

Lady Zia lays a hand on his arm and sends a hint of comfort to him. "I'm sure you can pull it together. Lord Stone and I will help in any way we can, so let us know." She removes her hand.

"Thank you and I will. Now, please excuse me, I have more to follow up on in other areas." He gestures to the empty booths next to the one Violet occupies.

"Ah, yes." Lady Zia moves aside. The knowing look shared between the two was all the acknowledgment needed.

With Darrock tucked into a communication booth,

Lady Zia gazes up at the sky through the top of the building. There wasn't as much traffic through the airship portal as the pedestrian ones. Trade of goods and supplies happens much slower than what she heard occurs in the ordinary world. The sky is blue with faint white clouds passing over.

"Lady Stone." A low, masculine voice interrupts her thoughts.

"Ah, Mr. Pravat." Lady Zia turns to stare into the dark glasses the pale man uses for protection.

"Lady." The gray wolf tips his hat.

"Sir Randolph. To what do I owe the pleasure of your attention, gentlemen?" Lady Zia asks.

"A change has occurred and our concern is great. The Order, as you know, feels things that disrupt the normal way." Mr. Pravat says. He continues to stand straight and still. His cane rests on the floor next to his finely tailored self.

"Yes, we have a problem." Lady Zia spoke. A glance over her shoulder shows Violet emerging from the booth. She reaches out in her young friend's direction, gesturing for Violet to join her.

Violet tucks her phone into her back pocket. As she nears the Governor, it became obvious she is not alone.

"My dear, I want you to meet two gentlemen that might help us get you home," Lady Zia said.

"I believe we have met." Mr. Pravat gave a slight tip of his head.

"Yes, at the Bee Cafe." Violet said. She tries hard not to stare at the wolf while standing next to him. A wolf on hind legs with his head above her own was disconcerting, no matter how spectacular his clothing and hat were. Tented goggles rest on the brim of his black and purple top hat.

"This is a dear friend, Sir Randolph." Lady Zia introduced.

"Miss." Sir Randolph whisks the hat from his head with a bow that had his fluffy tail swishing behind him.

Speechless, and a little rude, Violet tries for a pleasant smile. Despite his powerful presence, she smiles.

"We belong to the Order of Echoes. It is our duty to help you find your way back to where you belong." Sir Randolph adjusts his hat, then places his right fist over his heart.

"Thank you." Violet feels a tingle on her neck at the sound of his gravelly baritone. For one second, it seems as if he does not want her here. She forces her gaze up to the pale man. "What is the Order of Echoes?"

"Simply put, custodians of the magic in the world. We seek order and balance." Mr. Pravat said.

"I'm thinking it will be best for you to spend time with the Order to figure out what is keeping you from returning home. With or without that amulet, you should be able to cross." Lady Zia said.

"What if I want to stay?" Violet asks Lady Zia. The urge to glance at Sir Randolph was difficult to deny, but she locked her gaze on Lady Zia.

The quick glance Zia gives the gentlemen causes a pause before her response.

"Never mind. Obviously, I need to go back." Violet looks out the entrance.

Staying only avoids the mess with her dad. That would not be so terrible? He didn't care. And it is time she creates her own life, right? This place has so much to offer. Magic truly exists. That is worth exploring, surely.

"Lady Zia?" Violet asks.

"Yes." The lady steps to her side as the gentlemen move to give them privacy.

"I need to know. Is it possible magic could help someone change?" Violet asks as an idea forms in her mind.

"In what way?" Lady Zia asks.

"I know you have watched my dad and me for a long time. You know what he's like, right?" After her quick nod, Violet continues, "I want to help him. Help him stop drinking." The more she spoke, the more the idea tumbles together and comes boiling up.

"I want to help him WANT to stop drinking. Not just to quit, but to want to be better." Violet paces back and forth in front of Lady Zia. "You could help him with that thing you do, couldn't you? Just push intent or desire for life into him. Something like that would help him. I know it would." On that statement, Violet stops in front of Lady Zia to study her directly.

"I want to build my future, but I need him to be okay, you know? He needs his own happiness so I can have my own. I need this. Will you do it?" Violet asks.

Slowly, Lady Zia raises a hand in a motherly gesture to smooth Violet's hair. She then takes both Violet's hands into her own. "If it were possible, I would move all the stars in the heavens to fix him for you." Softly, Lady Zia continues, "Magic and people don't work that way."

"I've seen you do it, influence people. Can't you try?" Violet asks.

"It wouldn't have the results you are looking for." Lady Zia's soft watery eyes suddenly change as a crease forms in her brows. "What do you mean you've seen me do it?"

"Never mind. It doesn't matter. If you say it doesn't work, then fine." Violet takes an unconscious step back.

"Violet, what did you me—"

A loud, violent screeching of metal clanging and wood splintering rang out from above the building. Everyone turns to look up at the glass ceiling. The trade portal for the airships has closed with an airship nearly all the way through. Its back portion briefly hangs motionless in the portal until it didn't. The giant structure falls.

Screams erupt inside the building as citizens try escaping the inevitable destruction. Those that can't move drop to the floor, covering their heads. Glass rains down, making a terrifying kind of music as it hits the marble floor. Soon, the ceiling over the office area falls under the weight of the airship remains. One sail of the ship flutters through the opening that once held panes of glass. It drapes over the pedestrian portals that remain open.

Violet lifts her head from the cool floor to see a

cloud of dust fill the air where the office staff had been moments before. When reaching out a hand, she finds Lady Zia's arm.

"Lady Zia? Is she ok?" She asks Sir Randolph as he reached her seconds before.

"Yes, I believe so." Sir Randolph nudges Lady Zia gently, brushing her hair from her face.

"I'm fine, thank you. Stop fussing now." Lady Zia gingerly touches a dot of blood at her hairline on her forehead. "That floor is so hard."

"You pushed me to the floor, thank you." Violet sat up on her knees, brushing debris from her dark hair.

"No time for that. Let's help those in need. Let's go." Lady Zia stands at the help of Mr. Pravat and Sir Randolph. Without hesitation, she ignores their protests about giving herself time to recover. Lady Zia heads to what had once been the office. The space now had the tail of a large ship smashing it nearly to the ground. Dust, papers and bits of cargo from the ship float in the air.

"Has anyone seen Baldric?" Lady Zia calls out. "Baldric?"

"Here Lady." A strangled grunt calls.

Lady Zia moves closer to the massive structure to realize the ship is sitting on a beam that rests on the great rhino's back.

"Get them out." Baldric says with a grunt.

"Move back!" Lady Zia clears the area with the help of Sir Randolph and Mr. Pravat. Violet steps into the small area next to Baldric's side.

"Violet, wait!" Lady Zia calls out.

On a shudder Baldric says "Hurry!"

"Move through here." Violet pushes the terrified creatures through the opening. An ostrich, a monkey and a kangaroo all escape at the insistence of Violet. One last peek under the ship and she jumps through the narrow space as one of Baldric's knees gives out.

"Please, old friend, come this way before it's too late." Lady Zia says.

A final snort and push up on the beam and Baldric lands out from under the ship. At Lady Zia's feet, the great horned beast rests. She reaches down to pat his horn.

"You truly are a hero today, Baldric."

"Lady" Mr. Pravat says quietly.

"Yes, Mr...." Looking at the spot Mr. Pravat is pointing to, Lady Zia stops. A chunk of wood lodged in Baldric's side causes a crimson puddle on the floor.

"Don't move Baldric. Just be still." Lady Zia encourages.

"No worries about that." Baldric snorts.

"Gentlemen, I trust you will see to our friend while I organize the others." Lady Zia said quietly as she surveys the surrounding room. Chaos is everywhere as citizens in shock and disbelief stumble around the debris.

"What can I do?" Violet asks Lady Zia.

"Give me a minute." Lady Zia continues to assess. Upon seeing help arrive, calm settles over her face. Her husband, Lord Callahan, entering with Bijou, Gryphin, and Cacey on his heels. Queen Eldora of the bees enters from the now open ceiling with her swarm in a line behind her.

"Glass." Lady Zia says to the Queen, causing her antennae to vibrate, signaling her swarm to clear the danger from the room.

"Wounded." Lady Zia says to her husband, and he organizes the monkeys to help evaluate the many injured moving them through the front of the building.

"Violet, you can help direct those that aren't hurt to exit the building." Lady Zia looks at her daughter and points to Violet.

With the organized efforts, the area clears rapidly. Someone stopped anyone from entering through the portals until the building is safe for travelers to be present. Commander Sera and her team were already investigating the airship dock to find out what caused the closure on a ship to begin with.

Violet looks around at the progress. The dust had settled; the glass cleared from the main areas, and few individuals remained in the building. One small group was still trying to remove a beam from the communication booths. Violet herself had been inside moments before the crash.

"Baldric will make a full recovery thanks to his tough hide." Lady Zia said as they watch the enormous creature being carried out of the building by several gorillas.

"I can't believe how everyone just showed up to help." Violet said.

"Isn't it the same in your world?" Lady Zia asks.

"Sort of, I guess. We have people trained to respond to catastrophes. I haven't ever seen anything like this happen up close before. I wouldn't have gotten involved. What do I know?" Violet said. The reality of what they had all just been through crept into her mind.

"You did great today." Lady Zia continues. "Look at the blue sky today." They both gaze up through the roof. The bees were making their way up and out of the building. Large butterflies, pigeons, bats, and other members of the aerial security team are inspecting the structure to the side of the airspace.

"Things could have been much worse given a part of an airship just landed on a significant public building. Yet, the day is just as lovely as ever. We will continue on, won't we?" Lady Zia said, her voice so low Violet wasn't sure if she was talking to her or possibly herself.

"Perspective is a funny thing." Violet hadn't given a thought to her own safety today. She just wanted to help, if possible.

A gentle nudge on the back of her shoulder brought her attention back to herself. Just as softly, another bump to the back of her shoulder.

"What..." Violet turns but can't finish her thought. In front of her stands a creature she cannot name. A pure white horse with a two foot iridescent horn and wings tucked along its back. Slowly, it bows its head to her.

"It's true!" Lady Zia whispers next to Violet, and she lowers to one knee.

Violet tore her eyes from the exquisite creature to see the few citizens remaining inside the damaged building had lowered to the ground as well. Before she can force herself to do the same, the horn of the creature taps her shoulder.

There was no voice but an urging to follow where ever it wants to go. With near soundless grace, the creature turns towards the entrance. It pauses, looking back at Violet.

Violet looks at Lady Zia.

"You must go. The Alicorn has called you for a journey. What it will entail, I do not know, but try not to fear," Lady Zia assures, rising she takes Violet's hands into her own. "I will send Bijou, Gryphin, and Cacey to follow. You will not be alone. Besides, you can communicate with me if you need." Lady Zia taps the bracelet on Violet's wrist.

Violet nods and goes back to the Alicorn. She puts one foot in front of the other. From behind the unbelievable being, Violet watches the long hair of the tail sway with each step. The tips only just touch the smooth marble floor.

Behind her, Lady Zia calls to her daughter to form a small group to follow at a distance.

"It works!" Brune paces around the altar she created in the old castle ruins. The crumbled stone walls of the once great hall lay covered in vines, leaves, and moss. Grasses sprout up between the stones of the floor, evidence of nature reclaiming the forgotten palace. Brune uses a large fallen stone in the center to pile every magical object stolen on her behalf on top. She has lived with this injustice for too long. Now she will have her vengeance.

"I'm so close to having everything I want, as it should have been." Brune walks from the altar to the side of the room. The view would have looked out over the cliff. With her gaze looking over the forest below, she can see the kingdom that had once belonged to her ancestors.

"I will reclaim you and my child will rule you as is our right." Brune declares to the wind. She drops her focus to the base of the cliff where a small clearing sits. A ring of flowers grow despite the dense forest. Despite the height making it difficult to see, many of the blooms are out of season. Nothing much should grow so thick in this patch of forest right now.

"Could this be the spot? It must be." Brune remembers the strange birth she had been told of occurring deep in the forest years ago. Occasionally, a sighting gets whispered about it today, but with no proof, she couldn't be sure. Knowing peasants to be unreliable, she had not invested in hunting for the creature. But, if true, she can use it to boost her power, making it easier to close off the ordinary world from the enchanted. The horn of the Alicorn can make all the difference.

First, the most important piece of the puzzle had to be found. She must bring her daughter back here before they try to stop her.

13

LAND OF DECEPTION-TEMPTATION

"Wait! Hey, where are we going?" Violet asks. The only response she gets is the swish of the whitetail in front of her. Clomp, clomp, clomp. The hoofs make a steady sound on the cobblestones of the village.

"The other animals I've met in this land can talk. Just my luck. The one animal that wants me to join them doesn't say a word." The latter said more to herself than the Alicorn. Violet notices the road changing. She steps to the side and sees the edge of town is up ahead. The road became dirt and a narrower lane and a less traveled path than she had expected.

"Should I go back and grab food or something for a hike?" Violet was sure Bijou or someone would let her borrow a water bottle at least. With each step, the realization that she couldn't go to her own home for her backpack and her own jacket and hiking boots feels more real. Trees edged closer to the road. The path ahead was obviously going through a wood. A wood to where?

"Look, I don't know why you chose me." Violet

lengthens her stride to get even with the front shoulders of the beautiful creature. As she passed the wing tucked to its side, the urge to reach out and stroke the feathers was strong enough that she gave into it. The feathers rustled and then settled with the weight of her hand gliding along a feather the length of her forearm.

A great calm settles over Violet. Amazing how so many in the land could bring her such peace. The pattern was becoming so obvious she should give it more thought and maybe ask someone what was up with it.

"Can I ask a question and at least get a nod or gesture in response?" Violet asks.

The eye closest to Violet swivels to look at her and then back to the path ahead.

So she takes that as consent. Violet continues to think for the next several steps. She focuses on the brush on the ground. Then looks a little deeper into the surrounding woods. What seems to be oak trees spaced out enough to allow plenty of ferns and brush to grow thick and lush. Suddenly, Violet notices small animals sitting under the leaves of the ferns. Two rabbits huddle together dressed in hats and neckwear, watching the Alicorn. Peeking from behind the base of a tree is a badger holding his plaid cap in his paws.

Violet looks from one side to the other to see a variety of animals sitting still to watch as the rare creature passes, unaware of them. What makes this animal so special?

"Where are you from? No, never mind." Not a head

shake answerable question.

"Were you born in this land?" Violet asks. The low clomp of the hooves on the packed dirt is all the sound she hears as she waits. Just when she is sure the wait is pointless, the large head bobs up and down in a jerk. A hum of excitement fills her.

"Do you visit other lands through the portals?" Violet waits a little more impatiently than last time.

This time, the answer comes a few steps sooner. The long white snout jerks from one side to the other.

"OK, yes, you were born here and no, you don't use the portals to visit other lands." While looking up through the tree canopies to the blue sky, Violet has a thought.

"Do you visit other lands?" Violet asks.

Up and down the ivory head moves.

"When we are done with wherever you are taking me, can you take me back home?" Violet rushes on as another thought worries her. "I know that might mean I need to ride on your back, but I would be very grateful."

The eye wheels back to her and intensely conveys insult.

"No, you are right. Forget I asked. That was rude of me." Violet wasn't sure how she felt about not getting the answer she thought she should want. This world continues to amaze her. Maybe it could be a brand new beginning if she stayed here.

The pair continue to walk side by side. Violet keeps her gaze on the path, trying to ignore the watchful eyes of animals they pass. Without warning, her companion veers off the path. In her difficulty to step over or through the undergrowth, Violet falls back behind the pearly coated creature. It quickly becomes obvious to her that her canvas shoes are not the best option for this journey. Bits and pieces of leaves and dirt tumble around in both of her sneakers.

"Do you mind slowing down?" Violet calls out as the Alicorn gets farther away.

"I can't keep up with you. My legs aren't long enough to step over most of these plants." Violet tries to push through the lush foliage, now knee high and increasing the farther they go.

Her guide continues at the same pace. She can still see the white shimmer in the dappled sunlight. When Violet looks around while catching her breath, something draws her eye. Just to the left of the Alicorn, the floor of the woods becomes clearer. It would make it possible to catch up. Keeping her escort in view would be easy enough from there. So Violet opts for the easier path and pushes towards it.

One last step, pushing her legs between two prickly shrubs. On her first step, it became impossible to stop her momentum. The meadow grass gently slopes downward just enough that her speed increases until she is twenty feet farther than she intended to go. The realization that she had lost sight of the Alicorn moves her to try locating a way up the right side of the valley. Large stones stick out of the sloped walls with trees sitting on top.

Why hadn't she continued to follow the beast? It was difficult, but at least she had not been alone. Now what? A faint sweet scent fills her nose. Up ahead, she is sure it looks like a structure covered in vines. With no other option, Violet goes that direction.

Each step closer, the shape becomes more visible. Two woody vines grow up and meet above, forming an archway. Purple flowers bloom with each step Violet takes. Close enough to touch now, Violet traces the tip of her fingers along a grape-like cluster of blooms. Two more erupt next to her fingers, causing her to pull back, startled.

Mesmerized by the flowers dangling overhead, she walks under the archway. The life so clear, the feeling of loneliness fades away. After a few feet, Violet stands in what feels like a room created by surrounding trees and boulders and objects. The abandoned or forgotten objects lay half covered by forest growth. Vines, dead leaves, ferns, and saplings grow on top of, through, and around things. Things people use or dream of every day. An upright piano with ivy running along the keys. The legs lost to tall grass and saplings fused to the sides reaching to the sky are sitting forgotten. Stacks of books, easels with half-finished paintings and unused canvases all tuck in together. Patches of dead leaves make for stepping stone like places to wonder through the objects. A tuba with no polish to its brass sits on a chair without its fabric upholstered properly. On top of a rock, Violet sees pristine ballet pointe shoes with a coat of dust. In the grasses on the ground, several other kinds of shoes lay abandoned.

Each object pulls at something deep inside Violet. The scent grows stronger in her nose. Vanilla with some unknown spice and a hint of lavender has Violet looking around for the source. But resting her hand on a desk that slopes to one side, she realizes she wants to sit and rest.

"Just for a few minutes." Her voice is more a whisper than she intended. She shuffles her feet to the side of the desk, where an unfinished wooden chair waits. Violet brushes off a layer of dust and sits. Obviously intended to be a lounge chair for a deck. Violet snuggles back into the chair, trying not to close her eyes.

Her eyes rest drowsily on a dressmaker's mannequin with a lovely rich purple silk fabric hardly pinned into place. In the foliage below are drawings of clothing, shoes, and jewelry, all unfinished. Books lay open with unfilled pages everywhere her eyes can reach.

"What is this place?" Violet whispers to herself.

Her mind wonders. Memories from her childhood play through one after the next. Each one had her parents playing imaginary characters with her. Pirates was her dad's favorite. They used the couch as the pirate ship. The cardboard tube from some paper towel would allow her to see a deserted island in the distance. Violet was not aware of the faint smile as she remembers her dad being a kraken trying to climb onto the ship to sink it.

The memory that pushes a tear down her cheek is of her mother. Her mother liked to sew her play clothes for dress up and costumes to use any day of the year. Princess dresses, lion tamer safari outfits, and a mermaid warrior. But Violet's favorite was the time her mother made them matching nightgowns.

What had her mother wanted to become? Was being a mother enough? Her life had been so short. Did it give her mother enough? Surely not. What was there to show for her life now that she was gone? The little family was so broken it couldn't even be called a family, really.

"Maybe if I just sleep here for a while, I will feel better." Violet didn't know if she said it out loud or just thought it. She drifted off to sleep before she figured it out.

"Violet! Violet, wait, don't go in there." Bijou yells. Panic filling her body from head to toe.

"Run!" Cacey shouts from one of Gryphin's pockets. "We must get to her before it's too late." Cacey drops lower into the cargo pouch, trying not to get bounced out as Gryphin uses his lanky legs to push over and through the brush.

"Oh no, no, no." Bijou tries to keep up and does better than she might have had fear not been propelling her forward.

"Wait!" Gryphin says breathlessly at the arched entrance, Bijou trying to push past him. Hands gripping her shoulders, he looks into her eyes. "We can't go in there. You know this."

"But she didn't know. We have to help her." Bijou pushes, surprised that her slim friend has enough strength to prevent her from moving past him.

"We will. There must be another way." Gryphin holds her gaze. "But first, can I trust you not to go in there?"

Eyes pulling from the opening to center on the green eyes weighing her intentions. The only thing Bijou can manage is a curt nod of confirmation. This allows him to release her. The spot he had held grew cold without his touch.

Bijou paces back and forth in front of the entrance, rubbing her arms, trying to calm her fear that Violet could be lost to them forever, thinking it was her fault. She should have been faster. They shouldn't have taken time to grab the meager supplies. For a quick departure to follow the pair to who knew where, for who knew how long. Her practical side may have cost her this new person brought into their lives so recently.

A quiet sound up on the ridge pulls their gaze. Sir Randolph was making his way down the slope on all fours with every grace a wolf can possess. Given his large stride, mere moments pass before he stands with Gryphin, Bijou, and Cacey.

"I assume you couldn't reach her in time to stop her from entering?" Sir Randolph asks.

"Not because we didn't try." Cacey bounds out of the pocket to face the entrance. "I'm willing to try. Some of my kind can enter and not succumb to the grip this place has on the mind."

"No." Bijou won't allow another friend to be lost.

"No need, my dear." Sir Randolph steps closer and wraps his tail around the fluffy bunny for comfort. "You will all stay back while I see what I can do." Sir

Randolph said quietly in his deep, rough voice. Without further instruction, the trio move off to the side.

Sir Randolph reaches into a pocket, pulling out a long metal box with a domed lid. He opens it to read dials and gages. Then, speaking as he continues to study the instrument. "What you know of the Order of Echoes, I assure you, is not nearly enough to explain what you are about to witness." The quiet tone of his voice keeps his audience still.

"Our preference is to avoid sharing our secrets. Not for any reason other than no one should use them lightly. There is always a price to pay for magic of any kind." Closing the box, he puts it back into a pocket. He finds a small notebook and flips through the pages. When he finds what he wants, he continues to explain. "I won't ask you to not share what you are going to see me do, that is up to you." Finished with the book, Sir Randolph reaches for the goggles on his hat and lowers them onto his eyes and adjusts the strap.

Rolling his shoulders while he uses his tail to sweep a circle on the ground, leaping up with each foot as his tail passes. Arms out to his sides, he drops his head back and just when the others get antsy, a deep growl starts in his chest. It rolls up and out to a howl, causing Bijou to cover her ears. As the sound dissipates, the air swirls around the wolf standing tall at the entrance of the Valley of Forgotten Dreams. Bijou closes her eyes to blink and opens them to nothing but leaves drifting to the ground.

"Wait, what?" Bijou jumps from her seat on the

boulder next to Gryphin and Cacey. "I didn't know this magic still existed. We have been told it does NOT."

"Amazing!" Cacey hops up and down, clapping.

"Gryphin, did you know about this?" Bijou turns her focus onto her…what? Is he a friend or boyfriend? The dream is too secret to think of with him so close. So she pushes her feelings aside, trying to stay on track.

Gryphin rises off the stone. His gaze avoids Bijou entirely.

"You knew." Bijou says. Hands balling up to fist at her sides, she narrows her eyes. "Does everyone know magic is still possible in the realm?"

"No, not at all." Gryphin turns to her then. "It's not strictly a secret. Professor Bibli says that it stopped being practiced because it didn't work for so long. Then the practice died out, causing much to be forgotten."

"The Dead King dissolved the monarchy of the realms and dispersed power, causing the concentration to be diluted. At least that is the theory taught." Bijou said. She could still make out the circular pattern in the leaves on the ground from Sir Randolph's tail.

"As far as the professors can tell, that happened. Those that had powerful strength with magic had none. Others, like your mother's family, found a strengthening of a natural ability. To feel the feelings of others and to push feeling out to the world stronger than most." Gryphin said.

"So, what was this? Sir Randolph just vanished before our eyes." Bijou said.

"Over time, it seems magic has found its own

balance again. Because it is a living thing that no one being has all control over." Gryphin said, reaching into a pocket. "I have a notebook that might help you understand."

Before Gryphin found what he was looking for, the wind whirled over the circle again. Sir Randolph flickered in and out as if a hologram that couldn't hold a signal. He appeared to be trying to drag something with him, but it wasn't cooperating. Suddenly, he was fully present, but his grasping paws were empty. He fell back on his rump and rolled to his side, springing up on his hind legs.

"Grrrr, that was not good." Sir Randolph growls. He removes his goggles and fastens them to his top hat.

"Where is she? What happened?" Bijou asks with her voice raising with each question.

"She is in deep, I'm afraid. We are going to need help." Sir Randolph said. He takes a step back from the entrance and brushes leaves off his coat.

Violet opens her eyes moments after relaxing. The Alicorn had to be near this place. The urge to stand and find a way out got her to move sluggishly. A slow turn allowed her to see so many abandoned things. The forest was claiming each item as its own. Who had left them here? The question fading from her mind nearly as soon as she thought it.

One step forward brought her close enough to a stack of medical textbooks that she could touch them.

She brushes across the open pages, pushing dust and leaves off to see a picture of a human body with the major bones labeled. The next pile is a collection focused on animals.

"Veterinarian studies, just what I need," Violet spoke absently to herself. Two books in the stack found their way into her hands.

"Did I pick these up?" Violet looks around to realize she is at a desk. A breeze blows debris from the surface. With little thought, she lays the volumes down and opens the first one.

Unsure of how time might pass in this place, Violet cannot account for how long she sat studying. She glances back at the page. It wasn't obvious what she had been viewing. Gazing up at the sky was of no help. The tree canopies sway over any view she tries to get of the sun.

"I was looking for someone, wasn't I?" Violet rose from the desk. Across the way, a piano sits alone. "Maybe I have time to sit for just a minute."

One step, then another, and she was there before she should have been. "Do I play the piano?" Violet asks. The wood weathered and splintered, but she still puts her hands on it. Sheet music was what she felt instead of splinters pricking her hands.

The sound of papers shifting as she tries to brush it aside is the only sound to be heard in the woodland room. Violet looks at the keys. It is obvious many are missing, and a few sit at odd angles. Find middle c. Her mother's voice said in her head, or out loud? Violet places her hand in the proper position. She presses the keys with no sound being made. Tears fill her eyes.

"Where is it?" Violet searches the keys, hitting them harder and harder. It still makes no sound. The bench falls backwards at her sudden eruption from sitting. The upright piano, being too tall for Violet to see inside the back, still made no noise when her knees press the keys. Up on the piano, Violet pushes aside plants growing where the string mechanism should be and still are. Because of the roots of the plants tangling under the hammers, they cannot strike to make the tinkle of the instrument.

"No, this mess is not right! This can't be here." Violet pulls at the offending plants only to find more and more roots. One plant after another flies over her shoulder. Still no sound from the piano.

"I can do it. Truly I can, just let me try," Violet said. Tears falling freely from her eyes.

With every ounce of energy spent, Violet can feel herself ease back from the keyboard. Aware of going down, she can only continue the motion, letting the plants cushion her fall. A cozy slumber feeling settles into her entire being. Maybe she could close her eyes for just a moment.

She is still with no reason to move. Violet wonders why she is awake. The sleep had been so peaceful. A comfort after so long, with none. It was the lack that hurt so much. But here this place is so nice. The things are nice. Painting was never an interest, but why not try now? Or maybe she could learn to dance now that the shoes are at hand.

Or laying right here and closing her eyes is best. Later, she could try something else.

14
LAND FOUND THROUGH THE WOODS-TRAPPED

"I can't believe you. Why must you behave so primitive?" Berenger asks. Up on the roof of a stoop, he eyes his companion.

"Hush! The ordinary will hear you." Sketes sits on the cement banister running up the stairs of the entrance to the home. "This is how squirrels in this world behave." He pulls a seed from a cheek pouch and cracks the shell with his teeth while holding it in his front paws.

"At least tell me if you can see inside the residence." Berenger said, giving his wings a flap only to smooth them in place at once.

"She is in there alright." Sketes said, standing on his hind legs, giving the air a sniff. He resumes to pulling another seed out of his cheek.

"It's a good thing we came across Brune when we did. What is she doing in the ordinary world?" Berenger swoops down to the sidewalk in front of the house for a look in the street facing window. "I can't see a thing." He tries a tree branch at the curb near the window.

Sketes climbs down to the narrow patch of grass between the brick house and the sidewalk. With little effort, his rodent legs propel him up to the window box under the front window. He sits digging in the dirt, sniffing for the treat another had buried.

"Now, will you try to focus?" Berenger squawks and ruffles his feathers.

"You will draw attention, more than I can if you keep up that noise." Sketes finds the treasure and begins testing it with his teeth while looking in the window. A small slit between the curtains allow him to witness Brune talking to another woman. The other woman is older, if her silver hair is any indication.

"I see her." Sketes said.

Berenger stills on the branch.

"The old lady looks mad. She is holding an envelope out to Brune, but she isn't taking it," Sketes recounts for the raven. "Brune is pacing away from her, then back. I hear her yelling something about the girl is hers. Oh, here she comes!"

Sketes scoots away with his back to the front door and Berenger flies up to the roof of the house. Traffic passes, a dog barks on a leash across the street and the owner pulls it away from a cat in a window.

Brune rushes out of the home to the sidewalk, heading to the corner of the street. Never does she acknowledge any beings from this world or any other.

Berenger swoops to a trash can near the edge of the street. Sketes sits at its base, observing Brune retrace the path she had used to come to this place.

"We must return to report what we have seen here today." Berenger said.

"Don't tell me you want to pick me up and fly back faster." Sketes rubs his shoulders.

"It isn't fun for me either. You must have put on a few grams." Berenger gives the rodent a side eyed glance.

"What! I have not." Sketes runs his paws along his belly and his sides, checking for any extra pouches of fat. "It must be you that has put on a few grams with the perching and preening you do. When did you even fly before today?" Sketes narrows his gaze at the blackbird.

"Wait just a minute." Berenger leans over the top of the trash can to catch Sketes's nose twitch and a smile break out on his whiskered face.

"Got you, old fella. Let's get outta here. Lord and Lady will find this information very interesting." With a chuckle, Sketes flicks his tail, then runs down the sidewalk.

"I appreciate the help." Darrock said.

"Are you sure you're okay?" Lord Stone asks.

"Despite being trapped by a falling airship, I'm fine." Darrock brushes dust off his sleeve while surveying the damage to the surrounding building.

"I am sorry it took so long to get the beam moved from blocking the doors. But we had to tend to those that were more seriously injured first." Lord Stone clamps a hand on Darrock's shoulder. "You seem to be fine."

"I assure you, I am," Darrock said, with a slight grin as he continues. "The only wound I've sustained is from not being able to help you with the rescues."

The two men chuckle as they step out into the fresh air at the front of the building. Darrock looks to the side, noticing Pravat standing with a hand on a tree while holding a small copper box.

"What is that about?" Lord Stone asks.

Pravat snaps the lid shut. "Darrock." He said, turning to look at the young man through his dark spectacles.

Darrock looks at Lord Stone with a shrug.

Pravat was instantly at the base of the steps, addressing both Darrock and Lord Stone.

"I need your help, Darrock. Lord Stone, please inform your wife that Miss Violet has gotten herself into trouble. Sir Randolph contacted me, asking for our help. Time is of the essence. For Bijou could not stop Violet from entering the Valley of Forgotten Dreams." He takes a step back, making a slight bow, ending the conversation.

At the mention of Violet, Darrock rushes down the stairs. Lord Stone steps backwards and calls out, "We will meet you there."

"Back to back, young Mister Grail." Pravat speaks as he retrieves a black lacquered box from inside his jacket pocket. When opening the lid, he mumbles under his breath numbers and readings from dials and instruments displayed in the container. Continuing to mumble things the others can not quite hear, he presses his back against Darrock's.

"Stay close." Pravat said, barely audible as he lifts his cane above his head with both arms. After he makes two consecutive rotations above the men's heads, the air swirls around them, picking up force.

As the wind begins, Darrock closes his eyes. He knew this existed but has never traveled in this manner himself. He assumes his senses will take a beating with all the uncontrolled movement. Soon he is no longer on the stone walkway in front of the International Gateway Station. Just when he notices the floating feeling, he feels soft dirt of the woods under his feet.

"Blast! Oh, double blast!" Darrock leans over at the waist with his hands braced on his knees. He could only think how grateful he was that he had been too busy to eat anything for the past few hours, or it would surely cover the ground in front of him.

"Deep breaths, my boy." Pravat sounds amused. "First time, obviously."

"I might suspect you are enjoying this." Darrock slows his breathing and stands up. He notices Bijou, the apprentice to the professors, a caramel color rabbit he suspected was an official and Sir Randolph.

"No time for introductions. It's been too long." Sir Randolph steps forward. Pravat hands Darrock a silk scarf he pulls from his neck. Sir Randolph assists Darrock with wrapping it around his nose and mouth.

"I need you to wear this scarf. It's infused with the essence of honey, several herbs, and crushed crystals. These efforts of protection will only last for so long.

So we need your strength to pull Miss Violet from the grip of this place as swiftly as possible. Randolph tried, but she fought him." Pravat said all this matter-of-factly while he pulls the box out and observes the dials.

"She grabs at the vines and plants like they are her lifeline. I've seen no being ensnared this fast before." Sir Randolph speaks quietly. With the soft gray fabric tied securely at the back of Darrock's neck, the three stand back to back.

"I'm going to do this different this time. Until we locate our target, we will be half there and half here. It takes longer before we cannot resist the drugging effect of this abomination. Stay close." Pravat said, raising his walking stick above their heads. He makes two complete circles. Unlike before, he then lowers it in front of himself and continues twirling it with both hands from the center of the cane.

"I think I understand what the plan is." Gryphin said. "We will continue to see them just as they are here, but they will also be in there. Look!" Gryphin said, pointing to the faded, ghostly appearance of Pravat, Sir Randolph and Darrock.

"I still don't know how this is possible." Bijou said. Then she paces a few steps on the narrow path in front of the entrance.

"Everything is magic until we understand the science of it." Gryphin said. Casually, he moves to stand between Bijou and the doorway.

"Why hasn't anyone dismantled this whole valley yet?" Bijou swings her arms out, gesturing to the entire structure before them.

"Once someone understands the method used to create the thing, it will be done." Gryphin motions for her to follow him.

"Don't show her. You don't want to know, truly you don't." Cacey hops back from the pair.

"I'm fine, Cacey, I need to understand." Bijou said.

They walk along the outer wall formed by trees, vines, and boulders. So densely enmeshed is the foliage that not even a mouse can see through the tangle.

Gryphin stops, a pile of rubble protruding from the makeshift wall. And squatting down, he pulls at ivy and leaves until he is several inches deep. "Look here."

"Sticks?" Bijou moves closer. "Oh, no!" Falling backwards onto her backside, one hand covers her mouth. "Bones! That's a skeleton. Wh—when did this happen?"

Gryphin offers his hand to help her stand. He pulls her back away from the wall. They watch as everything he had pulled away moves back over the bones.

"Over the years, there have been many attempts to destroy this place. When a loved one goes missing, their families lash out and try to reach them. Who can blame them, right?" The pair walk back to the entrance path.

"It's just so sad. There is so much despair in this place." Bijou wraps her arms around herself. Gryphin puts his arm around her shoulder, pulling her close to his side. They watch the ghostly figures still half there.

"Bijou!" Lady Zia calls out as she makes her way down the slope at the edge of the valley. Lord Stone trailing behind her.

"Stay near one another." Pravat said to Darrock and Sir Randolph.

"We must hurry." Sir Randolph moves to lead the others. He sniffs the air. And turns his head this way and that between each snort. Desperate to locate Violet, his ears swivel, trying to pick up any sound.

"We can cover more ground if we split up." Darrock takes a step away from his companions. A hand grips his arm.

"You mustn't leave my side. I won't be able to keep you tethered in both spots if you don't. You will not be of any use to Violet or us if you succumb to the toxins as well." Pravat cautions as they walk.

The group pass by a piano. From the narrow path, they step into prickly bushes brushing at their ankles. Still anchored between the outside and this place, they do not see the scratches they sustain.

"Best to touch as little as possible while in here." Pravat warns Darrock. His hand lifts from Darrock's shoulder, to adjust the fabric on the young man's nose again.

Darrock pulls back from a stack of books and shakes his head. As they move deeper into the piles of forgotten objects, he reaches up to tighten the scarf on his neck.

"I think I've caught her sent. It's faint." Sir Randolph veers off to the right, knocking over a drafting table. The falling furniture causes unfinished architectural drawings of buildings to flutter through the air.

"Keep up!" Pravat said.

Darrock stumbles on the uneven terrain, tumbling face down in the undergrowth. "Wait!" he calls out. His hands bury in the soft piles of decaying foliage beneath him, making pushing up difficult. Finally, feeling his left palm hit a firm object, he pushes up to all fours. The distance between him and Pravat increases. His body becomes fully present. The ground underneath his knees feels bumpy and hard under the dead leaves. Slowly, he lifts his hand to see he grips a skull. He cups the round back of the head. Then, turning it around, the hollow eyes of an ape look at him. The gaping jaw with missing teeth dangles below. Dropping the weathered bone was a slower reaction than he thought it should have been. Something was trying to disconnect him from the thinking part of his own mind. The scarf! A voice inside screams at him to raise it over his nose and mouth. It must have moved when he fell.

"Get a grip." Darrock said out loud. Brushing at the debris under his hands exposes bones of all sizes and species. But looking more carefully at the abandoned things, partial and full skeletons were everywhere. The vines and leaves hide some bones, but many lay exposed. If you look for them, they are visible.

Mask secured in place, Darrock looks up to see Pravat reaching out to him, calling his name. Darrock shakes his head and focuses on Pravat. And letting his voice draw him out of the haze pulling at his mind.

"We found her. Come with us," Pravat said when

Darrock got closer. "Hurry!"

Weaving around broken, dusty furniture and the tools of many trades, Darrock finally finds Sir Randolph kneeling on the ground. The wolf pulls vines away from a mound. Pravat positions himself on the other side of the heap that the tendrils continually reach out for.

"What should I do?" Darrock rushes to kneel at the end of the pile. His hands plunge wrist deep in the tangle, turning cold. Like a late fall day with no sun shining, frigid. After a moment, he realizes he feels her shoulder. "She's close to frozen."

Pravat and Sir Randolph look at each other as they move faster. Pravat removes objects from his interior pockets. Randolph pulls a silver blade from a sheath at his waist. Pravat mumbles readings from dials and gadgets, performing calculations in rushed murmurs. Randolph cuts vines, causing them to wither back onto their self. Darrock sees something written on the blade shining in the cool dim light. He's unable to read the obscure script.

As one vine withers, another comes up alongside it to dive deep into the pile covering and twining around Violet. Little by little, a Violet shaped figure becomes visible. Darrock brushes debris from her cheeks.

"She's so pale. What do we do? What can I do?" Darrock asks, not taking his eyes off the face so near death.

"Grab her shoulders and pull. We need her to wake up. She must hear us." Sir Randolph growls.

One hand on her cool cheek, Darrock reaches with

the other to undo the scarf from the back of his own head. The warm fabric slithers down his chest. With both hands, he places the treated silk over Violet's nose and mouth. And ignores the growing blue tinge of her lips and hollow around her eyes. Darrock fights the foliage to secure the only bit of protection they can provide.

He takes shallow breaths, hoping to delay the effects of the toxic air. Darrock forces his arms under Violet's shoulders and pulls with all the strength he has. Despite this, he only moves her enough to rest her head on his lap. The vines don't reach her face, at least for the moment.

"Violet, please Violet, wake up!" Darrock speaks as he curls over her, preparing to pull again.

"Wait, don't move her too far until we can get her awake." Pravat said. He shoves the devices into pockets and holds a slip of paper with his scribbled notes. "Do it Randolph. Cover your ears, Darrock." Pravat covers his own.

"Violet!" Randolph growls, tossing his snout up to the sky. He closes his eyes, letting his wolf grow wild. "Viooolet." He begins a long loud howl that vibrates the surrounding air.

Darrock notices the atmosphere became lighter. He drops his hands from his head to shake Violet's shoulders.

Her eyelids flutter. Darrock nudges her shoulders again. "Violet, wake up!" He says.

As pale as her skin is, her eyes open to show gray irises glinting silver in the eerie light. Darrock gasps in shock.

"Violet, listen to me." Randolph says. Violet shifts her unseeing gaze in his direction. "Do you want to escape this place?"

After a moment of no reaction, Darrock shakes her shoulders again.

"You must choose to withdraw. We cannot take you from here without you choosing for yourself, Violet." Sir Randolph cuts through the tendrils, trying to climb up onto the mound covering her frame.

"What if she doesn't make the choice?" Darrock asks, looking at the wolf.

"She is too deep. We will lose her mind even if we remove her body from here." Pravat answers.

The three look at the unseeing eyes, waiting for a response.

15

LAND OF DECEPTION-DECISIONS

"Uh, I can leave here?" Violet said. "Mom, what should I do?"

The woman turns from the dress she had been pinning to the form, smiling. She looks over at the sunny light hitting the desk. Violet can see her father. "What do you think, Dad?"

He turns from the papers on the desk to smile at her. Violet looks into her lap to see a fluffy baby duck scratching at the pages of the open book underneath itself. The title at the top of the page blurs in her tired eyes, but it says something about veterinary medicine. The beak pecks at her thumb pinching the skin.

It should have hurt, shouldn't it?

Violet looks up, intent to ask her mom, and notices the sunlight dims. Her shoulder jerks. Then the other one. Despite the odd movements, she glances at the desk. Her dad is gone and a layer of dust covers the surface. Over at the dress form, the tattered fabric is no longer being pinned. Suddenly, she was lying on her back.

"Cold. I am cold," Violet said out loud, but her lips didn't move.

"Violet!"

"I'm here." Violet answered.

"…choose…"

"Choose what?" She tries a deep breath, but her chest is too heavy. Something pulls her down hard.

"I just want to go home. I'm so cold here." Violet didn't know if she was thinking or talking.

A breath in. Memories come to life in her mind of her mother, then her father, past and present. Another breath. Flashing police lights. Another breath.

"Violet?" Darrock says.

"…help me go home…" Violet tries to get up.

"Now!" Randolph said.

Darrock pulls Violet out of the vines far enough he had to move himself backward to pull again.

"She's free, now Pravat!" Randolph said. Pravat twirls his walking stick above his head while Darrock and Randolph lift Violet off the ground. In a blink, they are no longer trapped inside the deadly enclosure. But appear back on the outside in the exact spot they had left.

"Thank everything that is good!" Lady Zia gives praise.

"Yes!" Gryphin shouts.

Lord Stone rushes to cradle Violet in his arms as the three collapse, panting.

Cacey hops up to peer into Violet's face. When she reaches out with a paw, she touches the ghostly colored cheek. "She's so cool." Watery eyes look up at Lord

Stone.

"I know, little one. They need our aid urgently." Lord Stone speaks softly.

The scratches and scrapes unfelt during the search were now visible and felt by each one. The pale man had minor injury to his hands, but his feet had suffered in the soft leather of his custom shoes.

"Here, let me help you, Sir Randolph." Lady Zia said, reaching for his bloody paws.

Darrock collapses onto his back. Shallow breaths and groans of pain are the only sounds he can manage as he reaches to unfasten his embroidered tunic. Gryphin helps him remove the fine fabric only to gasp at the blood soaking the white shirt hidden by the garment.

"Lady." Gryphin said quietly.

"Still, we are not safe. We must leave this area. Contrary to our pleasure of having them with us, we are only somewhat better off now. We need to get up that ridge and make camp." Lord Stone looks around at the injured group. "Bijou go up and gather kindling to start a fire. Cacey search for a water source. Get it boiling right away." He carefully picks his way to the base of the path. And adjusts Violet over his shoulder, he finds steady footing to get Violet away from the place that could still cost her everything.

Together, they worked to help everyone leave the Valley of Forgotten Dreams. Lady Zia takes charge of cleaning wounds and making sure they tend to everyone's needs. Bijou keeps the fire hot and water boiling. The provisions she had taken time to retrieve helped to provide the makeshift treatments for now.

"Will this be enough?" Bijou asks Lady Zia.

"Enough for what, to travel? Yes, but will it be enough to cure them? I'm afraid not." Lady Zia uses the small metal cup to pour water on Mr. Pravat's bare ankle.

"We must rest for the night, I'm afraid." Mr. Pravat said.

"I agree." Lord Stone tore a sleeve from the shirt they removed from Darrock. Then rips it into strips, wrapping it around Darrock's middle to cover a gash low on his back. "Everyone, rest now."

"At first light, we must get them to the lady in the woods." Lady Zia said.

"Wilga the Witch?" Bijou turns from the fire. "Why would we do that?"

"She isn't a witch. That is just what children say because she's…" Gryphin said but couldn't finish.

"She's lived longer than any of us and knows more of healing than I do." Lady Zia said, stepping to the edge of the light pouring water on each hand drying them on the fabric of her split skirt, being sure to avoid her leggings underneath the fabric. "Odd to be sure, but we have no doctors in our land. At least, not the kind in Violet's world. We owe her the best care we can find here." When moving near the fire, she looks at the still figure of the girl with Cacey curled up in the crook of her neck.. "I should have gone with her."

"Why didn't you?" Darrock asks.

"I should have been with her. I own that mistake. But the Alicorn…" Lady Zia pauses. "I didn't for one minute think she would let anything happen to her." She wraps her arms around herself and gazes into the flames.

"Where is it anyway? Did any of you see it?" Lord Stone asks the group.

Shrugs and jerks of heads were the only answers given. Everyone moves to sit near the fire as the darkness grows deep in the forest. No one prepared for a night's stay in the rough, but they made do with leaning on each other or trees and rocks. Gryphin sits next to Bijou. She yawns and leans into his arm.

"Will Violet wake up?" Bijou asks, resting her gaze on her parents.

"Tomorrow, rest now." Lady Zia rests on a log her husband had dragged near the heat of the fire. His arm wraps around her back, chasing away a chill that had little to do with the nighttime breeze.

Violet and Darrock, having sustained the worst of the injuries, sleep soundly. Sir Randolph stretches his paws to the warmth and closes his eyes, but his ears continue to twitch with each subtle sound. Soon Bijou and Gryphin are resting with heads leaned on each other.

Pravat sat leaning against a tree with eyes closed behind his dark glasses. One hand rests on his cane laying along one leg, the other holds the brim of his top-hat on his lap. No one comments on how odd it is to see his pale bald head. So rare for him to remove his hat completely while in the company of others. None notice tonight.

The wolf lifts one eye, scenting the air. "Friendly incoming." He said so low only Lady Zia heard him. Silky wings flap in the wind. A rustle of leaves being disturbed nearby had Lady Zia turn to see Sketes plop in a heap at the edge of the light.

Berenger drops to perch on the log next to Lady Zia and removes his black top hat in a slight bow. "Lady."

"How did you find us, Berenger?" Lady Zia asks.

"It wasn't easy and took frightfully long." Berenger said.

"Too true!" Sketes flexes his shoulders and waddles to the fire, turning to wiggle his backside at the flames.

"That's right, catch your tail on fire." Berenger said, shaking his head clicking his beak.

"Please don't. It's been a long day." Lady Zia rubs her temple. "What caused you to seek us in the first place?"

"Of course, forgive us." Berenger turns to focus on Lady Zia. "We caught sight of Brune leaving through a portal and followed her."

"She went to the ordinary world." Sketes moves closer to Lady Zia and lowers his voice. "At a fancy house, we got a show! She was yelling at an old lady. Boy, was she spitting mad too."

"Sketes! That's quite enough." Berenger jumps down to stand next to the fluffy rodent and pecks him on top of the head.

"She did!" Sketes mumbles rubbing his head with both paws. He waddles to the other side of the fire and finds a spot to curl up and tuck his tail over his face.

"There was an altercation. The woman that lived in the home had a legal document, we think. It was difficult to hear what they said. A young girl was at the center of the discussion." Berenger said.

"Tell me everything you saw and heard." Lady Zia said and nudges her husband. Together, they both listen as the crow relays as much as he can.

"Do you think it is possible Brune has a daughter?" Lord Stone asks his wife.

"I heard no rumors to suggest this." Lady Zia tore her gaze from her husband to contemplate everything staring into the fire. It took a moment, but through the flames her eyes focus on Darrock sitting up looking at her.

"My father has a daughter?" Darrock asks.

First waiting for the crow to make his way over to sleep with the others, Lady Zia spoke. "Are you telling me you didn't know Brune had a child?"

"They sent me away to study and train in whatever suited my father's interests. That was before the wedding. My father came to visit me from time to time, but they did not bring me home." Darrock said. He lifted a bandaged hand, looks at it as if he hadn't known of the injury. Then, rubs over his eyes and down his face. The drowsiness closed in again, obvious in his lowering eyelids.

"Rest now, Darrock. We will help sort this out once you are well." Lady Zia said, but he was back asleep before her words were complete.

"What does this mean, Cal?" Zia speaks to her husband.

"I can't imagine. Tomorrow, I will leave once we settle them at Wilga's, and she agrees to heal them." Lord Stone glances at the wounded. "Then I will try to use the portal with Berenger and find this woman. With any luck, she will share her story with me."

"You know I don't want you to travel to the ordinary world." Lady Zia said. Her hand reaches out to squeeze his. "Darrock's father got killed in the ordinary world. It's too dangerous."

"I know, my love. You know as well as I do that something did not sit right with that incident." Lord Stone pulls his wife close.

"Someone shot him! They have guns and random violence that makes no sense." Zia rests her head on his shoulder.

"The investigation on our end was all but positive that it was a trap set for him deliberately. We can't assume that I will befall the same fate." Lord Stone lifts her chin with his hand to see the golden light of the fire shimmer in her unshed tears. "I won't go into the details, but I won't be alone. I never am. Now rest. It will be a long day following a long day." He kisses his wife, then Lord Stone chuckles.

When giving him a tight hug, Lady Zia closes her eyes, cherishing the rumble of laughter in his chest. She was afraid tomorrow may only bring many more questions.

The able in camp got moving before first light broke through the trees. They constructed a litter of limbs and branches found on the floor of the forest to transport the two sleeping bodies.

"Keep pulling, we will reach smoother ground soon." Lord Stone said.

"True enough." Pravat tries to pull, despite slipping with each step. The ties fashioned to keep his torn shoes on his injured feet didn't allow for traction on the dried leaves.

The wolf growls around the short bit of rope clamped in his teeth. In his primal stance of four legs, he limps with each step, trying to help pull the others.

Lady Zia casts her gaze to Violet and Darrock sleeping while the conveyance sways with each step. Gravity of the design force the two together as their weight strains the bindings. Sweat rolls along Darrock's temple. But Violet is as cool as death.

One last hard push through knee high brush and the litter hits even ground. "Stop here and rest." Lord Stone says.

"Cacey, come with us and we can scout for fresh water." Bijou said. Dropping the branch she had been using to help pull the load.

"We don't have time to stop." Lady Zia said.

"There is no choice. Look at everyone." Lord Callahan said.

Still at her place beside Violet's resting head, Zia turns to see Gryphin adjusting the bandages on Sir Randolph's paws. The wolf was sitting but looks as if he should lie down too. Mr. Pravat sat leaning on the trunk of a tree. He used a gray handkerchief from his pocket to mop his brow.

"You are right. Forgive my impatience." Zia closes her eyes and takes a deep breath. She releases the branch and rubs her hands on her hips.

Callahan takes one of her hands into his and turns the palm up for inspection. Lightly, he rubs his thumb on an angry red spot.

"You will have blisters by the time we get to Wilga's." Callahan kisses her palm and releases her hand.

"Do you know how much farther we have to go?" Zia asked. Upon hearing the giggles of their daughter and Cacey, she closes her palm over the sweetness of her husband.

"I don't believe it will be as far as we have come so far. There are those that say the distance to get to her place has more to do with your intentions than yards of earth." Callahan chuckles. "I expect to be there in the hour. I've spotted the markers on the path."

"That is right. I forgot your aunt was friends with Wilga when you were a child." Zia reflects on the past, trying to remember why her husband has a fondness for the notorious woman of these woods.

"Friends may be strong. Auntie brought me and her kids to see Wilga and exchanged fresh garden pickings for healing knowledge. Herbal remedies to help her neighbors during a time when we had no other options." Callahan picks a sprig from a small bush nearby. He rolls the leaves in his palm, using his thumb to bring out the oils.

"This will soothe your hands. I don't remember the name of the plant, but I recognize it as one Auntie used in a salve." Callahan reaches for her hands and presses the green mush into her palms. "Auntie had me pick this one many times when I was hardly bigger than Cacey. Wilga will know how to help them." The seriousness with which he looks into Zia's eyes helps to calm her fears.

"What price will she demand?" Pravat speaks quietly as he approaches the intimate conversation. "Excuse me, please. I am sorry to interrupt, but have you considered the price?" Pravat asks. He leans on his cane.

"Yes, it has weighed on my mind as we have traveled." Lord Callahan said.

"Lady Stone, you must refrain from letting your guilt over Violet's unfortunate circumstances interfere with bargaining. I know it will be tempting. It is common knowledge that Wilga is a crafty creature."

"We have known each other for some time, haven't we, Mr. Pravat?" Lady Zia asks.

"Yes, we have." A wrinkle formed on the pale man's brow.

"In that time, have you ever known me to let my emotions interfere with the best course of action in any dealings you have had occasion to witness?" Lady Zia clasps her hands in front of her hips. Shoulders back and hair dancing in the light breeze.

"Forgive me, Lady." Mr. Pravat tips his hat and removes his glasses and produces a handkerchief to dab his brow. "I can't seem to think. Under normal circumstances, I am certain I would never have presumed to suggest you lack the capabilities necessary to handle Wilga." Replacing the glasses, he continues. "I think we must hurry to our destination."

Lady Zia places a hand on his arm, squeezing gently. "You are burning up. I feel it through your sleeve." Zia looks up in concern.

"True, Sir Randolph and I ingested the toxins of the valley directly in our bloodstream and by breathing it in, I'm afraid. Let's be on our way, please."

Lady Zia helps Mr. Pravat back to his place on the other side of the conveyance. After cool water refreshment, she encourages everyone to make ready to finish the journey as soon as possible. Soon, they can see a tendril of smoke drifting dreamily through the trees. Thanks to Lord Stone, the path to Wilga had been swift.

Seeing the destination so close gives everyone a second wind. They are soon at the stone fence surrounding the yard of the small cottage. No longer able to stand, Sir Randolph collapses to sit, leaning against the stones. Uncontrollable shivers racking his fur covered body.

Mr. Pravat joins him but slower to lower to the ground. His cane making the descent gentler. Shivers claim him as well.

Bijou crouches in front of the two with a jug of water. She assists each one to sip as they can manage.

The second the wolf touches the stone wall, the door of the cottage opens. The earthiest herbal scent wafts from the home.

"What are you waiting for? Bring them in, silly girl, we must hurry. You have left me little time to save whatever is possible." The voice was as ancient as the hills in the land. They looked around, trying to decide if it came from inside their heads or drifted on the wind?

Lady Zia pushes the gate open.

"Take them first. They are worse than we are." Mr. Pravat's voice rasps for his parched throat. This prompts Bijou to raise the water for him once more.

"Uh, we will stay here till you need us," Sketes said. He pulls his cap lower on this head, moving along the base of the stone fence. He makes a cozy pile of leaves and curls up inside the mound. Berenger shakes his black head but perches on the stone above the squirrel's nest.

Lord Stone lifts Violet up into his arms. He steps through the gate. Gryphin and Lady Zia struggle to get Darrock's arms up on their shoulders to drag him through the gate much slower than Lord Stone.

"Lady of the Woods?" Lord Stone stands in the light pouring out of the cottage entrance.

"Enter, boy. We don't have time for this. Lay her on the cot there. They are struggling with young Grail. Hurry, now help them." The small lady in black lacy layers of silk, cotton, and satin rushes around the room. She lifts the kettle from the iron hook in the fireplace and pours hot water into two bowls to clean her guests. After placing the hot kettle back, she tosses the potholder on the butcher block island in the middle of the room.

"There on the table. Lift him onto the table." Wilga said. She rushes to pull out the chair to drag it to the side of the fire. "Go shoo, get the others! There is no time!" Clomping feet rush from the house as Wilga grips Lady Zia's arm. "Open the windows, light more candles. The stink is on each one of you. Now, do this now."

Lady Zia does as instructed, grabbing a match from the box on the fireplace mantel. She found seven candles around the room to set ablaze once the three windows were as open as she could get them. At the counter in the center of the room, Wilga shoves a mortar and pestle at her.

"Do as I do. Add dandelion." Wilga said. She grabs a sprig of green leaves, she drops it into her own bowl. "Burdock root," she uses a paring knife to chop a small chunk off a long tubular root. "This and my special mixture, along with a pinch of bentonite clay." She produces a jar from a hidden pocket with unidentifiable dried leaves. Then, stepping back, Wilga places a finger on her lips. "Ah, yes, almost forgot!" At a wall of shelves behind Lady Zia, the woman grabs two jars. "These blossoms and lemon crystallized with honey. Now, mash quickly." Wilga has the stone tools working faster than Lady Zia thought possible. She grabs her own stone handle and mashes the ingredients together.

"Now place the strainer on top of the cup. When you get all the mixture in it, pour hot water over it. You do this for each of your people. But first start with the most affected." Wilga took the medicinal tea she had created over to Violet. While blowing on the warm brew, she motions for Bijou to lever her up enough to get a few drops of the liquid in her mouth. Cacey sits on the pillow curled into Violet's neck. With her fluffy paws, she pulls her chin down enough to help her drink. Pushing her mouth closed, Cacey uses her paws to stroke her neck, getting the swallow reflex working.

"She's still so cold." Cacey looks up at the wrinkled face.

The old woman's gnarled hand pats the bunny's head. "Just keep doing this until all of it is gone." Wilga abruptly turns away. While crossing the room, she snaps at Gryphin with her bony fingers. "Turn him over." They work together to find the worst of the injuries at the base of Darrock's back. One red tinged pointed finger nail pokes and prods the gaping flesh.

"No, not good." Wilga absently reaches her green hand up to feel around the gray hair piled on top of her head. She pulls glasses from the tangled mess, unnoticed before, to rest on her nose.

"Out, you may not stay. Be gone with you." Wilga uses the pointy nail of her smallest finger to scoop into the dark red wound. "There you are, now no more of this!" Wilga crosses to the hearth. Carefully, she flings the squirming vine to the stone floor. And reaches to the work counter. She plunges her hand into a dish of salt and tosses it onto the invasive vine. As it tries to escape through a crack between the stones, the salt stuns it, rolling in place. Until Wilga pinches it between two sharp finger nails and flicks it into the fire. A black plume burst up the chimney.

"Everyone get back to work. More to do, so much to do." Wilga claps her hands at the faces staring at her.

She mumbles to herself about gawkers and the ignorance of people. As she goes back to cleaning the wound and gestures for Gryphin to do the same for Darrock as Bijou was doing for Violet.

The urgency slows once everyone has the brew to cleanse the toxins from inside their bodies. Now they wash hands and faces as well. Wilga inspects each person for signs of something unexplained. She finds a tendril as fine as hair tangled in the fur on the back of Sir Randolph's neck. And repeating the salt and fire treatment to rid them of the last living piece of the dangerous place. Everyone relaxes when Wilga declares them clean enough.

Mr. Pravat sits near the fire sipping his preferred black tea to rid his mouth of the foul tasting medicinal tea of earlier. "Thank you, kind woman."

"Kind, me? Ha." A chuckle burst from the old woman as she rocks in her chair sipping her own drink.

"Wilga, I must take my leave." Lord Stone knelt next to the wise woman.

"Good to see this face grown and with his own people," Wilga said.

"You remember me?" Lord Stone asks.

"Cal, boy, you are the same here." Wilga places a hand above his heart.

"I don't know about that. I haven't been that boy for many seasons." Lord Callahan said, not able to take his eyes off her lavender flecked ones.

"Sorry for loss of Patrice. Excellent student she had been." Wilga looks in the flames of the low fire.

"Thank you for that. Also, for all of this. How can

I repay you?" Lord Callahan gestures around the woman's home at the people he now considers his own.

"These days are in the balance. Hold it steady, help the next to keep it from tipping. The past tried to balance the future. Possible to try but failed. Together, two must be," Wilga said and sips from the earthenware cup.

Lord Stone stands to say goodbye to his wife and daughter. He had to seek answers in the ordinary land. This puzzle of words needs to wait.

"Lord Stone, Callahan, may I go with you." Mr. Pravat said.

"If you are sure you are up to the walk back to Maplehaven, I'm happy to escort you." Lord Stone answered.

"Yes, I'm not near as bad off as the others. The journey you are preparing to undertake interests me." Mr. Pravat said. He leaves the warmth of the fire to set the teacup on the counter, tapping his walking stick on the floor.

"Alexander, are you sure?" Callahan looks at the torn shoes with bandages peeking through the delicate leather.

"I can stop for a shoe change and then we can be on our way." Pravat tips his hat to the others and walks to the door.

"Wait." Darrock coughs on the drink being dripped into his mouth.

Everyone turns to the table where the shirtless figure lays. He raises up on one elbow.

"No, don't get up." Lord Callahan rushes to stop Darrock.

"I must come with you." Darrock tries to push his shoulder against the hand but makes no progress.

"You are in no state to do this. Stay put and I will tell you everything when I have something to tell. Stay here." Lord Callahan said.

The last of his energy spent, Darrock collapses back with a thud of his head on the wooden table. Trying to reach up to wipe the sweat from his brow, he falters. Lady Zia turns up at his side with a cloth and did so for him.

"My husband's word is good. Trust him to do this," Lady Zia said.

A slight nod came before Darrock drifts off to sleep. Everything settled, the men leave the cottage. Wilga goes into a small pantry and reappears with supplies. In a cast-iron pot she adds water, meat, and herbs. She moves to the fire, placing the pot on a hook. The little cottage in the woods soon smells divine as those inside rest.

16

LAND FOUND THROUGH THE WOODS-HEALING

"That cruel woman!" Brune screams and slams the door to her own bedroom. She paces the room, pulling the braided bun off the top of her head. One hair pin, then another makes a ping noise, hitting the mirror of the dressing table. Not aiming, just tossing each as they bounce off the mirror to land on the floor.

"I'm so close!" Her guttural growl bounces off the walls while her hands tug and pull her black hair loose from the braid. Hair finally free, she moves to the window. One hand on the latch, one on the other side, she opens it with so much force each sash swings back, bouncing half closed.

Bracing her hands on the windowsill, Brune stills. Eyes shut, clinching her jaw till the tears of frustration disappear. It isn't long before deep breaths come slow and steady. The fading sunlight with its show of colors across the sky going unnoticed. When she opens her eyes, she sees the overgrown gardens. The place in the stone wall, having fallen over to pile on the lawn. Her gaze moves to the stone below her window. Unruly vines crawl up the house. White paint on wooden trim cracked and pealing everywhere.

Disgust threatens to send her back into uncontrollable temper. The estate had once been charming, not nearly as nice as she deserves. Money, had she made sure the finances came to her as they should have, she could leave this dump. Better yet, he should have moved them to the High Lands as she wanted. Everything would be much different if only he had gone along with her plans.

That was her own fault. Her youth had made her underestimate the man he truly was. Now she was paying for her own mistakes. His betrayal had been so much worse than she had known. Not everything was her own fault, at least.

"Now what to do?" Brune asks. The horse whisper all she can manage after the burst of temper. She crosses the room to a sideboard to pour water from a pitcher into a crystal glass. In the middle of a sip, a knock sounds on her bedroom door.

"Come in Dom." She said.

"Mrs. Grail." Dom said. The six-foot gorilla enters the room, executing a slight bow.

"What have I told you about that?" Brune asks and raises the cool tumbler to her temple and closed her eyes.

"Sorry, Mrs. Brune." Dom said, dropping the offensive last name. He looks at the hallway to find it empty and closes the door. "You came back from your trip upset. Can I help in any way?" The hulking figure stands with his back, nearly touching the door.

"What could you possibly do to help me?" Setting the water down, Brune paces across the room. "Haven't you done plenty already? If you had helped years ago, my daughter would be here right now. None of this would be a problem." She refuses to look at him, nor does she raise her voice.

"I've explained many times. In the many years I knew him, served with him on battlefields, explored territories with him, never would I expect you, his wife, to be harmed by him." Dom lowers his gaze to the floor.

"He did unspeakable things to me and you never stopped him." Brune stood facing the window with her back to him. "You were in the same house. All the servants heard my screams and did nothing."

"Mrs. Brune, he told a very different story to us. I will forever regret believing him."

"Well, that doesn't help me now, does it?" Brune asks.

Letting the words hang between them, Dom waited. He continues to stand with his shoulders straight and formal. "Mrs. Brune, you were gone much longer than expected. I'm here to help, but you need to tell me what happened." Quietly, the deep voice remains calm.

"Since you refuse to argue with me, I guess I might as well tell you." Brune turns her back to the window and rests her hips on the sill. Arms to her sides, her hands firmly gripping the wood ledge at each side of her hips.

"When I received information on where to find his

great aunt Carmilla, I went to see her, as you know. Aubrey wasn't with her. She said something about school, whatever." Brune said and waved a hand in the air. "Whatever they do in the ordinary world with children, I'll have to find out more." Bracing her hand back beside her, she continues. "When I demanded to bring my daughter back with me, she pushed a package of papers at me. She believes I have no legal right to my daughter. Also, said that HE went to the High Council in both lands to see to it I could never have Aubrey with me." Brune shoves off her perch to pace the room again. Her hands clinch at her sides.

"I knew you were going to see her yesterday. Where have you been since?" Dom asks. "I have heard the International Gateway Station lost several openings before you went. Where did you cross over?" His deep voice fills the room despite his effort to keep it quiet.

"Yes, I heard about that too." She keeps her head averted, hiding her small smile. "I traveled through the station. They had one portal running. I think more were capable, but repairs were being made to the building." With a sigh, she rests on the window ledge once again.

"I came back planning to come here. Then I remembered there had been a solicitor in the High Land near the Capital Building that handled legal matters for the estate. So I turned around and went to the High Land." Brune said. Despair washing through her. The only outward sign was her white knuckles when her fingers laced together in her lap.

"It took time to find the right firm, but when I did,

it was more insults. That abomination refused to meet with me! They gave me a note explaining I have no claim to documents in their possession." Color fills her face and her fists clinch her skirts.

"That old woman was telling the truth. I have no recourse to claim my daughter. I have no currency to fight this in the courts. Besides, I don't know WHAT scheme my husband orchestrated." Brune stands, turning her back to Dom. Eyes bright with rage, she sees nothing outside the window.

"How can I serve you?" Dom asks, seeing the trembling shoulders before him. He clenches his large black hands.

"What can you do? You did enough the day you took my baby from me," Brune said in a venomous whisper.

"I didn't know what your husband had planned to do. You know that," Dom said, pulling his back up a fraction straighter.

"That is what you have always said." Brune said, she turns with eyes glaring at him. "Don't forget, you promised to stay in my service until Aubrey is back with me."

"Yes, Mrs. Brune." Dom said, stepping to the side and reaching for the door handle.

"You haven't forgotten what I promised, have you?" Brune asks.

Back facing her, Dom's shoulders slumped at the mention of his shackles tying him to her. "Your threats are unnecessary. I gave you my word."

"Contessa Fusco still believes she saw you pay that

assassin to kill my husband. She won't tell anyone what she saw unless I press her. Be sure to keep your word," Brune said. The thrill of pushing this giant of a creature to do her bidding sent tingles along her skin.

"You keep your word to leave Darrock unharmed, and I will continue on this path with you." Dom turns his head, leveling his dark eyes on her glittery ones.

"I don't understand your loyalty there. You should care more about your own neck." Brune said.

"Your confirmation, Mrs. Brune?" Dom asks.

"Yes, everything stands. I won't harm him. But he is in my way. I want the estate finances under my control and not his. You are lucky I like the challenge of finding alternative ways to get what I deserve," Brune said. A step towards the desk and a wave of her hand to dismiss Dom.

"Good evening." Dom said and closes the door behind himself.

"I don't know what I'll do if I don't break his loyalty to that boy soon." Brune said under her breath.

"Yes, you need to get that done soon." Contessa uses a feathered wing to push the sheer curtain aside on the window down the wall from the one Brune had looked out.

"It's about time you got here." Brune tapped her fingers on her crossed arms and walked to the closed door of her closet. "Wait here." She went to retrieve the book that holds the key to her plans for the future.

"I heard you say you had trouble. What are we going to do to get the girl?" Contessa asks. A rubbing of metal is the only sound in the room as she stretches the wing out and back. A few feathers are still on the shoulder, with old human knives, forks, and spoons forming the skeleton of the wing. In between the overlap areas are metal typewriter keys. The snip, snip sound comes from an old pair of scissors strategically placed for optimal use.

"Is it giving you trouble today?" Brune watches the exercise from the doorway, tapping a manicured fingernail on the cover.

"I manage. Doctor Kravin adjusted it yesterday." Contessa said.

"You would be far worse if I hadn't found you in the woods that night." Brune takes the journal to her desk and flips through pages.

"True, but did it have to be the old vulture?" Snip, snip, Contessa glides to an embroidered footstool near the desk.

"Are you here to help me, or to complain?" Brune said, staring pointedly.

"Violet's father did this to me. I want to take everything from her, too." Contessa said.

"You trapped her here for now. I just don't know how long it will last. Violet nearly succumbed completely to the Valley of Forgotten Dreams. She got lucky this time." Brune pulls a folded piece of scroll from between two pages. The delicate piece crinkles as she unfolds it on the desk.

"Some of the writing is missing, but I'm sure I can close the gateways to the ordinary land without Aubrey. It references the two being present. I am of the same branch of the bloodline as Aubrey, so it must work." Brune runs a finger over the words. "I already disrupted the connection, at least temporarily. You saw the destruction at the air portal."

"Brune, you are not the generation of the fair hair, it's Aubrey. That must mean something." Contessa leans closer to the parchment on the desk.

"It only says the ones divided in the past, see?" Brune slaps her hand on top of the paper.

"But a chunk is missing over there and along there." Contessa points at the parchment.

"Obviously. This must work! You don't understand how long I've waited for this." Brune tucks the scrap of the text back into the journal, closing it. She puts the book into a desk drawer and locks it. The key goes into a small pouch on the belt at her waist.

"We met years ago, and it was the only thing you talked of at one time. You know, when that man put the blanket over me and I fell out the window?" Contessa said, swiftly spinning her head around in the opposite direction from Brune.

"You're just lucky I was near the portal in that woods that night." Brune said.

"Do you even remember why you want this in the first place? We don't know what it will do to this world being severed from the other." The owl said.

"I am descended from kings! My whole life I've been powerless to stop others from taking from me. As a child, my parents treated me as if I was defective or something. They took me from one land to the next, trying to fix me. I lost everything so that they could pay charlatans for cures, treatments, and lies. Friends, toys, homes, everything lost." Brune said, dropping her head to stare at her empty hand laying in her lap.

"What was so wrong with you?" Contessa asks.

"Ah, I don't even know. I was willful maybe. Once someone said obstinate, with no regard for authority. My tantrums were legendary among staff, the few we had anyway. I remember little of it. It doesn't matter. I was eventually told that my parents were rundown from the travel and searching and became ill. One after the other, they died."

Brune stood going to a window, ready to end the conversation. It had been so long since she had thought over any of it.

"What happened to you when they were gone?" Contessa hops and glides her way to the open window.

"A distant uncle on my father's side took me into his home. He gave me freedom and left me alone at one of his estates. He had an amazing collection of books." The mention of the books causes a sparkle to shine in her eyes. Brune holds back the curtain, ready to close the window once the creature leaves.

Without a word, just a nod of the head, the large golden eyes search Brune's for a moment, and then the slight metallic scrape was the only sound of her exit.

The savory aroma of soup tugs Violet from a restful sleep. The sound of a crackling fire was loud in the stillness behind her eyelids. A gentle thump of a fluffy paw follows a slight movement beside her head. Her desire to open her eyes was hardly greater than the effort to do so. Darkness, with hints of the fire's golden glow, didn't entice her to keep trying to see the room.

Not wanting the peaceful sleepy feeling to disappear, Violet turns her head into the soft fluff of what had to be Cacey. Burying her nose into the soft fur brought a deep sigh before she could fully open her eyes.

The soft body moves. "Violet?" Cacey whispers loudly.

"Shh," Violet tries to hush the rabbit.

"No, Violet, please wake up. You must." Cacey bounces on the pillow next to the dark hair tangling on the pillow.

"Sleep." Violet squeaks out while clamping her eyes closed.

A movement in the room soon results in a hand pressing to her forehead. "No fever, good, up and drink now." Wilga said in a low voice as not to disturb Lady Zia, Bijou, and Gryphin sleeping on the floor across the room.

At the sound of the old woman's voice, Violet opens her eyes, blinking to focus. "Where am I?" Her raspy voice is unfamiliar to her own ears.

"Ah, I am Wilga. Some say Lady of the Woods, some say witch. My home is the place, but you must decide where you want to be," Wilga said as she holds out a mug of fresh water. "Sit up now."

Reluctantly, Violet tests her strength to sit up on the narrow cot in a little alcove tucked to the side of the open room. "What does that mean? Where I want to be?" Violet reaches for the water, sipping slowly at first. The cool liquid sooths her dry throat. She gulps faster.

"Slow down. Talk we must. Give your innards time to adjust to the drink. Soup too. Move to the chairs by the fire." Wilga reaches for a wooden bowl and a chunk of bread. At the hearth, she ladles soup from the black pot.

Violet drops her legs over the side of the cot to feel the cool stone floor. Someone had taken off her shoes and clothes. A white cotton nightgown hangs off her slight frame. Violet notices sore spots in random places. One on an ankle had a strip of white bandage wrapped around her leg. Another on her upper arm was painful. "What happened to me?" Violet wonders aloud.

"Go sit by the fire and talk to the lady. She will explain things, I'm sure." Cacey said with an enormous yawn. "I'm so glad you are better." She curls into a fluffy ball and falls fast asleep.

Violet stands slowly. With shaky arms, she wraps a blanket around herself while making her way to the chair. On a sigh, she drops into it hard enough to make a thump.

"I will talk while you eat. Don't interrupt, just let the soup restore your energy." Then, passing the food to Violet, Wilga places a small log onto the fire. "You strayed from the path of the one that needs you, didn't you?"

Violet watches the flickering flames licking the new log. Her memory of the white horse like beast floods her mind. The journey through the woods had been unexpected. The farther they walked, the harder it had become to keep up. "I—"

Wilga shakes her head and pins Violet with her piercing gaze.

Violet jerks her chin up and down, finally admitting that she had indeed strayed from the path.

"Easy is not important. The struggle is." The gray-haired woman relaxes back into the rocking chair. Her green skin looking dark gold in the firelight. Her wrinkles deepening in the shadow filled light. Each hair filled mole looks taller and more pronounced. While her eyes glisten in the light, her fingers smooth and pick at the layered lace covering her lap.

"Part of you wanted to stay inside the world the enchanted snare created for you." Wilga lowers her voice.

Violet sips and chews the vegetables of the soup. And dipping her bread in the broth, she nibbles, watches and listens. Soon she was unsure if Wilga spoke of her own experience or Violet's.

"A broken heart is a powerful thing. Some, most, don't see it that way," Wilga said. Turning to Violet, she speaks again. "They can cause great destruction. A broken heart clings to what could have been. So let that go, whatever it is. Only then can there be growth."

Violet heard the words but didn't want to look at the memories of her time while trapped. She looks down at the empty bowl in her lap. The dregs of broth and herbs sit in the bottom. The spoon was empty and resting on the side of the bowl. Hunger satisfied, she realizes she feels better than when she had first gotten up.

With the blanket secured around her, Violet stands and takes the bowl to the sink behind where she had been sitting with Wilga. She skirts around the worktable in the center of the room. She can see smooth, worn wooden surfaces polished clean. A simple home for a very complicated woman.

Placing the empty dishes in the sink for washing later. A small window over the sink shows stars twinkling in the sky. There was one wish bigger than any other her entire childhood. Never had she wished it out loud. Never had she told anyone the one thing that could fix everything. Violet went back to her seat. The Lady of the Woods waiting for her to settle.

"Your brief life has been full of pain. It is time to try different." Wilga looks over her own shoulder at a figure in the shadows on a table near the others sleeping on the floor.

"Is it possible —? I just need to know if magic can fix people in ways things in my world can't." Violet whispers.

"Speak plain, say exactly what you want. Magic is a tricky thing with repercussions we cannot plan for." Wilga fists her hand in the lace of her lap.

"Can my dad become the dad he was before my mom died, with the use of magic?" Violet asks, plainly. But places a hand on one cheek, knowing her skin is red. It felt so childish to say it out loud.

Wilga looks at the face of the young woman before her. With eyes filling with tears, her head moves from side to side.

"I had to be sure." A tear rolls down her cheek, but Violet brushes it away. "Love is too much if this is what it's allowed to do to people. His broken heart has ruined our lives." Violet let go of the blanket, letting it fall back on her shoulders. The warmth of the fireplace was lessening, but she was growing warmer by the second. Hands tangling through her hair, she lifts the mess off her neck.

Wilga glances around at the other guests in her home. The window over the sink shows the day will wake soon. "Tea, we must finish with tea." Up from her seat, she turns to Violet, "get cleaned up and dressed." Wilga points to a narrow door in a corner of the room near her cot. "The water closet has everything you need."

Violet drops her hair and looks to the corner, surprised by the sudden instructions. Standing, she follows Wilga from the fire, both women trying not to wake the others. Closet was an accurate description of the room. Only slightly larger than a public bathroom stall back home, the space holds a little sink and ancient style toilet. All the while, she relieves herself and cleans up with the meager supplies on a shelf. Violet hears Wilga in the kitchen. Mumbles beyond the thin wall had her thinking someone else had gotten up. Violet hurries to finish.

After opening the door, Violet sees Wilga seated back at the fire, holding two cups of tea. "Thanks for cleaning my clothes." Violet returns to the chair she had sat in moments ago.

Pointing to a figure on the floor across the room,

she said, "You have her to thank, mother hen she is." Wilga said.

Violet stores the information away to thank Lady Zia later.

"What do you know of love?" Wilga asks, sipping her tea after handing one to Violet.

"Nothing good." Violet sips and continues. "I enjoy a good rom-com, but I think I will do without." Unexpectedly, Will's face comes to mind. At Wilga's questioning look, Violet explains. "A movie, uh, entertainment like a play about romance that makes you laugh."

One hand waving in the air, Wilga asked. "Why no love? There are so many forms of it."

"Oh, well, I see my parents giving up so much for it with nothing in return but a broken heart." The images of her dad drunk so many times she could not count play in her head.

A glance over her shoulder at the sleeping bodies, Wilga suddenly scoots to the edge of her chair. "What I'm about to say comes from my experience of choosing to avoid the risk of love." The green hand grips Violet's own on her lap.

"My dear, love is not the giving up something of yourself. Love is the allowing of selflessness. It is the loss of greed. Love, true genuine love, is the setting aside of one's own desires. You still have them, but they lose importance." With a sigh, she pushes the point forward.

"The love of a child for a parent is a more self-centered love. It's more about the need for protection and shelter, sometimes even learning. Romantic love, now that is something more. It's an acceptance of submitting to the heart. You allowing your heart to be sacrificial with your needs and wants. When you place their happiness above your own, that is a pure selfless love." Wilga, the witch, pats the back of the troubled girl's hand. Then she wraps her own hands around her mug of herbal tea.

"Don't avoid this gift of love. If your heart is talking to you, listen to it. But don't make the mistake of assuming what your parents actually felt or did not feel." Despite her rough appearance, Wilga's face softens and a distant, wistful look fills her eyes. "Too many fall into that trap and miss out on the love of a lifetime."

As unexpected as could be, Violet thought she saw a slight smile at the corner of the old woman's mouth. When the glassy gaze pulls away from the window, her voice is hardly more than a whisper. "Always remember that your parent's tragedies do not have to be your own. Your choices create your own experiences and association with them does not doom you. Just be you, my dear." With that, Wilga finishes her tea and sits back in her own chair.

For just a moment, Violet could see the young woman Wilga must have been. The rough facade of the witch disappeared. She could see the brown hair, pale peachy skin of her cheeks and the long straight nose. But just as suddenly, a moan from the figure on the table fills the air and Wilga was the old crone again.

Violet watches as Lady Zia scrambles from her pallet on the floor. She still wore the same clothes Violet remembered seeing her in at the International Portal Station. Lady Zia went to the body shadowed on the table.

"Wait, let me check your bandage before you roll onto your back." Her back to the room, Lady Zia turns to her daughter, who sits watching from the floor.

"Bijou, please light the oil lamp and hold it close." Lady Zia washes her hands before touching the wound.

Violet continues to sit by the fire but watches as everyone wakes. Shaking off the night as dim morning light peaks into the cottage. Cacey is the only one to stay curled in slumber.

Sir Randolph ruffles his fur from the flick of his ears to the tip of his tail. With a tug on his vest, he spots Violet sitting by the fire.

"Miss, it's good to see you looking well." Sir Randolph walks the few paces between them. And lowering himself to eye level with her, he looks over her face carefully.

"I'm sorry, have we met?" Violet feels her eyes widen at the black nose and white teeth in front of her face. "You're a wolf?" She could not help but ask the obvious.

"My apologies Miss. Please forgive me. I forget sometimes how my appearance can overwhelm those unaccustomed to it." He moves to allow space between them, but continues to hold himself proud.

"No, we have not officially met. I was with those

that pulled you from the valley. I am Sir Randolph. Are you feeling any lingering effects from your ordeal?" He asks.

"Thanks to Wilga. I'm feeling better by the minute. Thanks for your part in my rescue." Violet lowers her eyes. "I'm sorry I caused everyone so much trouble." She forces her eyes up over his shoulder. She could see Gryphin moving to help Lady Zia with the patient.

"We are all sorry for failing to protect you in our land. I, for one, will try to keep that from happening again." The great wolf bows his head in a solemn gesture.

When the gray fur covered head lowers in front of her, Violet locks eyes with the man sitting on the table across the room. Time stills as the head raises and the eyes of the wolf block her view.

Violet's breath catches. Standing, she brings a hand up to touch the missing necklace. A step toward the shirtless man across the room. Sir Randolph silently moves back from her path.

"Violet, we should talk." The familiar voice said. He sits on the edge of the table while Lady Zia and Bijou unwrap the bandage from around his waist. He moves to stand.

"Darrock, you need to sit still." Lady Zia pulls the bandage from his back.

He winces, sucking breath in between clinched teeth.

"Will?" Violet asks, leaving several feet between them.

Lady Zia shakes her head at Bijou when she speaks.

Her eyes motion to the others to follow Wilga. Footsteps shuffle out the door of the cottage.

"Lady Zia called you Darrock?" Violet wraps her arms around her middle without the locket to fidget with.

"Darrock William Grail. Let me explain." Will reached for the gray-blue tunic folded on the seat of a chair next to the table.

"You must think I'm so stupid." Violet chuckles halfhearted as she takes her eyes from his handsome face. Fingertips of one hand press the spot between her brows.

"No, wait." Darrock pulls on the rich fabric.

Violet turns her back to him. The sight of his flexing muscles warms her face and causes a flutter in her belly. The clothes don't help, given his sleeveless arms still show. No wonder he felt hard as a wall when she had run into him at the bookstore. Self-consciously dropping the hand, she resumes holding her middle but grips the sides of her shirt for fear her hands will reach up to touch the smooth muscles of his arms. The betrayal of her attraction to him felt ridiculous. He lied to her, didn't he?

"I wanted to tell you. Especially when I realized what your necklace is. You didn't seem to know about this world, so I waited. My mistake, I'm sorry." Darrock said. She turns back around in time to see his outstretched hand suddenly plunge into his dark hair.

"What does my necklace have to do with anything?" Violet asks, her hand fluttering up to the place it belonged.

"Where is it? Did you lose it in the valley?" Darrock asks.

"Wait, what do I call you?" Violet asks.

"I go by Darrock here, but you can call me whatever you want," Darrock said. That one side of his mouth quirking up as he rested back on the table.

"Not a good idea. Now, why do you care about my mother's necklace?" Violet asks as her eyes linger on his mouth. The golden glow of the fireplace and oil lamp causing the mood to be far too intimate for her own good.

"I don't. My step-mother would love to have it. If she were to know about it," Darrock said and shifts to sit more fully on the table. He braces a hand on each side of himself. "Would you get me some water, please?"

"You look pale. Should I get Lady Zia or Wilga back in here?" Violet doesn't know why she cares. He is not her friend, after all. Not that she had thought of him in that way. Yes, there had been an attraction between them, but they obviously didn't know each other at all.

"I can get you some soup?" Violet offerers. Though telling herself it is the right thing to do, but not at all because of her attraction to him.

"I will take whatever you will give me." Darrock grins again. His long legs stretching out in front of him, clad in dark pants. He is too damn appealing.

Violet steps back and busies herself with finding a bowl and dishing up soup just as she had watched Wilga do for her. Stepping close to him, she hands the bowl and a mug of water to him. When he reaches out, his fingers linger for a second longer than necessary. She felt a hum run through her hand and up her arm before it dissipates. Violet steps back outside of arm's reach to be safe. Safe from him or her own actions was something she wouldn't look too closely at right now.

"Brune is your step-mother?" Violet asks. Safe ground that is not really safe at all, given what she keeps hearing about her distant relative.

"Yes." Darrock said in between spoons full of soup.

"You didn't tell her about my necklace?" Violet asks.

"No, I had planned to but…" Darrock stops, one hand holding the bowl, the other the spoon, lower to his lap. "I'm not sure exactly what stopped me from telling her of it, of you." Darrock's steady gaze holding hers.

"Why would she want it?" Violet asks, ignoring the temptations Darrock keeps providing her.

"To fix the past. But now, I don't know." Darrock resumes eating the soup.

"You suspect it has something to do with her daughter?" Violet takes a step closer.

"Yes, I knew she was hiding things from me, but not a child. I was away at school so much I didn't know where they were or what their lives were like. After my father died, they informed me of my legal responsibility. That did not include a sister." Darrock said. Then, finishing the soup and washing it down with the water, he puts it aside. The soup restoring his strength, he stands.

"I need to understand this. What does my necklace

have to do with any of this?” Violet takes another step forward.

“It’s complicated. Brune said there was a conspiracy to put her away in an institution before my father’s accident in the ordinary world.” Darrock said, his gaze resting heavily on Violet.

“I’m sorry for all of your loss, but I still don’t understand what any of this has to do with me. Someone stole my family heirloom, forcing me to be trapped in this world. Now you tell me that Brune wants my necklace.” Violet turns to pace away from him. His hand grabs her arm, preventing her from walking away.

“Wait, it’s gone?” Darrock asks, gently turning her to face him.

“Yes, that is the only reason any of this happened. I wouldn’t have been here otherwise.” Violet said. The truth of her words felt questionable, and it churns at the soup in her stomach. Avoiding his eyes, she pulls free and paces three steps in each direction in front of him. Back and forth across the stone floor until her thoughts force her to speak.

“That’s not exactly the truth. I don’t know why I said that. I’m here because I was upset with my dad for disappointing me yet again. Falling asleep on the bench gave someone the opportunity to steal my necklace. The white-winged unicorn thing is how I got trapped, kind of.” Violet stops, satisfied with setting things straight.

“OK. Now are we good?” Darrock asks, he tried to get her to look up at him but didn’t reach out to touch her.

"It's hard to trust you. You are not who I thought you were." Violet relented and brought her eyes up to meet his. "Didn't you tell me you worked for someone doing research?"

"I did that. But it was for Brune. She wanted me to find magical artifacts. There are quite a few in the ordinary world. Well, because I had some school in that world, I can blend in." Darrock said.

"You stood out plenty when I met you." Violet felt her cheeks warm.

"No, I didn't. I was wearing typical college kid attire, my hair was messy, and you know the typical 'dude' attitude." Darrock said and crosses his bare arms over his chest and scowls down at her.

"Again, no, you didn't blend in. How could you?" Violet scoffs at his defense. "You're more handsome than the typical guys I've met at school. Your posture is too good, the glasses were odd at best, and you were hiding a rat on the shelves."

"You think I'm handsome?" Darrock lowers his voice and leans towards her, grinning with a sultry heat.

"That is not what I said, exactly." Violet takes a step back, her eyes mesmerized by his mouth.

"I think you did, Mouse." Darrock steps closer. His stride, larger than hers, reduces the space between them.

"You're being impossible. I can't concentrate on what's important when you look at me like that." Violet tries to clear her head. He is closer now and his scent fills her nose, just like every other time she has been near him. Deny all her mind wants, but her body is making it clear what it thinks of him.

Darrock's grin grows, and he slides his tongue along his bottom lip. His eyes drop to her lips. One more step and he is close enough. To what?

"I've wanted to kiss you ever since you bumped into me, Mouse," Darrock whispers.

Mind racing, Violet clings to the memory of their first encounter. There is one thing that she recalls.

"No, you just couldn't take your eyes off my chest, not my mouth." Violet said and sidesteps out of his reach.

"What!" Darrock pulls back and his eyebrows nearly became one as they hood over his eyes in confusion.

"You heard me. You hardly looked up from my chest. At first, I wasn't sure if you were a pervert or not." Violet keeps pushing the insult to cool the heat between them.

"Ha!" Darrock laughs, a deep rumble, making her belly tense in pleasure at the sound. "You realize your necklace rests right between…" Darrock points in the general direction.

Violet instantly feels her face flush. The heat rushing down her neck likely covering the area he is gesturing to. "OK, stop, I'm sorry." Her hands feel cool on the blaze of her cheeks. "I can't do this. I'm not good at the whole flirting banter thing."

"You look fine to me," Darrock said. His intense eyes hold laughter despite the serious line of his lips.

Violet can't look at him. It wasn't like she was this

inexperienced. There had been guys she dated casually. What is her problem with Darrock or Will? This guy, what is it about him? One second, she can't stop pouring words out of her mouth and the next she embarrasses herself so much she never wants to speak again. Never had a man caused her to feel off balance the way this one does.

17

LAND FOUND THROUGH THE WOODS-SEEK

"Violet, come outside." Bijou rushes through the door of the cottage.

Without another look at Darrock, Violet crosses the room to follow Bijou out into the yard. The relief of escaping the awkward conversation is short-lived. Bijou steps aside. Violet turns to face the gate only to see the white beast that found her in the International Gateway Station. Violet stops. A solid body collides with her back.

"Sorry." Darrock said.

But ignoring him, Violet cannot help but stare at the white lashed eyes before her. Slowly, she goes closer to the gate. Voices behind her wonder aloud if she should follow the creature alone again. Her face warms remembering how she had messed up getting trapped in the Valley of the Forgotten Dreams.

Close enough to reach out and touch the long face, Violet waits. Not that she has any idea why she waits. The ears on top of the head swivel around at the different speakers in the conversation. Violet has lost track of the words said. The pale blue eyes blink and the head turns enough to focus one eye on her own.

Not questioning the action, Violet lifts her hand to rest at the base of the horn between the eyes. Thick strands of white hair slides between her fingers as she finds the coat underneath it. Without warning, she hears a soft voice inside her mind.

"Why do you not trust me? There is no time for this." The voice said only to Violet.

"What are you doing?" Violet thought the words. She could have been talking to herself as much to the animal in front of her. No response to her, but the head gently shook a negative response.

"Did you hear me? I don't understand," Violet thought the words and shakes her head.

"No time. I have much to show you before it becomes too late." The voice fills her mind, and then the connection ends. The winged animal backs away, but beckons for her to step through the gate.

Violet reaches a hand out to open the gate but stops. Turning to the people who had cared for her and saved her life, she made eye contact with each one. Wilga is the only one to step forward and speak.

"Only follow this path if you will stick to it. We may not be fortunate enough to save your life the next time you wonder on your own," Wilga said, moving to a small herb garden under a window of her cottage to tend the plants.

"Wait, great one. Let us give water and a few supplies for the journey." Lady Zia was near the stone fence as she spoke. Assured that the creature wouldn't leave, she turns to Violet. Bijou will be right back. Just give her a minute." She moves close enough to grasp Violet's hands in her own. "Please be safe. Don't get distracted. I don't know where you will travel, so I can't think of what to explain to you. Remember, you can communicate with me." Lady Zia taps a finger on the bracelet around Violet's wrist.

"I think I've learned my lesson." Violet said.

"I will keep her safe." Darrock said.

"No. You will not." Violet said. The moment he spoke the words, she furrows her brow.

"Yes, I will. You need someone that knows what the dangers are in this world. I do. I'm familiar with the ordinary world as well." Darrock said.

Bijou rushes up to Violet with a bag of provisions. She glances from one to the other and pushes between them. She raises the strap of the bag over Violet's head so it hangs cross-body. Bijou looks at the shorter girl and wishes her luck and dashes back to Gryphin's side. He grips her hand.

"Come back safely, my dear." Lady Zia said as she embraces Violet tight.

Violet looks back over her shoulder to see the impatient swishing of the long white tail. Back and forth, the hooves stomp into the earth while Violet hesitates to leave. She looks at Darrock, trying to see more than the handsome exterior. Her forced independence hasn't given her the best instincts with people. But it looks like he is her best option for getting things right this time.

"Fine, you can come with me." Violet spins away from him and passes through the gate.

"What makes you think you had a choice?" Darrock follows her.

"Really, that is how you want to play this?" Violet tosses over her shoulder, rolling her eyes. When he didn't respond, she tries to hide a glance back at him. That grin! Why did it cause a melting tingle to flow through her body so easily?

Could it be this world intensifies her emotions? With each step through the forest, Violet ignores the man and the sounds he causes behind her. He steps on the path far quieter than herself. This place suited him more. He looks more confident. That alone, is more attractive than the messy hair baggy sweatshirt look he had when she first bumped into him.

"You seem more confident here, in this world." Violet said, not meaning to say her thought out loud.

"If you say so," Darrock said.

"I just mean, it suites you better being here." Violet said, face getting hotter with each word.

"I explained to you, I was purposefully being a typical 'dude' from college in that bookstore. I wasn't being myself most of the time." Darrock said, moving up beside her on the path.

"That's right, you were after my amulet." Violet felt the cool reminder that he had just been playing her to get closer to the magical artifact.

Darrock gazes ahead, letting out a sigh.

They walk in silence, following their guide on the narrow path. Gradually, the pace picks up, causing

Violet's breathing to get heavy. The sun is high enough in the sky to be noon by now. Unsure how far they had walked or how much farther they would go, Violet flexes her toes in the borrowed shoes. A break is a must if they had to travel much farther.

"Hey, I need to rest a minute." Violet calls out. No sign the creature is listening to her.

"Alicorn, we need to stop." Darrock raises his voice.

And the white tail swishes, followed by a side look from a white fringed eye. With an irritated shake of the gigantic head, the creature stops in the lane.

Violet digs into the satchel Bijou had packed for them, finding a jug of water. And sips enough of the cool liquid to refresh herself, she passes it to Darrock.

"Thanks." With the jug raised to his mouth drinking, he dribbles the liquid as he rushes to lower it. "Do you hear that?"

Both strain their ears to locate the direction of the sound.

"What is it, bees?" Violet asks.

"That must be the queen." Darrock swipes his arm across his mouth, drying the water.

"As in the Queen Bee?" Violet asks.

"Yes, I don't know why she would be out here." Darrock said, looking around for a pollen source that might call for the queen herself to visit.

"I've been to the Confectionery with Bijou." Violet said.

"It's not common to see her out of the cafe. She normally sends her hive members out to do whatever bees need done." Darrock grins and his eyes light up as he looks at Violet. "This will be a treat for you."

Soon the sound gets closer. One by one, the bees gather to swarm through the trees. The attention of the Alicorn focuses on the bees. A muffled whinny sounds out over the birds and chirps of insects in the forest. Drone bees the size of plums circle around the head and neck of the Alicorn. A new sound fills the air.

Violet raises her gaze to the sky just as Darrock. Looking through the trees for the mysterious creature responsible for the tinkling musical birdsong. Far from Violet's expectation of a small exotic bird, her chin drops at the sight in the sky.

Gliding with wings spread to catch the wind current, the red and gold bird swishes its tail to make a lazy circular decent. The long feathers ripple in the wind as wings flap, soundlessly lowering long golden legs to a log in front of the Alicorn. Upon landing, the celestial sound is silent. The small head with a golden beak looks at each being in the small clearing of the woods.

The last arrival is the queen of the bees. Her small black feet land on a nearby boulder. The Queen stands on hind legs while the smaller attendants fly to adjust the purple tinted crown on top of her fuzzy head. After an exhale of breath, she makes eye contact with the long-legged bird. A slow graceful pause and the enormous eyes of the queen raise to meet Violet's dark ones.

Violet takes a step forward, instinctively bowing her head before returning the gaze. The honeycomb depth of the golden orbs draw her mind to quiet itself. Hardly aware of the smaller bees circling the group, she feels the buzz in her chest. Darrock stands next to Violet and receives a silent greeting from the queen as well.

This time, it wasn't necessary for Violet to touch the Alicorn to hear her words. The mythical creatures don't acknowledge her, though the conversation plays in her mind. Unaware of doing so, she reaches for Darrock's hand.

"Rare One, is it wise to interfere?" The Queen asks. The words hum through the earthy air of the forest.

"Not to try is the unwise action." The phoenix's musical notes fill the air, but words tinkle like chimes in Violet's head.

"I disagree. Something is on the rise. There are others changing the world and things may not be as they seem." Said the Queen.

"So, the Great One should lead these ordinary beings to greater understanding." The bird flaps its wings, causing gold sparks to pop into the air.

"Enough." The whinny and snort sound like an ordinary horse. Violet jerks her gaze to the white beast.

"Queen Eldora, I share your concern. Char, I share your concern as well." The long white head turns toward Violet and Darrock. For a quiet moment, the only movement is the blink of the white fringe of lashed eyelids.

Just when Violet felt the urge to squirm under the gaze, it turns away. She looks up to Darrock's dark eyes, only for him to shrug his shoulders and look back at the unlikely creatures.

"None can tell these two the best course to take, not knowing what they will discover on this path. The one called the Widowed King tried to guide the kingdom as best he could. Yet corruption sprouted as vigorous as a weed in his own house. What he did was to preserve the lands as best as possible." With the pause, Darrock and Violet lean towards the Alicorn.

"Now, something is trying to change things again. We are the only ancient ones left in the world. At least the only ones that have come into the knowing. Why do you think that is?"

"When you came into this existence, I listened to the call. I came." The claret colored bird answered.

"As did I. It is possible some did not come. I have heard rumors of dragons still among ancient lands. They are not here, nor did they come at your creation." Queen Eldora said. Her small ebony hands clasp together.

"There are whispers of an organized ancient group disposing of our kind. The fewer of us, the more power there is to be harnessed." Alicorn said.

The group remains silent while considering the information. Violet, feeling out of place in this conversation, wishes once again for more knowledge of her family's history. Nothing in her life, until recently, had prepared her for this. Who was she? It was far too recent that she found out her mother was a descendent of the Widowed King. He was her great-great-grandfather, or something. But that didn't make her like these creatures. Magic, if that is what any of this is, is not hers to control. And having always felt ordinary that sits perfectly fine with her. Just a normal-ish young woman with a mostly dysfunctional childhood. Just like most people in the world.

Unconsciously, Violet steps back. Darrock's hand being the only anchor to the spot she no longer wants to occupy.

"Are you okay?" Darrock asks.

Before Violet could find words to explain, the conversation continues as if the two witnesses don't exist.

"Knowledge of as much truth as possible is the only thing that will help this one and the other to understand the best path forward." The great Alicorn flips the long white hair streaming from its muscular neck. "Time is against us. The ritual, half done, can happen again. Even if it goes unfinished, it will do significant damage with each try. We may be stuck with the damage done." Alicorn ruffles the great wings folded along her back. The musky smell of horse fills the air.

Violet steps near the creature, lightly placing her hand on the warm twitching shoulder nearly as high as her head. The link between the three becomes a hum in Violet's blood. Looking from the now still beast on one side, then to the tall dark-haired man on her other side, Violet finds a calm grounding. The surrounding forest feeling more alive than ever.

There are more than trees and unidentified creatures living in the vegetation. The air sings electrically along her skin. The fragrance of the earth opens her understanding of the connection to every entity sheltered by the surrounding trees.

"I may not know your history, or understand what exactly will happen should I do nothing. But what I'm willing to accept is that I am a granddaughter of the Widowed King and I can't turn my back on this world or my own." Violet said. She moves forward to stand in the center of the gathering. "There are many things I am not. Only because I am new to being grown and no longer a child. I want to figure everything out. Honestly, I don't think you have any say in what I do." Violet said, she turns to walk out of the group to resume the same path before they had stopped.

"You are wrong, you know." The song of the beautiful bird fills the air, causing Violet to stop. After a moment, she looks back over her shoulder.

"I, for one, can play a song so calming you will sleep for as long as I desire," Phoenix said. Pushing up into the air with long feathers, moving gracefully to lift the bird. The long tail feathers swish when it perches on a branch in front of Violet.

"The Queen, with a twitch of her antenna, can have you stung with a special toxin that will either cause sleep or death. Then we have the Alicorn. Do you wish to know what prevention is available to such a legendary creature?" The song fades.

Violet turns to look at the Alicorn.

"Mouse, I can't understand the bird anymore. You have less color than the winged horse." Darrock said as he moves to place his back to Violet's while pulling a dagger from a hidden spot inside his tunic. "Is there danger?" He looks from one creature to the next.

"I think if there were, we would already know it," Violet reaches for his free hand. No words spoken, no threats carried out. She gives a light tug on his hand and they step on the path.

The trail bends through the trees and the others are no longer visible. Violet releases a held breath. "Mad? I should be mad, but I can't find it. Scared. I'm too scared to be mad."

"Wait, fill me in before you spin out. I don't know what you should feel." Darrock pulls her back to walk next to him.

"The fiery bird was filling me in on how many ways each of them could prevent me from continuing on this journey, should they think it best." Violet uses both hands to air quote the word prevent. Dropping both arms at her sides, she raises her gaze up to the trees.

"So kind to share information." Darrock reaches out to steer her around a rock in the path.

"Should I be doing this?" Violet stops. "Can I even do this? Why did I feel so sure back there? Now, I'm thinking I'm seriously a scaredy-cat?" Violet doubles over as her breathing increases. "I might faint, or puke."

"Come here, over here." Darrock guides her to a log on the edge of the path. "Sit."

"I can't answer any of these questions for you. Only you know what you can or even want to do." Darrock keeps his eyes on the path toward the creatures. He tucks the dagger away. "I know you can do whatever you set your mind to."

"You know?" Violet asks, her head snapping up to look at him. "What do you know about me?" She jumps up, walking back and forth in front of him.

"We haven't known each other long enough for you to know anything about who I am or what I'm capable of. You lied to me before, so why should I believe anything you say now?" Violet stops with her arms crossed, waiting for a response.

"Hold on a minute!" Darrock stands.

"I will not. I'm waiting for an answer." Violet said.

"How did we go from you holding my hand to you, not trusting me again?" Darrock asks crossing his arms nearly touching her arms with his.

"I did not hold your hand. You held mine." Violet said, dropping her arms and placing her hands on her hips.

"You did. You grabbed my hand, and I could hear those infernal creatures." Darrock drops his arms, leaning in to challenge her point.

For a moment, their hot breath mingles as they lock eyes. "You—" Violet said and didn't finish.

"What? I'm waiting to hear it." Darrock said, softer than the last words he spoke.

Both lean in slowly.

The sound of hooves on the path grows louder with each breath taken. They both pull back.

"There you are," Alicorn said as she slows to a stop. "We must hurry." Without explanation, the wings open out on each side of the long body. "Darrock, help her up on my back. You join her. We must go to the High Land."

"What?" Violet asks without moving.

"Quickly." Alicorn sidesteps closer to the two.

Despite wanting to squirm, Violet tries to rest easy against Darrock's chest. Her hands grip the strands of white hair at the base of the neck of the beast. One thought plays on repeat: don't fall off the back of the Alicorn.

"Fine, we did as you bid. Now explain." Darrock said as if reading Violet's mind.

"Darrock, are you aware that earlier generations of your father's family served the Widowed King?" Alicorn asks.

"I am." Darrock stiffens at the mention of his father's family.

"Did you ever see things that belonged to the last king?" Alicorn asks as her wings push on the air. With each movement, lifting them farther from the ground.

"No—well, as a child, there was talk of our wealth coming from a gift by the king to our family. I was too young at the time to remember much of it. Father never spoke purposefully of it to me." Darrock adjusts his seat on the back of the beast. "We spoke little after he met Brune."

"I see. Have you met with his solicitor in person?" Alicorn asks. The tree tops becoming specks below as clouds float past them.

Violet grows more comfortable with the feeling of the massive muscles moving beneath her. The creature is powerful in her flight through the clouds.

"No, he sends his paralegal, Ezer, to me when I must sign paperwork. I've only shared correspondence with Brigham. My understanding is he never meets with clients." Darrock said. One hand rests across Violet's thigh to grip the hair above her hands. His other hand releasing her hip as she relaxes.

"That is odd," Violet said, resting her back into Darrock's chest for warmth as the surrounding air grows cooler.

"That is where we must go first. You must inquire after your father's possessions. There must be something we are missing." The Alicorn glides on the wind currents with wings outstretched. "The magical things disappearing have caused confusion. We know the one performing the ritual has many, but not everything that is unaccounted for."

"How do we get to this place?" Violet asks.

"Up ahead, see the portal?" Darrock gestures.

His breath drove away the chill on her earlobe. Chills run along the side of Violet's neck to places she prefers not to analyze.

"Wait!" Violet said, her mind racing from tingling places to the memory of what had happened last time she tried to pass through a portal.

The Alicorn ignores her. Directly in front of the flying beast, the air looks to be raining shimmering specks. Blue skies, white clouds, and then sparkles faintly, sliding from the top of the portal to the bottom. But no marker to identify the place. No structure calling it into existence in this spot. Just a slight movement of pin dots of light dropping and then disappearing.

"I can't—" Violet tries to explain, fearful Alicorn and Darrock will continue through to the next land. But she will fall to the floor of the forest that she could no longer see.

She squeezes her eyes shut tight as the portal comes closer.

"You can't what?" Darrock asks.

"... cross over." Violet said, opening her eyes and realizing the hard muscles were still beneath her thighs. "The last time I tried, nothing happened." Violet said, bringing a hand up to her chest to steady her rapid heartbeat.

"What does that mean?" Darrock chuckles.

Violet feels the deep rumble through her back and the tingles threaten to come back.

"Just that I didn't go anywhere." Violet answers, glad he can't see her face. "Because of that, I was afraid I would plummet to the earth and you two would be in another world."

The laughter she expects doesn't come.

"Look." Darrock said, raising his free hand to point straight ahead of them. The clouds part. Violet's breath catches in her chest. Grateful she is not alone, for fear she could have toppled backwards off the steed.

An island looks to be floating in a shallow pool of clouds. Rocky earth pokes through the tops of the white vapor. Mounds of green sit on top of the earth like pillows. As the Alicorn flies around the land floating in the sky, it becomes obvious the grass is not the same as that of her home. It is more mossy and a deeper green than she finds familiar.

They filled most of the land with buildings. Stone or terracotta structures rising six and a few more stories high. It isn't long before they come to a bridge reaching from one mass of land to another larger mass. This island has few buildings and mostly farming. Then yet another bridge farther around linked to a mountainous island. Waterfalls rush down the mountains to a serene pool of water covering most of the land.

Violet realizes the air is no longer cool on her skin. Briefly, she closes her eyes, breathing deeply. The air smells as fresh as a spring morning after a night of rain. Carefully, she sits forward, trying to see each mass of land she can. Bridges connect lands from one to another. So many that she can't count.

Suddenly, she feels a shift in their direction. Darrock's hand finds her hip again. They descend to a small green patch on the first island they came to upon entering this world. The expert landing did nothing for the odd feeling Violet had while maneuvering on the back of the Alicorn.

"Steady, Mouse?" Darrock asks.

"I think." Violet said, waiting for her turn to dismount. Grateful for Darrock's help to the ground when her knees give out with her weight. The mistake she made was looking up into his dark eyes.

"Take a minute." Darrock said, the one side of his mouth quirking up just enough.

Knowing her cheeks had to be red, Violet pulls her gaze away and forces her legs to steady. There is plenty around them to explore with her eyes besides the handsome man so very near to her.

"I'm sure you can find the correct residence if you take that road just over there." Alicorn speaks to Darrock in particular.

"Where are you going?" Darrock turns as the creature steps away, wings readying for flight once again.

"Atop the waterfall." Alicorn said, but only inside Violet's mind.

"I suppose she told you?" Darrock ask, but didn't look at her as he straightens his tunic.

"Yes." This time Violet smiles and tells him while walking to the street pointed out to them.

They don't waste time finding the odd building that appears to be as wide as the arched door and just as tall as Violet's chin. A silver plaque reads Keijo Bringham Esquire. In font the same size, but in all capital letters underneath the name, it reads appointment required. Darrock gently taps his knuckles on the door.

After several moments, when no one answers the door, and no sound comes through, Violet looks from one side to the other. Each building boasts bright colors and is neat and tidy. This door has weathered poorly and looks unopened.

Again, Darrock knocks, louder this time. After a moment, Violet touches a finger to the last line of text on the sign.

Darrock looks more closely at the door. A mail slot, as low as his knees, has tarnished. A light hangs over the top of the door, but the bulb is black as if spent long ago. Cobwebs and grit cover every exposed crevice.

"Maybe he isn't at home," Violet said. She takes a step back from the door farther out on the wide sidewalk. Just as she turns her back to the door, a metal squeak sounds. She whirls back to the door and points at the mail slot.

"I'm sure I saw eyes peeking through that thing," Violet said, getting on her knees.

"Sir, please open up the door." Darrock pounds harder than ever.

"Shh, stop that." Violet said to Darrock between blows to the door. Once he stops, she waits a moment. With a tap next to the mail slot, she speaks. "Please sir, my name is Violet, and he is Darrock. We mean you no harm. We need your help. Please open the door so we can introduce ourselves properly." Violet waits.

"You have no appointment. I know this because I don't allow appointments. Go away." The gruff voice thunders through the door.

"I'm Darrock Grail, Mr. Brigham." Darrock said, but before he could take a breath to continue, locks rattle on the door.

Through the door, they hear two voices. One deep and thunderous, the other stern but softer. The handle jiggles and rattles. The stern voice loudly instructs, "Push from your side, please."

Darrock looks at Violet and shrugs. His shoulder makes a loud thud on the door as the wood scrapes through the threshold. A metal squeak comes from the hinges as the door moves the rest of the way open.

18

LAND ABOVE ALL-FOUND

The door opens to a darkness that looks even darker in contrast to the cheerful light outside the odd building. Violet strains her eyes to see past the door, to two figures standing past the edge of the entrance.

Darrock reaches out, swiping cobwebs away before stooping over to move through the passage. Once he did, Violet can see just how narrow the space truly is. He turns sideways to pass the door and the occupants. At least he can stand upright with a few inches to spare below the ceiling.

Violet slightly ducks to enter. She notes being taller than the two men struggling to shut the door.

"Continue on through, please." The taller of the two instructs.

"Thank you, Ezer." Darrock calls back over his shoulder. He is halfway there.

A partially concealed opening at the end reveals bright light. Violet hears the many locks moving back into place as she struggles to see through the dark hallway. Darrock's wide shoulders shield the dim light coming from the quarters beyond him.

One hand out in front of herself, she soon feels the fabric covering Darrock's back. Quickly removing her hand, she offers a tiny apology.

"My pleasure, Mouse." Darrock holds the tapestry in the doorway aside for her to join him in the much larger room.

It is rare Violet finds reason to roll her eyes, but his remark demands it. The room draws her attention. After being in the dark confined space, this room feels large. It is just as tall, but the wall opposite the entrance has windows letting in outside light. The scale of the furnishings stands out as odd to her. Her short frame will fit perfectly in the chairs. The book shelves on the other walls have the worn books much lower than expected.

The desk on one end is lower but large enough for stacks of papers and books piled around an ancient-looking desk mat. The other end of the room has a smaller desk facing the windows, with a stairway in the other corner. One set leading up and one disappearing into the floor.

"Young Mr. Grail, please allow me to introduce you to Keijo Brigham Esquire." The slim figure waves a delicate-looking hand between the two.

"It's nice to meet you, Brigham." Darrock holds out a hand to the much shorter, odd looking man.

Both hands wave away the gesture. The bulky figure lumbers his way around the room to sit behind the large black desk. He shuffles papers to the side, pulling a side drawer open.

Violet looks from the well-mannered man, in an old tailored suit with trim gray hair sticking straight out from his head in every direction, to the other man. The most gorgeous eyes she may ever have seen sit above a bulbous partially flattened nose. The things she can't take her eyes off of are the tusks protruding up from his bottom lip to cover his upper lip at the corners of his wide mouth. After several seconds, she notices his frizzy red hair.

"Never seen a mix breed before?" Brigham asks Violet in his deep baritone.

"Please, I'm sorry. No, I mean, it's everything. I'm new to all of this," Violet stammers. Finally, she stops speaking and turns her red face to Darrock.

"What Violet is trying to explain is she didn't know any world other than the ordinary existed until recently. This is the first land she has visited aside from her original entry to our lands." Darrock turns his ghost of a grin across the desk.

The solicitor grunts. From the drawer, he pulls out a long-stemmed bone pipe. Habitually places it in his mouth. He continues to grope around in the drawer.

"Sir, please remember you mustn't smoke that in here. The documents, remember the complaints we get when they reek of your boggweed blend?" Ezer steps around the desk to hold out a hand, waiting for the pipe to be placed on it.

"I can't find a match anyhow." Brigham drops the pipe in Ezer's hand. "Why did you come here? As I'm sure you know, Grail, I don't receive visitors."

"This is important, I assure you." Darrock said.

"If you don't mind my asking, why don't you see anyone?" Violet, unsure if his handsome eyes or the odd combination of them and his less desirable features cause her to be comfortable asking the bold question.

"I do mind." Brigham's voice booms, bouncing off the low ceiling. "But I will answer, anyhow." A rough cough erupts from his chest. Then he adjusts his position in the chair. "I'm mixed blood. I'm too tall for a fairy, too short for a troll. Too ugly for fairy and too ugly for troll. In short, I am an outcast from both. But the bigger issue is I'm a solicitor!" Brigham erupts into a laugh, causing his belly to jiggle. His thickly muscled shoulders shake as he leans back in his chair.

Violet can't help but smile at the odd being in front of her. "I've only seen a fairy once. I think I would remember a troll if I had seen one. So I can't judge either way."

"Please come, sit. I like you." Brigham gestures to Ezer to bring chairs to the desk for them. "You asked me direct, most try to be polite and ignore what hangs in the air between us." One of his thick hands slaps the desk. Red hair curled on the back of his hand, matching the frizzy hair on his head.

"You wouldn't know it, but Ezer here is part house brownie." Brigham says, gesturing to his assistant.

Ezer brings one chair from the side of the room to sit facing Brigham's desk. The delicate-looking man grins at Violet, causing his gray mustache covering his lips to curve up to cover his cheeks. His long-fingered hand gestures for her to have a seat. In a blink, he disappears. Violet turns, looking for him only to see him for a moment at the other desk. In the next blink, he was next to Violet with the chair positioned for Darrock to sit.

Violet realizes Darrock does not react to the strange things occurring. He takes the two beings and their behavior in his stride. She will need to strive for the same response. One thing nudges her anxiety. If these things are normal, how can she know when something isn't normal? Will she be able to tell when something is dangerous? The thoughts had to be put aside for consideration later.

"We appreciate you allowing us to take up your time. But we are in a hurry. You knew my father?" Darrock asks.

"Yes, he was one of the very few clients I have met. After working together on his estate for many years, he insisted on meeting with me. That said, I was told to keep everything private. He being gone is the only reason I'm allowing this meeting with you now." Brigham hooks his thumbs on the faded vest covering his round belly.

"Why is that?" Darrock leans forward in the too small chair. It creaks with each movement he makes.

"If I'm not mistaken, it was not long before his tragic death." Brigham pulls a ring of keys from a pocket. Ezer appears at his side, taking the keys and blinks away again. When Ezer is visible, he is near a bookshelf by the stairway. He unlocks a panel swinging open several shelves to show more shelves with leather folios filling the space.

"I was told not to inspect the documents, but to keep them safe." Brigham pulls small glasses from another pocket and places them on the smashed bridge of his nose.

"Let me understand this for a minute. Father came to you with documents for safekeeping and even though he died, you never told me?" Darrock's hands ball to fists on the arms of the chair.

"Be clear," Brigham's voice doesn't raise but fills the room, "there were no instructions other than to keep them safe. They were not a part of the estate specifically. We worked together to secure the business dealings and inheritance separate from the personal side. There, as you know, was another firm dealing with the business assets and a trust set for making sound financial decisions until you came of age." Brigham lowers his penetrating blue gaze.

"Sir, it has a note here that we have something in the holdings below as well." Ezer places the files on the desk.

"So we do." Brigham hunches over, examining the note. He sniffs in a 'hound on the hunt' kind of way. He unties the leather string wrapped around the dark brown folder. One finger slides over embossed letters spelling out Grail in a flourish of curls and strokes.

"Here now. I did not know this was here." Brigham pulls a gray linen paper envelope out of one side. He holds it across the desk for Darrock.

In Darrock's hands, Violet can see Darrock William Grail written across the front. When he turns it over, a black wax seal covers the opening. He flips it back to the front. A finger lightly sliding over the inked letters.

"My dad's handwriting." Darrock's words are faint. "I hadn't spoken to him for at least a month before he got killed." His eyes continue to rest on the envelope.

"They shot him in a, what do they call it, Ezer?" Brigham turns from the papers to his assistant.

"In the ordinary world, it's a mugging, sir," Ezer answers quietly.

"Wasn't it Grail?" Brigham asks as if he had said the words himself and not received clarification.

"Yes, shot and killed in the ordinary world." Darrock sighs before raising his eyes to the burly man on the other side of the desk.

"Hum." Brigham continues to look through the papers. Ultimately closing the leather packet, he wraps the cord back around it. Thoughtfully setting it in front of himself, he rests his hands on the top. He looks for a long moment at Darrock.

"There are many important papers in here that you will need to keep safe. I believe that you have a half-sister that needs to be kept from her mother. You didn't know this, I can see." He raises a hand to delay Darrock. "Wait, there is more you should know."

"No. I recently learned of the girl. But why wasn't I told of her, by you, as soon as I assumed legal responsibility?" Darrock stills his bouncing leg. His movement stills, but the air in the room grows tense.

"I didn't know. The documents are from an agency I recognize as based in the ordinary world. The girl has needs treated best in the ordinary world. As well as

Brune having questionable mental stability." Brigham eyes Darrock.

"THIS is the first time I've ever heard that." Darrock said. The temperature of his voice chills the room.

"The documents here suggest your father may not have known until the last months of his life. He spent his last week in the courts. In both the ordinary land and here in the High Lands." Brigham stands abruptly. "Follow me. We have to hunt the archives below for a large wooden box. I recall your father entrusted it to me. If I remember correctly, it has carvings of creatures on the top. When he brought it to me, I was told not to try opening it. A key didn't come with it, so no worries there." Brigham walks to the corner near the staircase.

Ezer, leading the way, turns on lights as he goes, descends the curved staircase that is entirely too small for Darrock to fit. Violet takes one step, then the next, noticing how each stair turns farther than the last one. One hand on the handrail, the other on the stone wall. The space tightens around her small body after several steps.

"I will not be joining you, obviously." Darrock's eyes raise to the ceiling with aggravation at the suggestion he could descend the cramped stairs.

"Sure you will." Brigham places his powerful hand on Darrock's arm and the next moment they are in the cool catacombs underneath the simple office.

"You could have warned me!" Darrock said. He bends over, breathing deeply. When standing up, his head brushes a ridge of stone arching above his head. The square rooms connect by archways, with each room domed to just over six feet high. No problem for the two proprietors, with only one being just over five feet tall.

"How did you beat us here?" Violet asks when her feet hit the smooth stone floor. She puts a hand on her chest. "The stairs made me dizzy."

Ezer lightly places his hand under her elbow. "Brigham's gifted with the Fairy ability to appear in a known location. In your world, it's teleportation."

"Thank you." Violet said, walking a few paces to Darrock.

"Ezer, do you have any idea where the trunk might be?" Brigham asks.

Without words, he goes to a large wooden cabinet with many drawers along a wall.

"Wow, I haven't seen one of these since I was little. My mom took me to a library that still had part of its books listed in one of these." Violet smiles at the memory.

"Card catalog. Yes, similar, but not precisely the same. We are enchanted here, remember?" Ezer said the last with a grin, moving the curls of his mustache to his cheeks. Violet, near his elbow as he opens a drawer bearing markings she is not familiar with, watches. Each card log inside is again in a text that makes no sense to her.

"It's a shorthand we use. Only the two of us

understand and know the cypher." That said, Ezer pulls one card from the drawer to place it on a crystal pad on top of a moss covered pedestal in the center of the room. Small mushrooms sprout around the base, up the sides and around the crystal. After a moment, the crystal glows underneath the card. Lights in each room beyond the entrance flicker off and on randomly. Finally, a path of light leads from the pedestal to the exact location of the treasure they seek.

"That is amazing!" Violet said. She smiles, bringing her hand up to where her necklace should have been.

"This way." Ezer said to the group. He leads them through one room, turning to the next, then through another and turning through another until the light stops over a group of wooden boxes.

Darrock ducks under the archway, surveying the crates, trunks, and wooden boxes. "That's it. I'd know it anywhere." Darrock moves forward. He and Ezer move several objects until they can safely pull out the wooden box with ornate carvings.

The group makes their way back to a room with a table against one wall. Darrock sets the box on top of the lightly dusty table top. Everyone gathers to see what is so important that the box needed hidden.

"My father showed this to me a when I was a child. There's not a traditional key. You must know the right way to open it. And he taught me how to work the combination." Darrock said, his fingers tracing along the emblems on the top of the box.

"Like a puzzle box?" Violet asks, stepping closer to see the details of the carvings. On the top of the dark wooden box, the center holds a raised carving of a seahorse in profile. She reaches out to touch the carved shape above the sea creature. The airship wiggles lightly under her fingertips.

"Don't press the shapes yet. I need to remember the right order of movements." Darrock rests a finger on the warrior shield below the sea horse.

Violet looks up to see Darrock shake his head as he taps each symbol on the top of the box. Gently, she places her hand on top of his to still his motion.

"Close your eyes and remember." Violet whispers.

Darrock holds her gaze for a moment and then does as instructed. She removes her hand and waits. After some time, he opens his eyes to see her questioning look.

"Thanks, Mouse." Darrock says, locking his eyes on hers briefly.

Violet returns a grin, accepting that he may always use the name she would rather he forget. Yet, she couldn't deny the warm flicker of something sweet every time he says it.

Darrock's fingers embrace the canna lily bloom to the right of the center. He turns it into a full clockwise rotation. She gasps when the symbol drops to be level with the surface. He then moves the airship above the center one and a half turn clockwise and it drops. Next, he pushes the shield, and it lowers into place. Lightly, he slides his fingers to the left of the seahorse to a dagger pointing down. Darrock turns it one full turn counterclockwise, and it slips into the lid. This causes the seahorse to turn on its own. Movement inside the wood is the only sound other than the breathing of those watching intently.

"Is that it? If you are wrong, what happens?" Ezer asks.

"I don't know. Father never allowed me to do it incorrectly." Darrock gives the small man a shrug.

Once the box is silent, the lid pops up a fraction. Everyone holds their breath. Darrock places a hand on each end of the lid, pulling. The thick piece of wood comes loose, and he places it upside down behind the box.

"It's empty?" Violet's voice is not much louder than a sigh.

"No, see here, a leather pouch." Darrock says. The antique wood is dark enough to miss the walnut colored leather lying flat in the bottom.

"Why such a small thing in this big box?" Violet looks at the men around the table.

Darrock opens the flap of leather resembling an envelope. Nothing but leather at first. He places a hand palm up underneath the opening of the pouch. After a couple of shakes, a silver coin flops onto his palm.

"Why this secreting for a not so rare coin from the Widowed King's time?" Brigham's deep voice fills the domed room. One large hand strokes his bulbous chin. "While it's not in use anymore, it certainly isn't rare."

Darrock flips the coin from one side, showing an image of the king to the back, showing a seahorse in deep relief.

"Would you agree this is odd?" Darrock hands the coin to the older man.

Brigham's thick thumb rubs across the seahorse. "You have a point. I can't say I remember the old coins being as thick as this carving. Better hold on to it until you find out why he saved the coin."

"Would the professors know of it?" Violet asks the men.

"Let's keep this quiet for now." Darrock says. His eyes fasten to the underside of the box lid. "I can't remember... there was something else." He rubs a hand over what looks to be metal plates concealing the mechanisms inside the lid.

Ezer whisks the empty box along the table so Darrock can pull the lid closer. Nothing moves or shifts when Darrock pushes, then he flips the lid right side up. A ribbon of scroll work borders the entire top of the lid. Darrock traces his fingers over the intricate work and closes his eyes.

"I remember my father telling me there is one last treasure the box can give. We never did it, but he told me it was only for the most dire of times." Darrock pauses, remembering. "Every soldier in battle can use a horse to help him see what he must see." With each word, his fingers trace a pattern through the carvings to rest on the seahorse. He opens his eyes to lock on Violet's. Gently he pushes the seahorse flush with the surface of the lid.

Clink.

And lifting the lid from the table, Darrock reveals to everyone gathered around the table the last treasure the box holds. A metal key the size of his hand, burnished black with age, resting on the table.

"Well done!" Brigham claps a hand on the center of Darrock's back, causing him to sway forward.

"Thank you, but I don't know what this key unlocks." Darrock picks it up, trying to see if any of the markings give any clues. Turning it over, shifting it to the light for better views. "Nothing." Darrock looks around at the others. "Any ideas?"

"Maybe the Alicorn will know. We can take the paperwork with us to look at and maybe we will find answers." Violet said, but looks at the other two for help.

"I'm not sure you will find answers in the documents. The best bet may be the personal papers your dad wrote directly to you. You may leave everything else here indefinitely." Brigham said, ushering the others back in the direction they entered the room.

"Yes, I will store everything until you send word you wish to have them brought to you," Ezer said. Although making it obvious they were not to return to collect the items themselves.

This time, everyone knew what to expect on the journey back up to the office level of the building. Still, it took a moment for the pair to breathe easy. Violet longs to be out in the fresh air again after the cool caverns underground. Sunlight and fresh air beckon to her.

"Might I suggest you find your way through the back garden? When we choose to walk for fitness, we use this door." Ezer crosses to the wall of windows opposite the entrance they had already used. Opening what appears to be a set of shutters exposes a door. Used often enough, the door opens silently with little effort. Darrock and Violet gather the important items. A brief farewell and the door slams behind them.

"I don't understand why they shutter themselves off from the world. They were great, I enjoyed them. I didn't expect that." Violet said, adjusting the pack on her shoulder as they walk on the spongy grass to a short gate facing a narrow stone path between buildings.

"Their reputation for discretion is impeccable. Yet, many refuse to do business with them. The ignorance of their race is based on fear, no doubt. I like them too." Darrock looks back at the building tucked between many others. His eyes soften.

"My father trusted them in his last days." Darrock said quietly and pauses. With a shake of his head, he steps through the gate.

"Any idea in which direction we should go to find our way to the bridge?" Violet asks, looking right, then left. Tall buildings shadow the narrow path in both directions.

Darrock stands behind her with his chest slightly brushing her back. The warmth of his nearness is both comforting and disturbing. She doesn't want to want him. Yet, he feels like home every time they get this close. A deep yearning to lean into him surfaces.

"This way." Darrock said, near her ear.

His breath warms her skin. The side of her neck tingles at the intimacy. Violet raises a hand to her chest, feeling her heart beat faster because of him. The effort to take that first step to put distance between them is more than she expects. With every nerve in her body tuned to Darrock's presence, she walks the long cool stretch between the stone buildings. But hearing each of his steps on the cobblestones under their feet, every brush of fabric as his muscular body follows her, Violet knows her cheeks must be pink if the heat is any indication.

"Let's go this way." Darrock said, stepping around her at the end of the path. His hand reaching for hers in a light embrace.

Violet avoids eye contact with him. She just can't face the confirmation of him seeing she is losing the battle with herself. A battle she was sure she could win in the beginning. The more time she spends with him, the more ground she loses in the battle. Now this, his powerful hand cradling hers to pull her through the streets. Was it truly necessary that he keep hold of her? No, it's not crowded. Just people walking, going about their own business.

Although the more important question being, does she want him to hold her hand? Violet's toe catches the edge of a cobblestone and her step falters. Darrock stops, looks over his shoulder at her. The stumble causes Violet to slam into his side. They stand looking deeply into each other's eyes.

So startled by the collision, her breathing is rapid and mingles with his. Violet feels her chest heaving and tries to pull her thoughts away from how warm his brown eyes glow. Just as slow as the magnetic pull of his lips, she realizes he is drawing nearer to her own lips. As soon as his musky scent fills her nose, her lips part. Darrock's eyes dip to her lips and then his eyes dart over her head, then back to her eyes. The tip of her tongue moves along her bottom lip. She wonders what his lips will taste like at this exact moment.

"On the count of three, run with me," Darrock says in the barest of whisper. "One, two, three."

"What!" The word jerks out of her as Darrock pulls her hand, running in the original direction they had been heading.

19

LAND ABOVE ALL-PERSPECTIVE

"Why are we running?" Violet asks after finding her stride behind Darrock. Her free hand gripping the bag, bouncing on her hip.

Darrock didn't answer. He looks back behind Violet, gripping her hand tighter. The risk of looking behind herself too great to try. Whatever the cause, she had to consider who to trust. Darrock had saved her from the Valley of Forgotten Dreams. She trusts him with her life. The realization spurs her to grip his hand more securely and quickens her pace.

Soon they can see the end of the road up ahead. They must choose a direction fast. Darrock guides her to the buildings on her side of the road. Without warning, something grabs Violet, pulling her into a narrow space between two buildings.

A leather covered hand is on her face until she is in the space far enough that Darrock can fit. A tall wooden slatted door slides into place with Darrock's help. There is no going back to the street. Suddenly, a small glass fixture glowing with golden light is beside her face. Violet is looking at a black nose she had seen recently for the very first time. Gray fur draws her gaze up to the dark eyes of Sir Randolph.

He gestures for them to be quiet and follow him. They can only move side step as the space isn't wide enough to turn their shoulders fully ahead. Violet cannot see past Darrock to the entrance, so her ears strain to listen for someone or, in this world, something following them.

After a moment, which feels like hours, the three reach the end of the buildings. The path reaches a much wider alleyway and they turn right. A few people mill around talking or entering doors, not giving the strangers any notice. The city is the site of official business for all the lands, citizens of every race, and breed come and go as a matter of course.

"I can't thank you enough, Sir Randolph, for alerting me to our trouble and our rescue." Darrock said.

"It's my duty, young Grail. If I had found your location sooner, I could have warned you sooner." Sir Randolph said and let a low growl rumble in his chest.

"Wait, when did you even see Sir Randolph?" Violet questions, her brows drawing together. She darts a look at Darrock. She didn't want to risk stumbling again, so her eyes move back to watch the path in front of herself. Soon she must get used to cobblestone roads if she planned to travel by foot while in these lands.

"He made me aware he was near at the path behind the solicitors." Darrock said, reaching for Violet's elbow to steady her on an uneven section of the alley.

"Once we reached the road, Sir Randolph alerted me to a tail we picked up on the road when we arrived."

"We are positive they have followed Violet from the night her amulet went missing." Sir Randolph said.

"Who are we? Who are they?" Violet asks the first questions that come to mind, but many follow and answers feel necessary.

"My dear, we don't have the time now. Because I know you won't let it go. Just accept this much for now. The Order of Echoes have been aware of a plot surrounding you. We are trying to keep you safe from whatever wants to cause you harm in this land." Sir Randolph moves in front of her and Darrock at the end of the alley.

His leather covered paw stretches out to hold them back. While sniffing the air in every direction, his ears swivel, listening before Sir Randolph motions for them to follow.

"Now can you tell me who is following us here right now?" Violet skip steps to catch up to the fluid movements of the upright wolf leading the way.

Yet glancing past Violet, he connects with Darrock before he speaks. Sir Randolph takes several steps before answering. "We fear the plot is bigger than we expected. You know that Darrock's step mother, Brune, is gathering magical objects for a spell. Recently, we found evidence that Brune had been visiting this city often." Sir Randolph said, turning on another road leading to the edge of the floating island.

"Yes, I originally scouted for magical items to help her. I can promise you I didn't know it was for a spell.

That was not what she told me," Darrock said with his jaw clinched and his gaze straight ahead.

"While the International Portal Station's damage got sorted out, the usable portals were so few, we spotted her crossing to this location. Once repairs began, the Order had a moment to look back over the records. We discovered her frequent travels." Sir Randolph ushered them along the rim to a bridge. Each of his senses was on alert for a follower. Luckily, few of the regular citizens have cause to frequent the bridge to the water land.

"You must hurry and cross. Once you get past the center of the bridge, no one can see you from this side. I will keep watching for anyone trying to follow. But you need to hurry." Sir Randolph said while opening the gate and using his bushy tail to slap at their feet to get going.

"I have more questions. Come with us," Violet said while tugging against Darrock's insistent pull on her hand.

"Next time, my dear, we will talk much longer. Find your Alicorn now." Sir Randolph closes the gate behind them and rushes away from the bridge to blend into the surrounding despite being a magnificent wolf. Violet lost sight of him while trying to watch her footing on the bridge.

"Fine!" Violet said in a low but firm voice. Her free hand balls to a fist and she jerks her other hand free of Darrock's grasp. Her steps quicken to a near run. So frustrated with the lack of answers, Violet does not give the view any thought. She keeps her eyes focused on the uphill road in front of them.

Darrock remains quiet by her side. He matches her stride until they pass over the peak. He slows once they are no longer visible from the mainland.

"What are you doing?" Violet asks. She stops in the middle of the road, facing him with both her hands on her hips.

"Taking in the amazing view." Darrock said, his lone dimple showing next to his half smile.

"We don't have time for this." Violet's voice losing its punch as she looks past the railing on the side of the bridge. The view, like a magnet, pulls her close enough to lean against the copper colored metal.

Endless blue sky dotted with transparent fluffy clouds stretches out before Violet. Any land found is being hugged on the bottom by dense white clouds. Each one connecting to one or two others by the high arching bridges that look impossible. The engineering of these structures would be impossible in her ordinary world. No giant pillars support the bridge from below, with no bedrock to anchor them. No great cables strung through the air holding up the roadway.

Violet, having seen this riding on the back of the Alicorn when they first arrived in the High Lands. Still, the style from the air had been stunning. To be on the bridge makes for an entirely unique experience. Up close, the structures are enormous. They allow you to be up near the clouds. The white vapor drifting near enough you can reach out and feel the moisture carried by the clouds.

That thought makes her fingers itch to reach out to

experience it for herself. Before she can remove her hand from the cool metal railing, warm fingertips slide over to touch hers. She looks down, seeing Darrock's larger hand resting next to her own, close enough she feels his warmth.

"I came here once with my parents. We stood on a bridge the same as this. Every time I visit this land, I pause and enjoy the amazing views, to remember them." Darrock says, then turns his head to look at Violet.

All tension and aggravation melts away with his confession. Both of his parents are gone. Violet looks deeper into his dark eyes. Beyond the glow of the dark amber, feeling more than seeing the loneliness he carries, buried in the depths. One step towards him and she lightly places her hand on top of his.

"This could be the beginning of something amazing." Darrock leans close enough his breath sends shivers across her skin.

"This could be the beginning of something disastrous." Violet said, lightly licking her lips.

Darrock's mouth curls at one corner. "Are we ready to find out which of us is right?"

Violet nods before stretching up to cover the last of the space separating them. His lips, warm and firm, gently touch hers. Then pull back for a beat of her heart, or maybe his heart. Then press into hers with more firmness than before, and again he pulls back, locking eyes. Her surprise mirrors in his eyes.

Home. He feels like her home, or the missing place she had been looking for and never understood how to find. Passion pulls her to him as an invisible force.

Darrock moves his hand on the railing to weave his fingers through hers on the railing. His free hand caresses her neck and jawline, causing an electric warmth to ignite something racing throughout her body. Still gently, their lips press together as if neither can believe the connection is real. His thumb rubs back and forth on her skin.

"You're crying?" Darrock says but rests his forehead to hers, not releasing his hold on her.

"I am?" Violet whispers. Clears her throat and opens her eyes, realizing the truth.

"Did I rush you?" Darrock asks.

"No." Violet says. Her free hand reaches up to grip his wrist, holding it in place. Unwilling to lose the contact they share. She closes her eyes and breathes his scent in deeply.

"Take your time." Darrock chuckles.

"There has been… a lot lately. This is the nicest thing to happen for months." Violet says, deliberately pulling back from him.

"High praise, given you got trapped in the Valley of Forgotten Dreams so recently." Darrock looks at the fading scratches on her arms.

"Well yeah, there was that too," Violet said, pulling her eyes from his as her face warms with the mention of the harrowing experience. The clouds that had been creating such an intimate seclusion from the world drifts away. She notices from the corner of her eye a green oasis in the vast blue sky.

"We should go." Darrock said, looking over her

head to the green edge of their destination.

Violet tries to ignore the now awkward attraction hovering on the surface between them. The view of the land helps distract her wish to find a new normal with Darrock. She does not have time to think about how to date someone from an entirely different reality than her own. Not just a different country, but a place of talking animals. Unusual technology or lack of tech compatible with her own world. Not to mention that someone wants to separate the worlds, and no one knows what will happen if a person from one land was in the other at the moment of separation.

A slight knot of panic forms in her stomach. Could she give up her land? Could Darrock give up his? More worrisome to think of, is if they could live in the land not of their origin. This had to be stopped. This plan of destruction. Whether her link to the two lands truly exists or not is unimportant right now. If she can stop the scheme of untold repercussions, she will do it. Then, and only then, can she be free to explore whatever place Darrock might have in her future.

The last step off the bridge was onto spongy, green grassy vegetation. Gently sloping hills prevent the view of the interior of the land mass. And to the left they see an enormous tower of land with rocky pillars stretching into the blue sky. The sound of birdlike creatures is a distant noise to the rushing water pouring from the top of the mountain of land hovering above. A few trees with white blossoms scatter around the landscape. The sweet floral scent perfumes the air as they walk toward the base of the mountain.

"We need to find the Alicorn's hiding place. He didn't want to draw any more attention than we did when we arrived." Darrock said, while walking in front of Violet.

"Have you ever been to this island on your past visits?" Violet asks stepping over a small plant she could only think of as a kind of fern.

"No, and I'm surprised none of the locals are enjoying this place. It is worth hiking for the views alone." Darrock said.

"Since you say it that way, I've noticed the citizens don't…" Violet said, pausing. Her hand reaching up for the necklace that she no longer had. Her hand moves up to brush hair from her eyes. "Recreation in the enchanted world is not the same as in the ordinary world. We spend so much time occupying ourselves with entertainment. Or we just try to escape our ordinary way of being by watching things that have no real meaning to our survival."

"Exactly! I see that survival is more of an enchanted land occupation. Even personal interactions like gatherings, conversation, and face-to-face communications are more common in the enchanted lands. We value experience with each other differently in the two worlds." Darrock said, slowing his pace to allow frequent looks over his shoulder.

"Look at that." Violet steps next to Darrock to gaze over the crystal clear lake.

"See that? Let's go there first." Darrock said, pointing at a dense group of trees at the base of the waterfall. He waits for her to walk nearer to the pond's edge to follow behind her.

"Why isn't anyone here?" Violet asks, eyes surveying the land from one side of the floating island to the other. She fidgets with adjusting the straps on the bag she has been carrying. "Birds are the only creatures I see."

"Stop!" Darrock grabs her arm, turning her to the water's edge. "Look, there."

Violet looks the length of his arm past the point of his finger to see a blue pin dot glowing in the water. She scoots closer to the water. While holding onto Darrock's hand, she steadies herself on the soft wet ground.

"There are more lights now." Violet said.

"Move farther along the edge." Darrock said, waiting to let go of her until she was on steady footing.

"Whatever it may be, it's following you." Darrock said. He looks at his feet along the dappled grassy edge. He grabs two small rocks. And looks at Violet, then back to the lake. With ease, he sends one rock, skimming the surface of the water until it drops, making ripples radiate to the edge where they stand.

"Here, you try one." Darrock said, holding out the second stone.

"Ok, but I'm not sure what you expect to happen." Violet steps close enough to grab the rock and do as he had. As soon as the stone leaves her fingers and moves near the surface of the water, the dots of blue light appear in mass and race with the object. The moment it drops into the water, an explosion of glowing water bursts up into the air. When the last drop of water lands back on the surface of the pond, the two witnesses turn looking at each other.

Violet realizes her mouth is hanging open only because she notices Darrock's is as well. She looks at the edge of the water to see the dots of light populate in front of her again. Without hesitation, she takes a huge step backwards.

"I don't know what that was but, yah let's not get too close." Darrock said, moving with her to a safe distance up the slight slope of the bank.

While walking along the edge to the destination in silence, Violet looks towards the water again. The lights were fewer than before, but following their progress.

"Every single time I get a grip on the crazy, I get the wind knocked out of me with something else that can ultimately turn into a nightmare." Violet said, taking her gaze from the water to navigate the uneven ground in front of her.

"We just have to figure out if we have a life and death thing or not." Darrock chuckles.

"Too soon Darrock." Violet said and groans, "You haven't mastered ordinary world humor yet."

"Sorry. It's getting late. We need to find the winged beast soon." Darrock said.

Violet looks toward the sky with no idea where to look for the sun, if it had one. True, the sky has dimmed to a darker blue, but the shadows don't have a direction as a sun creates. Everything fills with shadows in a horror movie way.

"I agree. I don't like this darkness." Violet moves faster. Up close, the trees are not as dark as she thought. The canopy of the treetops muffling the noise of the waterfall. Bushes border the only path.

"I know how different our worlds are, but this smells like home. The damp earth and mossy scent is similar." Violet raises her face to the sky. So that she cherishes the moment, she closes her eyes and takes a deep breath.

"Violet, don't move." Darrock whispers. Looking at her feet, he stands in front of her.

"What?" Violet asks.

"You're standing in a small creek. Step to one side, slowly." Darrock said, watching the blue lights gathering at her feet.

Violet holds her breath and moves one foot out of the water. The foot remaining begins glowing with the blue light moving up onto the white canvas of her shoe. She looks for Darrock's hand to steady herself, to pull her foot free from the water and shake loose the particles of light.

"Is that all of them?" Violet bounces around on one foot, wriggling the other one.

"Yes." Darrock said, still holding her hands.

"I wish we knew what that is." Violet drops her foot, sloshing in wet canvas.

"It may even be a who." Darrock winks at her and his lone dimple appears. That one special way she now finds familiar.

"Ugh, I hadn't thought of that. I may never get used to this world." Violet said, realizing how vulnerable they are. Before she could get lost in his kiss again, she pulls away to find the path. It follows the creek. No wonder she had stepped into the water.

"The path ends up here." Violet said to Darrock.

"Let me see." Darrock moves around her to see what looks to be a wall of leaves surrounded by trees and brush. He reaches to pull a knife from his boot. With care, he cuts through long vines to squeeze through to a small clearing. He steps through, reaching out behind for Violet.

"Wait, I can't get through without stepping into the water. Darrock, wait." Violet calls but he doesn't answer and his hand moves farther into the vines. The vines loosely drape back over where Darrock cut them. She looks at her feet, then back at the curtained opening, worried how long she had before the vines seal back closed. The choice clearly lay out in front of her. Either step in the water and find Darrock again or lose the way in and be alone with darkness falling fast. The blue lights had not hurt her so far, and she had to get to Darrock.

Regardless of feeling stupid, Violet takes a deep breath and steps into the creek while reaching for the vines. Blue lights multiply and move up her shoes. While ignoring the glowing light the best she can, she pushes the leaves aside until reaching the clearing on the other side.

Darrock stands near a tree trunk in the center of the opening, his back to Violet. Still in the water, the light particles have reached up to her knees but have slowed their movement. The water coming alive with the blue glow.

"Hey, Darrock." Violet calls out. She keeps walking in the shallow creek to avoid the rocky ground under the canopy of the weeping tree. The path of the water spirals around the tree several times. But stepping from one loop to the next, Violet avoids walking in circles.

"Darrock, who are you talking to?" Violet asks between grunts from stepping over large rocks in between the arcs of water.

"They are waiting for you." Darrock said, but doesn't turn to face her.

"Who?" Violet gets to his side and looks up to see his face glowing in a light like the one in the water, but more purple than blue.

"You, they are waiting for you." Darrock speaks in a dreamy voice as he continues to gaze at the trunk of the tree.

Violet looks at the tree, seeing orbs of the light up in the canopy. There are no words spoken aloud. The only sounds are that of the water in the distance and birds chirping in other trees. The moment the blue specks began touching her, the scent of moss and earth fill her nose and continues to grow stronger.

Despite her eyes watching the lights in the tree, she reaches to shake Darrock's arm. He doesn't respond.

"What are you doing to him?" Violet calls to the orbs.

Nothing.

"Release him." Violet says. She looks from one purple light to the next. Up high, nearly obscured by the other orbs, Violet sees one light move. First, it tries to maneuver around the others hovering in place. Not able to get far, the light suddenly bursts downward. While knocking into any ball of light in its path, it halts eye level with Darrock.

"Please forgive their behavior." A sweet little voice with a musical lilt comes from the light in front of them. Darrock shakes his head and blinks hard before turning to Violet, wiping a hand down his face.

"Who are they, or you?" Violet asks, tugging Darrock's arm. He won't move, instead he clasps her hand with his.

"We are of the fairy heritage." The orb said, but slowly its light dims. Wings appear and then an outline of a feminine body is in silhouette in the purple light. Every light in the tree dims. Both male and female winged forms take shape within each light.

"Why did you hypnotize, or whatever, my friend?" Violet asks. Looking at the one speaking to her. She looks up into the tree to confirm the feeling that every orb is watching her.

"You have a familiar imprint, but he does not. Our kind have not bargained with his line in any significant way. We prefer not to do so now." She says, floating out from the tree and around their heads in a circle.

"Are you their leader? Will they obey you?" Violet asks, looking up at the others again.

"No." A giggle tinkles similar to jingling bells. "We are more of a tribe. There are elders, but each of us leads." She pulls back to be near the other purple lights.

"I think I've heard of you. There are only a few of the more ancient fairy folk left." Darrock said, his eyes wide, moving around the tree's inhabitants. He turns to Violet. "I don't know of anyone that has seen them in person." Darrock's voice a loud whisper.

Violet carefully makes her way around the tree wearing the blue pin dots of light on her feet and legs. Her dark hair taking on a royal purple shimmer from the light raining down from the beings filling the weeping tree.

"You are favored." The one light continues to move with her until they are back to Darrock.

"If you don't mind my asking, what does it mean to be favored?" Violet looks from the figure in the light to Darrock and back again.

"Our water mites recognize you. They know you." Saying this, the orb drops low to the tiny stream of water winding around the tree and then glides around Violet's legs and back up to her eye level.

"I've never been here before now. That isn't possible." Violet says and chuckles.

"Wrong words. Your life liquid is from the past, your line." The orb jingles again. This time, several others in unique tones join the choir. The sound becoming part of a song drifting up through the tree as each orb plays the tune.

Darrock looks at Violet, his face glowing with the purple tint emitting from the beings. His smile widens when the orbs drop from the tree, moving rhythmically along the creek. Violet reaches for his hand, letting him spin her in a dance as the cheerful music fills the air. The movement of the globes following their ring around the tree. With each step, the water splashes electric blue lighted dots into the air. Darrock laughs with Violet keeping her hands in his as they move and splash.

"Wait, stop. I'm so tired." Violet laughs between gasps for air, lowering herself to the ground. And sitting on a root at the base of the tree, she leans her back on the trunk. Darrock releases her hand once she is comfortable. When Violet removes the bag from her shoulder, Darrock offers to carry it for her. As soon as he loads the weighty pack onto his shoulder, he wonders off, looking around.

The friendly fairy light glides to her side. Violet lets herself relax, looking up into the tree where the purple orbs gently move around the branches. When she lowers her gaze back to the weeping branches, she catches movement in her peripheral vision. The light transforms into a toddler sized girl. The dots of blue pin light form a dress over her body.

When Violet looks directly into her eyes, the being dips her chin and lowers her blond lashed eyes. The pale skin of her cheeks turn pink.

"Hello." Violet says with a smile.

"I don't use this form often. I am curious about you, so they gave me permission to present to you." She said, her voice growing stronger the more she spoke.

"This is the best time I've had in the enchanted world. Thank you for that." Violet knew the energy she had gained at the Lady of the Woods' cottage was fading. Her head leans back on the tree without her being able to resist.

"Then I dislike what I need to tell you." The girl's

smile falters.

"What is your name? Can we start with that? What should I call you?" Violet asks with a smile, trying to keep the mood light as long as possible.

"Um, well, you have no language for what I am called." She said, shaking her head.

"Can I give you a name? It feels odd talking to you without knowing who you are," Violet said.

"Yes, and then you must listen." She said, moving her little legs up underneath herself. Then, placing her hand on her knees, she rests her weight on them, leaning into Violet. "You must not slumber." Although the size of a toddler, her form is that of a well-proportioned young woman. Her delicate hand reaches out to the water next to them. Blue lights race around her hand. When she pulls out of the water, the lights zip over to Violet's feet.

"I think," Violet looks up to the leaves hanging on the branches reaching to the ground. "I could use a name for the tree back home that this one reminds me of, but no. Fay suits you more than Willow." As Violet speaks, her head clears. The sleepiness instantly fades.

The water mites encircle her legs, racing around each of her limbs. Violet looks from her legs to her new friend with a question in her eyes.

"I asked them to restore you. Because they are fond of you, they did." Fay said.

"Thank you. I feel amazing," Violet said. But she looks more closely into the eyes of the being next to her. The color of her eyes was an undefinable depth of light and color. The overwhelming sense of knowledge and understanding fills Violet.

"Fay is good. What am I to call you?" The creature of light and universe asks.

"I am Violet." She said, feeling questions bubble up from every new experience of the past several days. The calm quiet of Fay rapidly makes the need for answers seem unimportant.

"Violet, you are not on the journey alone. Many want your success. We cannot take your place. It is not ours to continue." Fay said and one graceful hand touches Violet's.

"I understand it's a prophecy of some sort. The whole chosen one thing feels ridiculous coming from my world, where we are all ordinary people. We just get through our days trying to live with whatever the world throws at us. What makes me so special?" Violet waits for the answer to the one question bugging her from the beginning of finding the enchanted world.

"You were born for this. The line of your ancestors, the parents you were born to, and the person you have become are what make you special to this world. This place and time is your moment to be special." Fay said, smiling widely. She looks up into the tree at her companions and closes her eyes. Still, the smile remains.

"Fay, I don't feel ready for any of this. I don't think I'm special," Violet said in a whisper.

"Oh little flower, it's not about how you feel. It's about who you are and what you will choose as right. What you choose will tell you what to feel," Fay said, head tilted to one side.

"Where I come from, our feelings guide our choices," Violet said after a moment of contemplation.

"Wrong way around for making sense." Fay giggles. One of the other orbs drifts near her shoulder. She stands, and the merriment vanishes.

"You must hear this, friend Violet. The one from your split line of ancestors has been trying to gain fairy favor. We cannot do as she desires unless she traps one of us into a bargain. I cannot say that each of our kind can outwit the human kind. While nothing preordains us to sway this outcome, we each get to make our own choice." Fay wrings her hands.

"Brune." Violet whispers.

"There is suspicion she is being counseled by another." Fay said.

"We know she works with others." Violet said, her brows drawing together.

"It may be more than that. We protect our island in this world. There is one that keeps trying to gain audience with us. We allow many to visit the pool of water outside of this secluded place. Our guests here are limited to those the water sprites recognize." Fay looks up at the purple lights. More than her hands become restless.

"You mean we got in here because the Sprites knew one of my relatives?" Violet said, trying to understand the increasingly anxious energy coming from Fay.

"Trust yourself Violet. You will know what to do when the time comes." Fay said, her form changes, shrinking back into the small orb with her dark figure visible in the purple light. "We will meet again, little flower." Fay said, and the figures disappear into the orbs they had been when Violet first encountered them.

No more laughter jingles in the air. No more movement in the tree. The lights in the tree were now back as they had been when they mesmerized Darrock.

"Violet, over here." Darrock calls out from the edge of the clearing.

"Coming." Violet responds, reluctant to leave the delightful place protected inside of the tree's weeping canopy. As she stands, she is aware they restored her energy. Before stepping from the spiral of the creek, she turns back to look up at the orbs. "Thank you."

When her feet leave the water, the blue dots of light fade away and the purple light dims significantly. Violet waits a moment for her eyes to adjust to the deepening shadows before walking to Darrock.

"There is a path through here." Darrock said, moss-covered, pushing aside leafy branches. He holds out a hand to Violet. Each step being placed carefully on moss-covered rocks. Darrock follows her through what had moments before been a wall covered in vines. The sound of the waterfall grows louder as they continue on the narrow path around boulders taller than their heads.

Violet places her hand on one wet outcropping of rock to squeeze around it. She pauses. Darrock steps up close behind her.

"Finally." Darrock says under his breath. They both watch as the Alicorn stands on a flat slab of stone at the base of the waterfall, drinking from the lake. The sound of water splashing into the pool below is loud enough to drown out the sounds of the birds.

Violet looks around for a quieter place to sit away from the water. Before waving for Darrock to join her, she moves away from the Alicorn to another rock slab.

"Thank you for the fun back there." Violet bumps her shoulder into his. Darrock sitting with his arms wrapped around his bent knees, watches the faint ripples dance across the water. Lazily, his smile spreads wide.

"You're welcome, but I'm not entirely sure it was our doing." Darrock turns to look at Violet, resting his face on his arm so that his smiling eyes are all she can see.

"No, honestly?" Violet tilts her head, watching his eyes while her brain analyzes what his words mean.

He says nothing, only jerks his head in affirmation. When the smile leaves his eyes, he speaks. "I'm OK with it, are you?"

Violet continues to think about the consequences of another being controlling her actions. This was fun and innocent, but would it be next time? Making her own choices is increasing in importance to her. Would she have let go and played with Darrock on her own? At that moment, probably not. We should take the plot to rip the worlds apart serious. Right? This isn't the time to play around.

"Mouse, you are thinking too hard about this," Darrock said, dropping his arms and stretching his legs out in front of himself.

"Guilty." Violet avoids looking at him by turning to

the sound of the hooves clomping on the rocks nearby.

"I'm going to look over my father's papers." Darrock pulls the bag open. He roots around in the supplies until he finds what he needs.

"I will go see if we can figure out what to do next." Violet stands, brushing her backside off before picking her steps carefully over to grass the Alicorn found nearby.

"You have many questions, as you should." Alicorn said as Violet approaches her.

"True, but I'm not even sure where to begin." Violet said and pauses. Unsure, she looks at the cream-colored hoofs of the magnificent beast and crosses her arms. "It's all overwhelming."

"You are aware the Widowed King, as you know him, had twin daughters. Violetta is your ancestral line. Nila is the other daughter. The Queen died immediately after the birth of the princesses." Alicorn taps around on the ground, finding a comfortable spot to curl the long white legs up under the muscled body. Violet follows suit and sits leaning her back on the warm shoulder of the creature.

"Because nearly every enchanted land fell under his rule, the King traveled much of the time. Or that was the excuse for his absence in his daughter's lives. Ultimately, he stayed at the palace more. The damage was done by then. Magic was stronger in those days. The ones that wielded it had political power as well." Alicorn said, then gives a snort, shaking the long head.

"I was told the Princesses had very different natures about them. One was sweet and kind, but the other not so much." Violet said, looking out at the waterfall in the distance.

"Truth, we have lost details in time, but that is close enough." Head swinging to the side, one enormous eye looks at Violet. "When the King drained the magic, he did not seek council from his advisers, he didn't tell anyone in his court, Vergilius Starosta accomplished his task and died."

"Why would he choose to do it in that way?" Violet looks deep into the pale ice blue eye.

"That is not the answer we seek now." The ears on top of the head twitch, then the long snout swings back to look out at the water. "Young Darrock must find the treasures his father hid away, just as his father had. They are what the dark one is seeking. That is why the artifacts keep disappearing."

"You mean Brune?" Violet turns to lean her side on the creature. Distractedly, her fingers comb through the white hair draping the neck, nearly touching the ground.

"In part it's Brune. The Dark One is not a single being. It is more of an idea or group wanting to put magic back the way it once was." Alicorn gave another snort.

"To close the ordinary world off from your lands." Violet tries connecting the few dots she thinks she knows.

"The lands were born connected." Alicorn ruffles the wings, laying relaxed behind Violet.

"There is so much I don't understand. The professors gave me a crash course on the way this world works and the history, but I have so many holes in my knowledge." Violet looks up to see a white feather drifting in the air near her. So, holding her palm open, she let it land there. Twirling it in her fingers, she waits to see if the Alicorn has more to share with her.

"Did your mother have time to share with you how the amulet came into her possession?" Alicorn asks.

"No, she didn't. What does it matter now?" Violet shakes her head stronger than necessary even though the creature wasn't looking at her.

"It had belonged to Violetta, but went missing somewhere along the way. So much lost in time. If we had more answers, there might be a way to prevent more damage to our world," Alicorn said. Wings flutter and muscles twitch, signaling to Violet the creature is moving.

"When I have time, I can try to talk to my dad to see what he might know. I can't promise any answers just that I will try." Violet stands too, brushing off her pants and tucking the feather in her pocket.

"Hey, we need to go back. I found something I need to check out at my family's home." Darrock stops in front of Alicorn while stuffing the documents back into the bag.

20
LAND FOUND THROUGH THE WOODS-HUNTING

"Are we truly going to see Brune? Are we ready for that?" Violet asks, turning her head back to face the wind to keep her hair out of her face.

"My father was sure that Brune was planning to do something drastic. He was worried about my safety. I just wish he had told me." Darrock clears his throat and continues. "I'm not sure I understand everything he was trying to tell me. He was very careful with his words in case Brune got her hands on the papers."

Violet can sense the tension in his body behind her on the back of the Alicorn. Instead of worrying she might fall through the sky when crossing through the portal, Violet focuses on the possibility of a confrontation at Darrock's family home.

"Explain to me again what we are looking for when we get there," Violet asks. Seeing the shimmer in the sky, she closes her eyes tight.

"I think my father hid something in his study. The key unlocks something in that room." Darrock said, but his voice fades in thought.

"You don't have any idea if it goes to a door or another trunk?" Violet had no lasting effect from the crossing this time. Maybe she will get used to it, just as Lady Zia had said.

"No, not really. I'm trying to remember what the room looked like the last time I was there, but I can't. Once my father was gone, I tried not to look too closely at his things. I only dealt with what I had to for the sake of the estate." Darrock reaches around Violet to grip the hair on the Alicorn's neck tighter. "Hold on."

Violet doesn't mind the flying, but landings are not her favorite. As the ground rushes in fast, her legs squeeze tight on the belly of the beast. Alicorn gave a great whinny at the pressure. She didn't falter on her landing despite the discomfort.

"I'm sorry. I will try to trust you more next time." Violet pats the twitching shoulder and she steps back from the white-horned creature.

"If there is a next time." Alicorn said quietly. "I don't know how much longer we have before someone figures out how to close the rest of the portals."

Darrock adjusts the bag on his shoulder before they step to the gate of the property. He couldn't help but notice that the more aggressive vines and brush were no longer choking the entrance. He had hired a grounds keeper but had no time to check in on his progress.

As he and Violet walk up to the entrance of the small estate, he could see improvements to shrubs and trees. Soon things will get cleaned up enough to have the stone walls cleaned and pealing wood trim around the windows painted. There was just so much to figure out first, such as what to do about Brune.

Climbing the stairs to the front entrance, Darrock pauses. Hand resting on the handle of the black door, he closes his eyes.

"Nothing will be the same after today." Darrock said quietly.

Violet didn't know what to say to that. She reaches out to rest her hand on his arm.

Darrock tilts his head to her, showing the lone dimple. He winks. And with a slight pause, he opens the door.

The entry hall is empty and dim. They step into the long room. Darrock closes the door behind them. Pausing, they listen for a hint of anyone else being in the house. Nothing.

"This way." Darrock says leading Violet further along the wide hallway. Nearly at the end, he stops to face a closed wooden door. "This is my father's private study." One hand on the handle, the other on the wood, he waits.

"I know this will be hard, but we need to get it done while no one is around to question what we are doing." Violet said, looking up and down the hallway.

"I find it difficult to believe we will find this treasure trove that once belonged to the Widowed King." Darrock shakes his head and opens the door.

Inside the room, windows with heavy drapes slightly open, allow daylight to pour into the room.

Dust particles float through the light.

Once inside the room, Darrock closes and locks the door behind them. Assessing the possibilities for something hidden in the space, Darrock points to a small sitting area.

"Look there, check for secret spaces or hidden objects. I do not know what we are looking for, so just try to find anything odd."

Violet moves to the small area with two deep sitting sofas facing each other. She runs her hands over the top of the cushions. The soft, worn leather shows no sign of anything out of the ordinary. She keeps feeling around the furniture.

Darrock stands in front of his father's desk. "I have been in this room countless times recently. And I still haven't looked through his things. I haven't even moved the impersonal objects just sitting here waiting to be used. The letter opener would be useful, but I haven't touched it." Lightly, one finger touches the tip of the silver serviceable object.

Violet, on her knees, lifts her head up from searching underneath the small sofa. "I am sorry you have to do this now, Darrock. Really, I am. But I am feeling a strong sense of urgency. I don't know why, but we need to get moving." Violet tried not to let his sadness distract her from the task at hand. She continues searching.

"Right." Darrock pulls his shoulders back, looks out the window at the late afternoon sunlight. He moves to the back of the desk and pulls the chair away. Fingers slide under the edge of the desktop. Opening drawers he feels for false bottoms, hidden objects, or levers of any kind. Nothing.

After several minutes spent on each space, the two look over the book shelves surrounding the sitting area. They pull books out and slide them back, touch wood edges, push and pull near seams in the trim work. Nothing.

Across the room, beside the desk, sits an empty fireplace. Though it looks abandoned and cold, there is a lack of dust on the wood mantel. The stone work above reaches to the ceiling. Each taking a side, Violet stays on the end nearer the desk. Soon she finishes and stands at the window on the same wall as the fireplace.

"Darrock, what is past this room in the hallway?" Violet asks, looking out of the window at a hard angle towards the wall continuing beyond the room. "Didn't the hallway continue on some and end at a door?"

"Yes, but the room beyond was once a servant's space. As expected, it's cramped and opens up to a small kitchen and small rooms for utilitarian purposes. We don't use them to tell you the truth. They store things from the past, I suppose." Darrock moves to a narrow stretch of wall with wood detailing to match the woodwork around the room. This differs from most as it goes floor to ceiling. The bookcase on the wall beside it runs to the doorway where they had entered the room.

His fingers push and tap, looking for anything odd. When his knuckle taps a hollow sounding spot, Violet calls him to the window.

"Something isn't making sense structurally." Violet

finishes saying, locking eyes with Darrock.

"I know why," Darrock responds. He looks out the window as she had. "I'm thinking I found a compartment or something behind that wall." His arm raises, pointing past the fireplace. They move along the wall. First, looking at the details in the woodwork.

"I don't see any obvious latch to open the wall." Darrock said, his fingers trace each notched piece of molding. On the last raised wooden notch, he pushes.

A tiny metallic click fills the silence.

Darrock looks at Violet, then back at the wall. A narrow doorway swings into the space behind the room. Too dark to see what lays beyond the entrance, Darrock turns to leave the room.

"We need light." Darrock said, coming back carrying an old-fashioned lantern. The flickering light sends golden sparks through the warm color of his eyes. After flashing Violet a grin, he turns, holding the lantern to the opening.

The light fills the forgotten space. Darrock must turn sideways and duck to fit through the passageway. Both of his feet are on the rough stone steps and he can stand up completely. With the light held high, he descends the stairs.

Violet turns herself to squeeze through the opening. With one foot in, her toe catches the bottom lip of the passage. Her right shoulder bumps into the door as she stumbles back to the left. The small door bounces closed. The metal latch echoes in the stone passage.

"Crap!" Violet says.

"Are you alright?" Darrock turns with his free hand

out to steady Violet.

"Yes. No." Violet says, getting her feet steady beneath herself on the second step.

"What?" Darrock holds the light up, running his eyes up and down Violet's shadowed form.

"I'm fine." Violet rolls her eyes, then waves a hand at the space behind her. "The door closed." Violet grabs his wrist holding the lantern, raising it up to better see the back of the closed door.

"Is there a latch to get back out?" Darrock moves closer, crowding Violet.

"There has to be, right?" Violet looks sideways at Darrock. Her free hand slides over the wood. She sees the hinges the door had opened on. Across the center, a bar meets another piece of metal running vertically along the opening edge. Then she notices the latches at the top and bottom connect to the vertical bar.

"Yes, we can get out this way when we are ready." Violet breathes a sigh of relief.

"Good. Are you ready to see what is down here now?" Darrock holds the light out over the stairs again. His shadowed gaze looks back at her. Violet nods. The realization of being in the secluded place with such a handsome man making her grow warm. Although she finds minor relief when he turns to navigate the steps descending into an unknown space.

One turn, then another, and the last step is a door somewhere under the study. A stout door with more metal than wood fortifying the entrance to an unknown place. Suddenly, Darrock feels around inside of his tunic. In the lantern light, he holds up the key from his father's box.

Violet holds her breath when the key fits inside the square metal framework with the keyhole in the center. Darrock turns the oval bow on the end of the key. The lock snags and will not turn far enough. He turns it back to the starting point. So he holds his breath and turns again. The slow spot allows the key to continue this time. The full half turn and the lock opens. Darrock pushes the door with his free hand, causing the hinges to squeak.

"If the dust wasn't enough of a clue, then these dry hinges would make it obvious that no one had been here for a long time." Violet says

In any other location, the room would be called a cellar. Stone floor, rough stone walls and a low stone ceiling with no other exit but the one they came through to get here.

"Look at all of this!" Darrock whispered.

"Oh, my." Violet absently reaches for her missing necklace standing next to Darrock in the snug room.

Old wooden shelves hold documents, scrolls, and artifacts of every kind. Darrock walks to the far wall in only a few paces. And right there, hanging on the wall, blade down, is a sword.

"This, do you know what this is?" Darrock stands in front of the silver metal holding the lantern up high.

"Of course not." Violet laughs at the child-like excitement displayed in his eyes.

"Eternos Arcanis is the Widowed King's sword. This is a legend hanging right here in my…secret room." Darrock looks around hastily to find a hook on the ceiling to hang the lantern.

"The sword has a name? As in folklore and novels of kings and knights of the round table sort of things?" Violet asks. "Sure, why not? I'm in an enchanted land with talking animals. Why wouldn't the stuff of legends be hanging around in someone's cellar?" Violet speaks to herself more than Darrock, who was trying to remove the blade from the cradle under the cross guard with gold filigree.

"Please tell me it's not a sword in the stone thing?" Violet asks.

"You are lucky I've studied in the ordinary world. You would sound crazy to most others in this world." Darrock grins at her while wiping his face across his arm. "No, that is not what is happening here." Darrock takes a step back, crosses his arms and stairs at the object hanging on the wall.

"Look at this." Darrock reaches out, pointing at the spot in the center of the cross-guard. "The decoration makes it hard to see but, it's indented in a specific shape." His voice tails off. One hand reaches inside of his tunic, pulling out the outdated coin. The golden light makes the metal of the coin glitter brightly.

Eyes connecting, they both move to the sword. The only sound in the small underground room is metal on metal as the coin seats into its home. The air vibrates at the same time as a metallic rainbow arcs down the blade and up the grip and pommel. Darrock gently wraps his fingers around the grip. His breath stills until the sword lifts from its mount on the wall.

He turns to Violet, not breaking eye contact. They

breathe with eyes wide.

"Did that just happen?" Darrock asks.

"You're from here. Why are you surprised?" Violet makes a confused, breathy laugh.

"This doesn't happen here anymore. We are talking about the ancient history of our lands. Magic isn't a thing seen in this strong of a way." Darrock surveys the room quickly.

"I don't see a scabbard or sword belt in here. I might find one that will work in our training room." Darrock steps to the door.

"You have a training room? Like, for working out or something?" Violet asks, her eyes lower to his broad shoulders briefly.

"Training as in sparing with weapons. My father insisted I learn to use swords, knives, and hand to hand combat skills. That makes since now." Darrock looks down at the beautiful sword in his hand.

Once the treasure room gets locked, Violet grabs the lantern, following Darrock up the stairs. The air, only a little less stifling, causes Violet to look around the narrow space. Holding the light overhead, she can only tell the space is at least up to the second floor of the house.

"Hold this while I get the door open." Darrock hands Violet the sword. With his back to her, he works the mechanism to let the door swing into the space.

"Why did you bring this with us? It's awkward juggling the lantern and this sword in this small space." Violet said, going down a step so Darrock can do the same to allow the door to open. Then back up the step so he can take the sword from her. Because she had never held a sword before, she couldn't figure out how to hold it without getting cut. And it was heavier than she expected it to be.

"I didn't even think about it." After Darrock steps through the narrow space, he reaches for the lantern.

"What does that mean?" Violet asks after the secret door latches behind her.

"It wasn't a decision to bring it. I just did." Darrock shrugs.

"Ok, so now what?" Violet asks.

"Stay here while I go hunt down a belt to carry this thing. We can decide what's next when I get back," Darrock said, looking around the room, then at Violet. "Make yourself comfortable." He looks at her for a second longer, then leaves the room. Hands full, the door doesn't latch behind him.

Violet looks around the room, allowing her attention to pull her to the bookshelves near the sitting area. All the books are from the enchanted lands. She doesn't know any of them. Her curiosity undeniable, Violet reaches for a leather-bound book. The smooth feel of the leather was a delight. The temptation to smell the paper and leather combination was almost greater than her resistance.

Behind her, she hears the door open and floor boards creak.

"Have you read every book? I would love to." Violet speaks while running her hand over the cover, trying to imagine what words lay on the pages.

"What is the point of that?" The woman's voice

rings out in the room.

Violet startles, dropping the book at the unexpected presence in the room.

"Oh, I'm sorry. I thought you were Darrock." Violet says, picking up the book and placing it back on the shelf. Then she turns to face the dark-haired woman, guessing she must be Brune.

"Obviously I am not. Who are you?" Brune asks, standing still inside the now closed door.

"I'm Violet, a friend of Darrock's." She says wishing he would find what he was looking for and get back ASAP.

"That is interesting." Brune walks over to the desk, leaning back against the edge of the heavy furniture. "I don't believe Darrock has any friends, at least none he has ever brought here. In particular, none he would bring into this room. My husband's study is off limits to outsiders. Now, tell me why you are truly here, Violet." Brune smiles, but it doesn't touch her eyes.

"We just stopped by for a minute. He told me to wait for him here. I don't know what's taking him so long." Violet resists the urge to look at the door. Wishing Darrock would walk through it was not helping her nerves. She had not come up with a plan to confront Brune. Now she was regretting it.

"I know precisely who you are, cousin." Brune said, and this time, the wicked smile fills her eyes.

"So you are Brune." Violet gave the best smile she could manage but could sense how taut it was.

"Stupid girl, I have no time for this dance of pleasantries. I had only just concluded that I need you to make this thing work and here you're delivered right to me," Brune said and pulls the chain at the neck of her low cut black blouse. Violet's amulet spins as Brune holds it up.

"That boy did promise he would deliver what I need. He came through this time, didn't he?" Brune laughs, her eyes sparkling.

"That's mine. How did you get it?" Violet asks, but her instinct is to grab it away from here. Something in Brune's eyes makes her hesitate.

"We are family. And this is our family heirloom that has power I need. Besides, you don't even know what exactly you had all this time." Brune says, twirling the pendant dangling on the chain.

While Brune fixates on the necklace, Violet looks her over carefully. A black blouse and skirt with ankle boots drape her curvy figure. But the intrigue comes when noticing a small dagger handle on the inside of the left boot. Is it just for decoration? Brune's overall style, being a bit goth, could account for that.

"What makes you think Darrock would be friends with you?" Brune suddenly, dropping the necklace. She tilts her head to one side.

"I don't understand why you think he wouldn't be. Besides that, what does it matter to you if we are friends or not?" Violet didn't want to give her any information that might cause trouble later. Telling her they had met in the ordinary world didn't seem right.

Brune takes a step closer to Violet, studying her.

"He might enjoy playing with you, I'll give you that. I have been working on him longer than you have."

Brune smiles.

"I'm not working on him." Violet says, narrowing her eyes but holding her ground.

"You can either help me create the world that should have been mine all along or…"Brune moves close enough for Violet to smell spiced coffee on her breath. "…you will help me and I'll destroy you when I'm done." Brune's glittering eyes pin Violet in place.

"Who do you think you are?" The moment of disbelief causes Violet to lose the only seconds she could have used for escape.

Brune leans into Violet, wrapping her long fingers tightly around her upper arm. "I am the next Queen."

Violet gasps.

"Don't scream. If you do, Dom will take care of your precious Darrock." Brune pulls Violet to the center of the room.

"I don't know who Dom is. Let me go!" Violet tries to pull her arm free.

"Stupid girl! Dom is my servant, loyal only to me. It just so happens he is a gorilla." Brune pulls Violet to the door. The madness in her eyes was raw and unhidden for all to see.

Violet can't find words. The instinct to fight back gets lost at the mention of a gorilla. It doesn't matter when Violet suddenly feels something sharp pierce the skin between two ribs on her right side.

"You didn't notice this dagger, did you?" Brune asks, pressing harder.

Violet stops struggling.

"That's right, I'm the one in control. We are leaving

now and you are going to do as I say." Brune pushes Violet to the door, waiting for her to open it.

The trembling in Violet's hand doesn't prevent her from opening the door. Nor does the weakness in her knees prevent her from passing through it when shoved. She closes the door as instructed.

"Not a sound or this blade will deflate your lung and I will be gone before you hit the ground." Brune whispers against her ear. "This land has no way to heal you, so don't forget." The moisture of Brune's breath makes Violet squirm. The blade slices skin and Brune's hand clamps on her mouth. Violet swallows the scream caused by the pain of her cut skin and panic. Every thought of using the self-defense moves from a long ago class disappears. The woman holding the dagger seems to enjoy causing pain.

Brune keeps Violet pulled firmly in front of her own taller body. One hand holding the blade now lodged into skin enough to make blood drip on her side. The other hand pressing her mouth closed so hard Violet can't move her head. Together, they walk out of the house, silently closing the door behind them.

"Mouse, I want to introduce you to someone..." Darrock is looking down at the leather belt. He adjusted with one hand while opening the door to the study with the other.

"Violet?" Darrock looks from one end of the room to the other. The pack they had carried with them still lay where he had dropped it when they arrived. The secret door remained closed.

"Mister Darrock, where did she go?" Dom asks maneuvering his wide shoulders through the doorway. He looks at the floor around the furniture. "How small is she?" The small round eyes of the gorilla raise up to Darrock expectantly.

"Ha! No, it's a nickname. She is a human girl, Dom." Darrock half laughs but rapidly frowns.

"What can I do to help you, Mister Darrock?" Dom asks, standing in his stiff, formal way.

"Stop with that, mister crap! We are alone in here." Darrock says. He waves a hand as if swatting a fly. But his gaze touches on the secret door again. Violet couldn't have gone back to the treasure room because he had the key to its door. The pack with supplies and documents lay undisturbed. Surely she would have taken the provisions with her if she hadn't wanted to wait for him to get back to the governors.

"Dom, I don't have any idea where Violet is right now. What I am positive of," Darrock looks at the bag holding the documents his father had left behind, "is that you need to know what my father found out before he died."

"I was always loyal to Mister Grail until I found out what he had done to his lady wife." Dom bowed his head, unwilling to meet Darrock's eyes.

"You are wrong about my father. She is wrong about my father." Darrock moves directly in front of the six-foot gorilla. The dark brown eyes recessed deep into the black skin lined with sadness.

"We don't have time to go through this right now.

Just know that my father was not harming that woman. He didn't kidnap their daughter either. The high courts of the land had approved the placement of Aubrey in the ordinary world away from Brune." Darrock said, seeing the truth wash over the hulking figure in front of him.

"You have proof?" Dom asks.

"Yes, and I suspect more will come to light than we have discovered. Right now, I need to find Violet." Darrock gives Dom's huge shoulder a pat as he walks past him into the hallway.

"I'm going to look for Violet." Darrock said as he walks toward the front door of the house. He lengthens his stride, heading to the sitting room. But walking into the room, he finds it empty. One hand raises, and he drags it through his hair. He drops the hand so both rest on his hips.

"Mister Darrock?" Dom says from the entrance hall.

Slowly, Darrock turns to face his lifelong friend.

"Dom, I don't know where to look for h-" Darrock hears a horse whinny and the sound of wings flapping.

"Is that an Alicorn, Young Grail?" Dom asks, though his voice is low enough to be for himself.

"The Alicorn!" Darrock grins with relief. "She must be with the Alicorn." Darrock rushes past Dom and out of the house.

"Come now!" Alicorn calls to Darrock. The great creature prances on the grass lawn near the entrance. The long white tail flips back and forth.

"She's not with you?" Darrock leaps down the

steps, one hand bracing the sword on his hip.

"No, but I know who took her. She is in danger." Alicorn stills long enough for Darrock to climb on her back.

"Mister Darrock, what can I do?" Dom asks from in front of the open doorway.

"Where is Brune?" Darrock asks as he grabs the white hair of the Alicorn.

"She was here when I arrived, just before I ran into you." Dom reaches up to pull loose the neck wear of his servant uniform. His black fur, now free, gets ruffled by the breeze.

"Follow us the best you can," Darrock said, over the sound of the massive white wings lifting the great Alicorn off the ground.

Dom rolls up his white sleeves at the same time as he kicks off shoes she ordered him to wear. Suddenly, he heaves a snort of air before vaulting himself over the railing of the small entrance space. With the grace of a wild animal, he lands in the grass practically where the Alicorn had been waiting, impatient to leave.

Massive, leathery black hands pound into the earth as Dom swings his body forward. The combination of running and vaulting keeps him close enough to follow behind the creature he had never seen in person before today.

Soon, the destination was obvious. The old castle ruins lay at the end of the rise the white-winged creature is aiming for.

21
LAND FOUND THROUGH THE WOODS-RUIN

Violet could still feel the point of the blade touching her skin. While walking with the taller woman's arms wrapping around her, the blade pricks at her flesh. The whole side of her tee-shirt, now bloody, clings to her side.

"Please, I need to slow down," Violet tries to reason with the woman.

"Shut up!" Brune hisses and mumbles to herself something unintelligible. "You are a disgrace, same as your ancestors." Brune continues to converse with herself.

The terrain raises elevation steadily. Violet stumbles. Brune stabs her fingers into Violet's shoulder length hair on the back of her head. Because she grips a fist full of hair, she drags Violet up the path to the stone ruins.

"Ah! Brune, you've got to stop." Violet scrambles on her hands and knees to keep up with the deranged woman.

"How dare you give orders to your queen!" Brune shoves her into the base of a pile of objects in the center of what must have been a room. Her outstretched arm holds the dagger pointed at Violet. Chest heaving, disheveled hair trailing down her back, Brune's eyes glisten with madness.

"I will help you. Just tell me what you want me to do." Violet said with only a slight quiver in her voice.

"I don't need you. You need me to do this. You have no future in your world or this one. If your life is going to have any purpose, you need me to use you to make a better world." Brune lowers the blade, pacing in front of Violet huddled at the base of the altar.

"How can you say that to me? I'm related to you, distant cousins. Can't we be family?" Violet feels a familiar pain triggered by the woman's words.

"You are too weak to be my family. My Aubrey is my only family. They took her from me," Brune says, her free hand rubbing her forehead.

"Who took her?" Violet asks, gradually working her legs underneath herself to a crouch.

"Her father. He did it." Brune pulls the necklace off herself, breaking the chain.

Violet rubs her wrist. While the pendent distracts Brune, Violet turns on the bracelet given to her by Lady Zia. Frantically, her eyes hunt for a tree or something near enough to touch and try to contact Lady Zia. On one side of the altar, a half dead woody vine hangs on to the pile of stones. Violet scoots sideways. When the vine is behind her shoulder, she places her bare hand on the wood. By devoting as much attention as she dares away from the dagger waving near her face, she tries to concentrate on Lady Zia.

"Brune, can you at least tell me what this place is?" Violet asks loudly, continuing to touch the vine.

"You are such a disappointment. This is our family's home. I will rebuild the castle as soon as my reign begins." Brune stops trying to open the amulet that once belonged to Violet's mother. She looks around as if seeing tall walls of stone where rubble lies.

"Did you ever see the castle while it was still standing?" Violet asks. Gradually, she slides her hand up along the vine so she can stand. Each movement pulls the cotton shirt across the cuts on her side, causing a pricking pain. Despite trying to hide her wince, her breath catches.

"How old do you think I am?" Brune whips her head around in time to see Violet wince. "That's right, don't forget I can cause you even more pain than that minor scratch." And pulling the dagger away from her target, Brune lightly taps one finger on the tip. The necklace dangling in her fist distracts her from the dagger.

Brune steps towards Violet, still pointing the sharp metal at her.

Violet nods in acknowledgment. When the tip of the blade twitches to the side, Violet jumps back a step, losing contact with the vegetation growing on the altar. The dagger continues towards her. Violet bumps into the magical objects piled on top, causing a silver wand and tortoise shell hair comb to fall to the ground.

"You careless brat! Pick those up, now." Brune hisses, stepping around Violet as she does as ordered.

"Sorry. What is this?" Violet asks. While casually doing as ordered, her mind races to soothe Brune's temper. After placing the last of the fallen items, her hand lingers as she looks to comprehend the variety of everyday objects.

Brune reaches out, grabbing Violet's wrist before she can pull it back from the hair comb.

"To anyone else, it's all useless. To me, it's all part of my plan." Brune said, shoving the large black mirror back on the raised stone altar more securely. "You will soon see—"

The sound of wings flapping in the air gets louder. A rustling sound in the trees nearby soon follows.

"You stupid girl! Come!" Brune reaches up into Violet's dark hair and fists her hand into the shiny strands. Her arm pulls back hard, forcing Violet to stumble back into the taller woman. The blade of the dagger once again presses into the fabric of her shirt on her wounded side. Brune backs towards the cliff edge.

"How did they find us so fast?" Brune mumbles.

"It's all right. Tell me what you want me to do for you." Violet glances at the tumbled stones near the edge of the once grand room's floor. Just a couple of feet and they will both be over the edge.

At the sound of footsteps, Brune tightens her grip of her fist and pulls so hard Violet's head leans back into Brune's shoulder.

Hardly able to see across the room of rubble, Violet

tries to locate where the running is coming from.

Darrock climbs over a crumbled wall of stone blocks. His eyes lock on Violet's.

"Darrock, I'm fine. Stay there. Brune and I are just talking." Violet tries to pull her head up to see him clearly.

"Be quiet, stupid girl." Brune jerks her hard enough to cause tears to blur Violet's vision.

"Brune, let Violet go and we can figure this out together." Darrock looks squarely at his stepmother. Hands out away from his hips, palms out.

"I know where you have been. You haven't been helping me, you are helping her!" Brune yells. Her eyes jump from the magical objects in front of her to Darrock and to the cliff over her shoulder.

Violet notices movement to the side in the trees has stopped. An uneasy feeling of being watched tingles along her skin. As Brune focuses on Darrock, her grip lessens a fraction. Ever so slightly, Violet lifts her head enough to survey the trees on two sides of the ruins.

"That's not true. I've been trying to find answers for us." Darrock gestures from himself to Brune. He fiercely holds eye contact with her.

"Why didn't you bring her to me right away?" Brune steps closer to the altar nudging Violet.

"You didn't tell me to. Look, I found my father's treasures." Darrock points to the sword on his hip. Two steps closer to the altar, but he stops when Brune points the dagger at him, then back at Violet's side.

"How did — but where was — give it to me!" Brune shoves Violet face first, onto the pile of objects on the altar. A jumble of metal clatters with the shift and several objects drop to the stone floor.

Violet, bent at the waist, leaning over with arms outstretched on the collection of pieces. The necklace, still dangling from Brune's hand with the dagger, thuds at Violet's back when the dagger points at her neck.

When Violet carefully raises her cheek up off the smooth surface of the mirror, a faint shimmer of light flashes. It's just enough for a gray face to wink at Violet. The electric pulse of adrenalin surges through her veins before she can control her reaction. The warm hand splayed on Violet's back doesn't respond. Violet winks back at the empty mouthed face.

"Can't you let the little mouse go now?" Darrock asks, dropping his hands to rest on the belt of the sword. He takes a step sideways, closer to his stepmother.

"Of course not! I need her blood to work this thing." Brune lifts the hand holding the dagger to show the amulet dangling from the chain wrapped around her hand.

"There's plenty on her side. Just use that." Darrock motions with one hand while taking another step closer.

"You fool, she must choose to do it." Brune says removing her hand from Violet's back to push her hair off her sweating forehead. Her eyes search the trees and brush surrounding the castle ruins. Subtle noises in the leaves fill the warm evening air.

"I won't help you." Violet says before her brain has time to consider the words.

The tip of the dagger moves up from between her shoulders to the base of her skull.

"Do you know what happens if I slide this blade into you right here?" Brune leans closer to the side of Violet's head, whispering.

Suddenly, the branches hanging above the ruins shake, causing leaves to fall. Between Darrock and Brune, a large dark figure drops to the ground.

"Dom! What took you so long?" Brune jumps. She pulls the dagger back to see red on the tip of the metal. "Look what you nearly made me do! I need her alive for now, you worthless—"

"Brune, I couldn't find you. We were to meet at the estate. Only because I saw young Grail rushing here did I even find you." Dom stands facing the woman as if he is bringing the mail and not witnessing her holding a young woman at dagger point.

Violet clinches her jaw with the stab of pain at the base of her hairline. Movement in the mirror under her face catches her attention. A small scroll unrolls where only she can see. Then writing materializes as if written by an invisible hand.

Behind Dom, wings stir up the wind, drawing the attention of everyone but Violet. The great owl lands on a partially erect wall of stone blocks.

"Contessa, I don't recall inviting you here," Brune snaps.

"I don't need an invitation to be sure you are successful, now do I?" Contessa Fusco flexes her metal fabricated wing, punctuating the movement with the snip of a small pair of rusty scissors at the tip of the wing.

"Where is my daughter, Dom?" Brune leans back from Violet, waiting for the answer.

"I could not get to her. You know I am not free to travel in the ordinary world." Dom said, the six-foot silver back gorilla unmoving.

"You failed me." Brune drops her chin to her chest. Her disheveled black hair shielding her face from the others.

The sound of hooves clomping on the remaining stone tiles covering the floor fills the air. Darrock glances over his shoulder, Dom turns to face the white creature, and Brune lifts her head.

Eyes glittering, Brune vibrates with tightly wound excitement at the sight of her best chance at accomplishing her plan. "Dom, I want that horn," Brune says in hushed tones, as if afraid of scaring the creature away.

The magnificent creature stands facing the altar with tail swishing. A loud whinny echos up through the trees as a hoof pounds the stone where it stands.

"That I cannot do, Brune." Dom says just as quietly.

"You will! Don't make me tell the world what you have done. You will lose everything." Brune hisses the words, keeping her glittery eyes on the rare magical creature.

Dom turns to Darrock. "I must do this." The gorilla says, advancing forward.

"I can't let you." Darrock draws the Widowed King's sword.

Dom draws his own sword and the two clang

together between them.

"Dom, kill him. I have no use for him now." Brune says in a tone used for ordering tea from a servant.

"Why would you do any of this?" Violet asks.

"Why wouldn't I?" Brune pulls Violet upright by her hair. "Take this and make it work."

Darrock steps back as Dom advances with his giant muscular arms, expertly maneuvering his sword.

"I'm too strong for you, mister Darrock." Dom's black lips part, showing his white fangs.

"True, but I know your every move." Darrock blocks his opponent's sword and spins to his left. While crouching, he swings out his own sword at the black gorilla's knees.

The tip catches the outside of one fur covered leg, causing a dark bloody scratch to form.

"You're not too light on your feet, old friend." Darrock stands waiting for the next move from his opponent.

"Don't make me hurt you, young Grail." Dom says with a loud snort.

"She doesn't deserve your loyalty, Dom." Darrock says when they come together with swords clanging against each other.

"What old Grail did to her was unforgivable." Dom shoves the weaker man back.

"Father found the best care for Aubrey. He had no choice but to take her away from Brune's madness." Darrock found himself backed into the Alicorn.

As the gorilla advances, he hears a voice in his head tell him to use the sword as its design intended.

"What?" Darrock asks, scowling at the large white head near his shoulder. The wing at his back shoves him forward.

One hand on the grip, the other on the pommel, Darrock looks at the coin sunk into the cross guard. The Widowed King comes to mind as Dom advances.

A hair's breadth before the swords clang together, Darrock's hands sense a vibration in the steel. As before, a metallic rainbow runs the length of the blade.

The sound of metal hitting metal bounced off the crumbled stone. But Dom gets forced back two steps by the impact and Darrock remains in place.

Again, the opponents come together with swords swinging with controlled strength. The same force propels Dom backwards.

"Whatever Brune has told you my father did is a lie," Darrock says, lowering his own sword.

Dom stands still. Sword in one hand, he uses the other thick leathered hand to rub his own face.

"She has many lies on many people." Dom lowers his sword and turns to Brune.

"Why can't any of you just do what you're told?" Brune's voice raises.

The owl stretches out her wings, drawing the attention of everyone.

"Young man?" Contessa's voice calls out.

Darrock looks to see where Brune's dagger is before responding. "Yes?"

"I think it's time you learn the truth." Contessa says, leaping into the air. She swoops low in a slow glide before flying up to land on the back of the Alicorn.

The pale beast snorts as horses do, shaking its head hard enough to toss its mane side to side.

"What truth?" Darrock backs from the circle, looking one direction to the other. The great horned owl is dangerous even without the hidden weapon in the feathers and metal parts of her wing. The beak and talons could do great harm on their own.

Violet watches the drama unfolding in front of her. Brune, being distracted by the others, continues to mumble to herself. While having forgotten, she told Violet to use the family heirloom now clutched in her hand. But controlling her breathing is the only thing she can focus on so as not to catch Brune's attention.

"Your father is dead because of Dom. He arranged it." Contessa purrs the words from her perch on the Alicorn's back.

Darrock whips his head around to Dom standing stiff as the soldier he had been while serving with his father.

"That's right, Contessa saw Dom make the arrangements." Brune spoke with such excitement, everyone turns to look at the wild-eyed woman.

"Dom?" Darrock questions with such steely quiet, the forest around the ruins still.

"I never intended—" Dom said, taking a step in Darrock's direction. He stops when the tip of Darrock's blade raises to the base of his black-haired neck.

"I've known you my entire life. How could you?" Darrock's voice, thick with emotion, is hardly a whisper.

Violet feels Brune loosen pressure on her back. The drama unfolding in front of them, capturing her full attention.

"Darrock, wait. Think about this." Violet set aside her own fears, pulling away from Brune. Desperate to get Darrock's attention and avoid Brune's grasp.

Behind Dom, they can hear many footsteps coming along the path. Still, no one moves. The questions hang in the air.

"Enough of this! Get me that horn, Contessa." Brune grabs Violet's hand containing the amulet. "Make it work."

Before Violet can respond, the amulet falls to the stone floor, rolling behind Violet towards the edge of the cliff. Lord Stone steps around a pile of tumbled blocks of a long ago wall. He places his hand on top of Darrock's sword hand, pushing it away from the hulking gorilla.

Out of frustration, Brune lets go of Violet, bending to grab the necklace. Violet turns as the long fingers of the other woman reach out. While she grabs at the chain slipping through a small opening in the crumbled stones. Violet readies as much force as she can and shoves into the side of Brune's hip. The woman screams as her long hair tangles around her face.

Violet grabs the black frame of the magic mirror and runs around the altar to Darrock.

"You need to see this," Violet says, looking around at the stones piled around the edge of the once grand room. Sure to place it securely, she props the intricately carved frame on a ledge. And she stands beside

Darrock for everyone to see the reflective glass. But they only to see the people and things around them being reflected.

Darrock runs his free hand down his face. All traces of unshed tears blinked away. His rigid jaw was the only sign he was still dealing with the betrayal of his father's closest friend.

"Magic one, in the mirror, tell us the truth." Lord Stone rests a hand on Darrock's shoulder.

"I will shatter you and grind your glass into powder if you obey any command but my own." Brune says as she brushes her hair from her face and shakes out her skirt. Her back to the cliff as she stands with the dagger at her feet.

"Lady of the Last King's lineage, you know I am bound to respond according to the enchantments placed upon my being." The mirror glows with a blue gray light, giving the face an unearthly glow. The hollow mouth grins devilishly.

"I have learned this widow has spun a tale to trap this most faithful servant to do her bidding. What can you show us?" Lord Callahan Stone steps back, allowing Darrock and Dom a clear view.

"Thank you Lord, I long to do as you bid." The mirror fades to a smoky black with gray clouds coiling and swirling as if the mirror is not flat but as deep as infinity. Gradually, the light brightens to display a figure, Brune's late husband. He walks hand in hand with a young girl. The voice of the enchanted looking glass speaks.

"Grail found help for his young daughter in the

ordinary world. She once had no words to share. The magic she needed did not exist in this land. When Grail returned to his broken wife, she devised her revenge." The image changes to show Brune searching the estate for something unidentified.

"But it doesn't matter. You can't stop what I've already begun. The portals are unstable now. Closing them is the only answer." Brune lifts her skirts, looking for the amulet along the edge of the cliff.

"What were you looking for, Mother Brune?" Darrock turns to ask her. His eyes crease at the corners, waiting.

"You are wearing it, boy," Brune said. Her eyes dart to the sword. "Stop calling me mother. I never wanted to be your mother. You would have been gone a long time ago if I had my way." Brune moves over to another pile of stones along the edge, bending to look in the cracks. Stopping, she stands to face Darrock.

"Your father was so infuriating. He blocked my efforts at every turn. Once my child was in the world, he changed so much." Brune's head tilts to one side and her eyes drift to another place in time.

"The treasures from another time indeed. She could never convince Grail to share his knowledge of the Widowed King." Mirror brightens with his words, then dims.

"You got your way. Father sent me away nearly from the moment you married." Darrock forces the words past clinched teeth.

"That is not what I wanted. I wanted you dead." Brune turns to continue looking for the amulet.

Contessa gives up on picking at the Alicorn's horn. Then she flies to the stones near Brune and tilts her head awkwardly to search in the rubble as well.

"Fine, you didn't want his dead wife's child in your way. Tell me the truth, Brune. How did my father die?" Darrock moves until the altar is the only thing preventing him from reaching her.

"Stupid boy, I did it! I paid to have him killed in the ordinary world. He kept getting in my way. He took my daughter. The blood I need to make everything right. Your saintly father, while alive, turned everyone against me. Everyone obeyed HIM. In my home, I had no power." Brune stops looking and begins pacing. The dagger moves from one hand to the other while she wipes her palm on her skirt. Back in her right hand, the woman points at Violet.

"That brat had the amulet that should have been mine. I don't know how you got your little hands on it, but you couldn't keep it from me once you came into this world." Brune shook with anger, but suddenly a smile pulls the corners of her mouth taught.

"As soon as I find it, you are going to put your blood on it and close this world off from the ordinary one. I will be queen and everyone will bow to me." Brune reaches for the fallen magical objects clumsily, putting them back on the altar.

"This must stop. We can see you get help, Brune." Lady Zia says from behind Dom's wide form at the edge of the ruins. She steps between the men near the mirror.

"Help?" Brune calls out from her bent posture,

searching for the object in the stones.

"Brune, please hear me." Lady Zia holds her hand out behind her to prevent any other from following her. Her daughter, Gryphin, and Cacey crowd into the edge of the room. "The ordinary world has made great strides in medical care for things we don't yet understand in this world. Your husband's Great Aunt Carmilla told Callahan that was the plan all along." Lady Zia stopped beside the altar when Brune suddenly stands facing her.

"Lies! He was no saint. I know what happened in my marriage." Brune looks around at the faces of each person present. A crease forms in between her eyes. Tears gather, but she doesn't blink.

Violet moves to the other side of the altar, holding out a hand. "Please let me help you Brune." Chest unmoving, she watches the pale face of the woman in front of her.

Brune reaches out but pauses just inches from clasping Violet's open hand. The antique gold pendent falls to dangle below Brune's fisted hand.

A harsh gasp of air pulls into Violet's chest, followed by a squeal of pain. The glint of silver visible before the dagger in Brune's other hand swipes across Violet's palm. She slams the amulet on top of the red streak.

Once her own fist is open, Brune more carefully slices her own flesh. The long fingers wrap around Violet's hand, pressing the amulet between the two bloody palms. Brune pulls Violet to face the altar and raises their hands into the air.

Mumbled words pass between Brune's lips as her eyes close. Her head raised to the sky, she repeats the same mumblings.

Nothing happens. No one moves.

At the far side of the once grand room, movement draws everyone but the chanting lady's attention. Slowly, the figure draws nearer to the ruins. The silhouette of a pointed hat with a wide brim is obvious. Layered lace skirts swish with each step up to the floor. When the dark hat trimmed with a peacock's feather raises to reveal the green complexion of the lady of the woods, the onlookers step back. Violet locks eyes with the lady. The barest of nods from the woman is the only permission she needs to speak.

"Brune, this won't work. I think you know it won't." Violet says softly. Turning to the taller woman still grasping her hand. No visible reaction.

"Child, it is pointless." Wilga says in her no nonsense way.

The words stop when Brune's entire body flinches at the sound of the woman.

"What do you want, witch?" Brune sneers.

"You are not the one in the words of the old scroll. Your Aubrey is the only one of us that can do this with Violet." Wilga steps closer to the altar. "Let the girl go. Return these useless objects."

The magic mirror coughs with indignation. Wilga flashes it a brief glare, and the light goes dark.

"Brune, take the help you're being offered and let go of a past that is not yours to lay claim to. Your ancestors chose their path as you must do. Erasing their choices is not the way." Wilga holds a hand out to Violet. Her eyes leveled on Brune's.

Suddenly, Brune releases Violet, leaving the amulet on the younger woman's hand. While using both hands to clutch her black skirt, she still holds the dagger. A step backwards from the altar. Her head bowed with black hair falling around her face, she takes another step away from the magical objects.

"This didn't have to be this way. If all of you had helped me do this, I could have been a great queen." Brune said. Her shoulders slump so much as to appear shrunken.

Defeat in the air, Contessa takes flight. She perches outside of the ruins, in the trees. Several onlookers move back, allowing a bit of privacy for the defeated woman.

"I will go with you until we find you the best help." Lady Zia speaks softly. She leans closer, but when Brune doesn't look at her, she steps back.

"Brune?" Violet asks, trying to see through the dark waves of hair shielding the eyes of the woman in front of her.

"Don't." Wilga says simply.

Brune looks up, locking stark eyes on the old lady of the woods. Two calm steps back and Brune leans backwards. As if in slow motion, she disappears from view.

No sound, no scream, not even a moan when the thud comes to those still rooted in the ruins on the cliff. Disbelief keeps the onlookers rooted in place. It happened so calmly. No crying, no goodbyes, as Wilga was the only one that could see the intention in the woman.

Lady Zia and Violet step to the edge to look at the broken body of the broken soul. She lay in the center of a ring of flowers blooming out of season at the base of the cliff. Violet brushes away the tears on her cheeks. Lady Zia clears her throat as her right hand rests on her chest. She closes her eyes.

"Come ladies, we must try to repair the link tying the lands together. I fear the longer the instability lingers, it may become lost to us," Wilga says. Yet her gaze remains cast out to the treetops beyond the edge of the cliff.

"What should we…" Violet looks at Lady Zia, then to the sorrow filled eyes under the wide brim of the hat.

"I will see to her once we finish." Wilga pulls her eyes to Violet briefly. "Come now, gather around the altar. Perhaps we can make this mess useful." Her green hands motion to the pile of objects. Then they rummage through the layers of lace and black cotton folds of her clothing. One hand disappears long enough to pull a worn leather-bound book from the deep recesses.

The odd woman arranges the objects in front of her, making a flat spot to open the yellowed pages of the book in front of herself. The dark red fingernails slip between pages near the back of the book. Soon her long index finger follows the handwritten text on a particular page.

"Come everyone, gather around here." Wilga says

without raising her gaze. The wide brim of her dark hat shields the old book from inspection of anyone coming to the altar. Lord and Lady Stone stand next to each other. Darrock moves up next, followed by Bijou and Gryphin holding Cacey. Alicorn steps back from the ruins, continuing to be a witness to the choices the beings of both worlds make.

Wilga tilts the brim of her hat to the side enough to see the position taken by the white-winged creature. No words, just a slight shake side to side of her head and she returns focus to the book.

No one questions what the ageless woman is doing. Those gathered wait for instruction, but the only sounds are that of the woods.

"The magic to do what we require does not exist in any one being in this generation. The power of life got dispersed throughout the worlds. It echoes in every living thing. In theory, when enough of those echoes gather, one may harness them. Set your intentions to healing the portals. Think only of the balance between worlds." The Lady of the Woods speaks tenderly. Her voice filling the ruins despite the intimate tone.

"The amulet." Wilga holds out her hand to Violet.

Without hesitation, Violet places the object with the broken chain in her palm.

Wilga turns the piece over in her hand so the back, with a very slight dimple, is visible. Her long bony thumb gently presses the spot. Long enough passes that those watching look at each other curiously. Still as a statue, Wilga waits until suddenly the magical object hums in mechanical vibration as it did for Violet before these events unfolded.

22

LAND FOUND THROUGH THE WOODS-RESTORE

"You do the same." Wilga says to Violet, handing her the amulet. Violet repeats the same act that had shocked her the day she first passed through the portal to Maple Haven. She and Wilga each rub their thumbs to soothe the prick of the skin.

The Lady of the Woods motions for Violet to place the necklace on the altar with everything else magical. Once placed, Wilga bows her head to read from the book.

"Set your mind with intention." A reminder to the onlookers, she returns to saying words they cannot hear or understand.

The air around the ruins becomes heavy with the atmospheric pressure of a large storm. With the summer sky clear, the blue dazzles. Yet the woods become quiet.

The ground under their feet rumbles hard enough everyone reached for the altar to keep from falling. A few stones tumble to the ground outside of the ruins.

Heads turn to be sure nothing threatens to fall on anyone present.

Above the altar, above the trees, the air sparks and flashes. A musical sound draws near the spectacle. Heads raise to see the phoenix circling through the pop and crackle of light. The tune growing louder. With each spiral, the bird rises higher, pulling the light with it.

The crimson and gold bird moves to the center of the mass. Head pointing up to the heavens, wings stretch out with the mass of tail feathers pointing to the altar. The creature spins as a toy top. It becomes a blur of red and glows gold, bursting with flickering flames.

A collective gasp comes from the ones gripping the altar for stability as they crane their necks to see the spectacle. The rumbling in the ground slows, and the air grows lighter while more energy pulls into the orb.

"Focus on restoring balance." Wilga's voice blankets the participants. As the light gets too bright, heads bow and eyes close.

A burst of energy pushes out from the center of the golden glow. Quiet now, calm and back to normal, eyes open. A flurry of feather light ash flutters from the sky to land on hair, skin and the ruins. A black ash with a subtle burnt spicy scent.

By the time the sky is empty, the clomping of hooves draws near the gathering. Soon, each one present is waiting expectantly for the great Alicorn to speak. And for the explanation of the event they just saw.

Violet nods to the Alicorn and walks around the altar to stand in front of the gentle creature. The two converse in their own private manner. But the only sign to those watching is a tear on Violet's cheek. The velvety muzzle of the horse-like creature rubs into the young woman's shoulder for a moment.

"Soon I will send a gift to this one. Do each of you vow to protect my last gift?" Tall and proud, the thick neck fringed with long white hair twitches with the waiting.

Every head nods in agreement. The beast raises up on hind legs, letting loose a whinny toward the sky. Hooves pound the stone tile floor. Several hard snorts and Alicorn steps back from the ruins and takes flight.

"What just happened?" Gryphin spoke the words everyone had been thinking.

"Precisely what needed to happen." Wilga blows the flakes of ash from the pages of the book before closing it. She tucks it away in her garments. One hand, then the other, rooting around in the folds of her clothes. She pulls out an empty glass bottle with a stopper. Swiftly, she opens the bottle and without touching the ash, she fills the bottle and returns the stopper.

"The ash of a phoenix is a rare thing indeed." Wilga said. Once she has the now black bottle squirreled away, she pats the stash and the lines on her upper lip smooth, nearly to a grin.

Turning to leave the ruins, Violet is in her path. Wilga raises a hand, palm open, facing Violet.

"I know questions are racing around that head of

yours. No, no need to talk and explain everything. You saw and were a part of something that saved the connections to our worlds. You and I used our blood on the amulet, yes. That answer will come to you someday, my dear." She grabs the folds of her skirts, raising them to step over and around the fallen stones.

"I have work to do." Wilga pauses and steps back to Violet. In order to lock eyes with Violet, she tilts her head to one side. A quick nod and she produces the old book she had only just stored away. With both hands clasping the book, she holds it out to Violet.

"What?" Violet asks, a crease between her brows appearing.

"Take it." Wilga said. With book outstretched, waiting.

"I can't." Violet holds her hands up, palms facing Wilga.

Wilga steps forward, shoving the book into Violet's hands. One hand under the book with the other forcing one of Violet's onto the top of the book.

"This was mine. Now, yours. Keep it safe and use it for its natural purpose only." Wilga speaks with her eyes continuing to see into the confusion filled eyes of Violet. Then she releases her grasp and Violet drops her gaze to the scuffed up leather cover.

By the time Violet looks up, Wilga is a dark shadow in the tree line beyond the ruins.

"Wait!" Violet calls out, remembering Wilga's words she will see to the broken woman at the base of the cliff.

"Oh! Look!" Bijou is standing at the edge, leaning

over stone rubble.

Everyone crowds around to see the mossy patch at the base of the stone wall. The body of Brune Grail is gone. No patch of blood. Nothing to tell the story of the woman that grew too mad for the world in which she lived.

Violet looks at Lady Zia and pulls back from the edge.

"Those flowers were not so overgrown as that when we looked earlier. Were they?" Violet hugs the book to her chest, still clutching the amulet in one hand.

Lady Zia can only shake her head in agreement with Violet's assessment of the ring of flowers.

"It's time I try to get back home." Violet says to the two people standing in the cobble stone alleyway with her.

"You are welcome back anytime. Don't forget." Lady Zia wraps her arms around Violet for another quick hug.

"I have heard this a dozen times just while walking here. Bijou said it another half dozen before she went home too." Violet rolls her eyes, but the smile never leaves her face.

"We mean it. Please let us know how you are and what you find in that book." Lady Zia walks backwards to wave and then turns to leave.

"You have made quite an impression on the people here." Darrock says, leaning on the brick wall behind him.

"Are you kidding me? They have made an impression on me!" Violet says, voice raising somewhat.

"What about us now?" Darrock asks, emptying his face of emotion.

"Is there a need to rush this?" Violet levels her gaze to his.

"Nope." Darrock says, motionless.

"Then can we just find our normal before we decide what we are?" Violet eases forward and clutches the strap of the bag on her shoulder.

Darrock's one-sided grin warms Violet in a tingling way. He takes both of her hands into his.

"I think we both have a lot to understand first." He releases one hand and walks her to the end of the alleyway facing the stone wall.

Since she knows it's time to cross in to the ordinary world, Violet reaches for the bag containing the book and amulet. She knows the chain needs repaired soon. Crossing would be more convenient if she could wear it.

"Wait, try to cross without it. A lot has happened since you tried this. Maybe you don't need it." Darrock leans his forehead to Violet's and squeezes her hand. And just as swiftly, he lets go and steps back. "I see the woods and a pointed pillar, do you?" He asks, looking through the portal.

Violet feels nervous energy rolling through her body. What did it mean if she couldn't do this without the amulet? Did it even mean anything? So, pulling her hand out of the bag, she turns from Darrock to the wall. With her eyes closed, she takes a deep breath. Another deep breath. She shakes her shoulders to loosen the tensions there.

So she opens her eyes to see shimmering waves of light sparking in front of, in, and through the wall. The stones fade and deep green trees materialize. Violet's hands clutch at the dirty tee shirt on her stomach.

"I can see it!" The words whisper past her lips.

"Maybe you could the whole time but didn't believe you could," Darrock said quietly. His eyes fixed on the young woman leaving the world he was born to serve, as was his heritage.

"Darrock?" Violet turns her head back to see him.

"Yes."

"Come see me tomorrow." Violet says.

"I thought you'd never ask." Darrock smiles widely.

Violet steps through the portal with a smile she can't force herself to stop. The reason she had run to the enchanted world in the first place felt removed from who she became on this journey. Yet the cause of that pain must get sorted out now. A shower and then she will find her dad.

23
HOUSE BY THE WOODS-
UNDERSTANDING

It didn't surprise Violet that her dad was not home when she walked into the house. So many things were rolling around in her head she better not talk to him first.

She drops her bag on her bed, grabbing clean clothes for a relaxing shower.

"Wow." she pulls her nose away from her underarm. The smell is coming from more than her clothes. She laughs to herself.

Turning around in the middle of her room. This home coming feels different from her time away at college. But nothing had changed. No one had touched the things in her room. Even Cacey's cage sat in the same spot. It needs to go; she notes to herself.

The room she had, even before her mother's death, suddenly felt so different. Even the walls seem closer or something. The colors, less bright than they once were. Old notes on the bulletin board, faded and unimportant.

As much as she wants to get clean, she knows the cuts will sting. Violet had avoided taking stock of her small wounds but dreads the soap calling out each one. She walks out of the room to get the much needed shower.

Only while rinsing her hair in the shower's spray does the random observances align. Parts of her relationship with her dad bubble up with different perspectives than she had considered. Her grief at losing her mother shifts as well. Observations from the past few days try to surface, but she pushes them aside.

The lavender scent from her body wash fills the steamy air. Safe in the warm cocoon of the bathroom gives her courage to face the reality of her past and present with her dad. The memories of her mother don't seem so painful as she looks around at the cheerful butter yellow walls. After tying the sash on her robe, her hand reaches out to touch the white ruffled curtain on the window at the end of the room. The window, open a few inches, allows the late afternoon air to flutter past the fabric.

A memory of sitting on her mother's lap at the sewing machine drifts in her mind as if the breeze carries it. A radio plays somewhere. The scent of freshly washed fabric mingles with the shea butter lotion her mother had just used. Not recalling the words, she remembers the hum of her mother's voice in her ear telling her where to place her hands to keep them safe from the needle.

The pain she thought would stab her chest never came. And the joy of the love her mother gave to her warms a lonely place. Her tears also never came. This little room, the others in this house, will continue to spark memories she had been pushing away to avoid the pain. She understands this pain does not have to come.

Violet unfolds that knowledge while she dresses and readies herself for the conversation she needs, and wants, to have with her dad. Only when she feels ready does she go to the kitchen for a snack. She is not as hungry as she should be. Violet realizes she needs to speak to her dad before she can enjoy a full meal.

The porch steps call to her as much as they had as a child. As the screen door creaks and thwacks closed, the feeling of being home fills her like she hasn't felt in years. Violet sits in the same place she did as a small girl. A sense of nostalgia washes over her. While looking out at the woods, she rests her chin on her palm. Knees holding her arms, Violet just breathes in the familiarity.

Crickets chirping, birds calming to settle into their nests, just a few lightning bugs wink at the line of trees. The season is too late for many to still be active. Randomly, Violet wonders if lightning bugs can talk in the enchanted lands. Along with considering the questions she could ask them? And then what could they tell her? She smiles to herself, continuing to let her mind wonder.

Not realizing her eyes had closed, and the stars had appeared. Violet heard her dad's truck pull into the gravel drive. With no need to move, she waits for him to come around to the steps.

"I need to talk to you, Dad." Violet says from her spot, leaning on the post next to her perch on the steps.

"I didn't know where you were the pasts few days." He said, putting his hand into his pockets.

"You didn't call my phone." The words she speaks are just a statement.

"True." After a moment, he sits next to her on the top step. They both look out across the grass lawn, beyond the tall tree to one side, on to the woods.

"I want you in my life in whatever way you can handle." Violet says in a low, firm voice. Before going on, she clasps her hands between her knees. "That said, I'm not taking part in your drama, dysfunctional coping stupidity or whatever you choose. I'm not helping you get out of messes or taking care of you. That is on you." She waits, eyes jumping from his profile back to the woods.

"You're right." He sits with an elbow on his knees, dropping his gaze at the step between his dirty worn-out boots.

Violet waits to see if he will say more. Afraid there will be. Afraid there won't be.

He is silent.

Assessing what she needs from this broken man is the only thing she can safely do. The smell of beer wafts from his direction. Nothing clinches in her gut. No disappointment jumps to the front of the cue, ready to spill out onto the injustice of her life.

"I'm choosing to have my own life now, Dad." Violet said.

He nods jerkily.

Along with releasing a deep breath, Violet lets go of expectation.

"I met a guy." She grins and, despite being a grown woman, she wraps her hands around her ankles and rests her chin on her knees.

After a moment, his head lifts, and he gazes at the woods again.

"When can I meet him?" The weight of the world lies in the words, but the effort shows.

"Well, he's coming over tomorrow." Violet chuckles and lifts her chin. "I'm hungry. Want something to eat?" Violet stands up and moves across the porch to the screen door.

The night before, sleep came easy. She slept deep and didn't wake as early as she normally did. Unaccustomed to late morning wake ups, she felt the day was passing too fast. But it did not surprise Violet to find the kitchen empty, her father having gone to work.

The weight of having lots to do keeps pressing in on her. Moving through cleaning her room, taking out trash in the kitchen and general cleaning from their late meal the night before still didn't squash the feeling.

Now, walking into the edge of the trees bordering her house energizes her to hurry to the stone marker. The dappled sunlight soon was gone completely as the woods become more dense. The path narrows as ferns and low brush crowd over it.

Before Violet has time to examine her happiness,

the path turns, and she hops over the hidden boulder this time. She stops at the stone pillar and rests a hand on it. Violet realizes she didn't bring her necklace, the Proclivitas Amulet. She turns the name of the object over in her mind several times. Then she looks at the base of the old land marker. A large fern is obscuring what looks to be brown fabric.

Violet squats, pushing back the arching branches of the plant. The fabric looks two feet long. One arm holding back the leaves as one hand reaches out to retrieve the unknown object the fabric covers.

Her hand pauses suddenly. Is the object intended for her? Then she remembers the Alicorn's words. She promised she was giving something to her. Her hand lands on the rough brown fabric. She pulls back as if scorched. The woods are quieter than usual. She realizes not even the magnificent stag is lurking around the way he always had done.

Confident she has no witnesses, Violet lifts the object from the brush. She stands to assess it. Heavier than she had expected it to be. It wasn't as slick as it looked, either. Again, sure no one is watching her, she pulls a lacing cord loose from loops along the length. She maneuvers the long piece from the wrap carefully. Unable to stop the shallow breaths, she works as delicately as possible.

When the fabric falls to the ground, her fingers connect with the pearly iridescent, tapered horn. Knowing it had been on the crown of the Alicorn causes mixed feelings. A warm tingle pulses at every point of contact her skin makes.

A lone tear falls from her eye. Knowledge of the Alicorn no longer living in this time and place stuns her. While her emotions run high, the weight of the sad mission takes over. She will figure out the purpose of this gift and many other mysteries, eventually.

Violet takes care to wrap the exquisite piece back into the brown fabric. She needs to find a room at home to keep the enchanted objects safe. It will be time to start veterinarian schooling too soon. She didn't want to leave them for just anyone to find.

The portal next to her shimmers with movement. Surprise promptly turns into warmth when Darrock walks into her woods. One arm holding the gift, Violet reaches up to wrap the other around his neck for a quick hug.

"Hey, Mouse! How's it going?" Darrock's eyes touch her while his hands pull back to hook on his jean pockets.

"I'm surprised you're here, especially when I'm standing right at the portal, but I won't question it. I'm just glad to see you," Violet says. And she moves back a step, forgetting her surroundings. So she trips over the boulder under the brush. Darrock reaches out, grabbing her arms, preventing the fall.

"Crap, thanks." Violet says, cheeks turning pink.

"No worries, Mouse." He rubs his thumbs on the bare skin of her arms before letting go.

"Mouse?" Violet asks. Her giggle floating in the air as she ignores the electric tingle on her skin.

Darrock nods, chuckling. She shakes her head, sure she will never tell him how she secretly likes when he uses the nickname.

"You are just in time to help me figure out a problem." Violet says, leading the way back through the forest on her favorite path.

"Haven't we dealt with enough problems for a lifetime?" Darrock wearing blue jeans and a tee shirt from the ordinary world continues to follow her.

"Oh, I agree with that. This is less than life or death. I need a place to hide valuables when I'm not at home," Violet lifts the brown fabric when she mentions valuables.

"Do I want to know?" Darrock asks.

"I doubt it." The grin Violet tosses over her shoulder teases more than she intends. Darrock follows her with his own chuckle. Emerging from the woods side by side, talking in hushed tones until they reach her house by the woods.

"My dad is at work. I think he wants to meet you later if he gets home before you leave." Violet says, standing on the bottom step leading to the front door.

"That's fine. Fair warning, I have little experience with this parent meeting thing, so keep your expectations low." Darrock steps so close his toes touch the base of the step. He hardly needs to look down to be eye level with her.

"No pressure. Honest. No labels yet, right?" Violet said. She finds it difficult to breathe with Darrock so close. Although his fresh, musky scent feels familiar and exhilarating at the same time. She had to remind herself to avoid falling too deep, too fast with Darrock. Temptation is far too real.

"Right." Darrock looks at her lips, then back to her eyes and waits.

Violet leans into the gentle kiss. When she pulls back, she leans her head on his shoulder. His arms wrap around her. They stand this way for seconds, both breathing in the other's nearness. Nothing wrong with enjoying the moment, the wonder of feelings never experienced. Violet grins when she pulls back.

"Now, come help me figure this out." Violet turns, leading the way into the house and up the stairs. Darrock follows without question.

At the top, they stand in the hallway. One direction is her dad's room and the bathroom. She turns to her room and the unused room at the end.

"I'm thinking this unfinished space will work." Violet opens the door opposite her own and brushes a cobweb from the air. "It was likely used long ago." They both step into the space full of cast off trunks, furniture and plenty of dust.

Darrock walks in as far as he can and faces the doorway. He squints, looking up at the loft. "What is up there?" Darrock points to exposed wall joists reaching higher than the ceiling. Atop the second floor is unfinished and open to the roof peak.

Violet turns near the door and flips a switch, turning on power to exposed bulb light fixtures throughout the space. "I've never been up there. I only explored this room." Violet says, pointing to the floor. So she stands next to Darrock on her tiptoes, trying to see as much as possible of the attic space.

"Look around in here for a ladder. I remember

seeing one once, I think. I'm going to get the amulet and book from Wilga. We can hide them up there if it looks safe enough." Violet says. Laying the horn on an over-stuffed chair with torn fabric on one armrest.

She was back to see Darrock's feet leave the ladder to stand in the open space. The bag with the book and necklace on one shoulder. Violet grasps the horn in one hand, ready to climb the ladder herself.

"Here." Darrock reaches out to grab the horn. Once he sets it aside, she climbs onto the floor beside him.

"That ladder nearly isn't tall enough for me to make it." Violet says with a smile, brushing dust off of herself.

"Any idea what is in these?" Darrock asks, pointing to old boxes and trunks.

"Nope." Violet walks the center of the space to the far wall. "My dad came up here. I remember once for sure. We had a bat trapped in here." A domed trunk with vintage leather straps sits waiting, covered in dust.

"Let's see if we can open this." Violet listened to whatever was drawing her to it.

Unlocked, but takes both of them to force the unused latches to release the lid. Everywhere they touch leaves clean spots in the dust. Soon gold lettering becomes visible on the front.

"Wait, what does this say?" Violet asks. She and Darrock both swipe across the letters until it was clean enough to read.

"Princess Violetta Starosta," Darrock looks to Violet.

"Princess?" Violet clarifies. "Wait, let me think." She pulls back with one hand to her forehead and she paces in the small space.

"There was something my mother said the last time she could talk to me." Violet fumbles through the bag for the amulet.

"She gave this to me. I was so upset I didn't listen." Violet held the pendant to her chest.

"It was something about a box she could never open herself, but I thought it was small, a trinket thing. She didn't say exactly." Violet steps closer and nods to Darrock.

He places one hand on the top and one on the bottom and pries the lid open. A creak of the hinges and the lid leans back on the wall. Both lean into see something lacy filling the space. Violet reaches her empty hand in to push the silky lace aside to reveal a leather-bound book.

After pulling it from the dark interior, she holds the journal in one hand. Darrock reached into the bag hanging at Violet's side. He pulls out the book Wilga had given to her. Side by side, the leather is the same. Despite one being more used, but the original scroll work and craftsmanship are the same. The top third of each cover has a name embossed and filled with gold. One says Violetta and the other Nila.

"How can this be?" Violet asks, looking up at Darrock.

"Look there." Darrock says, pointing to the lower third of the covers.

"Wait, what if, —" Violet places Violetta's book on

top of Nila's. And looking over the amulet in one hand, she turns it over so the dimple is down. Calmly contemplating something she can't define, she sets the amulet on top of the books on the lower spot of the cover.

Both books in Darrock's hands, Violet places her hands on top of his. A bright light erupts out of the amulet. They both close their eyes. When it dims, they open them to find the amulet is gone and two books are now one.

Violet lifts the cover to see what was once the works created by each princess are now one story. The time of the Widowed King's daughters.

The End

ACKNOWLEDGMENTS

My love of story started as a child. It has followed me all of my life. Many people I've met have lived the best stories. But most of all I want to say God has been with me in my darkest and brightest of times. My gifts come from him and the determination planted in me.
My husband, Matt has been my constant and more than I imagined to have in a partner.
Not only our children but our team-Whitney, Matt, Brett and Cooper.
Lori and Harry constant through the good, bad, ugly, fishing, and going out for great food.
I never realized my journey with art would find me the most like-minded friend possible-Wendi. The best portrait artist I've met in person but also, a true friend.
This book caused me to doubt myself but these women shored up my confidence-Whitney, Kayla, Wendi, and Lori. I'm forever grateful.
Many characters are actual pieces I made that now live with some amazing art collectors. Candy and family love some of my most unique works to date. Thank you all.
There are so many more, but I hope you know who you are. My thanks, prayers, and gratitude are with you.
Thank you from the bottom of my heart.
Smile!
P.S. Ladies, don't forget to check your whiskers!

ABOUT THE AUTHOR

W. L. Simon is known for her whimsical Cartoon Taxidermy sculptures as a full time sculptor. Those character's personalities inspired her to bring them to life on the page. Artist by day and writer at night and still she has plenty of imagination for many more creations.

She is also wife to her high school sweetheart and mother of two adult children, but includes her son-in-law as one of their own. One grandchild to play with in the studio keeps her extra busy. To keep life exciting they share their home with Kodiak the keeshond pup and Gerty the hedgehog.

TO FIND OUT MORE CHECK OUT THESE OPTIONS

www.wlsimonauthor.com

www.perhapsandpolkadots.com

www.ingramcontent.com/pod-product-compliance
Lightning Source LLC
Chambersburg PA
CBHW031840310726
48972CB00005B/1345